Wedding Bells for Woolworths

Also by Elaine Everest

The Woolworths Girls
The Butlins Girls
Christmas at Woolworths
Wartime at Woolworths
A Gift from Woolworths
The Teashop Girls

Ebook novella
Carols at Woolworths

Elaine Everest

Wedding Bells for Woolworths

MACMILLAN

First published 2020 by Macmillan
an imprint of Pan Macmillan
The Smithson, 6 Briset Street, London EC1M 5NR
Associated companies throughout the world
www.panmacmillan.com

ISBN 978-1-5290-1591-1

1 3 5 7 9 8 6 4 2

A CIP catalogue record for this book is available from the British Library.

Typeset by Palimpsest Book Production Ltd, Falkirk, Stirlingshire
Printed and bound by CPI Group (UK) Ltd, Croydon, CR0 4YY

To the people of Alexandra Road, Erith, past and present, and remembering with fondness our friend, Stella White, who will be much missed.

To the people of Alexandra Road, Erith, past and present, and remembering with fondness our friend, Stella White, who will be much missed.

Prologue

October 11th, 1948

Police Sergeant Mike Jackson viewed the scene before him. In all his years in the police service, he had never experienced such an outpouring of grief and love. Although he was present in an unofficial capacity, he had worn his dress uniform as a mark of respect. Now, with an unseasonable chill wind blowing across the graveyard of St Paulinus Church in Crayford, along with a smattering of the rain that had been threatening all day, he wished he had his muffler to pull round his ears and the woollen gloves knitted by his wife, Gwyneth. He shuffled from foot to foot as he stood close to the lychgate, saying goodbye to mourners as they left. Everyone was heading back to Alexandra Road for a boiled ham tea, and something to drink to warm them up.

Gwyneth had gone on ahead to put on the large kettles loaned to them by friends at the Arthur Street mission hall. She was also keen to check on their baby son, who was being cared for by a neighbour. Mike's heart swelled with pride as he thought of young Robert. Still only seven months old, he already possessed the sunny disposition of his Welsh mother and the sturdy build of the Jackson men. He smiled to himself as his thought of his father's opinion that the lad would make a fine policeman; Robert already showed signs of having the required large feet, which would help when walking the beat. Yes, it would be good to have a fourth generation of coppers in the family, he thought with pride.

'It's a sad day,' an elderly man said as he stopped to shake Mike's hand.

'It is, Derek, it is. It was good of you and the lads to turn out to sing at the service. Especially on a such a miserable day.'

'It's the least we could do,' the man replied. 'Not one member of the choir would have missed paying their respects. It's an honour.'

Mike nodded and shook hands with the retired police officers who filed past. The Erith Police Male Voice Choir was part of the local community, and he had found it very moving to hear them singing 'The Old Rugged Cross' with such feeling. There was hardly a dry eye in the church.

Stamping his feet to keep his circulation moving, he spotted a police car pulling up and a young officer hurrying towards him. He hoped he wasn't required to go in to work. Not today of all days. 'Hello, Dave. Is there a problem?'

The constable whispered in his ear, aware of mourners close by, and then waited for Mike to make a decision.

'Go and wait in the car and I'll be with you as soon as I've said goodbye to the mourners. It's not right to be hurrying people on their way,' he said to the young lad, even though he knew speed was of the essence. He headed up the narrow cinder path, nodding to the vicar and shaking his hand. He found himself repeating the words he'd used with other mourners. It was hard to think of original comments on such a sad occasion.

As he came closer to where his friends were standing, he could see the headstone of Irene Caselton, late wife of his stepbrother, George. He stopped for a moment to pay his respects to the woman who had been killed by enemy action when a V2 rocket landed on a Woolworths store in New Cross almost four years earlier. Close by was the grave of Eddie Caselton, George's father. So many people Mike knew were now interred in the grounds of this ancient church, along with the occupants of a German plane shot down over the nearby golf course, who were now at rest in one corner of the graveyard. He hoped to see the day when these lads were taken home so their families could pay their respects in their homeland. War shouldn't mean young men could never be repatriated. Even though it was three years since the war had ended, its consequences lay heavily on everyone's minds.

Mike snapped out of his reverie as an elderly woman dressed head to toe in black approached with a stern look on her face. 'Good afternoon, Mrs Munro,' he said, hoping the woman wasn't going to stop him for a chat. Vera Munro, who lived up the road from Ruby Jackson in Alexandra Road, was a person who could find the dark side to a rainbow and enjoyed nothing more than a good gossip. 'It's a sad day,' he added.

'If you say so, Sergeant,' she muttered angrily, hurrying past him.

Mike shook his head. 'Nothing changes,' he murmured to himself. Up ahead he could see the women he wanted to speak with. The three musketeers, he thought to himself as he approached, watching them huddled together while looking at the wreaths that lay beside a freshly dug grave. These three women had been through much during the war, but their friendship hardly ever wavered. Sarah Gilbert, George and Irene's daughter, was wiping her eyes as the two other women, Maisie Carlisle and their younger friend, Freda Smith, gave her a hug. What brought them together today was nigh on as bad as the war, but these women were tough and would pull through, he was sure. 'I've just had word from the cottage hospital. There's a police car waiting just outside the lychgate, if you're ready to leave?'

The women all nodded, and without saying a word they linked arms and set off down the path away from the grave.

Mike took a final moment to bow his head and say his goodbyes. 'This world will be a sadder place without you,' he whispered, as his words were carried away on the wind.

1

July 1947

'It is with the greatest pleasure that the King and Queen announce the betrothal of their dearly beloved daughter, the Princess Elizabeth, to Lieut. Philip Mountbatten, R.N., son of the late Prince Andrew of Greece and Princess Andrew (Princess Alice of Battenberg), to which union the King has gladly given his consent.'

'It's so romantic,' Freda Smith sighed as she leant over her friend, Sarah Gilbert's shoulder to read aloud the betrothal announcement from the newspapers spread over the table. They were in the staff canteen of the Erith branch of Woolworths, taking their morning tea break. 'Listen to this: "The Princess wore a light grey coat over a yellow silk dress as she walked with him on the terrace of Buckingham Palace." Maisie will want to know the fashion details. Her customers at Maisie's Modes are bound to be asking for yellow frocks to copy the Princess.'

'I doubt they'll be silk, and with our rationing there'll not be many women in Erith decking themselves out like royalty,' her friend laughed, as she turned the page to look at the handsome naval Lieutenant.

'Maisie can turn her hand to most things. She'll find the fabric from somewhere, even if she has to pull apart dresses from the back of someone's wardrobe. She's the queen of make do and mend, is our Maisie.'

'You can say that again. However would we all have coped without Maisie and her sewing skills? Nan reckons she'd give those London fashion houses a run for their money if she upped sticks and moved her business to the West End.'

Freda chuckled. 'Ruby is right, but the West End's loss is our gain. Oh, look: it says here that the wedding will be in Westminster Abbey. It would be wonderful to go up to London and watch all the pageantry! We missed out on the celebrations up town on VE Day because of Ruby and Bob's wedding. A part of me wishes I'd danced in the fountains in Trafalgar Square.'

Sarah almost choked as she took a sip of her tea. 'Freda, you don't even like getting your feet wet when it rains, so I can't imagine for one moment that you'd have jumped into the fountains. You're also forgetting that we went to London for the Victory Parade last summer. So it's not as if we missed out.'

Freda shrugged her shoulders. 'It was a special occasion, I'll give you that, but all rather formal, with the forces marching past and the bands playing. My feet ached from just standing there and cheering all day long. It says here that people went to Buckingham Palace last night and cheered their heads off to show the young couple how much they all thought of them. This is just what we need after all the years of war: a lovely wedding to look forward to.'

'A pity she isn't marrying an Englishman,' one of their colleagues muttered from an adjoining table. 'He's a foreigner, and a Greek at that.'

'Oh, for heaven's sake. He grew up here, and relinquished his foreign title. He's as British as you or me,' Sarah snapped back.

'Don't let her rile you,' Freda whispered. 'She's only just accepted me, and I moved here from Birmingham nine years ago. I swear she thinks anyone born outside of Erith is a foreigner and would murder her in her bed.'

Sarah agreed, and turned back to the newspaper just as a bell rang loud and clear through the store. 'Oh crikey, our tea break is over already. I'd best get a cup of tea for Betty, to take back with me to the office.'

Freda didn't hear a word as she gazed at a large photograph of Philip Mountbatten. 'It's just like a fairy tale, with the handsome Prince meeting his beautiful Princess and getting engaged.'

There was a roar of laughter from a nearby table where a trainee manager and a stockroom boy were having their tea break. Each held a hand over their heart and fluttered their eyes as they took the mickey out of the girls. Freda scowled. 'That new trainee manager is so full of himself,' she said. 'Give me a royal prince any day over the lads who work here.'

Sarah laughed. 'Life isn't like a fairy story, Freda, although our Princess Elizabeth seems to have kissed the right frog. She's a lucky woman – but I still prefer my Alan,' she sighed, reaching for the silver sixpenny piece hanging on a chain around her neck. Alan had given her the necklace some years earlier, when he coined the name 'sixpenny' for her in recognition of goods once costing sixpence at the F. W. Woolworths store, where they had met and fallen in love.

'You are very lucky, and I envy you, meeting your Alan right here in Woolworths,' Freda said as she spotted a dreamy look cross Sarah's face. 'I only seem to kiss frogs that turn into wart-covered toads.'

'Oh, you'll find your prince one day. And I reckon it'll be sooner than you think,' Sarah said. She stood up, ready to return to her desk in the corner of the office she shared with store manager Betty Billington. Before walking away, she started to collect the dirty plates from the table.

'It's not for want of trying,' Freda said as she brushed a few crumbs from the blue checked oilcloth table covering. 'I wouldn't say I've had many beaus, but they've amounted to nothing. I reckon I'll end up an old maid, working in Woolworths until I'm too old to serve behind the counter. What's that saying? Always a bridesmaid, never a bride?'

Sarah laughed at her young friend. She'd known Freda since the day they'd started work together at the Erith branch of the well-known high street store, back in 1938 – in the months before the war became a reality. The girl in front of her now looked nothing like that frightened, half-starved waif in a threadbare coat who'd seemed scared of her own shadow. Freda was now twenty-six, and a confident supervisor for Woolworths. She'd kept up her interest in motorbikes, which she'd been involved with while a volunteer with the Fire Service at the nearby

Erith fire station; and when she wasn't working in the store she could often be found in Sarah's husband's workshop, tinkering with engines and suchlike. Freda's face had a healthy glow from the time she spent in the open air either with the Brownies and Girl Guides or out and about on one of Alan's motorbikes.

'You've been a bridesmaid many times because you have lots of friends who love you and want you to be part of their happy day. I wish I could say *I'd* been a bridesmaid at the wedding of Johnny Johnson, and waltzed with David Niven.'

'It is tradition for the best man to dance with the chief bridesmaid,' Freda replied, her cheeks turning pink at the memory of the happy event she'd taken part in. 'All the same, it was rather surreal, wasn't it? Who'd have thought that our Molly, an ironmonger's daughter from Erith, would marry a matinee idol and hold her wedding right here in this town? It was like a dream to be part of Molly's happy day.' A faraway look came into her eyes as she recalled the Christmas wedding at Christ Church, followed by the journey to London in a Bentley for a swish reception at the Ritz. 'It still feels like a dream.'

'And she gave you her house in Alexandra Road – so if you are going to be an old maid, at least you have somewhere to live,' Sarah joshed. She didn't begrudge her young friend her good fortune; Freda had not had a very good start in life before coming to Erith.

'I'm truly lucky, and that's why I like to rent a room to some of the young women who work here at Woolies while they find permanent homes. I know what it's like to live in a strange town and not be able to find a decent lodging house. Which reminds me, I must put a card up on the staff noticeboard. My last lodger has just left. It's a shame I can't put up one or two of the young chaps who come here as part of their management training.'

'My goodness – could you imagine the gossip if you did? The old dears in Alexandra Road would have a field day,' Sarah said, thinking of her nan Ruby and her neighbour and sparring partner Vera Munro. 'Best you stick to young women from respectable homes,' she grinned as she collected tea and a sandwich from her mother-in-law, Maureen, who was working behind the counter in the staff canteen. Balancing them carefully to take to Betty, her boss, she headed for the door. 'I'm working for a couple of hours this afternoon, so I'll say my goodbyes now.'

Freda waved back at her friend and tidied up their newspapers, thinking of the happy days ahead for the young Princess. It was half-day closing, and she had something to look forward to as well: a whole afternoon spent helping Alan Gilbert in his workshop stretched before her. The weather was lovely, and with luck she would be able to take one of the motorbikes out for a spin.

Her life was good, and she shouldn't worry about being unmarried and without a boyfriend. To be honest, men were often more trouble than they were worth, she thought to herself as she straightened her uniform. It was time to go downstairs to the busy shop floor, to continue working for what remained of the morning.

Later that morning Freda waved goodbye to Betty, who was standing with a bunch of keys in her hand waiting to lock the front door of the Woolworths store after her staff departed for the afternoon. The sun was still shining, and she could see George Jones over the road at Misson's Ironmongers, taking in the buckets and pans hanging from the display at the front of the shop. She waved to him. The old man waved back, as did several other tradespeople who were shutting up shop for half-day closing. Freda loved living in the town of Erith, set on the south bank of the Thames. It had become her adopted home after her sad childhood in Birmingham. Freda enjoyed working at Woolworths, and with the security of owning her own house thanks to the generosity of her friend, Molly Missons – or should that be Molly Johnson now she was married to the handsome matinee idol – she had her roots firmly in the friendly town, and couldn't imagine ever leaving the area.

Crossing the bottom of Pier Road into the high street, she headed on past the Odeon cinema, where an advert for *A Matter of Life and Death* caught her eye. She must remember to see whether Sarah and Maisie fancied a night out to watch the film. At once, the memories of attending the special Royal Film Performance in London came back to her – how she'd loved watching the film, and in the company of film stars and royalty. Yes, a night out with her chums would be fun. She smiled to herself, thinking back to the days when, without children, her mates could drop what they were doing and head out to enjoy themselves – be it at the cinema, dancing at Erith Dance Studios or taking the train to London to see a show, air raids permitting. Now, with the war firmly in the past, it was as if a weight had lifted from their shoulders and even though they still had rationing and the word 'austerity' had entered the nation's vocabulary, spirits could not be dampened as they thought of a war-free future ahead of them all. Lifting her face to the sun, Freda felt the warmth on her face. Yes, it felt good to be alive, and with the excitement of a royal wedding in the offing, things were certainly good.

'Hey, Freda!' a voice called out as she approached Manor Road. 'Wait for me, and I'll walk with you.'

'Hello, Sadie – are you doing some last-minute shopping?' Freda asked as she stopped to wait for the red-faced young woman to catch her up. 'Arthur's getting a little big for that pushchair, isn't he?'

'You can say that again. He was whining to come with me, and if I'd let him walk we'd not have caught the shops before they closed. Nan needed her liver salts, and she'll never let me forget it if she goes without due to me not getting to the shops. Last time she sent me back as I'd picked up the wrong kind. It seems Fynnon's Liver Salts aren't as effective as the Andrew's ones. I swear she waited until the last minute before asking me to go, the cantankerous old so-and-so.'

Freda snorted with laughter. Sadie's grandmother, Vera Munro, was known for her forthright opinions and stubborn ways, and she knew Sadie suffered at times because of the woman's sharp tongue.

Freda liked Sadie, who'd had more than her fair share of bad luck in past years, although she now had her darling son, Arthur, to make up for it. Freda bent down to tickle the lad under his chubby chin, and was rewarded with a toothy smile. She thought Sadie was lucky to have the little lad in her life, and felt a twinge of envy. Would she ever have a child of her own? 'Do you have time to pop in for a cup of tea, or will Vera be at the gate waiting for you?'

Sadie checked her wristwatch. 'Oh, go on then, she can wait for a while,' she said as they crossed over into Alexandra Road and headed towards the Victorian terraced property opposite the house where Freda had lodged for most of the time she'd lived in Erith.

'I still can't believe this is my home,' Freda said, opening the door then lifting young Arthur out of his pushchair, watching as the lad toddled off down the long hallway.

'You are lucky,' Sadie sighed as she put the pushchair in front of the bay window in the small garden, and followed Freda inside. 'Although I don't begrudge you this for one minute. You've shared your luck with others, and I for one think that's admirable.'

Freda knew without asking that Vera Munro would have been imparting her views on her good luck to all and sundry. 'All I've done is to offer rooms to a few young women who work in Woolies. I know how hard it was to find decent lodgings when I first came to the town. If it wasn't for Sarah and her family, I don't know what would have become of me,' she said with a catch in her voice. 'I'd hate any person to be homeless.'

A cloud passed over Sadie's face for a few seconds before she gave a knowing nod of her head. 'Yes, I was at my wits' end before this little chap was born. If Ruby hadn't convinced Nan to help me, I'd have had Arthur taken away from me at the home for unmarried mothers. I had nowhere to go, after . . .'

Freda patted the young woman's arm. Sadie had blossomed of late, now that she was living back home with Vera and had some money coming in. The petite blonde girl had filled out slightly, but she'd been all skin and bones a little while ago. Freda knew the story of how Sadie's nan had all but disowned her until Ruby Caselton, as she was known then, stepped in and made Vera see sense. 'It all worked out for the good. I take it you haven't had any problems with Arthur's dad seeing you all right?' she asked as they walked through to the kitchen and Freda struck a match to light the gas under her kettle.

'Although I want nothing to do with the horrid man, he does pay a little towards the lad's upkeep. I do my best to save it now I'm working for Maisie looking after her brood. She has the little ones this afternoon, what with it being half-day closing,' she added, seeing a small frown cross Freda's face. 'I've not left them on their own if that's what you're thinking?'

'Not at all,' Freda said quickly even though that was exactly what had crossed her mind. 'Does that mean Maisie is taking the afternoon off for once? She works so hard in that shop of hers.'

'She'd finished a special order for the mayor's wife and decided to have a few hours off to get some sun on her face. For once her sewing workshop is closed and they've gone for a walk down to the river front. Maisie did ask if I'd like to join them, but I knew Nan wanted me to run some errands for her, so I declined. By the way, have you found someone to take on your back bedroom yet?' Sadie asked. 'That was a super idea to take in lodgers. Even Nan approved. She did say you should keep it to female guests who have good references, what with you being . . .'

'A spinster living on my own?' Freda finished for her, aware that on more than one occasion Vera had questioned her unmarried status. 'I'm only advertising in the Woolworths staffroom, and Betty Billington is advising me. It's such a shame my last lodger left to get married – she was such a sweet girl, and so quiet. Hopefully the room will be taken soon.'

Sadie looked wistful. 'I'd kill to have rooms for me and Arthur, but if I moved it would have to be far enough away for Nan not to be knocking on my door every hour asking me to run errands. Speaking of which . . .' She drained her cup and got to her feet. 'Sorry to run so soon, but you know what Nan can be like.'

'I do,' Freda grinned as she caught hold of the little boy and gave him a kiss on his cheek. 'I'll see you later, young man. I'm going to put a few hours in at Alan's workshop once I've changed out of my work clothes. By the way,' she added as she followed them back to the front door, 'I'm thinking of asking Maisie and Sarah to join me for a trip to the Odeon at the weekend. *A Matter of Life and Death* is on and I'd love to see it again. Would you like to join us?'

Sadie beamed. 'I'd like that. Thank you for including me. It means a lot. People can be quite harsh with me not being married to Arthur's father. Only the other day that horrid Mrs Martin up the road called something quite untoward out to me. Nan gave her a right old mouthful, I can tell you.'

The girls looked at each other and burst out laughing,

as it was Vera Munro who was usually the one dishing out the comments to those she looked down on. Freda gave Sadie a quick hug. 'Oh Sadie, what happened to you could have happened to any of us. Who are we to judge? I'll look out for Gwyneth and see if she'd like to join us as well. Why, we could perhaps have afternoon tea in the Oak Room at Hedley Mitchell's beforehand and make it an extra-special treat.'

'That would be wonderful. Perhaps it would cheer up Gwyneth. She's been a little down since the news from Wales about her dad's job down the pit. I'm not one for politics, but I can't help wondering if this nationalization of our coal mines will suit everyone. Why have the country run someone's job, when a local boss would be better? I'm not sure I'd like it if I was a miner's wife.'

Freda nodded. She'd noticed that their friend Gwyneth was rather down lately. An outing would do them all good.

As she watched Sadie set off up the road towards her nan's house, she spotted Ruby wiping down the window ledge in front of the large downstairs bay window and crossed the road to say hello.

'I thought you'd be off round to Alan's place?' Ruby said as she dabbed at an invisible spot on a windowpane.

'I'll be going shortly. I came home to change and stopped to have a cup of tea with Sadie. She's a nice girl,' Freda said as she rested against the wall and leant her elbows on top. The sun was warm on her face and she closed her eyes, enjoying the sensation.

'You look tired, love. Why not put your feet up for a few hours?'

'No, I'm fine. I promised Alan I'd help him out. He has

a motorbike in for repair and I'd love to give it a spin before the owner collects it. It's a Brough Superior that's been under canvas since before the war, and the owner wanted Alan to give it the once-over before he ships it off to Canada. You don't see many of them,' she said with a dreamy look in her eyes.

Ruby shook her head. 'I can't tell those motorbikes apart. It could be a penny farthing for all I know. They're all noisy and dangerous, and then there's the grease you get on your clothes. I don't know, you've always been the same, wanting to get yourself mucky messing around with machinery and such-like . . .' She tutted to herself. 'Would you like to come here for your dinner later? It's not much, but Bob's up the allotment and I asked him to bring back some veg. I've told him we should think about giving up one of them. He can't keep up with it all like he used to.'

Freda felt guilty. Since moving out of number thirteen, where she'd lodged for many years, she'd not helped Bob and Ruby as much as she used to. 'No, he shouldn't do that, not when everything is in such short supply. Let me have a word with Sarah and Gwyneth. Perhaps we can all muck in to help? After all, you help us all out with the veg Bob grows.'

'That would be kind of you, lovey. I do worry about the state of things at the moment. I thought when the war ended we'd get back to normal within months. Here we are two years later and we still have rationing and have to make do as best we can. Mike was up there the other day, helping Bob put a lock on the old shed. Someone had been in and pinched some tools and seeds. Mike reckons we aren't the only ones it's happened to lately.'

Mike Jackson, the local police sergeant, was Bob's son. Ruby was proud to have a policeman in her family since marrying her Bob on the day the war ended. She often warned Mike of any wrongdoings she heard about on the town's grapevine, and in return Mike advised Ruby and her friends on how to stay safe. She'd been as proud as punch when he gave a talk to her local Women's Institute recently.

'Don't worry about it, Ruby. We'll all muck in and make sure everything is as it should be. By the way, have you read the news about Princess Elizabeth's engagement? We were looking at the newspaper this morning on our tea break. The wedding will be a big boost to the country.'

'You're right there, love. I'm going to cut out all the pictures and put them in a scrapbook so the little ones can see them when they are older. Just think – she will be our Queen one day. Not that I'll be around to see that happen,' she said, picking up her bucket and cleaning cloth.

Freda's face dropped. 'Oh Ruby, please don't speak like that. There's nothing wrong, is there?' she asked, her heartbeat quickening. The stout, grey-haired woman was the matriarch of the family that Freda was proud to be part of, if only as a dear friend. Please God she wasn't ill.

Ruby chuckled. 'No, love, I'm as fit as a fiddle. It will be many years before the King goes to meet his maker, and I was only thinking how the likes of me and Bob probably won't be here here to see it. Life goes on,' she added as she saw Freda's sad face.

'I suppose you're right, but let's not think about it,' she pleaded.

'Well then, you get yourself off to those messy motorbikes. And if you see my Bob, tell him to pull his finger out. He's been gone ages.'

Freda promised she would look out for Bob, and hurried back over the road to her own house. Upstairs in her front bedroom overlooking the street, she took off her work clothes and pulled on a pair of navy blue dungarees and an old shirt that had once belonged to Alan. Folding a headscarf into a triangle, she tied it round her head, tucking in the loose ends and poking her curls underneath to keep them clean. Maisie had advised her to grow her light brown hair a little longer, so that it could be styled in many ways and wouldn't look as childish as the short bob she'd had for many years. Freda had been surprised at the curls that had appeared with the longer length, although the upkeep of the new hairstyle was something she was still getting used to. At least she could tuck it all away while she worked on her beloved motorbikes.

Picking up her handbag, she hurried out of the house and round to nearby Crayford Road, where Alan ran his business in a rundown workshop set behind the two-up, two-down houses. She inhaled the smell of oil and petrol as she stepped in through a small door set in a larger door that was always kept locked. She was ready to work – but she wasn't prepared for the angry voices that assailed her ears, wiping the smile from her face.

'There's something pleasant about having the store to oneself,' Betty Billington said as she leant back in her seat in the office she shared with Sarah Gilbert.

Sarah chuckled. 'Don't let head office hear you speak like that! They may remind you that customers are the lifeblood of Woolworths. Joking aside, I know just what you mean. These few hours allow me to catch up on paperwork and have the decks cleared before I set to with the wages tomorrow.'

Betty placed her pen on the desk and folded her arms. Now in her mid-forties, she looked young for her years, although her brown hair, always pinned up whilst at work, was peppered with steel grey hairs. 'Are you still happy to work here, Sarah, rather than be at home with the children?'

Sarah turned on the wooden seat to face her friend. 'I won't deny there are times I wish I didn't have to pack Georgina and Buster off to be cared for by someone else while I go to work. But I like my job here, and the money comes in handy – especially at the moment,' she added, her bright smile dimming for a second.

'Is there a problem at home?' Betty asked, looking concerned. 'You know that anything you tell me will not leave this room.'

Sarah shrugged her shoulders. 'It'll pass, I'm sure. It's just that these last couple of months, the motorbike workshop doesn't seem to be as busy as it has been in the past. When I pop in to see Alan, the place only seems half as full as it used to. I've tried to discuss it with him, but you know what men are like.'

Betty smiled to herself. As the busy manageress of a Woolworths store, with a husband whose business she knew inside out and who she often advised during meetings with his business partner, David Carlisle, she'd never had a problem. But she did know that even after a war, during which many women had held down responsible jobs, there were men who considered it their responsibility to be the sole breadwinner and manage the family finances. She'd thought better of Alan Gilbert than to keep his wife in the dark; but who knows what goes on behind closed doors?

'I'm sure things will sort themselves out soon, Sarah. Business can be like that. Someone once told me it can be feast or famine, and I'm inclined to agree. Look at how one minute we're run off our feet here, and then the next it goes quiet and we're worried that head office will start asking questions and making changes. It will all come out in the wash, as your nan would say.'

Sarah nodded in agreement. 'I can see the sense in what you're saying. But with Maureen about to move out to marry my dad, we'll have the rent and upkeep of the house to find on our own. However, I do believe I worry too much,' she added, trying to brush off her own comments. She didn't wish to tell Betty that on a few occasions Alan had been unable to give her enough money for the housekeeping, and she'd dipped into her savings. He'd never given a real reason, which worried her greatly, but she didn't like to ask what was happening in case it dented his male pride. Alan tended to get quite prickly if Sarah offered to pay for housekeeping items. He viewed providing for the family as a man's duty.

Betty absorbed her friend's words. Since leaving the RAF, Alan Gilbert had decided not to continue with his trainee manager job at Woolworths. Instead he had followed his dream of running a motorbike repair business.

Betty's own husband, Douglas, was an undertaker, and he had been able to advise Alan about going into business for himself; but he had confided in Betty that he feared the young man would try and run before he could walk.

'I know Alan had big dreams, and he started out with such high hopes. However, you mustn't forget what I said to you at the time: your Alan is welcome to return to Woolworths any time he wishes. Please do tell him that from me,' she said, wondering at the same time if Woolworths was the right place for Alan to work after all this time.

'I will. I'm sure it's just one of those things that happens in business sometimes,' Sarah said, trying to look brave. 'As you say, trade goes up and down all the time.' She didn't add that she was worried her dad, George, who had helped them financially when they started out, would discover there was a problem. He'd been so generous, helping Alan set up the business. George Caselton had enough on his plate, what with his forthcoming wedding and also being a popular town councillor, not to mention holding down a responsible job at Vickers.

'I'm surprised you're paying rent. I thought Maureen owned her house?'

'She does, and as she often says, the house will be Alan's one day. We are the ones who insist on paying the going rate. Of course, she refused, so I've set up a post office savings account to put the money aside and will give it to her every quarter. I'll not listen if she argues. Money will be tight, but we will just have to manage.'

Betty nodded thoughtfully. Maureen Gilbert, who was also Sarah's mother-in-law, had been courting Sarah's father George Caselton for the past couple of years, after Irene Caselton had died during a horrific rocket attack on the New Cross branch of Woolworths. 'I was wondering if you could put in a few more hours here? I know the plan was for you to be part-time, but you can see how stretched I am with all that head office now throws at us. I can't think of the last time I was able to stroll through the shop floor without feeling guilty that work was waiting for me in this office. I've even been taking work home with me! Douglas and the children are not amused.'

Sarah gave a small frown, suspecting that Betty was simply feeling sorry for her.

'An hour a day would be just wonderful, if you think you could help me?' Betty continued. 'If not, I should really place an advert in the *Erith Observer* for a part-time office assistant.' She looked expectantly at Sarah.

'I'm not sure I could find someone to take on the care of the children. Georgina is at school most days, but Buster is only two and a half . . .' Sarah said. At the same time, she was thinking that if Betty hired someone to work in here, the Woolworths head office might decide she herself was no longer required.

'I'll leave you to think about it,' Betty said.

There was a tap on the half-open door and Maureen walked in, carrying a laden tea tray. 'I'm slipping off now, Betty love. I thought the pair of you would like a fresh pot of tea to keep you going, and there's a slice each of my bread pudding. The dried fruit's a bit on the scant side, but the flavour is still there. I've left young Peggy scrubbing the floor, so she'll be here a little longer, in case you were thinking of locking up.' She collected the empty cups and gave Sarah a peck on the cheek. 'I'll collect Buster from next door, and we can walk up the school to meet Georgie. That way you won't need to rush yourself,' she added, leaving the office and closing the door behind her.

Outside, in the long corridor, Maureen stopped to think about what she'd overheard. She wasn't one to listen at keyholes, but the door had been open, and she'd heard Sarah mention her own name as she left the staff canteen. With the building being almost empty, voices echoed along the upstairs corridor.

In a way, she was thankful she'd overheard what she had. Sarah and her Alan were ones for keeping things to themselves, and would not want to burden her. She squared her shoulders and made her way back to the canteen. She'd have to do something to help her loved ones, as she hated to think of them scrimping and scraping – but what? She would have to bide her time and be there if and when it was obvious the young couple needed help. Perhaps after the wedding she'd have George get more involved in Alan's business again. If only she'd taken that tea tray to Betty a few minutes earlier, she might just have heard why Sarah was being offered more hours at work and why Betty sounded concerned. However, one thing she did know was that the money Sarah intended to pay her for rent would be returned – she was adamant about that.

2

Three pairs of eyes looked towards Freda as she pushed open the rickety wooden door and stepped into the workshop. Pretending she hadn't heard the men arguing with Alan, she picked up a broom and gave him a smile. 'Sorry I'm late. I bumped into Sadie and we had a quick cup of tea, then got chatting. I'll make you one when I've swept up. Are your friends staying?'

The two burly men, dressed in long black overcoats with wide shoulders, pushed past her as they headed towards the door. 'Don't forget. If you know what's good for you, you'll have the money with us by Friday – or we'll be seizing goods to the value, as they say,' the taller man said, as his eyes roamed over the workshop.

'Accidents can happen in places like this,' the second one added. He smiled menacingly at Freda before tapping the rim of his hat and following his companion through the door.

Alan slumped against his workbench and ran a hand through his sandy-coloured hair. 'You shouldn't have heard any of that,' he said in a low voice.

'It's a good job I came in when I did or goodness knows

what would have happened,' she said, throwing down the broom and going to his side. 'I could hear them threatening you from outside.'

'Then you should have turned round and gone away. The last thing I want is for them to harm you, kid.'

Freda perched herself on the workbench so she could easily look into his face. 'What if that had been your Georgina or your mum that came in? They could have been hurt if those chaps had turned their threats into actions. I'm going to put the kettle on, and then you are going to tell me all about it. A trouble shared and all that,' she said as she hopped down and went to fill the battered kettle at a tap over a chipped sink. Alan's eyes were bright with tears, and she didn't want him to see she'd noticed. It would have hurt his pride to cry in front of her.

'I'll tell you everything, but you are not to repeat what I say to a living soul. Do you promise?' he said gruffly, blowing his nose.

Freda stayed silent until the tea was made, and she placed a mug in front of him before dragging over a packing case to use as a seat. 'Come on – let's be having it. If I'm to share this secret, I want to know it all. I want to help you, Alan,' she added gently, not wanting to appear too bossy. Alan had been like a big brother to her, and he called her his kid sister – hence the nickname of 'kid' that he'd given her. She didn't like to see him in trouble, no matter what it was.

He stared into the mug of tea rather than look her in the eye. 'The takings haven't been so good lately, kid. You might have noticed I've not had any bikes in from the GPO since they hired their own mechanics.'

'Oh God, Alan. I'd hoped that was a temporary problem.'

'A change of manager in the depot didn't help. By all accounts the new chap has his own contacts in the trade. I'd begun relying on that work, and now it's dropped off you could say I'm on my uppers. The rent on this place was due and I didn't have the wherewithal to pay it, so . . .' He picked his mug up and took a gulp without noticing it was still scalding hot.

'So you borrowed the money?' Freda prompted him. 'But who from, and why did those men come knocking?'

'I overheard someone down the pub mentioning a chap who lent money to businesses, and I followed it up . . .'

Freda slammed down her mug. 'You bloody idiot. You mean you went to a moneylender, and then you couldn't pay him back? Christ, Alan! They charge the earth in interest as it is, and once you don't pay back, they double, treble what's due and then . . . I thought any fool knew that. If you don't pay . . .' She stopped speaking for a moment to catch her breath.

'They beat people to death and dump their bodies in the Thames,' he finished for her.

'Oh, Alan, you bloody, bloody fool.' A sob caught in Freda's throat and she threw her arms round him. 'There's any number of people who could have helped you.'

Alan pulled her away and held her at arms' length. 'That's the thing; I don't want help, or to be beholden to family and friends. I want to sink or swim on my own merits.'

'If we don't get you out of this mess, you'll sink, all right,' she said forcing a grin to her face.

'Yes, wearing concrete boots, like one of those gangsters in the films you like to watch at the Odeon.'

She snorted, brushing off his suggestion even though she knew it could well be true. 'I have a bit put by you can have, if it helps? You know I've always fancied working for you. I could be your sleeping partner. How much do you need?' she asked, already imagining her name above the door. 'Gilbert & Smith' had a certain ring to it.

Alan didn't speak as he leant across the workbench and slid a sheet of paper towards her.

'Blimey, Alan,' she exclaimed, clapping a hand over her mouth. She didn't often swear, but this time there just weren't the words to explain her shock. She realized she'd been fairly vocal in that department this afternoon, and it wasn't ladylike. 'I didn't realize you'd borrowed this much.'

'I didn't – it was a quarter of that. They've added on a bit of interest.'

'Couldn't you have asked for time to pay?' she said as she picked up the piece of paper and stared closely at the numbers written at the bottom. At the top were the words 'Frank Unthank and Sons, Financial Investments'. 'I take it your visitors were the sons?'

'I wish. The sons are better dressed and more polite, even though they can be just as threatening. Those chaps were the hired help. I've got two weeks to pay them, or else.'

'Then we've got two weeks to come up with a plan,' she said as brightly as she could. 'What work do you have outstanding that we could turn into cash?' Watched as Alan looked up from his tea, she saw the despair in his eyes.

'Hardly anything at all. The Brough goes back later

today, but the owner paid me a large deposit and that's already been accounted for. Sarah needed her house-keeping; I couldn't refuse her, and the rest went on parts to go back into stock. In fact, I need to collect them this afternoon and hand over the payment.'

'How much does Sarah know, Alan?'

He gazed into the distance, deep in thought, not seeing the rough brickwork walls and the tin roof of the workshop that dripped water every time it rained. 'She doesn't know I'm a failure, if that's what you mean.'

'Oh, Alan, you can't keep secrets like this. Sarah will be so angry if she knows you kept this to yourself. You've been married for how many years?'

'It'll be eight later this year,' he muttered, avoiding her eyes.

'And I was there in church when you made your promises to each other. I don't recall you saying you'd not tell her when you had a problem.'

'And I never said I'd get myself in trouble with a bloody moneylender either,' he said bitterly, slamming his fist down on the wooden bench. 'She must never know about this. I couldn't face her if she knew how much I've let her down. It would be the end of our marriage. I know it would,' he exclaimed as his anger surfaced.

Freda could see how emotional he was. 'You'll get through this, Alan, and I'll be here to help you all I can. You can have the money in my post office book, and I'll see what else I can do to rake in some more,' she promised. This time he reached out and hugged her.

'I don't want to take your money, kid. It feels like stealing from my little sister.'

Freda felt herself choking up. 'Well, I'm giving it to you, so shut up and take it. It'll only make a small dent in the debt, but it's a start.'

'I'll not take it all the same. I'm going to sell Bessie. She's old but she's sound,' he said, looking to where his faithful motorbike stood close to the workshop wall covered in a tarpaulin.

'Oh no, you can't do that. You love that bike. Why, it was your dad's, wasn't it? You need to hang onto your memories, Alan, whatever happens. Besides, Sarah will notice if it's missing. I know she's never liked motorbikes, but she knows what that one means to you. How will you explain why you've let it go?'

He shrugged his shoulders. 'I'll say it's too old to ride so I let it go for spare parts.'

'Please don't start to tell untruths because one day you will find your life is built on lies and you won't be able to talk yourself out of them. You owe it to Sarah and the kids to be honest.'

Alan looked glum. 'I couldn't get away with anything, let alone murder, with you watching me, could I?'

Freda shook her head and sighed. 'I hope you don't ever consider such a thing. I'd rather see you walk away from this business than tell lies and, God forbid, think of murder. Now, let's see what can be done this afternoon to improve matters, shall we?' She tried hard to keep her voice upbeat. 'Did you say something about some spare parts needing collection? I can do that, while you make yourself a list of work that can bring in some money. I'll help when I get back. Can I borrow a motorbike to fetch the bits?'

'Take Bessie and the duffel bag. It's all small stuff.' He turned to open a drawer under the workbench, pulling out an envelope. 'Here's the cash. Remember to ask for a receipt, won't you? I wish I'd thought about this more; I could have done without the spark plugs and carburettors. Too late now, as I can't renege on an order,' he shrugged.

Freda grinned. Even with the cloud of Alan's debt hanging over them, she was thrilled at the thought of riding a motorbike once again. During the latter years of the war she'd absolutely loved her work with the Fire Service as a dispatch rider. The money in her savings account had been going towards buying her own motorbike, but that could wait. For now, she'd enjoy the wind in her hair and being able to ride the beloved Bessie, even if it might be for the last time if Alan had his way. 'Do they know someone's collecting the parts this afternoon?'

'Yes – I was going to shut up earlier and go to Bexleyheath myself for them. If those thugs had arrived ten minutes later they'd have found the workshop doors locked and bolted.'

'I'm glad you didn't because now I know what's happening and I'll be able to help you all I can. I may have another lodger soon, so I'll give you the rent money to add to what they're after.'

'It's good of you to think of me, kid, but it won't help much. I'm thinking it may be better for me to take the beating and get it over with.'

Freda became angry. 'You mustn't do that. They could kill you, and then they'd just go after Sarah for the money. Keep your chin up, Alan, and don't be so defeatist. We will sort this out between us.'

Alan hugged her. 'What would I do without you? We have to keep this secret to ourselves, as it will destroy Sarah if she finds out.'

From outside the workshop, Maureen Gilbert froze with her hand on the door handle. Why was it that she kept hearing news at half-opened doors these days? She hoped no one thought she was a nosy parker. Knowing Sarah was working late at Woolworths, she'd decided on the spur of the moment to take her son a sandwich; otherwise he'd not bother eating until he came home later. She'd not expected to hear him speaking in confidence to young Freda. A secret between them – what was this all about? She rapped on the door loudly and called out in a cheerful voice. 'Are you there, Alan? It's your mum with food!' As she stepped through the door she spotted Freda pull away from her son's arms, and they both pinned smiles to their sad-looking faces. Whatever was going on here?

Betty reached for a cardboard box on a side table in her office, and slid it towards Sarah. 'Goodness, I forgot to put these in the staff canteen. Would you be a dear and unpack them? Remember to keep one back for Maureen, as she has a day off tomorrow.'

'I can't believe Maureen will be marrying my dad next week,' Sarah said as she opened the top of the box and pulled out a handful of magazines including *The New Bond*, the Woolworths magazine. 'Ooh, that's good, I do enjoy reading *The New Bond* – if only to be nosy about what's happening at the other Woolworths stores.'

Betty smiled at her friend's excitement. 'It wasn't that

long ago you would have had more to say about George and Maureen marrying.'

Sarah looked up. 'I was rather an idiot, wasn't I? With them being so close and not a year having passed since Mum . . . left us, it was all too much for me,' she said with a slight wobble in her voice. 'But with Maureen being my mother-in-law, and her looking after Dad so well, it made me see what a wonderful woman she is, and life has to go on . . .'

Betty knew it had taken a lot for Sarah to accept that her father had found new love with Maureen Gilbert. But by all accounts they had been friends long ago, before he'd married Sarah's mother, the elegant and rather superior Irene. Irene hadn't been everyone's cup of tea, but Betty had got on well with her and had grieved when she'd died, not long before Sarah gave birth to Alan Junior. Betty shuddered inwardly at the young lad's nickname of Buster, but the name, given to him when he survived a near miss at the Hainault maternity home when only a few hours old, had stuck fast. 'All's well that ends well,' she said, giving her friend a gentle smile before starting to open a pile of correspondence on her desk. 'Hmm – this looks rather official.'

'Please don't say it's another letter about the trainee manager programme?' Sarah said as she placed several copies of *The New Bond* on her boss's desk. 'I'm forever calling these young men, who arrive for a few weeks then move on to another store, by the wrong name. They all look the same in their brown warehouse coats. Why can't we have one sent to us for office training, instead of being the store where they learn about warehouse and stock control?'

'Because Erith 397 has a reputation for keeping a tight

ship, that's why,' Betty replied proudly. 'I do confess to calling one young man Barry when his name was Malcolm. I'll make a note for them to start wearing name badges. That will solve the problem. Hmm,' she added, looking more closely at the letter. 'I fear this is a bigger problem than our trainee manager programme. Head office has noticed Erith 397 has not contributed to *The New Bond* of late. They suggest that we enter one of our female staff members into the cover girl competition.' She looked up from the letter.

'Don't look at me,' Sarah said, taking a step back from the desk with a fearful look. 'I can't think of anything worse than seeing my face on the cover of the magazine! I enjoy reading about fellow workers, but it's not for me. We need a young, single staff member who has been with Woolies for a while and who has led an interesting life.'

The two friends looked at each other and in unison said, 'Freda!'

'She would run a mile if we suggested it,' Betty said. 'Perhaps if I had a quiet word and told her it was for the good of the store. Remind her how you were featured in *The New Bond* when you were Erith's carnival queen.'

'Gosh, that was back in 1939,' Sarah said, thinking fondly of that time. 'Before the world went to war, and before I married my Alan.'

'I was still unmarried, too,' Betty added, remembering again how fortunate she was to have found her Douglas in her forties after facing a life of spinsterhood.

'And now you have two stepdaughters, and your own daughter,' Sarah said. 'Oh, that gives me an idea . . .'

Betty raised her hands as if to ward off whatever Sarah

was about to say. 'Please don't suggest I should appear in the magazine. I'm too long in the tooth, and I've worked for Woolworths far too long to be considered a cover girl.'

Sarah chuckled at her horrified expression. 'No, not that I don't think you'd look super on the cover. I was thinking we could send in a photograph of Maureen and Dad when they get married. Look at all the wedding announcements and photographs,' she said, opening the magazine to show rows of blushing brides and grooms in their wedding finery beaming out of the pages. 'Dad has loaned me his Box Brownie to use on the day, so I'll make sure that there's a nice one I can contribute to the editor on behalf of Erith 397.'

'What a marvellous idea. I'm sure the happy couple will be pleased to be included in the magazine to represent Erith. Well done, Sarah!'

Sarah nodded as she slipped a copy into her handbag. Another thought had come to her, but she'd keep it to herself for now.

'It's only me,' Vera Munro shouted through the letterbox after banging loudly on the door of number thirteen Alexandra Road. She ran her finger along the bottom of the glass panel and inspected the dust she found. 'You need to clean your windows,' she sniffed as she pushed past Ruby and led the way to the living room, plonking herself down on a wooden seat with a sigh. 'You'll not guess what I've just seen.'

'No doubt you're about to fill me in,' Ruby said, expecting nothing better of her neighbour.

'It was a shock, I can tell you. I'm fair whacked after hurrying to let you know.'

'Well? Spit it out, woman, before the anticipation kills me.' Ruby sighed, knowing it would be something and nothing. She was busy washing mud off the vegetables Bob had brought back from the allotment before thinking about their dinner. Was that what Vera had really come for, she wondered? She never missed a trick to beg a free bit of food. Mind you, there was a time when Vera was on her uppers, Ruby thought to herself, so she'd try not to think too badly of the woman even though she was a pest.

'I saw one of them darkies, and he was talking to our Sadie,' Vera huffed, with a pleased look on her lined face. Time had not been good to Vera, and the war could not be blamed. It was as if all the years of moaning had added more lines than necessary on her round face until not a single one more could be squeezed in. Her grey hair, cut in a short, harsh bob to just below her ears, did her no favours and she continually squinted through a pair of wire-framed spectacles. 'Do you think he's chasing after her, knowing she's a loose woman?'

Ruby sat herself down at the table. This wasn't going to be a quick visit after all; she could feel it in her bones. 'Whatever are you talking about?'

'Well, I'd popped out to look for our Sadie. She'd gone and picked up the wrong liver salts and I'd sent her back to change them. That girl would lose her head if it weren't screwed on. Only the other day . . .'

Ruby knew that if she didn't cut into what Vera was saying, they'd be there all day. 'What did you see, Vera?'

'Oh yes, well, I got down as far as the Co-op and spotted her talking to one of those darkies at the bottom of Crayford Road. She hadn't seen me as she was busy pointing something out to him, going by the way she was waving her hand, so I ducked up the alleyway and made my way back to Britannia Bridge and came down our road the long way.'

'And?'

'Well, that's it really.'

'You went a good quarter mile out of your way rather than speak to your granddaughter? What's wrong with you, woman?' Ruby was starting to lose her temper.

Vera squirmed in her seat. 'She might have seen me, and I didn't want to be seen talking to the . . .' She looked at Ruby's angry expression. 'I didn't want to be seen talking with him. What would people think?'

'People would see you were talking to someone in the street. Why would they think anything else?'

'Because he's different from us!'

'Who's different from us?' Bob asked as he came in through the back door from the garden, followed by their dog, Nellie.

'A gentleman Vera saw chatting to her Sadie,' Ruby said quickly, before Vera could comment.

'What's wrong with this gentleman?' Bob asked, knowing only too well Vera would soon fill him in with all the details. 'Let me wash my hands and I'll stick the kettle on,' he added, giving Ruby a sly wink.

'You don't know he's a gentleman,' Vera huffed. 'How can he be, when he's not like us?'

'What's he got – two heads or something?' Bob called out.

'Worse – he's a darkie,' Vera snarled, sensing Bob was about to take the mickey out of her. 'And he was chatting to our Sadie, and people will talk. She's already got a reputation.'

Bob joined them at the table, still wiping his hand on a towel. 'Now look here, Vera. Your Sadie is one of the nicest girls you can meet, and she loves that kiddie. She works hard and she will do anything for anyone. Why should one mistake in her life mean she's about to jump on some poor chap and get pregnant again?'

'Well, I never,' Vera squirmed. 'There's no need to talk like that. Men should keep such thoughts to themselves. I'll not have that tea if you don't mind, Ruby,' she said, rushing out of the house the way she'd come in.

Ruby hurried after her and checked the front door had closed. 'There was no need to be so blunt,' she said, trying not to laugh. 'She does get her knickers in a twist at times. I wonder who Sadie was chatting to?'

Bob snorted with laughter. 'Blimey, woman, you're getting as bad as Vera. Next you'll be saying we'll all be murdered in our beds by a stranger visiting the town – and you can stop looking at me like that. It doesn't matter what colour a man's skin is, there's good and bad in all. Now, shall I make that tea or will you?'

Freda fired up Bessie and headed down Crayford Road towards the centre of town. Considering what had gone on in the workshop, she felt remarkably calm and relaxed. Maureen had arrived just before Freda left, and she knew that although he'd not share his alarming news with his mum, at least Alan would have company for a while as they shared the sandwiches she'd brought along for his lunch. Freda considered taking the motorbike for a longer spin, enjoying the wind in her hair and the thrill of the open road; but mindful of the task ahead, and her own plans, she followed the row of terraced two-up, two-down houses to the junction of Avenue Road before heading up the High Street until she could see the expanse of open ground that bordered the Thames.

The river had been like a magnet to Freda ever since she'd arrived in this small Kentish town. She was fascinated with the people who earned a living on the river and also the large ships, many painted battleship grey, that were anchored there. On a clear day, she could see the Rainham marshes and the small figures going about their day-to-day lives. Trips on the Thames down to the seaside towns on the Kent coast were always a treat, especially when the trip was on the *Kentish Queen* paddle steamer owned by friends of the Caselton family.

Soon she was travelling through a much seedier side of town. West Street was full of river-related businesses, pubs and old houses that had seen better days. She soon spotted the address she'd memorized from the piece of paper Alan had shown her. She parked Bessie close to the property and called to a group of scruffy children who were playing in the street, 'Here, would you like to earn yourself thruppence?'

The older child looked at her suspiciously. 'Who wouldn't? But what d'yer expect us ter do fer yer?'

'If you keep an eye on my bike while I go in there, I'll give you the money when I come out. Deal? If I come out and find you've messed with it I'll tell my friend, Sergeant Mike Jackson. I take it you know him?'

'We all know Sergeant Mike. Is he really yer friend?' he replied, giving her a respectful look. The local bobby was well known and admired by the law-abiding people of the town, and also those who moved outside the law.

'He's a very good friend, and he's my neighbour,' she said, holding the coin out so they could see. 'Keep an eye on my motorbike and this is yours when I come out.'

'All right, missus,' the lad said, stepping closer to the bike and folding his arms across his chest. 'Nuffink'll 'appen while I'm 'ere.'

Freda nodded her thanks, and entering the building she found a small room with a high counter. Beyond it stood a weasel-faced woman holding a telephone to her ear. She made her goodbyes and gave Freda a hard stare without speaking a word.

Freda pulled herself up to her full height and did her utmost to speak the way she'd heard her boss, Betty Billington, address people whom she did not favour. 'I would like to speak with Mr Frank Unthank, please,' she said, wondering too late if her plan to visit the money-lender and beg for time to pay Alan's debt had been rather foolish.

'Mr Frank Unthank Junior is away on business. You will have to leave a message,' the woman said without smiling.

'It is the senior Mr Unthank I prefer to deal with, if you don't mind. I can wait,' she added as she saw the woman check a large round clock on the wall behind her.

The woman nodded her head, still wearing a stern look. 'Take a seat,' she said before disappearing through a door and reappearing a minute later. 'You will have to wait. He's busy.'

'I can only wait five minutes, so if he wants the money I have, he will have to hurry,' Freda glared back. She knew she'd have to hold her nerve if she were to get results.

The woman disappeared through the same door, closing it behind her. Freda sat with her insides churning until the door opened again and the stern woman popped her head through the opening. 'You can come through.'

Walking behind the counter and entering the room, she was faced with an elderly man sitting behind an oak desk. The two rough-looking men she'd seen earlier in Alan's workshop stood close behind him.

''Ere, boss, that's the one I was telling you about. Her that walked in while we was paying a visit ter Gilbert's place.'

Freda felt her heart start to thump fast in her chest. She had to stay calm. As long as she could escape out of the door behind her, she would be safe. That's when she realized the stern-faced woman had slipped behind her and was guarding the door. Without turning, she said in as harsh a voice as she could muster, 'I want to talk to Mr Unthank on my own. Surely you don't think a mere slip of a girl could cause trouble?'

Frank Unthank nodded his head, and Freda felt a cool draught as the door was opened and the woman left. Freda stepped aside to make room for the two large men to follow her. Unthank nodded to a chair set opposite his desk. She took it thankfully as her legs were beginning to turn to jelly, but she'd be damned if she was going to let him see how frightened she was. 'Thank you for seeing me . . .' she began before he raised his hand to stop her.

'You mentioned money,' he said in a low, gravelly voice. 'I take it you're here to settle the foolish man's debt?'

'Alan's no fool,' she spat back at him. 'He was unlucky and you took advantage of him. We can pay you what he borrowed and a little on top, but not the extortionate sum you've added that your thugs were demanding this afternoon. Why, that's daylight robbery. You should be ashamed of yourself. A man of your age should know better.' She bit her lip and felt worried. Perhaps she had gone a little too far. Now what would he do? She waited, watching his face for a sign of anger.

Frank Unthank stared at the young woman in front of him, rubbing his chin thoughtfully. 'I like you. Not many women would come in here and give me a piece of their mind. I take it you and this Gilbert are fond of each other, and he sent you here to negotiate with me? He's not much of a man to send a woman to do his work for him. I assume you don't have the money, and are here to pay me in . . . in kind?' He gave a thin smile, his tongue running along his lips.

Freda shivered. This was not going the way she had expected. Alan would be livid that she'd put herself in danger. Apart from the kids outside, no one knew she was here. If she didn't reappear before long they'd most likely take off with Bessie. God, whatever should she do? Reaching into the duffel bag, she pulled out the envelope full of cash that was supposed to pay for the motorbike parts. 'Here – you can have this, and I'll get the rest of it to you by next week. That is, I will pay you ten per cent on top of what you lent Alan Gilbert. We don't have any more money, so you can take it or leave it and I'll go to the police,' she said, not feeling at all brave as she placed the envelope onto the desk.

Unthank took the envelope and pulled out the notes, counting them carefully before stuffing them into a drawer and turning the key. 'It's a start, but I want more. Much more. And before you answer, remember this, young woman: I call the tunes around here. Not some chit of a girl. Not even one as pretty as you . . .'

3

'What's going on in your mind?' Ruby asked as she observed her husband. 'You've not turned the page of your newspaper in over ten minutes. I didn't know you was that interested in the engagement of Princess Elizabeth?'

Bob looked up and blinked. 'What?'

'I was asking what's on your mind. Do you have something to tell me?' she asked as she pulled one of his woollen socks over her darning mushroom and poked a large hole with her finger. 'I do wish you'd cut your toenails more often. There's more darns than original wool in this sock.'

'You can read me like a book, Ruby Jackson.'

'If I could, I'd know what you've been brooding over. Why not tell me?'

Bob put down his newspaper and took a deep breath. He had no idea how Ruby was going to take his suggestion. 'I'm thinking we should have another dog,' he said quickly, before he could change his mind.

Ruby frowned. 'What's wrong with the one we have? Nellie's no more than two years old and I'm fond of her, what with her being our Nelson's daughter.' Nelson was

Ruby's much-missed old pal, who'd been constantly by her side during the war. Her heart ached just thinking of him.

'No, I meant get a second dog,' Bob said, trying not to make eye contact with Ruby. He was sure she could read his mind and would know he hadn't quite explained why he wanted another dog. 'You can't deny they are good company.'

'I'll give you that – but with our family and young Nellie here, it's not as if we are lonely, is it?' she frowned.

Bob shrugged his shoulders and went back to his newspaper. 'Have it your own way,' he said chickening out of saying what he really meant.

'You're not wriggling out of it that easily, Bob Jackson. I know you of old and for you to come up with a comment like that, I just know you're up to something – so spit it out.'

'I met a chap down the pub the other day. He reckoned there's money to be made if we had a decent greyhound. I've got the time to train it and still look after the allotment,' Bob added wistfully as he finally looked at Ruby's face. He didn't like what he saw. 'The chap said he could get me one at a good price.'

Ruby laid down her darning mushroom after stabbing the needle into the toe of Bob's sock, making him wince as he waited for her reply.

'No one has ever said I'm an unreasonable woman, Bob, and I'd not stop you having a dog if you really wanted one. However . . .'

She was interrupted by a loud bang on the front door followed by Bob's son, Mike, letting himself in with the key that was always attached to the inside of the letterbox. Ruby's expression softened and she gave him a smile. 'Hello, Mike, we don't usually see you at this time of the day. There's nothing wrong, is there?' Using the edge of the table, she pulled herself to her feet and winced before walking slowly to the kitchen. 'There's some tea in the pot. I bet you won't say no to one?'

'Do I ever?' Mike laughed as he put his policeman's helmet on the table and sat down. 'You look a little on the stiff side, Ruby. I hope you're all right?'

'Don't you worry yourself about me. It's just me old bones taking a bit longer to get going these days,' she called back to him. 'Would you like a slice of fruit cake? You might be lucky and get a few sultanas in it. I'll be glad when life is back to normal and we don't have rationing and going without. What are those politicians calling it again, Bob?'

Bob gave his son a grin before answering. 'It's called austerity, love.'

'Bloody austerity.' Ruby snorted. 'I bet those up in Westminster don't go without and have to make do and mend. The whole lot of them are crooks. I just hope our George gives 'em a shake up now he's in politics.'

'Being a local councillor is not quite the same, love,' Bob said, licking his lips as Ruby put a plate on the table containing two slices of her home-made cake. 'However, he will do a good and honest job here in Erith. Not having some yourself, love?'

'I'm not hungry. There's a suet pudding on the go for tea that'll more than fill me up. I was going to send some over the road to you as well, Mike, if you don't mind? I know your Gwyneth's been working today, and Myfi never says no to her nan's cooking.'

'Don't leave yourself short,' Mike said, biting into the cake. He was more than pleased with how Ruby welcomed everyone into the fold, what with him being her stepson and Myfi being his adopted daughter. No one was made to feel different at number thirteen.

'I made far too much, and I know you'd do the same if the boot was on the other foot,' Ruby replied, returning with his cup of tea. 'I lick my lips every time I think of that batter pudding we had at your place the other week.'

Mike gave them both a smile. 'Save your suet pudding for tomorrow and I'll join you for lunch, as Gwyneth will be working. I hope I didn't interrupt you by popping in like this?'

'Not at all,' Ruby said before Bob could open his mouth. 'Your dad was wondering about getting another dog, and I was about to tell him why it's not a good idea at the moment. You're a sensible man, Mike, perhaps you'll be able to help.'

Mike grimaced. He had to tread carefully, as he didn't want to come between his dad and Ruby. 'I don't know a lot about dogs, I'm afraid. We give ours a few scraps and between the three of us we take it out for a walk. What else is there to know?'

'A lot, as it's to be a greyhound,' Ruby said, raising her eyebrows at Bob. 'I'm wondering if your dad wants to race it at the stadium over in Crayford . . .'

Bob raised both his hands in surrender. 'I was about to get to that. I don't believe it would cost a lot, as I was thinking of us having a syndicate amongst the family, and we could all share the winnings. Fred Trevillion has been doing a blinder with his dog, Trev's Perfection. You never know – there could be another champion dog in Erith.'

Ruby looked expectantly at Mike, who swallowed a mouthful of hot tea and cleared his throat. 'The little I know about such things comes from the lads down the station. There's a dark side to the racing game, and only last year an undercover investigation led to someone going down for doping. You need to buy a dog from a reputable breeder who will guide you through what to do and how to feed it. They have to be fighting fit to win races, which means giving them the best food.' He looked between his dad and Ruby, hoping he hadn't alienated either of them. 'Who is the breeder? I take it you've chosen and spoken to one?'

Ruby burst out laughing before wincing and rubbing her lower back. 'Don't make me laugh, as it hurts,' she grinned.

Bob was downcast. 'It was a bloke down the Prince of Wales. He did seem knowledgeable, though.'

Mike felt a flicker of sympathy for his dad. 'Look, I reckon it's a good idea. If we form a syndicate with family and friends, it could be fun for all of us if we don't take it too seriously.'

Ruby shook her head, looking stern. 'I don't want to be involved in anything that has a shady side to it. We had that pig club during the war and that was tricky enough, what with the government inspectors and all. What if our dog was to be doped and it died? Rather than be fun we'd have all the kiddies upset – and I'd be none too happy either. What about breeding rabbits or budgies instead?'

'Ruby's right,' Bob said. 'I'd not like anything to happen to the poor dog. It was bad enough when we lost our Nelson, and he was an old boy – why, if his offspring hadn't been dumped on our doorstep we'd still have been mourning him now.' One look at Ruby and he could see he'd hit a raw nerve. 'I still miss the old bugger,' he said sadly, patting her hand. She gripped his and squeezed tightly.

'What say I look into all this and let you know what I find out? Perhaps take a bit of time and do it right, if we want to own a champion racer?'

'I'd go along with that,' Bob said, giving Mike a grateful glance.

'Me too. We can still go to watch the racing and have a dabble, can't we? I've not been dog racing in ages,' Ruby said, knowing that for now the question of them having a second dog had been put to bed. 'Now we've agreed on that, what brings you over here this afternoon? It couldn't just have been my baking.'

Mike chuckled. 'I don't need a reason to visit you both. It was Dad I came to see. I thought you might be interested in some gardening items I've been offered. Old Joe down at the nurseries in Lower Road is retiring, and he said I could have first pick of his equipment. If you aren't doing anything at the moment, I could give you a lift in the car to take a look?'

Ruby frowned. 'Should you be using the police car for such goings-on?' she asked, slightly shocked that Mike would do such a thing.

Mike guffawed. 'There's no need to worry, Ruby. I'm there on official work, so to speak.'

Ruby wasn't so sure what he was saying was the whole truth. 'If it's official business, why would you be taking your dad with you? What's going on?'

'Joe's got a box of old crocks that he's offered to the police station from when his wife used to run a cafe. They're odds and sods, so no one else is likely to use them. They can't be any more chipped than the ones we use at the station, so I've been delegated to drive down and collect them.'

'That's all right then. What are you waiting for, Bob? Be off with you while I get on with repairing these socks,' Ruby said, giving her son-in-law a wink. Bob didn't need any second bidding, and was reaching for his coat before she picked up the wooden darning mushroom.

Mike kissed her cheek. 'Don't overdo things,' he said, making a mental note to ask his dad about Ruby's aches and pains.

Freda took a step back as Frank Unthank watched her.

'I'm not here to play your games,' she said, sounding braver than she felt. Why oh why had she come here? She should have known better, and now she needed to think fast. 'I have some money to give you, but please – can you not ask for so much interest on top? You may not know this, but Alan Gilbert served this country in the war. He flew Spitfires and was shot down by the enemy, and just missed being taken prisoner. He's doing his best to run a business to keep a roof over the heads of his wife and young children. Can't you see your way clear to be just a little lenient, if only for a war hero?'

Frank Unthank watched Freda as she stopped to draw breath. His eyes never left hers and she held his look, not wanting to be the one to give in. Slowly a smile formed, showing his yellowing teeth. 'You've got some pluck, girl, I'll give you that. I like a bit of sport, and taming you would please me.'

Freda gasped. She had to get out of here. Why the hell had she stood up to this creep? Alan would be so angry with her when she told him what had happened – that's if she ever saw him again. She feared Unthank and his gang didn't take to people like her giving them trouble. She shrugged her shoulders. 'Oh well, it was worth asking you. I'll bid you good day and be on my way,' she said, giving what she hoped was a smile and not the fearful look she was fighting to suppress.

'Not so fast, missy,' he said, getting to his feet and walking towards her from behind the desk.

It was the first time Freda had seen his full height, and her eyes widened in surprise. He was only six inches taller than her – if that – although he was almost as wide, and looked quite menacing with his black overcoat and greased-back hair that was a dark as the night. His appearance gave Freda renewed strength to stand up to him; somehow she didn't feel intimidated any more, even though she knew his henchmen were just through the door in the outer office. 'My friends will be expecting me,' she said, looking pointedly at her wristwatch. 'They will be concerned if I don't show up soon. It's been nice to meet you, but as you aren't prepared to help me, I'll be on my way.'

Her mistake was to hold out her hand to shake his. In

a flash he had grabbed her arm, twisting it behind her back until he had her in a vice-like grip. 'Not so fast, my love,' he breathed into her ear as he pushed her against the wall face first, slamming his body against hers.

'Get off! You're hurting me,' she yelped in pain, her voice muffled by the wood cladding on the partition wall. Although she could feel the blood pulsing through her head, she tried to calm down and do her best to think clearly. Alan had once told her how vulnerable men could be in certain positions, and she had once had cause to make use of his advice. Could it work again now? She would need a few inches to be able to raise her knee, so shuffled back a little, her body getting closer to the man's.

'That's more like it. Decided to become a bit more friendly, have you?' he grunted in her ear.

Freda did her utmost not to shudder as the stench of stale cigarettes wafted in her face. It was now or never, she thought to herself. She raised her knee and bent it forward before kicking back and catching him with the heel of her shoe where it would hurt most. He groaned in shock and staggered backwards, giving her time to reach for the door handle. Bolting through the door, she crashed into the arms of a tall man who caught hold of her tightly. Was there no escape? She felt a wave of oblivion wash over her, and her knees buckled.

'Hey, Freda,' she heard a distant voice call to her as she shook her head and tried to pull away. How did they know her name?

'Leave me alone – let me go,' she cried, trying to fight against the person holding her close.

'It's all right, Freda – it's me, Mike Jackson. Calm down, love,' he said. 'No one's going to harm you.'

Freda looked up into the friendly face she knew so well. 'How did you find me?'

'You can thank Bessie for that. We spotted her parked up against the wall, and came in to look for Alan. Shall we go outside?'

She nodded as Mike led her by the arm from the building. He muttered civil goodbyes in an authoritative tone that made it clear he didn't expect any answers. Outside, she blinked in the bright sunlight and took a deep breath. 'Thanks, Mike,' was all she could manage.

'So the kids were right – she was in there,' Bob said, giving Freda a quizzical look. 'Do you want to tell us about it?'

'Not here, eh, Dad?' Mike nodded towards Frank Unthank's office. 'I don't trust the chap to stay in there and behave himself. There's a cafe down the road a bit. Are you all right to push Bessie down there?' he asked Freda. 'I'll follow you in the car.'

'I'll stay with Freda,' Bob said as he tossed a coin to the crowd of boys, who'd been watching all agog for something to happen.

'I'll be fine, Bob,' Freda said as she swung a leg over the bike and prepared to push off. 'I'll see you down there.'

'Well, go slow, because I'm not leaving your side in case that mob comes after you – and I'm not so good at running,' he said, stepping beside her. Freda threw him a grateful look, and instead of turning on the engine she freewheeled alongside him towards the cafe.

After parking up the motorbike they joined Mike in the

steamy cafe, where he'd already placed an order at the counter. 'It'll be with us shortly,' he said as he joined them at a table by the window where they could keep an eye on Bessie and the police vehicle. 'Now, what's this all about? The last place I'd have expected to see you was in Unthank's office. You know what he does for a living, don't you?'

Freda looked glum. 'Yes, he's a moneylender.' And now he has all the money I'm supposed to hand over to pay for the motorbike parts, she thought to herself.

'He's got his fingers in all kinds of pies – moneylending is just one thing he dabbles in,' Mike said. 'He's a nasty bit of work, and could have hurt you.'

'Why were you there?' Bob asked, as a waitress wearing a none-too-clean apron approached with a tray containing three large mugs of tea and three bacon rolls. 'Bacon and decent rolls?' he added, forgetting Freda for a moment as he licked his lips. 'You don't see those every day of the week.'

'It's a perk of the job,' Mike winked before his expression grew serious once more. 'Yes, why were you in there, Freda?'

Freda looked suitably ashamed, but as much as she loved these two men and thought of them both as family, she couldn't give away Alan's secret. With Bob being married to Ruby and her being Sarah's grandmother, the secret would soon be out and Alan's problems would become common knowledge.

'I'd borrowed some money from them, and was paying it back,' she said, crossing her fingers under the flowery tablecloth and feeling worse than she'd ever felt in her life for telling such fibs. She pushed the plate away, feeling sick to her stomach. 'I'm not hungry, thanks all the same,' she said. 'I need to get off as I've got something to collect for Alan. Thanks for the tea and for rescuing me,' she added before getting up and leaving the two men to their thoughts. Outside, she could just see to climb onto the motorbike as her tears flowed unchecked.

'Well, that was rather queer,' Bob said as he tore the remaining bacon roll in two and placed half on Mike's plate. 'I've not known the girl to be in debt before. I'd best have Ruby speak to her.'

'Would you mind keeping this to yourself for the time being, Dad? I don't think our Freda is telling the whole truth. And for her to lie to us like that means she's covering for someone.'

'Could it be Alan? She's always hanging about his workshop.'

Mike nodded his head thoughtfully. 'Something doesn't add up.'

'Then let's keep it between the two of us for the time being until it does,' Bob said, biting into his roll. 'Eat up, before your bacon gets cold.'

Freda fired up Bessie's engine and headed back towards Erith. Alan would be wondering where she'd got to, and she wasn't sure how to tell him she'd paid off part of his debt, furthermore annoying the owner of the motorbike spares shop when she cancelled the items they didn't need. At the time she had been thinking only of the cash that could be saved, but now she wasn't sure if she'd lost Alan a supplier.

After leaving Mike and Bob in the cafe, Freda had popped back to her house to collect her post office savings book. She'd withdrawn the same amount of money she'd given to Frank Unthank, before hurrying to collect and pay for the spares. What a mess she'd made of everything! And Alan still owed Frank Unthank a vast sum of money.

She powered up Bessie and turned down Pier Road, knowing she had to get back to the workshop as quickly as possible. The street was almost empty due to early closing, and despite her worries she enjoyed the warm sun on her face, wishing only that she'd worn goggles to shade her eyes. The next moment she heard a cry and, blinded by the bright light, found herself being propelled over the handlebars and landing on something soft that began to protest loudly.

'Damn you, woman! Why don't you look where you're going?' a voice exclaimed before groaning loudly. 'Arrgghh – my leg!'

Freda scrambled to her feet, looking to where Bessie lay on the pavement by the main Woolworths entrance. She stretched her arms and legs, surprised that nothing seemed to hurt – Alan's motorbike jacket had helped to protect her – before turning to look in bewilderment at the man on the ground, who was still protesting loudly. His bicycle lay crumpled against the kerb. 'Where did you come from?' she asked, shading her eyes from the sun.

'I was turning to come out of the alley beside Woolworths, and you appeared from nowhere.'

Freda frowned. She knew that voice. 'Aren't you that rude trainee manager?' she asked without thinking. Perhaps it was the shock, but she felt oddly detached from the situation and wished he'd get to his feet and go away, as she really should be back at Alan's workshop. What if Mike or Bob should say something to Alan before she'd managed to explain what had happened at Frank Unthank's office? He would be furious.

'Yes, I am a trainee manager. Are you going to help me up, or let me stay here on the road until someone else tries to run me over?'

'You are a most disagreeable person,' Freda muttered as she took his arm and hauled upwards, expecting him to get onto his feet. Instead he rolled on the ground, groaning loudly.

'My leg is buggered,' he managed, before falling into a dead faint.

'Oh, good gracious! Whatever has happened here? We heard the noise from the office,' Betty Billington said as she rushed from the staff door of Woolworths, closely followed by Sarah.

'It was an accident,' Freda said. Her bottom lip started to quiver. 'I was blinded by the sunlight, and he came out of the alleyway and I didn't see him.'

'Did you fall off Bessie?' Sarah looked to where the bike still lay.

George Jones hurried over from Misson's. 'I saw it happen,' he puffed. 'He came out of nowhere. Freda didn't stand a chance. I've sent the lad up to get the doctor – although I think we need an ambulance, looking at the state of his leg.'

'It's on its way,' a woman called from an upstairs window of the Hedley Mitchell store. 'If you want a witness, I saw it happen. She ran straight into him.'

Betty tried not to smile at the conflicting witness observations. It didn't seem right when both involved were staff of F. W. Woolworths. 'Should we make Anthony more comfortable, do you think? We have some blankets in the first aid room.'

'I'm fine, apart from my leg,' Anthony said weakly as his eyes opened. He tried to prop himself up on an elbow.

'I'll get the bike stood upright,' Sarah said, backing away. She had never been very good at coping with the sight of blood, and felt quite faint.

'I'll help you, love,' George said as she struggled to lift the motorbike. 'Why, you'd hardly know it had been in an accident. Just a few scratches and a small dent. It's certainly a sturdy old motorbike. Your husband's, isn't it?'

'Yes, it was Alan's dad's. It's his pride and joy.' Sarah felt quite weepy, thinking how much Alan loved the bike and how easily Freda could have been killed. That girl must have more lives than a cat, the scrapes she's been in, she thought as she gave Bessie a look over.

George just nodded, then coughed to clear his throat. He liked young Freda, and she could have killed herself today rather than just ending up with a small cut on her chin that she'd yet to notice.

'I'm going to walk the bike back to Alan's workshop,' Sarah called out to Betty, who was kneeling beside Anthony. 'I'll see you tomorrow morning.'

'Can you lock the side door for me before you leave please, Sarah? I'm going to accompany Anthony to the hospital.'

'There's no need,' the lad protested. 'Can someone take care of my bicycle until I can collect it?'

'I'm going with you, and that's final,' Betty said, dismissing his protests. 'If I recall from my staff records, you live around here in lodgings. Do you have family I can contact?'

'There's no one,' he muttered, looking embarrassed.

'I'll take the bicycle up to Alan's workshop. Perhaps he can fix it,' Freda said, feeling she should offer to help.

'Thank you, but it could be past repairing,' Anthony said sullenly as he glared in her direction. Freda blushed.

'I truly didn't see you,' she said. 'But if it helps, I'll chip in with the cost of the repairs,' she added, thinking how her savings had taken a nosedive today.

'Here, I'll push the bike and you take Bessie,' Sarah said, relieved that she didn't have to handle the motorbike. 'Don't forget your duffel bag,' she added, nodding to the bag full of motorbike parts which lay on the pavement.

Freda grabbed the bag and hurried over to where Bessie stood, hardly any the worse for wear. 'I'll ride Bessie up to the workshop to check she's not suffering after the crash,' she said to Sarah, and hopped on without waiting for an answer. She needed to speak to Alan urgently, before his wife appeared on the scene.

Alan was deep in thought as he swept the floor of the empty workshop. Why he'd stopped to write a list of paying jobs, he had no idea, as he knew there were only two small repairs outstanding and they'd bring just a few pounds to the kitty. If he didn't have to wait for Freda to return, he'd have locked up and gone home early – and possibly stopped at the Prince of Wales for a pint on the way.

A loud bang on the wooden door had him almost jump out of his skin. It was too loud a knock for it to be Freda, even though she was late coming back, he thought as he looked at the clock hanging on the wall. Perhaps it was Unthank's men, come back to complete their unfinished business. Picking up a crowbar, he approached the door with caution. He'd not go down without a fight. 'Who are you and what do you want?' he shouted as he flung back the door, raising his weapon for protection.

'Whoa, man – I come in peace,' a familiar voice called out in alarm.

The late afternoon sun flooded in through the open door, and for a moment Alan was blinded. Surely it wasn't . . . ? Could it be . . . ? 'Lemuel, is that you?'

'The one and only,' said the tall, well-built man as he stepped into the workshop. 'Would you mind putting that down, man? It's making me nervous.'

Alan looked at the crowbar in his hand, then dropped it before leaping onto his friend and hugging him in delight. 'Well, blow me down. What are you doing in this neck of the woods? I thought you'd gone home to Trinidad after we were demobbed. What are you doing here, when you could be living in the sun?'

Lemuel placed his small, battered suitcase on the ground and returned the hug, slapping Alan's back until he almost tipped over. 'What is this, if not glorious sunshine?' he said, holding his arms wide. 'I thought I'd hang around and see what this country had to offer me. We fought for its freedom, so it seemed only right for me to stay and help it back onto its feet.'

Alan beamed. He was enormously pleased to see his

friend from the RAF days. Lemuel had been part of the ground crew who kept the planes flying despite everything the Luftwaffe threw at them. 'Come along in and I'll put the kettle on,' he said, closing the door behind his friend after a quick look up and down the road.

'I'm not holding you up am I, my friend?'

'No, no, not at all,' Alan assured him as he shook the kettle before topping up the water from the tap. 'Freda's due back with some spare parts, that's all.'

'Freda? Wasn't your wife called Sarah, if I remember correctly? You have two children . . . ?' A puzzled look crossed Lemuel's face. 'I hope nothing has happened?'

Alan laughed out loud. 'Sarah and the children are fine. More than fine. Freda is our friend. She helps me out when she can. You may remember, I told you how she rode a motorbike for the Fire Service?'

Lemuel slapped his leg, laughing at his own confusion. 'Yes, you did tell me. So now she works for you here?' He gestured around the empty workshop.

'No, I work on my own. There's barely enough work for me, let alone someone else,' he started to explain as he saw a shadow cross his friend's face. 'If you had hoped I could throw some work your way, I'm sorry, Lemuel. I could easily close the door and walk away if I didn't have bills to pay. My dreams have come to nothing,' he said glumly, as the kettle started to whistle.

'Man, I'm sorry to hear that. Running your own motorbike workshop was all you talked about before we followed our different paths.' Lemuel removed his jacket and rolled up the sleeves of his bright patterned shirt.

'I see your taste in clothes hasn't changed,' Alan grinned.

'I may no longer live in Trinidad, but I'll not forget my roots, and my roots are filled with colour and sunshine. Tell me more about your business and your plans.'

Alan was glad to share his worries with his friend. They'd spent much time together at Biggin Hill airfield and, over a beer in the NAAFI, would chat about their future after the war finished. 'I'm not so sure about plans. I've as near as dammit hit a brick wall. I don't know what the future will bring now,' he said, running his hands through his hair. 'If things had been different, I would have hired you like a shot. I'm sorry, my friend; truly very sorry. Where are you planning to stay?'

'I was hoping you could recommend somewhere. At the moment I'm staying down near the river and paying for my bed by the night. I can tell you, there are some strange bedfellows in that house,' Lemuel said wryly.

'The only places I know like that are some dosshouses down off Wheatley Terrace. It's come to something if a friend has to stay down there. If only my business was doing better,' Alan said, looking sad. 'Look, if it helps you can put your head down here in the workshop. There's a camp bed in our loft and we can spare some blankets. You can eat with us, if you like? We live just down the road. What do you think?'

Lemuel held out his large hand and gripped Alan's as they shook on his suggestion. 'I'll do what I can to pay for my board,' he said.

'There's no need. I doubt I'll be here more than a few weeks. I had a run-in with a local moneylender, and his lads have already come visiting once. Trouble is sure to come knocking before long,' Alan said as he poured the tea.

'Then they will find me opening the door to this trouble.' Lemuel gave him a generous smile. 'What does your wife say to all this?'

Alan looked shocked. 'I'd not worry Sarah with my business problems. Her father gave us some money to pay the rent and buy tools when we started out. If I tell her I've failed, it will be as if I've let her down. I can't do that. She has such dreams of a cottage with roses round the door that I dare not say anything,' he said hopelessly.

'When that trouble comes a-knocking, your wife will know for sure, my friend.' Lemuel's tone was sympathetic, but his words made Alan flinch. 'You need to tell her before she finds out for herself.'

Both men jumped as the door creaked open, and Alan sighed with relief when Freda put her head in. 'Can you open up the large door so I can bring Bessie in, please?' she said before noticing Lemuel. 'Oh sorry, I didn't realize you had a customer. It can wait a little while. She's out front. I'll put these parts away and not bother you while you're busy.' She hoped Alan wouldn't notice there weren't as many parts as he'd sent her to collect.

'Freda, hang on a minute. I'd like to introduce you to Lemuel Powell, a friend from my days in the RAF,' Alan said. Watching her put the duffel bag into one of the metal store cupboards, he added, 'That looks a little on the light side.'

'I'll explain later.' Freda avoided his eyes and held her hand out to Lemuel. 'Pleased to meet you,' she smiled, trying not to gasp as her small hand was engulfed by the large hand of the Trinidadian, who had stood up politely when she came in and now towered over her. 'I do recall

Alan telling us about his friends in the RAF. Are you staying in Erith?'

'I'd hoped to, ma'am, but circumstances may have changed.'

Alan ran his hand through his hair again, as he often did when something was worrying him. 'I'm sorry, Lem – if things were different . . .'

Freda looked from one to the other of them. 'I take it you've told your friend about your money problems with Frank Unthank?' The look on Alan's face showed she had put her foot right in it. 'Oh, blast! I'm sorry,' she said, feeling embarrassed. 'And now I've made things worse.'

'I have no secrets from Lemuel. I shared many of my plans with him when we were both at Biggin Hill.'

Lemuel nodded. 'I know only that Alan is going through a bad time, but believe me, I will help if I can. He is like a brother to me.' He gave Freda a broad smile that made her heart flutter.

She thought for a few seconds before deciding to come clean. 'You are going to hate me for what I tell you next. I've made things so much worse,' she said, trying to stay calm and not panic as she went on to explain her encounter with Frank Unthank, and then her attempt to make a deal with the spare parts supplier. 'I did persuade them to take back some of the spares, but I'm afraid it's just made them suspicious.'

Alan looked at Freda's sad face as she recounted what had happened, then turned to his friend, who was nodding his head as he listened. Then Alan burst out laughing, which shocked them both. 'I'm sorry . . . but it's like one of those comedies Mum likes to watch at the cinema. Just when you think things can't get any worse, along comes something else,' he guffawed.

'I'm glad you can laugh, as there's more,' Freda sniffed, feeling slightly put out. 'On the way back here, I knocked someone off his bicycle and dented Bessie. He's been carted off to hospital. I thought perhaps you could help fix his bike?'

Alan grew serious. 'Aw, kid – you could have been hurt, and here I am joking.'

'I'm all right; your jacket protected me. And Bessie will be fine. But I'm afraid the man may have broken his leg. Betty's gone with him in the ambulance.' Freda sighed heavily. 'I'm so sorry I made a mess of things with your money, and with Frank Unthank. I'm just glad Mike and Bob came along when they did to rescue me. And I've left them thinking I have financial problems, what with visiting the local moneylender.' Unexpectedly she felt the urge to laugh, and her lips twitched as she fought it. 'My goodness; whatever will happen next?'

Alan gave her a hug. 'The business may well be going down the pan, but at least we can still smile.'

The wooden door creaked open, and a surprised Sarah peered through. 'What's going on here? Have I missed something?'

4

It was late when Freda arrived back at her house in Alexandra Road. Her stomach growled as she went to the kitchen in search of something to eat. With all that had gone on today, she'd not thought to shop for herself. It was a long time since her sandwich in the staff canteen, and that had been nothing special, being made from the much-loathed National bread. Maureen had done her best by putting a generous portion of Spam between the two pieces of bread and adding sliced tomatoes brought in from home; Freda's mouth watered as she thought of it. Perhaps she could walk the short distance into town and buy herself a bag of chips? Yes, she'd do that right now. Her one lodger, Lily, worked in the Odeon, so she wouldn't be home until the last picture had finished.

Freda knew she would have to do something about advertising her other spare room before too long, especially now her savings had been eaten into. She had a postcard in the sideboard, so would write a few words about her available room and put it on the staff noticeboard tomorrow. Usually she found short-term lodgers from among the staff at Woolworths, but Lily had come with a recommendation from Mike Jackson – and who better to approve of someone than the local bobby?

Thinking of Mike took her back to earlier this afternoon, when he had rescued her. At some point she'd have to explain to him what was really going on. But she'd need Alan's permission first, as so much of what happened was linked to his problems and was not hers to share.

Reaching for her handbag and checking she had her door key, she hurried out into the street and down Alexandra Road towards the town.

'Hey, Freda,' Gwyneth called from her garden gate. 'Are you going somewhere nice?'

Freda stopped and headed towards number two, where Gwyneth Jackson lived with Mike and their adopted daughter Myfanwy. 'Hello there! I thought you were away down to Wales?'

Gwyneth shrugged her shoulders. 'It wasn't to be this time,' she said, looking sad. 'I was feeling poorly and couldn't face the journey by train.' She lifted a hand to her stomach for a fleeting moment. 'Another time perhaps,' she added quickly, trying to smile.

'I didn't know you were off colour. Weren't you in work earlier?' Freda said, noticing how pale she looked.

'It doesn't take much to stand behind a counter and smile at customers. Besides, we had a half day, so only half the work,' Gwyneth added in her soft, lilting Welsh voice. 'Do you have time for a drink? Myfi is playing with Maisie's children and Mike's on a late shift.'

Freda felt her stomach growl again with hunger. 'I was just popping down the road for some chips. Why don't you put the kettle on, and I'll bring back two portions?'

'The kettle won't take long to boil. Let me grab my bag and I'll come with you. If they have some rock salmon, I'll get a portion for Mike and keep it warm in its newspaper in the oven.'

'What time's he due home?' Freda asked as she watched Gwyneth close the door behind her. She didn't really want to bump into Mike just yet; the afternoon's events still weighed heavily on her mind.

'Some time after midnight. He's covering for a colleague who has gone off sick. I don't think I've seen him for more than an hour a day for weeks,' Gwyneth said, linking arms with the younger girl as they set off down the road. 'But I can't complain, as he's a good husband. I just wish I could give him . . .' She trailed off.

It was clear she was upset about something, so Freda guided her over to a low wall in front of a house, and they sat down. 'What's bothering you, Gwyneth? Can I help?'

Gwyneth shook her head and didn't reply.

'If I can help, I will,' Freda persisted, hoping it wasn't money problems. She certainly wasn't in a position to do much about those, what with her own dwindling finances. 'But if you'd prefer not to say, I'll understand,' she added, squeezing Gwyneth's hand reassuringly.

'Oh, Freda, you have been such a good friend to me since I came to live in Erith. How can I not confide in you? I'm afraid . . . auntie has come to visit again.'

Freda was confused. As far as she knew, all of Gwyneth's relatives lived in South Wales and weren't ones to visit at the best of times. Her friend looked so sad, though. Freda wondered how she could help, until an idea came to her.

'I have a spare room, if your auntie would like to use it? I know how hard it must be, what with Mike being on shift work and all.'

Gwyneth frowned for a moment. 'I don't mean that kind of auntie,' she said, glancing round to make sure no one was walking by, and then leaning in to whisper in Freda's ear.

Freda's face flooded with colour. 'Oh, I feel such a fool,' she giggled. 'Is that why you look under the weather? Perhaps you should go to bed with a hot water bottle held to your tummy? That's what I tend to do.'

'No, I'm fine. It's just . . . I was hoping it wouldn't happen this month. I hoped so much, and now I feel so disappointed,' Gwyneth said, rummaging in the sleeve of her cardigan for a handkerchief and not finding one.

Freda felt rather an idiot. Of course, it stood to reason that after being married for a few years, Mike and Gwyneth would want to start their own family. Pulling a clean handkerchief from her handbag, she passed it to her friend and waited for a couple to walk by before putting her arm around Gwyneth to comfort her. 'I don't know what to say. Is Mike very upset?'

Gwyneth looked down into her lap, and twisted the handkerchief into a tight ball. 'It's not something we talk about – well, women don't, do they?'

'I've only ever spoken to Maisie about women's things. I was young when I came to Erith, and quite ignorant of what . . . what goes on down there . . .' Freda answered, feeling more and more uncomfortable by the minute. 'I know about it all now, but I haven't necessarily put it into practice.'

'That's as it should be, and I can see I've embarrassed you. You've been a big help when I needed it most,' Gwyneth said, leaning over to kiss her young friend's cheek. 'What will be will be. Come on – let's get those chips. I may even get a saveloy, if they have one.'

Freda straightened her skirt and followed Gwyneth across the road. Mike and Gwyneth were such a wonderfully caring couple, it seemed a shame that they weren't surrounded by babies. Not like some people who had a child out of wedlock, she thought as she spotted Sadie Munro approaching them – and then immediately felt contrite. She liked Sadie, even if, rumour had it, she had been rather generous with her affections towards her old boss, much to her nan, Vera's, chagrin.

'Just the person I wanted to see,' Sadie grinned at Freda as she reached the two friends. 'I wanted to ask you about the tall dark stranger.'

Freda groaned inwardly. Was she missing something here, like she had with Gwyneth and her imaginary aunt? 'Whatever do you mean?'

'I thought you would have met him . . . you know . . . the darkie . . . He stopped to ask me directions to Alan Gilbert's workshop. I thought you might have been there, what with you always hanging around Alan like some lovelorn child.'

Before Freda could speak, Gwyneth turned on Sadie and wagged her finger at the girl. 'You'd best watch yourself, Sadie Munro, or the wind will blow, and you'll find yourself turning into your grandmother.'

'Well, I never!' the younger woman said, giving a fair impersonation of Vera. It was only when she laughed that the girls knew she wasn't offended by Gwyneth's remark. 'I'm sorry, Freda. It's living with the old bat for so long. She is rubbing off on me. I hope you didn't think I meant anything by my comment.'

Freda laughed. There was no point being offended. She did spend a lot of time with Alan, and so what if people thought she loved him? She did – but not in that way at all. She loved him like she would a big brother. 'Are you talking about Lemuel Powell? As it happens, I did meet him. He's a very nice man. Why do you want to know?'

Sadie gave a nonchalant shrug of her shoulders. 'I wondered if he had his family with him. We haven't seen many of his . . .'

'His kind, do you mean?' Gwyneth finished for her, looking indignant.

'Well, yes, I suppose that is what I mean – but there's no need to look at me like that, Gwyneth Jackson, just because I stumbled over my words,' Sadie snapped back.

Freda could see that Gwyneth was ready for a fight, no doubt because she was feeling out of sorts. 'He was on his own, Sadie. Lemuel was in the RAF with Alan during the war and has decided not to return to Trinidad for the moment.'

'A pilot, eh?' Sadie's eyes gleamed.

'Ground crew,' Freda quickly corrected her, still wondering why Sadie was so interested.

'I suppose he's staying with Sarah and Alan while he's here. Will that be for long?' she asked with an innocent air.

'Oh for heaven's sake, Sadie!' Gwyneth exploded. 'Why don't you get straight to the point and ask if he will be in Erith for long, and if he has a wife? That is what you wanted to know, isn't it? Why not spit it out – me and Freda are wanting our tea.'

The young woman looked affronted. 'I was just being a good neighbour. If you can't keep a civil tongue in your head, I'll be on my way.' She nodded goodbye to Freda, and flounced off towards Alexandra Road.

'Well, fancy that. You'd think Sadie would have learnt her lesson after last time,' Freda said, looking worried. 'I will say, Lemuel does seem like a very nice man and I'm sure Alan wouldn't be friends with just anyone – but it's as if she's set her cap at him after one conversation. Each to their own, I suppose,' she said as they started to walk towards the High Street, where the chip shop was situated.

'If she has, then she's bitten off more than she can chew,' Gwyneth said seriously.

'Sadie's old enough to make her own mistakes, although you'd think once was more than enough. What's that saying? You make your bed, so you must lie in it?'

'It's not so much her bed as her grandmother I was thinking about,' Gwyneth said, looking back to where Sadie was turning the corner into Alexandra Road. 'She doesn't welcome strangers easily.'

Freda nodded her head as she thought back to when Gwyneth had arrived in the road and was supposed to have lodged with Vera. 'Very true. She thought you were a foreign spy, what with having an accent she didn't understand, having never met someone from Wales before.'

'I was thinking more of her being wary of any man who

was interested in her granddaughter – let alone him having dark skin.'

Freda shuddered as a sense of foreboding swept over her.

Betty replaced the telephone handpiece and gazed out of the first-floor window, deep in thought. The matron at Erith Cottage Hospital had been as good as her word and had telephoned with news of Anthony. She'd stayed with him at the hospital yesterday afternoon until his wounds had been cleaned and stitched up and his leg put into a plaster cast before he was settled on the men's ward.

'You seem to have something on your mind?' Sarah said, as she entered the office with the midday post in her hand and spotted Betty was not her usual self. 'Would you like some time on your own?'

'No, not at all,' Betty said, giving a small laugh. 'I was thinking of Anthony and his situation.'

'He hasn't taken a turn for the worse, has he?' Sarah asked, looking alarmed. Her blood ran cold as she thought of the accident in front of the Woolworths store the previous afternoon.

'No – in fact, the matron informs me he is doing as well as can be expected after what happened. He will be in hospital for a while yet, but I doubt he'll be fit for work for a long time with his leg as bad as it is. The cuts on his arm have been stitched up, and being a healthy young man before this will be in his favour. No, it's the coming weeks that I'm worried about. Did you know he has no family?'

Sarah stopped opening an envelope and placed Betty's paperknife back on the desk. 'Oh, the poor lad. Was he a Barnardo Boy?' she asked, thinking of the orphaned young children who were put into such homes and then sent out into the world once they were old enough to work. She gave a shudder.

'Yes. I've been looking through his employment record, which holds brief details about his private life. Head office have the fuller file. This one follows the trainees as they move from store to store until they are given permanent work placements.'

Sarah leant over Betty's shoulder to see what she was pointing to. 'Hmm – he lives in lodgings, and not very nice ones at that.'

'Do you know this address? I know I've worked here for many years, but with so many small streets around the main town, I'm at a loss to recall them all. I may have a street map somewhere . . .'

'I'll save you the trouble,' Sarah said, putting a hand on Betty's shoulder to stop her rising from her seat. 'Wheatley Terrace is a small road close to the docks, off Manor Road.'

'So, it will be like Freda's house in Alexandra Road?' Betty nodded in approval.

'Not so you'd notice. Most houses there are of the two-up, two-down kind, some are larger and let out beds to men off the ships.'

Betty frowned. 'Beds? You mean they don't let out a whole room?'

'If they're lucky, they get a bite to eat thrown in.'

'Oh my; I just hope Anthony isn't living in a guest house like that.'

Sarah gave a grim smile. Dosshouse would be more the name she'd use, but Betty wouldn't be aware of such places. Erith had some beautiful streets and homes, but like many towns bordering the Thames, it also had a dark side. She did wonder why Anthony would be staying in such a place. 'I take it you need to collect his clothes for him?'

'Yes, and to inform his landlady that he's in hospital and when he is released he will need a room on the ground floor for quite some time. We have no way of knowing how long he will have to rest his leg,' Betty said as she looked at her wristwatch. 'I'll take a walk round there after lunch.'

'I'll come with you,' Sarah said with a determined look on her face.

Betty looked pale. 'Oh dear, is it that bad?'

Sarah didn't wish to alarm her too much. 'You may need a hand carrying his belongings,' she explained. Betty wasn't entirely reassured by this, but she said nothing more as they went back to the pile of post.

They'd all but finished when there was a tap at the door. 'Come in,' Betty called out.

'Sorry to bother you,' Freda said as she entered. 'There's a young lady waiting for an interview. I also wondered if there was any news on Anthony's bicycle? I'd not like Alan to be out of pocket, and I can't get up the workshop to see him for a few days.'

Betty frowned as she noticed Sarah visibly bristle. 'Is there any news, Sarah?'

'Not that I know of. But then, Alan doesn't tell me everything that goes on at the workshop. In fact, he discusses very little with me these days,' she said abruptly, turning away from Freda, who looked shocked.

Perplexed at Sarah's manner, Betty gave Freda a gentle smile. 'I believe we are about finished here. Please show the lady up, Freda. Oh, and we were just chatting about going to Anthony's lodgings to collect his nightclothes and inform his landlady that he will not be out of hospital for a while. As it's close to your home, perhaps you would like to join us? I thought we could go in our lunch break. What do you think?'

Freda glanced at Sarah, who now had her head down, checking figures in a ledger. 'Yes, I'd like to help, seeing as I was partly responsible for the accident.'

'I'll ignore that comment, Freda. The glare of the sun was to blame, and that young man should share the responsibility, from what the witnesses say. Why, the police have told us it was purely an unfortunate accident.'

'All the same . . .' Freda said, looking miserable for a moment.

'I'll hear no more of this, and will meet you both at one o'clock,' Betty said.

'I won't join you after all, if you don't mind,' Sarah said, speaking directly to Betty and ignoring Freda. 'I've remembered an errand I have to run in my break, and it can't wait.'

Betty could see there was a problem, but now wasn't the time to discuss such things. 'Not to worry. I'm sure we can manage between us,' she said, ignoring the frosty atmosphere. 'Show Miss . . .' She looked at a sheet of paper on her desk. 'Show Miss Effie Dyer in, please, Freda.'

Sarah waited until Freda had left the room, then got to her feet before Betty could ask her if there was a problem.

'I'll be downstairs checking our stock of carrier bags. These numbers don't seem to add up,' she said, escaping before Betty could ask her what was bothering her.

'Do you think this coat will do?' Ruby asked as she handed it to Maisie Carlisle to look over. 'I know you're busy, what with your dress shop and your kiddies to look after, but if you tell me it's past its best, I'll see if my coupons will stretch to a new one. The more I stare at it, the shabbier it looks. Bob said he'd treat me, but it does seem a waste to have a best coat sitting in the wardrobe for high days and holidays.'

Maisie took the coat from Ruby and draped it over the tailor's dummy she kept in her workroom behind the dress shop. That too was a bit on the shabby side, what with Maisie having found it on a bomb site during the latter days of the war. The room was stuffed to the ceiling with bolts of fabric and piles of old clothes waiting to be unpicked and turned into something wearable. There were shelves overfull of patterns, and a box full of reels of cotton thread sat on the floor. 'Why don't you stick the kettle on while I have a think?' she said, already wearing a faraway look as she stepped back to stare at the navy-blue woollen coat. 'You've 'ad this a while, 'aven't you? I remember you wearing it when I moved in wiv you years back. It's a good bit of cloth, though, and the lining's held up all right.'

Ruby nodded in agreement. 'It did cost a fair penny, but back then we didn't have clothing coupons, and we bought things new that would last. If I remember rightly, the kids chipped in for my birthday present.'

Maisie grinned as she pulled out fabric from boxes and held it up to the light to check the colour. 'I can't think of your Pat and George as kids, what wiv 'em being grandparents themselves. 'Ow is Pat these days? It seems an age since we've seen her family.'

'I had a postcard only the other day. She's gone back down to Cornwall to visit that family who took in the kiddies during the war. She did ask me if I'd like to go with them, but to be honest her kiddies run me ragged.'

'There's a good few of 'em,' Maisie answered, thinking they were nigh on feral when they were younger. She couldn't tell one from another, and wasn't sure Ruby could either. 'Cornwall's a place I've not visited, but they say it's pretty. Surely it would be like a busman's 'oliday what wiv your Pat living on a farm 'ere, then going to stay on one down there?'

'Oh, it's a different world, Maisie,' Ruby replied, smiling with pride at the thought of her Pat and husband. They had taken on a farm not far from Erith, close to the marshes and the Thames between Slades Green and Crayford. 'They work all the hours God made, and they've done a good job since that chap who ran it passed away and they took on the tenancy. Now, where do you keep your cups?' she said, looking around the untidy room.

Maisie pointed to a small cupboard. 'They've been more than generous to you and your friends over the years,' she said, thinking of how Pat supplied produce to the shops in Erith and Belvedere and often dropped off a box of veg at number thirteen. Ruby always shared it with friends and neighbours, along with whatever she and Bob grew on their allotments.

'She's a good kid,' Ruby said with a gentle smile. 'I've been lucky with both mine – and now we have another wedding in the family. Who'd have thought of my George getting married again? Mind you, he's got a good one in Maureen, although it's a bit confusing what with her being our Sarah's mother-in-law.'

'It's a match made in 'eaven,' Maisie said. 'But we'll all be thinking of Irene and never forget 'er. You know I was rather fond of Sarah's mum, even though she could be a right snob at times.'

Ruby chuckled as she poured boiling water into a small china teapot before checking the gas ring, which Maisie used in her shop for her copious cups of tea, was turned off properly. 'You're right. It's strange to think she used to hang about with Maureen when they were younger. I often wondered why George chose Irene over Maureen.'

'Love can be strange at times. Who'd 'ave thought my David would have picked me, what wiv 'im being proper posh and 'is family nigh on being landed gentry?'

'He's lucky to have you, love, and to be honest his parents are pretty down to earth considering they own what amounts to a stately home and all,' Ruby said, clearing a space at the edge of Maisie's worktable and placing down a cup of steaming hot tea. 'Mind you don't knock it over,' she warned.

Maisie snorted with laughter. 'They call it an estate. It's got a farm and everything. The whole lot of us could move there and not make much difference. Now what do you think of this?' she asked as she held up a child's black velvet coat.

Ruby eyed it carefully, cocking her head to one side as she did so. 'It's a bit on the small side for me.'

'No, I mean to cut it up and trim your coat. I can make a new collar and cuffs out of this and also cover the buttons. It'll look like a new coat.'

'It seems a shame to spoil such a nice coat, though, what with so many kiddies needing decent clothing. No, I'll make do with my old coat. No one will be looking at me anyway – the bride will be the one with all eyes on her, and that's as it should be.'

'Don't be such a daft bugger. Do you think I'd destroy a good bit of clobber?' Maisie said as she turned the coat round to display the back. 'Look, the little tyke it belonged to stood in front of a coal fire and scorched the back so much it's of no use to man nor beast. His mum gave it to me in a bag of bits and pieces. I ran her up a skirt and put elastic in a couple of pairs of drawers and she was as 'appy as Larry.'

'In that case . . .' Ruby said, beaming as she felt the softness of the fabric, 'I'd be very grateful, and I'll pay you for your time and all.'

Maisie frowned. 'I'll not take money from you, Ruby Cas— Jackson,' she said, almost calling the older woman by her previous surname. 'After all you've done for me over the years. I dread to think where'd I'd be if it wasn't fer the friendship of you and yer family. Why, I could be pulling pints in some sleazy pub; or even walking the streets,' she added, thinking back to her past life.

Ruby gave Maisie a hug. 'Then I'll pay you back by taking your kiddies out for the day and giving you some time alone with that handsome husband of yours,' she said, knowing that what Maisie had said wasn't far from the truth. Out of all of them Maisie's life had changed the most since she became friends with Ruby's granddaughter Sarah on the day the three girls started work together at Woolworths. 'Now, drink your tea up before it gets cold.'

'Coo-ee,' a voice called as they heard the shop door open.

'We're through here, Maureen,' Maisie called out. 'You must have smelt the teapot. Can you put the door on the latch, please?'

'Hello, love,' Maureen said as she kissed Ruby on the cheek. 'I could do with that cuppa. George has had me up the house looking at his handiwork. Why on earth he's decided to decorate the main bedroom one week before our wedding I don't know.'

'That's men for you,' Ruby chuckled as she checked the teapot before pouring out a cup of tea for her soon-to-be daughter-in-law. 'My Bob wanted to distemper the toilet the day before our wedding. I had visions of everyone getting white marks on their best clothes. I'd been nagging him for months to get the job done. He couldn't understand why I said no. Then of course he didn't bother to do it for another six months.'

'Best we don't let the pair of them get their heads together to plan to decorate our homes, then,' Maureen chuckled. 'What's your David like at getting jobs done?' she called to Maisie, who had gone to a tall wardrobe that stood at the back of her workshop.

Maisie's cheeks turned pink as she returned with a

garment on a hanger covered in a white sheet. 'Oh, he tends to get someone in,' she blushed.

'Now that is posh,' Ruby laughed as she explained to Maureen how they'd been talking about David Carlisle's posh parents.

'Hmm, perhaps I'll turn posh and get someone in, if it means getting the work done quicker. Not that I'm saying you're posh, Maisie,' Maureen said, wrinkling her nose at the thought.

'Common as muck, me,' Maisie retorted, seeing Maureen's reaction.

'Oh goodness, what am I saying?' Maureen said, looking embarrassed. 'I wasn't implying anything by it . . .'

'No offence taken, ducks. What you see is what you get wiv me, and my David's just the same. To be honest he's bloody useless at doing things around the house so it's me who suggested we get someone in, or it'd never get finished. Now, your dress is finished – would you like to try it on?'

Ruby got to her feet, wincing as she did so. 'I'll leave you to it. You don't want anyone seeing your special frock until the big day.'

'No, you stay where you are,' Maureen insisted. 'I don't have a mum to help me with this wedding, so a mother-in-law-to-be is just as good.' She hadn't missed the look of pain that crossed Ruby's face. She'd have to remember to speak to George about his mum's health – perhaps Ruby needed a check over by the doctor?

'I'd be proud to,' Ruby said as she eased herself back down onto the seat. 'Why, I never gave it a thought that I'd have another daughter.' She reached for the handkerchief that was tucked up the sleeve of her cardigan. 'I've always thought of you as family, what with you being our Sarah's mother-in-law, so it's a bit of a shock.'

'If the truth be known, I still feel as though I'm hopping into Irene's shoes, and it's an uncomfortable feeling.'

Ruby leant over to where Maureen had perched herself on Maisie's work stool and patted her knee. 'Never you fear, we are all overjoyed you're marrying George. And if you are half as happy as Sarah and Alan have been these past eight years, then all will be well. There isn't a problem?' she asked as she noticed a frown cross Maureen's face.

'I'm probably worrying over nothing,' Maureen said as she turned to where Maisie was uncovering her wedding gown. 'I've most likely thought too much about nothing . . . My, but that looks lovely.'

Now Maisie frowned. 'Come on, Maureen, you can't leave it like that. Spit it out,' she said as she hung the dress on a hook attached to the wall and turned to face the pair with her hands on her hips. 'I'll not sleep wondering what's going on.'

Ruby watched the two women. She wasn't about to say anything, but she had noticed Sarah was rather distant when she'd popped into number thirteen yesterday to collect the children, and she hadn't stopped for a chat like she usually did. 'A problem halved is a problem shared,' she said, encouraging Maureen to explain.

Maureen sighed, wishing she hadn't said anything; but at the end of the day they were all as good as family. 'I went up to the workshop the other day and overheard something just before I went through the door. I wasn't listening at keyholes,' she said quickly. 'My God, I'd hate anyone to think I was deliberately listening to what my son was up to. It was just that the pair of them stopped talking when I went in, and both looked rather embarrassed. I thought something was going on. I could have been wrong,' she added, feeling as though she'd betrayed her son.

'So, you overheard Sarah and Alan talking privately. It happens, ducks. I'd not worry about it.'

'It wasn't our Sarah – it was Freda,' Maureen said, feeling worse than she'd ever felt in her life. 'What if something . . . something's going on between them?' she said fearfully.

'Blimey. That would be a problem, what with you marrying Sarah's dad,' Maisie said, putting into words what the three women were all thinking.

'I suggest we don't let what's been said leave this room,' Ruby instructed. 'Let's keep our eyes and ears open and if anything is going on, we should not interfere – unless one of them needs a shoulder to cry on. It's probably nothing at all,' she added.

Maureen quickly agreed, feeling happier than she had in days.

Maisie turned away to reach for Maureen's dress, knowing she needed to speak to someone . . . and the best person was her friend, Betty Billington.

5

‘It’s just down here,’ Freda said to Betty, who was looking at a piece of paper showing the address of Anthony’s lodgings. ‘I was told the house is no more than a hundred yards from the New Light.’

Betty looked around in consternation. ‘I’m completely confused. What is this New Light?’

Freda chuckled. ‘Now I do feel more of a local. It’s the nickname given to that pub back on the corner – the Royal Alfred. It was the first public house to have electric lights installed – or it may have been the first building . . . Oh well, that’s what it’s known as locally. I suggest we cross the road for a little while,’ she said, taking Betty’s arm and steering her across the narrow road as a group of men started to call out to them.

‘Oi, love! I’m yours for half a crown. Throw in the old girl and I’ll make it three bob.’

‘Oh my, did they say . . . ?’ Betty blushed.

‘Ignore them, Betty, and don’t look back,’ Freda muttered as they walked a little faster. ‘I’m afraid you get men off the ships around here, and some are looking for . . .’

'I know what they are looking for, Freda. I was just startled to think they assumed I would provide it,' Betty started to giggle. 'Perhaps I should treat it as a compliment.'

It was Freda's turn to be shocked. 'Betty, really! Whatever would Douglas say?'

One of the men, thick-set with dark hair that covered his ears, had followed them and tapped Freda on the shoulder. 'I was talking to you, darling.'

'I'm sorry. I think you've got the wrong person,' she said as she grabbed Betty's arm. Together they tried to hurry back over the narrow road.

'Not so fast,' another man called out. 'Isn't our money good enough for you stuck-up tarts?'

'This one's mine,' said the dark-haired man who'd tapped Freda on the shoulder. 'Come on, darling, no need to be so stuck up. There's an alleyway over there . . .' He took a firm grip on her arm.

'Run, Betty!' Freda cried out as he pulled her away from her friend.

'Oh, no you don't,' Betty shouted, landing the man a hefty blow across his left ear with her handbag and giving Freda time to pull away from his hold. 'We are not the kind of women you're after. Be on your way!'

Two other men standing nearby joined in the chase as Freda and Betty ran for their lives.

'Hey, there – what do you think you're doing?' a loud, deep voice boomed from behind them. Please don't let there be any more of them, Freda prayed, as she tried to catch her breath. Her heart was pounding in her chest. She'd lost one shoe as she fled, and her arm ached where the beastly man had grabbed her.

Betty tripped and stumbled against the window ledge of one of the shabby-looking houses set directly onto the street. Unlike roads nearby, this long terrace of two-up, two-downs didn't have front gardens. She rapped on the dirty window, hoping to attract the attention of someone inside who might come to their aid.

The men pursuing them, roaring loudly with laughter, now pounced, treating Betty and Freda's discomfort as fair sport. 'I've got you now, my little darling,' grinned the dark-haired one as he pinned Freda's arms to her sides and tried to kiss her.

Freda turned her head aside, barely avoiding his mouth but wincing at his foul breath. 'Help,' she managed to scream as she spotted the other chap grab hold of Betty.

'Let go of the ladies,' the deep voice said from close by. 'I'll ask you just once more. I'm not an aggressive man, but I'll not see you harm these women.'

Freda, although fighting with all her might to beat off the offensive man, couldn't help wonder where she'd heard that voice before.

'I said leave the ladies alone,' he growled, as Freda felt her assailant being wrenched away from her. As she turned, she saw her attacker fly into the road and lie there stunned. His mates fled, quickly followed by the man who'd been grabbing at Betty.

'Oh my,' Betty said, straightening her jacket and tucking a loose strand of hair back under her hat. 'I don't think we've met?' She beamed up at the tall, handsome man. 'I must thank you for saving us. You are saving us, aren't you?' she added suddenly, looking a little worried.

Freda hurried over to where Betty was politely shaking

the man's hand. 'Betty, this is my friend Lemuel Powell. He was in the RAF with Alan. I met him at the workshop the other day,' she explained, as a questioning expression crossed Betty's face. 'Lemuel, this is Mrs Betty Billington. She's my boss,and the manageress of Woolworths.'

'I'm a friend of Alan Gilbert and his family,' Betty explained as she shook Lemuel's hand for a second time. 'You are truly our saviour.'

Lemuel nodded, a broad smile filling his face. 'I have heard so much about your Woolworths store, and all of Alan's good friends. We filled many nights talking about loved ones while waiting . . . waiting to see what the dark hours would bring.'

'You flew planes?' Betty asked, wondering how the tall man would fit into the aircraft.

Lemuel roared with laughter. 'No, ma'am, I worked with the ground crew. We kept the pilots in the air,' he explained. 'You've heard the saying "on a wing and a prayer"? There were times when it felt like the Almighty had deserted us and it was only a few men keeping our brave pilots up there.'

'Then we have a lot to thank you for,' Betty said. 'Not least for turning up again in our hour of need. May I ask why you are in this less than salubrious area of Erith? Not that I'm not pleased you appeared,' she added, glancing around to reassure herself once more that the gang of men were nowhere in sight.

'I've been staying around here for the past two nights. But I'm on the move today,' Lemuel explained as he adjusted a heavy-looking rucksack he had slung over one shoulder. 'I also wondered why you are here. It is not really the place for ladies,' he said, looking at the road that bordered the docks, where cranes were loading and offloading goods onto ships. Everything seemed grimy, with a layer of dust that made the houses look neglected and unloved, unlike those only a few streets away with their gleaming windows and scrubbed doorsteps. 'Perhaps I could escort you, to spare you any more unwanted attention?'

'That's very kind of you, Lemuel. I must say, the sooner we are away from here, the sooner I'll feel safe. We are looking for number twenty-nine,' Betty said as she fell into step beside him with Freda on the other side. Both women had to crane their necks to look up to their tall, well-muscled companion, and they felt much safer in his company.

'Here it is,' Freda said as she stopped by a door and used a heavy brass knocker that could have done with a spit and polish to make their presence known to whoever was inside.

'I'll wait a while over there,' Lemuel said. 'I'll feel better knowing you have concluded your business and gotten away from here.'

Betty beamed at him. She'd never felt so safe. She'd noticed people who passed by give them furtive looks. 'Thank you. It shouldn't take more than a few minutes to carry out our business. Ah – here comes someone now.'

The door was opened by a short, wiry woman who was wiping her hands on a frayed tea towel. She took in Betty, who was wearing her smart tweed suit, and looked defensive. 'If you're from the authorities, you've got the wrong house. It's her two doors down you want. It's criminal what she gets up to, with women to-ing and fro-ing at all hours. I told your people I don't hold with such things, but those poor women need help from someone – just not her.'

Freda didn't understand what she was going on about. 'I'm sorry – we aren't from the authorities, we're from Woolworths.'

It was the woman's turn to look confused. 'I didn't know you made deliveries. Not that I've ordered anything. You've most likely got the wrong house,' she said as she started to close the door. 'If you'll excuse me, I have things to do.'

'Please – I'm here on behalf of one of your boarders, a Mr Anthony Forsythe?' Betty interrupted, before the door closed completely.

'He's not here. I've not seen hide nor hair of him these past few days. He disappeared without taking his things. If he's in trouble with the police, you can tell him from me I'll be selling his property to cover the rent he owes me. I'm within my rights,' she added indignantly.

'Oh, my; I do believe we are talking at cross purposes,' Betty said, trying hard not to become irritated. The woman still seemed hell-bent on shutting the door on them. 'I am Mrs Betty Billington, the manager of F. W. Woolworths, and Mr Forsythe is one of our trainee managers. He met with an unfortunate accident yesterday . . .'

'If he's dead, I'll still be selling his bits and pieces. And that includes his bikes. They're cluttering up the yard, and I'm still owed rent.'

'Please, hear me out,' Betty said. 'Mr Forsythe isn't dead. He's in the cottage hospital and likely to remain there for a while. I came to collect his nightclothes and washing implements, so he's able to be a little more comfortable during his enforced stay.'

The woman didn't seem moved by the news of Anthony's predicament. 'So who is going to pay his rent?' she asked, folding her arms over her thin frame and glaring at Betty. 'I'm not a charity, you know.'

'Perhaps showing a little charity would help at a time like this,' Betty said primly. 'The poor man had an accident. He didn't mean not to be here and pay his rent on time. I'm sure we can come to some agreement . . .'

'On time? He's never paid his rent on time since the day he moved in,' the woman spat back. 'He's too bloody busy tinkering with those damned bikes or taking off cycling the streets. He's a rum one and no mistake. I'm glad to be shot of him.'

Freda was worried. Surely Anthony wasn't going to be made homeless because of an accident for which she was partly to blame? She looked to Betty for help, but her boss was speechless and clearly angry. 'Could we take his possessions?' Freda asked impulsively. 'They could be taken care of until he is fit to leave hospital.'

'That's an admirable idea,' Betty beamed, attempting to take a step over the threshold.

'No one's taking a thing until I've been paid what's owed to me,' the woman snarled. 'And if I'm not, then I'll be flogging his stuff to cover it.'

Freda felt more and more as though this was all her fault. The little she'd seen of Anthony Forsythe, she hadn't liked; he seemed rude and prickly. But she felt that it was down to her to help in some way so that when he left hospital, he still had his worldly goods and this woman hadn't sold them off, leaving him without a stitch to his name. 'Betty, I feel perhaps we could settle Anthony's debt and take his property. We wouldn't want this lady to be out of pocket, would we?' she asked, hoping Betty understood what she was getting at.

'Of course not,' Betty answered, giving her a discreet nod. 'May I see Mr Forsythe's rent book, please, and I'll settle what is due and give you something on top for your trouble.'

The woman thought for a moment before replying. 'Wait here,' she said, closing the door in their faces.

'I didn't expect any of this,' Betty said, taking a couple of steps away from the front of the house and checking her wristwatch as she did so. 'I have an appointment in fifteen minutes with a local supplier and I daren't miss it, as it could be beneficial to the store. I'm also unsure what we are going to do with Mr Forsythe's property. It doesn't seem right leaving his things in the warehouse. It could be an age before he returns to work, and the responsibility if anything should go missing is unimaginable.'

'I could store his things at my house. I do have a spare bedroom at the moment, and if I should take on a new lodger, we can think again about storage. I'm not sure about the bicycles, though.'

Betty nodded absentmindedly as she rummaged in her large leather handbag. 'Thank goodness I'd not been to the bank yet. I can borrow what is owed from this morning's takings, and alter the ledgers when I return to work.'

Freda forgot about the predicament of where to store Anthony's property and gasped as Betty pulled out a bundle of ten-shilling notes in a paper band. 'Put that away, before someone notices and runs off with your handbag! Gosh, what would have happened if one of those rough men had taken it?'

Betty pulled out four of the notes and tucked them into the pocket of her jacket before pushing the rest to the bottom of the bag and closing the brass clasp with a snap. 'For goodness' sake, Freda. They were not interested in our handbags. They were after our bodies,' she said briskly, before looking up into Freda's shocked face. 'Oh, I'm so sorry. I've shocked you, and there was no need. Why don't you go over and ask Lemuel if he will accompany us back to the store? A little protection would not go amiss.'

Freda agreed, and hurried over to where Lemuel stood watching discreetly. He rested his rucksack on the ground and wiped the perspiration from his brow as Freda explained what had happened with the landlady.

He nodded thoughtfully. 'May I ask if the young man is the kind of person to be in debt to someone?'

Freda screwed up her eyes against the hot sun as she looked up at him. 'I hadn't given it a thought. I only know him from work. The trainee managers move from store to store for their training. I think he's been with us for only a few weeks.' She didn't like to add that they'd had more contact after she ran him down while on Bessie. 'I'm pretty certain that anyone in training to run their own store one day would have to be honest and reliable.'

'Perhaps you should have a word with Mrs Billington?' he advised.

Freda agreed and beckoned to Betty, who waited for a

man with a wheelbarrow to pass by on the narrow road before joining them. 'We've been thinking that perhaps the landlady isn't being completely honest, Betty. Why would one of our trainees not pay his rent money? If the landlady had cause for concern, she could have complained to Woolworths and it would have been the end of his career. Something stinks here.'

'I agree – something does stink, and it isn't the river,' Betty said, as she wrinkled her nose. 'Look, the door's opening. Would you join us, Lemuel?' she asked, before heading back to where the landlady stood with her hands on her hips.

The three of them waited for the woman to speak. She gave a quizzical look at Lemuel before clearing her throat. 'I hope you aren't wanting to rent a room from me,' she said pointedly, nodding to a small card propped in the front window that bore the words NO DARKIES HERE. 'Nothing personal,' she added, 'but we've had problems.'

'You seem to have a lot of problems,' Betty said, giving her a hard stare and holding out a hand. 'May I see the rent book?'

'Well, there's a funny thing. I had it the other day, and now I can't find it.'

'Then we will come back when you have found it,' Betty said, starting to turn away. 'My friend, Police Sergeant Jackson, can visit later to help you search for it.'

Freda did her best not to laugh out loud as the woman turned pale.

'There's no need for that. I just want what's mine,' she muttered sullenly. 'As I told you before, I can sell off his stuff and cover my costs.'

Betty reached into her pocket and pulled out the notes. 'You can take this, and I'll forget to speak to my policeman friend. It is your choice.'

The woman looked at the proffered notes and licked her lips thoughtfully. 'All right,' she said, reaching out to take them.

'Not so fast, dear lady,' Lemuel said, pulling Betty's arm away before the money could be touched. 'We want the young man's possessions. When we have them here on this doorstep, you can have the money. I am sure that, from the goodness of your heart, you will be agreeable?' He gave her a charming smile.

'I can't do it all on my own. Those bikes are heavy, and I'm an old woman,' she answered, not taking her eyes from the money.

'I'll come with you to collect his personal effects,' Betty said, stepping forward.

'You make it sound as though he were dead,' Freda said, inwardly squirming at the thought that if he had been, it would be her fault. 'I can help with the bicycles, if you'll show me the way?' she said to the woman.

'There's a gate down that alley. They're in the shed.' The woman did not move from where she stood. 'You'll have to get them yourself, as my back won't let me lift things.' Turning to Betty, she added, 'His room's up the staircase on the left. I've already emptied the drawers and wardrobe. It won't take you more than a few minutes to pack his suitcase. What did you expect me to do when he vanished without a word? I've got people wanting to rent that room,' she said, noticing Betty's look of disdain.

'I'll come along and help you,' Lemuel said to Freda, following her towards a narrow alleyway between the houses.

'Don't you go into my house! I don't want no darkies in my home. It'll give me a bad reputation,' the woman screeched.

'Don't worry – your reputation's none too shiny anyway,' Betty muttered as she hurried up the stairs, intending to be as quick as possible.

'I'm sorry people are so vile to you,' Freda said to Lemuel.

'Don't give it another thought. What's that saying . . . water off a duck's back? I don't let people like her worry me. Let's get those bikes, shall we?' he said, continuing to the back yard as Freda followed, wondering what they'd fought for in the last war if people could still be so horrid to each other.

'Crikey, who needs three bikes?' Freda said out loud as she wheeled each one from the shed in the small back yard.

'Four, if you count the one in Alan's workshop,' Lemuel noted as he lined them up side by side and lifted them in one hand as though they were as light as a feather. Throwing his knapsack over his shoulder, he headed back through the dark alleyway out into the sunshine. Freda followed, protesting that she should be helping, but he brushed off her comments with a broad smile before setting the load down on the small pavement in front of the house. 'Have you thought what we are going to do with these?' he asked.

Freda hadn't, what with her mind being full of guilt

over her part in Anthony's injury. 'I can store his clothing and personal items.'

'Perhaps they should join the other bike up at Alan's workshop. I can keep an eye on them during the night.'

Freda frowned. 'You're sleeping at Alan's workshop?'

'I've slept in worse places. It worries me none, so don't look so concerned, little lady.'

'I have a spare room. I did put a card up on the board at work advertising the room, but I can take it down . . .' she offered, wondering at the same time if the single bed would be large enough for this giant of a man.

'No, no,' he protested, raising one of his large hands to stop her words. 'Without an income I'm not able to pay my way and until I can, I'll make my own bed – even if it is on the floor of Alan's workshop,' he added with a grin.

'Oh, I feel so sad about your situation,' Freda said, noticing the sign in the woman's window again. 'Life and people can be so beastly at times! I'm sure Alan would give you work, if he had any. He's a decent sort.'

'I'll help him out where I can for a roof, of sorts, over my head. He's been a good friend to me, and knowing his situation, I'll hang around to help as long as I can.'

'You are a good man, Lemuel Powell,' Freda said, reaching up as far as her arms would stretch to give Lemuel a big hug. As he engulfed her in his arms and swung her round, she saw the sign in the landlady's window and felt sick at the thought that such things could be happening in her beloved country. Then something else caught her eye. Two doors down, at the house the landlady had hinted had women coming and going at all hours of the day and night, the door was open. A young woman appeared, then hurried off in the opposite direction. Freda recognized her as Effie Dyer, who had come to the store for an interview earlier that day. Goodness – was a woman of ill repute about to join the staff at Woolworths?

Maisie stuck her head out of the door to her shop, Maisie's Modes, and shouted across the busy street. 'Oi, Betty! Can you spare a minute?' Ignoring the women browsing inside the shop, she put her fingers in her mouth and made a shrill whistle that pierced the ears of those around her. She gave a smile as Betty turned and waved before crossing Pier Road and entering the shop, following the glamorous Maisie.

Anyone seeing Maisie Carlisle for the first time would have thought she'd just stepped from the screen of a Hollywood movie. She not only sold the favourite fashions of the day, but was always impeccably turned out in styles copied from the pages of *Woman and Home*, *Woman's Weekly* and various others in her collection. What made the affable Maisie so popular amongst the women of Erith was that her outfits were all handmade in the workroom behind her shop, where she also sold remodelled gowns from second-hand clothing.

Maisie greeted her old boss with a kiss on the cheek. 'Can you spare a couple of minutes? There's something I need to talk to you about.'

'Have you decided to ask for your old job back? I can always use another supervisor if you've fallen on hard times,' Betty joked. She knew how much Maisie loved running her own business, which was next door to the premises of Billington and Carlisle, Funeral Directors. Betty still found it hard to believe that Maisie's handsome ex-RAF officer, David, had joined forces with her own husband, and together they had expanded Douglas's small undertaker business into a chain of four in the area. Their two surnames were now resplendent in gold lettering on black above all the shops, and both women were extremely proud of their hard-working husbands.

'That'll be the day,' Maisie roared with laughter. 'Let me just serve these ladies, and I'll be wiv you.'

Betty checked her watch. She was running late for her appointment with a potential supplier, having been held up for so long in Wheatley Terrace with Freda and Lemuel. 'Can I use your telephone, please? Then I'm yours for as long as you need me.'

Maisie pointed to the curtained-off part of the shop where she had her workshop. 'You know where to find it,' she said, turning back to a woman who was looking at a pattern for a summer dress. 'Put the kettle on while you're there? I'm fair parched.'

Betty filled the small kettle and put it onto the single ring before picking up the telephone and putting a call through to her office across the road. It felt rather indulgent for her to make such a call, but she knew that if she actually went into the store, she might not escape again for some time. Such was the life of a busy manager – a life she loved as much as her husband and family.

Hearing Maisie call out goodbye to her last customer, she poured the tea and added milk. Reaching into her handbag, she retrieved a bag of broken biscuits she'd placed there earlier to take home for the girls. 'I have a treat for you,' she said, picking out some of the larger pieces and placing them on a saucer.

'I miss these,' Maisie sighed as she sank into a shabby armchair in the corner of the workroom. 'If you do need me back at Woolies, just lure me wiv biscuits. In my 'ouse they vanish in seconds. I swear my kids can sniff a biccie from a mile away.'

'Who'd have thought we'd get so excited over a few broken biscuits! Let's hope it won't be too long before children can eat as many cakes, sweets and biscuits as they want without having to worry about shortages and ration books,' Betty said, looking sad.

'Sod the kids. I wouldn't mind eating my way through a large box of chocolates without feeling guilty,' Maisie snorted.

'Not that we can lay our hands on such things.'

Maisie tapped the side of her nose knowingly. 'I always know a man who can lay 'is 'ands on things,' she grinned. 'Now, I know you are a busy woman, so I won't delay yer too long, but something cropped up when I was chatting to Maureen and it's been playing on me mind a bit. 'Ave you got any idea what's going on wiv Alan Gilbert?'

Betty sipped her tea thoughtfully, wondering how much she could tell her friend. What little Sarah had confided about the Gilberts' money worries was not to be shared – at least not by her. 'He has a charming man called Lemuel Powell visiting. It seems they knew each other from their RAF days. I'm told by Maureen that Lemuel will be sleeping in the workshop, and helping out a little where he can.

It seems he was a dab hand at keeping planes in the air during the Battle of Britain.'

Maisie smiled, sure that Betty was not telling her everything. They'd been friends long enough to know when something was being held back.

'I was thinking more of how Freda and Alan are getting too cosy,' she said, noticing Betty blink rapidly. 'You know something, don't you?'

Betty sighed. 'I don't think what I know has anything to do with that. Please don't ask me,' she pleaded.

'But others have noticed.'

'What do you mean?' Betty asked, looking startled.

'Maureen overheard Alan and Freda talking up at the workshop, and they shut up as soon as she made her presence known. She told me and Ruby about it when she came for a final fitting for her dress. I reckon she thinks her son is carrying on with Freda.'

Betty looked distressed. 'Oh my, this doesn't bode well, does it? I may as well say now that Sarah intimated things were rather difficult at home. But I would never have imagined that . . .'

'Alan's 'aving a bit on the side, and wiv his wife's best friend?'

Betty winced. Maisie's turn of phrase could be a little fruity on occasion. After all this time, she was still surprised that such words could come from a woman's mouth. 'Possibly,' was all she said in reply.

'I could bloody kill him if it's true. In fact, I've a mind to go up that workshop and 'ave it out wiv him. I'll shut the shop for an hour and do it right now,' Maisie added, looking round for her coat.

'No, don't!' Betty exclaimed, placing her hand on Maisie's arm to keep her seated. 'He won't be alone.'

'What – you mean Freda's up there?' Maisie said, looking indignant. 'Shouldn't she be at work, or is she sneaking off during the day to carry on wiv him?'

Betty wanted to laugh out loud. The whole situation was ludicrous. 'No, it's not like that at all. She left me to go with Lemuel, to take our trainee manager's bicycles to be stored in Alan's workshop. The poor man's lodgings left a lot to be desired.'

Maisie gave a blank look. 'You've lost me now. Are you saying Freda's not carrying on wiv Alan? Or are you saying she is, but you don't want me going up there ter bang their 'eads together?'

'I'm saying I have no idea what is going on, but this afternoon is not the best time to say or do anything. With Maureen and George's wedding only a few days away, we can't afford for the family to fall out. I'll be very disappointed in Alan if he is dallying with Freda.'

'She's always trotted around behind 'im like a lovesick puppy,' Maisie observed as she reached for her now cooling tea.

'It's more like him being a big brother, and her liking motorbikes. I wouldn't think in a million years that there's anything untoward happening. Thinking positively, they'll not be alone at the workshop now that Lemuel is going to be spending most of his time there. I suggest we do nothing for now, and see how the land lies.'

'Then we'll 'ave to 'ave a word with Maureen and Ruby, in case they do decide to say something and upset the applecart.'

Betty nodded her head in agreement. 'Perhaps if you have a word with the two ladies, and I'll see if I can get Freda to tell me whether she is courting. She just might let something slip, and then I can advise her.'

'What about Sarah?' Maisie asked.

'She already knows her marriage is not that happy at the moment. I suggest we just be around to support her through the bloody mess.'

Maisie raised her delicately shaped eyebrows. 'Bloody 'ell – things must be bad fer you ter swear.'

'I thought you could do with this?' Freda said as she placed a cup of coffee on Betty's desk. 'I don't know about you, but I'm exhausted after our lunchtime adventure.'

Betty gave a vacant smile as she placed her pen down. 'It was something I wouldn't wish to experience again in a hurry. Can you spare me a few minutes, Freda?'

The younger woman looked up at the clock. 'I have five minutes before I need to be back on the shop floor. I'm keeping an eye on the two new girls. They seem to be shaping up all right, but it doesn't hurt to watch all the same. Actually, I wanted to have a word with you about the girl who came for an interview.'

'Effie? She starts on Monday. I felt it best to have a few days' gap between new staff joining us. Do you know something I should be aware of?'

Freda wasn't sure how to word her concerns. 'Er . . . it's just that I spotted her while we were in Wheatley Terrace at lunchtime. She was coming out of that house two doors along from Anthony's lodgings. The house we were told women come and go from night and day . . .'

Betty frowned. 'Do you mean . . . ?'

Freda nodded, thankful that Betty had got the gist of what she was trying to imply. Now she could say it properly. 'Yes, a house where prostitutes work.'

'You have it wrong, Freda. I have it on good authority that it is where women go when they no longer wish to carry a child.'

Freda clapped her hand to her mouth in embarrassment. How could she have been so wrong? Then the penny dropped. 'But that could mean that Effie . . .'

'It could mean many things, Freda – and until we know all the details, I insist we don't talk about such things. We could be scarring a woman's reputation, and that would never do. Do you agree?'

'Yes,' she mumbled, thinking that all the same she'd be keeping an eye on Effie Dyer when she started work on Monday. 'But shouldn't we tell the police about that house? Isn't it illegal?'

Betty thought long and hard as she stirred the cup of coffee. Perhaps now was the time to ask Freda about her friendship with Alan. It had only been a couple of hours since she'd left Maisie's shop, and her mind was still swimming with what they'd discussed. She'd completely muddled her appointment with the supplier, accepting a price far higher than she ought to have paid for produce. In some ways she wished head office dealt with local suppliers, rather than putting the onus on the store managers. No, she'd keep to what had been agreed with Maisie; but there was no reason she couldn't keep Freda busy, so that she had fewer opportunities to hang about the workshop with Alan Gilbert.

'Mike Jackson is aware of what is going on in the house, so please don't think about it again. I'm afraid the world can be a very sad place at times, but in some ways those women provide a service for women in a fix.'

'But . . .'

Betty raised her hand to silence Freda. 'Let's not discuss it again. I have something to ask you, and it is of a personal nature. Would you like to sit down for a moment?'

Freda racked her brains to think of anything she might have done wrong at work. Although Betty was a good friend, she knew that while she was at work the woman was her boss, and she shouldn't take advantage. Whatever had she done that Betty needed to talk to her about? She sat down nervously and waited.

'I was wondering how you felt about having a male lodger?'

Freda was taken aback. 'Well . . . I haven't thought much about it. If you mean Lemuel, he prefers to put his head down at Alan's workshop until he can afford a proper place to rent. He's not very well off at the moment,' she tried to explain, wondering why Betty was interested in someone she'd only met earlier that day.

'Although I'm saddened by Lemuel's predicament, it is a different young man I'm thinking of.'

'Who?'

'Anthony Forsythe. I had a word by telephone with the cottage hospital, enquiring about his situation and when he could expect to be discharged.'

Freda stared sullenly at her boss. She was not enamoured

with the young trainee manager, and she felt he had a similar opinion about her. There was no love lost between the two of them. 'I was under the impression he'd be in hospital for weeks?'

'I've been told that with crutches he could soon be out of hospital. He is healthy apart from his mobility problem, and if he had somewhere to go, he could be allowed out by the weekend. As he has no next of kin, the almoner at the cottage hospital asked that I find him suitable lodgings. I explained his previous room is no longer available.'

Freda looked thoughtful. 'The room I'm letting is upstairs, and I have a steep staircase. He'd not be able to get to his bedroom with his leg in plaster,' she said.

'I'd already thought of that. We have a single bed at home that is not in use. I could have Douglas bring it round and install it in your front room – it would be just right for Anthony. What do you say?'

'But if he didn't pay his rent money at the last lodging house, then surely he might not pay me either?' Freda could hardly conceal her triumph at having found what seemed like a reasonable objection.

'Freda, we both know that awful landlady was telling lies in order to extort money from us. I will admit to being galled at having to hand over more cash in order to retrieve Anthony's possessions, but it's much better he is away from that place and can make a fresh start. You will consider my proposal, won't you?' There was a look in Betty's eye that challenged Freda to say no.

'But the rent money . . . ?'

'I will ensure you are paid promptly each week. You

need not fear – it is not my intention to see you out of pocket. Now, if that is all agreed I'd like you to take his clean pyjamas and wash things up to the hospital this evening and give him the good news.'

'I'm going to the pictures with Sadie and Lemuel this evening,' Freda said. Her sulky expression made Betty raise her eyebrows.

'Then I'll give you permission to leave half an hour early. I'd hate your plans to be ruined because of some poor, homeless soul who is confined to a hospital bed,' she replied. It seemed to her that Freda had changed, and was no longer the girl Betty had thought she knew. What could have occurred to make her become like this?

6

Freda sat back in the cinema seat, arms folded across her chest. Even the Pathé News report on the engagement of Princess Elizabeth to her handsome beau could not lift her spirits. Next to her, Sadie snuggled against Lemuel, taking advantage of his large frame filling the plush seat high up in the balcony. It had been Freda's treat, to thank Lemuel for his help carrying the bicycles to Alan's workshop. Sadie, bumping into them as they'd headed up Crayford Road with the bikes, had wheedled an invitation to join them. She seemed smitten with Freda's handsome new friend.

'Try not to be so obvious,' Freda hissed in Sadie's ear. 'You must be embarrassing poor Lemuel.'

In the dim light, Sadie turned and hissed back, 'There's not much room with him being so large. Besides, he isn't complaining,' she smirked, leaning further into the man's arm. Lemuel, engrossed in the news feature, hardly seemed aware of his admirer.

Freda huffed and glared at the screen. Everyone seemed to have a boyfriend apart from her. As far as love was concerned, she'd always picked the wrong men, or she'd been deceived by them. No doubt she would eventually become an aged spinster with a couple of cats for company. Visiting Anthony Forsythe in hospital earlier had simply confirmed to her how irritating men could be. She kicked the back of the seat in front of her with frustration, causing the man sitting there to grumble over his shoulder. Oh, how annoying Anthony was!

Now, if she could only find someone like Alan Gilbert, it would be a different kettle of fish, she thought with a smile. Although Alan was like a brother to her, she could see he had the qualities she'd like in a husband. If only he would tell Sarah of his problems and his debts. Perhaps she should say something . . . Yes, she'd have a quiet word and put her in the picture.

As the titles came up for the main film, she put these problems out of her mind. She'd been waiting to see *The Piccadilly Incident* since its release the previous year, but had missed it first time round. Now she checked for her handkerchief, ready to have a good cry, as she'd heard it was a weepy. She didn't wish to spoil the moment by thinking of the Gilberts – or Anthony, come to that. When she'd told him that Betty had arranged for him to live at her house once he came out of hospital, he'd not said much, but she'd been able to tell by the clench of his jaw and the distant look in his eyes that he wasn't pleased. Blow him, she thought as the film started. It serves him right if I didn't say that Lemuel has fixed his damaged bike and the others are being kept safe.

Later, Lemuel offered his arms to both Sadie and Freda as they stepped out into the dark evening and headed towards Alexandra Road.

'It was a beautiful film,' Freda said. 'I like nothing more than a good cry. I'll have to tell Bob to take Ruby,' she said, before explaining to Lemuel that Ruby was Alan's grandmother-in-law.

'You have a large family. That is good, as family is the most important thing in the world,' he said with a slight catch to his voice.

'You must miss yours, with them being so far away,' Freda said, although she didn't wish to pry.

'I am the only one to remain here after the war. My brother James went home to Trinidad, but he has plans to return and will be bringing my sister and her family. Perhaps my mother will come. That will be good. My plan is to have a home for them when they arrive – whenever that will be.'

Freda noticed the break in his voice. 'You are fortunate to have a family. I only have my brother and his wife, but they now have two children, which is wonderful. And they live not far away, so I get to see them often.'

'I just have my nan and my son, Arthur,' Sadie said, joining in with the conversation.

'You lost your husband in the war?' Lemuel asked, sounding concerned.

'No . . .' was all Sadie said before changing the subject. 'Are you both going to George and Maureen's wedding?'

'I wouldn't expect to be invited, as it is a family wedding, and although I've known Alan from the war his family don't know me.'

'They make everyone welcome, Lemuel,' Freda said, giving him a warm smile even though it could hardly be seen in the darkness. 'Both Sarah and Alan's family treat me like one of their own, and have done since I came to Erith as no more than a frightened child. I suppose now Alan's mum is marrying Sarah's dad, that makes them all one happy family.' She laughed as if the idea had just come to her.

'My nan said there's something wrong in marrying your own family,' Sadie sniffed, sounding very much like Vera Munro.

'Well, I'm surprised she's going to the wedding, if she thinks like that,' Freda bristled.

'It is a good family,' Lemuel said in his deep, thoughtful voice. 'I wish mine was closer. I've missed many weddings and births, and also the passing of a few respected elders. There are times I wish I was back there.'

'Don't say you are thinking of going home,' Sadie cried. 'Why, you've only just arrived in Erith.'

Freda thought the woman was being rather dramatic, and tried hard not to snort with laughter. 'Lemuel is free to go where he pleases. In some ways I envy you, Lemuel.'

'Don't envy me, Freda,' he said as they arrived at the gate to her house. 'I'm hankering after putting down roots and growing my own family. Erith has a lot to offer a man and a family.'

Freda reached up and kissed him on the cheek. 'We'd be happy to have you in our community, so please don't go racing off just when we've got to know you. Alan needs you as well right now,' she added, saying no more in case Sadie picked up on her words and passed on a juicy piece of gossip to her nan. As much as she liked Sadie, the apple hadn't fallen far from the tree in the Munro family. As she opened her front door she heard the woman's tinkling laughter in response to something Lemuel had said and prayed that the pair did not become fond of each other. Vera would throw such a rage, the whole of the town would hear her. Besides, Lemuel was far too good for the likes of Sadie Munro, she thought, as she closed the door on the evening and thought about the wedding. It would be wonderful to see Maureen married to George. They suited each other so well. Perhaps it would be that she didn't find love and settle down until her fifties, she thought, as she headed towards the stairs and her bed before stopping suddenly as she spotted a letter propped against the bottom step. Ripping it open, she saw with dismay that her current lodger had needed to rush off suddenly, as her father had been taken ill. Knowing it could be some time, she had given notice and enclosed the last of her rent money.

Freda shrugged her shoulders. Perhaps it was handy that Anthony was moving in on Saturday, even though the thought of him made her blood boil.

'I've never seen this place looking so spic and span,' Sarah said as she gazed around the workshop. The floor was swept and washed and there wasn't a tool out of place. 'Lemuel, this must be your influence. I can't thank you enough. Alan has rather let the place go of late, and it can't be through being overworked; you never seem to have much here to work on,' she added, giving her husband a harsh glance.

Alan ran his hand through his hair and bent his head to hide the anger he felt spreading over his face. He didn't need this right now. 'Give it a rest, eh, Sarah? Why don't you take Lemuel down home and give him some food? He hasn't stopped all day.'

Sarah's anger dissipated as fast as it had blown up. She shouldn't take her feelings out on Alan in front of this lovely man. 'I'm sorry, Lemuel. I'm a bit on edge what with the wedding tomorrow and a hundred and one things to do. Here, take my door key and go clean yourself up, if you like. There's hot water in the copper if you want a bath. Just drag the tin bath in from out the back. You'll have an hour before I come back, as I've got to pop in to work and see Betty. We are going to discuss our outfits for the wedding,' she added with an edge to her voice. Alan had promised her a new outfit for the occasion, but nothing had come of it.

'That's very good of you, Mrs Gilbert,' Lemuel said politely.

'Please, call me Sarah,' she smiled back.

Alan frowned. The way his wife nodded her head and spoke to Lemuel reminded him so much of his late mother-in-law, Irene. God forbid that his wife was turning into that old trout, he thought uncharitably. That was all he needed. 'I'll catch up with you later in the Prince of Wales, Lemuel,' he called as the man headed towards the large wooden doors, which had been opened to let in the sun.

'Why are you going to the pub?' Sarah frowned as she picked up a used mug from Alan's workbench. 'We have a lot to do for tomorrow. Don't forget, it's the last night your mum will live in the house with us. I thought we'd make it special for her.'

'Sarah, it's your dad's stag night. Surely you've not

forgotten? It is a tradition, after all, and you're one for doing things by the book.' Alan felt as though everything he did or said was not good enough for Sarah.

Sarah stepped back as Alan's harsh tone hit her like a slap in the face. She fought back tears, not wanting to face whatever it was that had upset her husband. Crying would not help. 'I'm sorry if me liking to do things correctly no longer pleases you. I thought you admired the way I kept our home and family together and managed to hold down a job that put food on the table?' she threw back at him, knowing deep down she had overstepped the mark. 'Perhaps it is time you realized this workshop idea is not working and you should ask Betty to take you back on at Woolworths.'

Alan turned on her, anger blazing from his eyes. 'And wouldn't you love it if I was bringing home a regular pay packet. I know only too well how you wanted me to manage a Woolworths store so you could have a home with your bloody roses round the front door.' He turned away from her, clenching his fists and fighting hard not to slam them down on the bench. 'Go home, Sarah, before I say any more.'

'Hello, you two, isn't it a lovely day?' Freda said as she appeared at the open doors. 'I hope it stays like this for the wedding tomorrow. I wondered if you wanted a hand with anything? I've done all I can to prepare for my new lodger. Betty's Douglas delivered the single bed she'd promised and even assembled it for me, so I only had to make it up. My front room looks quite cosy as a bedroom.'

'You should have let me know and I'd have come down

to help him with the bed,' Alan said, his face brightening at the sight of his young friend.

Freda chuckled as he slung his arm casually round her shoulders. 'Would you believe, he delivered it in the back of a hearse. That'll give the neighbours something to talk about.'

Alan roared with laughter. The kid was always such a tonic and, God, he needed cheering up at the moment. Another letter had arrived from Frank Unthank in the mid-morning post. It didn't bode well. 'I'd like to have seen Vera Munro's face if she'd spotted that.'

Sarah watched the way her husband joked with Freda. She couldn't remember the last time they'd laughed together, or been intimate. There might as well be a brick wall down the middle of their bed, she thought bitterly. Why was it Freda brought a smile to his face, while around her he was morose and miserable? It was as if he had shifted his affection elsewhere. The thought hit her in the stomach like a sledgehammer. She all but staggered back – there must be something going on between the pair of them, as she feared. That's why Alan was no longer interested in building the business, and he didn't bother coming home on time or contributing to the housekeeping as much as he used to. She picked up her handbag, and with as much dignity as she could muster, she turned towards the open door and walked away without saying a word.

'My goodness, Sarah, you look terrible. Are you going down with something? Oh, please don't say you are – not the day before George and Maureen's big day.' Betty had been standing by one of the large shop windows, supervising the building of a special display, when she spotted Sarah walking slowly towards the store and hurried out to greet her. The young woman was in a world of her own as she all but staggered through the busy Friday afternoon shoppers, being knocked from side to side and hardly noticing. 'Come into my office and I'll use my telephone to get hold of Alan and have him collect you.' Betty took her arm and guided her into the store, where they bumped into Maisie.

'Bloody hell – 'as there been an accident? You look ghostly white,' she said, laying her purchases on a nearby counter and taking Sarah's other arm. Together they led her through the door marked 'staff only' and guided her up the steep stairs and into Betty's office. 'You sit yourself down there,' Maisie ordered, 'and I'll go rustle up some hot tea. I don't suppose you've got something stronger hidden away in your desk drawer, have you?' she asked, but seeing Betty shake her head she hurried away towards the staff canteen. Maisie had not worked for F. W. Woolworths for two years, but still treated the store as if she was an employee and was welcomed by all who knew her.

Betty frowned. 'There's a small bottle of brandy in the first aid kit, but I'm sure a strong cup of tea will do the trick,' she said, kneeling in front of Sarah, who was now sitting down and staring ahead, in a world of her own.

Maisie turned at the door to look as Betty took both Sarah's hands in hers and held them tight. Giving them a little shake to bring the stricken woman out of her reverie, she spoke firmly. 'Now, Sarah, what is this all about? Have you seen an accident? Has something happened to make you upset?'

Sarah gave a small shake of her head and mumbled, 'Alan.'

'What's 'appened to Alan?' Maisie said, forgetting she was going for tea and hurrying back to kneel next to Betty so she could look into Sarah's vacant eyes. 'Is he ill?'

Sarah shook her head, causing strands of hair to escape from the now untidy French pleat at the back of her head. 'Nothing can ever be the same again . . .'

'What do you mean, Sarah – have you done something?' Betty said, shaking the distressed woman's hand to try and keep her with them.

Sarah tried to force the words from deep inside. 'We had such dreams . . . at least I did,' she said as a single tear ran down her cheek. 'He's betrayed me, and he's betrayed the children and everything that ever mattered to us,' she said as she tried to hold back a shuddering sob.

'Bloody 'ell – 'as he murdered someone?' Maisie exclaimed. 'This is just like those crime books Freda reads.'

Betty glared at Maisie. 'Now is not the time for joking,' she hissed as Sarah pulled her hands sharply from Betty and stood up, the chair scraping and screeching on the linoleum floor, putting their teeth on edge, before it fell over with a crash. 'Is that the problem – has Alan become involved in something, Sarah?'

Maisie's face grew serious. ''As he been arrested?'

Sarah put her hand to her lips and chewed frantically on a well-manicured nail before blurting out, 'He's having a love affair with Freda,' and collapsing against Betty's shoulder in a fit of uncontrollable sobbing.

Betty wrapped her arms around the woman, soothing her with gentle words before looking to where Maisie stood with her mouth wide open. 'Now's the time to find that bottle of brandy,' she said, looking grim.

Maisie hurried from the room, leaving Betty to calm Sarah. It took a few minutes before she managed to ease her back into the chair she'd quickly righted and then reach for a clean handkerchief in her desk drawer for Sarah to wipe away her tears and blow her nose. Pulling her own chair closer, she rubbed the girl's back until Sarah was a little calmer, although she still gave the occasional small shudder before taking a deep breath, doing her utmost to compose herself. 'I'm sorry to bother you with my problems. I didn't know who else to turn to,' she said. 'I couldn't tell Dad, what with him marrying Alan's mum tomorrow. He may have divided loyalties. And as for Nan – well, she'd be round there with a rolling pin to sort him out.'

She might also have sat you both down and given you a good talking to, Betty thought but didn't say. 'What are friends for, if not to help in times of need? You told me not so long ago that things were strained between you and Alan. Has there been some kind of falling out, for you to come to this conclusion?'

'No, we hadn't fallen out – it was more what I saw, and realized. Granted we'd just exchanged a few sharp words in the workshop, and the air was tense, but his whole demeanour changed when Freda appeared. It was as if he was glad to see her, much more than he has been of late to see me. It can only mean one thing.'

Betty thought there was little there for her to comment

on. It would have been different if Sarah had walked in on Alan and Freda in a compromising situation; but there again, when a couple had been married for as long as Alan and Sarah, surely a wife could tell . . . ?

'I've decided to confront Alan and tell him I no longer want him sleeping under my roof until he closes the workshop and finds himself a proper job,' Sarah said, jutting out her chin in a defiant manner. 'Perhaps back here?' she added, looking to Betty for support. 'I know it's been a few years since he was a trainee manager, but he could soon learn any changes in the management system since he left,' she said, almost pleading.

Betty thought of the self-assured man who had returned after the war. She had wondered at the time whether he would be able to cope with the often mundane life of working in a Woolworths store. She doubted he could. Besides, he had a long-cherished dream of owning his own business, and Betty felt that dreams should never be crushed, even if the road to success was a rocky one. Alan's seemed to be rather rocky at the moment, from what she'd observed and from what Sarah had told her. No – Woolworths would not suit Alan Gilbert any more, and Alan Gilbert would not suit Woolworths.

Taking what she thought was the cowardly way out, she nodded as Sarah spoke. 'But if there is something between Alan and Freda – not that I'm doubting you,' she added quickly, seeing Sarah's expression, 'would it be wise to push them together day in and day out?'

'Gosh, I'd not thought of that,' Sarah replied. She fell silent for a couple of seconds. 'Then Freda will have to go. Can you not transfer her somewhere? Birmingham would be good, as she came from there.'

Betty thought the idea preposterous, but she couldn't say so, seeing the fragile state Sarah was in at the moment. 'No, I don't think it is,' she started to say, and raised her hand as Sarah was about to protest. 'You must think of your children. How would Georgina and Buster –' she still flinched at the nickname – 'feel if their father moved away, which would be sure to happen if he truly loved this woman and decided to follow her to the ends of the earth?'

A fresh flood of tears followed, making Betty wish she hadn't been quite so harsh. However, Sarah needed to take a hold on her emotions and think of the consequences of any form of action. 'I've lost him, haven't I?' she sobbed, as Maisie returned with a tea tray that also contained the medicinal brandy.

'Here we go. A nice cup of Rosie Lee and a nip of brandy will soon perk you up,' she said, giving a false grin while summing up the situation.

'My question to you, Sarah,' said Betty, looking closely at the woman sitting in front of her, 'is do you want to lose Alan? Or are you prepared to put up a fight for the man you truly love?'

'Blimey, this sounds serious,' Maisie said, perching herself on the edge of the desk and reaching for the brandy.

'It's the end of my marriage,' Sarah said dramatically, looking Maisie in the eye and defying her to crack a joke.

'Are you sure about that, Sarah?' Betty was concerned at the finality of her friend's words.

'Yes,' Sarah insisted. 'I'm going to sort this out once and for all, whether the pair of them like it or not.'

'But what about the wedding? You don't want ter spoil Maureen and yer Dad's big day, do you?' Maisie asked, thinking of the repercussions on the whole of the extended family. 'P'raps you need ter take some time to think about things. Give it a few days and make some plans.'

'I agree with Maisie. How will it look to the outside world if you spoil the wedding day with your own personal problems? It could also damage any business Alan does have, which would in turn be disastrous for you and the children. You need to think of the ramifications in all this so that when the news comes out, which it is bound to do, people will see you as the brave young woman who carried on regardless of her husband's . . .' Betty stopped, trying to think of a word that wouldn't set off Sarah's tears all over again.

'Affair?' Maisie said without thinking.

Fortunately, Sarah was focused on Betty, and nodded her head in agreement. 'I can always rely on you to make sense of a situation, Betty. I should bide my time and make plans. But if Alan thinks he and Freda are going to skulk behind my back seeing each other, he has another think coming,' she said defiantly.

'In the meantime,' Maisie said as she handed out the tea, 'I think you should show Alan what he'd be missing if the marriage was ter break up.'

Sarah frowned. 'Do you mean I should have an affair or something, and let him find out?'

Maisie spluttered into her tea as she hooted with laughter. 'No! I mean you should look like a million dollars at the wedding tomorrow. Be the most glamorous woman in the room.'

Sarah's eyes lit up for a moment before she again became downcast. 'There's a fat chance of that. I was only going to treat myself to a new hat, and if I don't get a shove on Hedley Mitchell's will have closed and it'll be my old navy felt coming out for another outing.'

'I've got something that came in the other day. It almost looks like new. A two-piece red woollen suit and an ivory silk blouse. I think there's a titfer and a bag in my cupboard that would match the ensemble.'

'A titfer?' Betty asked, not understanding Maisie's language yet again.

'A "tit for tat" – a hat,' Sarah explained. 'It's rhyming slang.'

Betty giggled as she thought about it. 'Well, I never. Whatever next!'

'It's decent of you to offer, Maisie, but I can't have you lending me your stock, really I can't,' Sarah said, raising a hand as Maisie started to insist. 'I'm grateful all the same – to both of you. You must think I'm an awful cry-baby, running here like that . . .'

'We don't think you're a cry-baby. In fact, we'd be proper offended if you didn't come to us in times of trouble. We'd do exactly the same, 'cos that's what friends are for. As fer the clobber, you're going to 'ave it even if I 'ave to tie you to a chair and dress you myself,' Maisie added, wagging her finger at Sarah.

The three women looked at each other and burst out laughing. 'Oh Maisie, you're a tonic,' Betty said. 'I do think you should take up the offer, Sarah. In fact, I think you should make sure Alan doesn't see you in your outfit until you're both in the church. I take it he is giving his mum away?'

'Yes, and I'll be at Nan's tonight to keep her company, as it seems the men are going to have a stag do. Bob's going too, so Nan will be alone.'

'Then I'll come down and do your hair in the morning and help with your make-up. I'll get our Claudette and Bessie to walk your two round to Maureen's place to get into their bridesmaid and pageboy outfits; that way no one will see you until you make your entrance. Alan won't be able to take his eyes off you – well, not if I 'ave anything ter do wiv it.' Maisie smiled reassuringly.

The smile suddenly dropped from Sarah's face. 'But Freda was coming over to Nan's to go to the church with us . . .'

'Don't give it another thought. I'll nab her to help take my lot to the church. She won't suspect a thing.'

'That's very kind of you, and a great weight off my mind.'

Betty looked concerned. 'Please don't do anything to spoil the wedding. Remember, revenge is a dish best served cold,' she said, hoping that given time Sarah might think more sensibly about the situation.

'Blimey, you're going ter get your revenge on them? That could be interesting,' Maisie guffawed, before noticing Betty's prim look and falling silent for a moment. 'Betty's right. Leave it until after the wedding – a few days at least. You may see differently by then. You know, water under the bridge and all that . . .'

'As I agreed before, I won't spoil the wedding,' Sarah

replied, but her friends could see a defiant glint in her eye. What was she going to do? 'I need to collect the children. Can I pop over to your shop in about an hour?' she asked as she kissed her friends goodbye and thanked them for their help.

'Blimey! I've forgotten about me shop. I only popped over the road to buy a zip and a reel of cotton,' Maisie exclaimed as she went to follow Sarah out of the office.

'Maisie – can you spare me just a few seconds?' Betty said as she waved goodbye to Sarah before closing the door.

'What can I do fer you?' Maisie asked, looking puzzled.

'I wondered what you made of all this?'

'I know I'd kill my old man if he went running after another bit of skirt,' Maisie replied, folding her arms across her front and taking on a fierce expression. 'I thought Alan was better than all this. And as for Freda, I just don't know what ter think. But Sarah seems to know her own mind.'

'I'm not so sure Alan and Freda have done wrong. This is so out of character – my gut feeling is that there must be something else going on. I think perhaps I can do something . . .' Betty added thoughtfully. 'I just wanted to run it by you.'

'Fire away,' Maisie said, sitting down in the seat Sarah had just vacated. 'Me customers can wait a while longer.'

'I've decided to see if I can keep our Freda away from Alan as much as possible. My thoughts are that if we don't interfere, except for keeping them apart, whatever's happening may all blow over.'

''Ow are you going ter do that? She's up that workshop

working on those motorbikes whenever she ain't at work,' Maisie asked, looking mystified. 'You know it's her dream ter work wiv him one of these days. Surely she wouldn't do anything to mess that up? Especially as Sarah's been so good to her too.'

'I know; and under normal circumstances Sarah would be fine with that. I would like to know what's happened to change their happy marriage. I will keep Freda as busy as possible in order to give her no time to be Alan Gilbert's sidekick.'

'Good thinking. If I can 'elp, just give me a shout,' Maisie said.

'I'll come down with you to see how the window display is developing. I'm hoping our customers will enjoy our homage to the royal engagement.'

Maisie looked downcast. 'It's sad ter think as one marriage is about ter start, another one could be finishing. One that started right 'ere in this store wiv Alan proposing to Sarah by the pots and pans counter.'

'Extremely sad – so we must form a pact to do all we can to help our two friends,' Betty agreed as she straightened her jacket and prepared to go downstairs to supervise her staff once more.

'Three people,' said Maisie. 'Our Freda has a lot to lose, just like Alan and Sarah, if this all goes pear-shaped . . .'

7

Freda checked her dainty wristwatch. It was the one her friends had clubbed together and given her for her twenty-first birthday. She saved it for special occasions, and the day of Maureen and George's wedding certainly qualified as one of those. It still seemed strange to think that Alan's mum was marrying Sarah's dad, she chuckled to herself as she checked her hat in the front-room mirror for the umpteenth time. Well, she was in the front room but, with a bed and chest of drawers installed it was more like the bedroom she hoped Anthony Forsythe would enjoy staying in as he completed his convalescence. Douglas had informed her, after visiting Anthony, that what they had assumed to be a broken leg was in fact a torn ligament. Anthony also had a nasty gash on his thigh. Freda shuddered as she remembered the blood on the road after his fall. With luck, she thought, it would mean the man would be out of her hair sooner rather than later, although she was no medical expert. He was due at any moment, but if he didn't turn up soon, she'd miss out on seeing everyone outside St Paulinus or being able to chat with her friends, and instead would have to dash into the church and sit somewhere at the back. Where was Douglas Billington? Surely it was a simple enough job to collect the patient from Erith cottage hospital and drop him off not half a mile down the road.

She picked up a discarded copy of the *Erith Observer* that had been left open at the page announcing the betrothal of Erith's favourite councillor to a local lady. There was an official photograph of George on the day he had won the local council election, and another of Maureen taken when she was helping out at the last Woolworths Christmas party for the old soldiers. She was smiling into the camera, having just sung a rousing rendition of 'Waiting at the Church', which was rather funny considering what the article was about. There was also mention of Maureen's son, Alan, being a business owner in the town. Maureen would be so proud.

A prickle of fear ran down Freda's spine as she wondered whether Frank Unthank knew about the wedding. Almost everyone took the local newspaper; it covered not only news and social events but sports results, prosecutions and what was on at the cinemas and theatres. If Unthank was aware of the wedding, would he cause trouble knowing it was Alan's family? Even with the pittance they'd managed to scrape together, which Alan had delivered to Unthank yesterday, aided by Lemuel, he'd still been well short of the sum owed. It had been fortunate only Unthank's secretary was in his office; they'd left the envelope containing the money and a letter of explanation, and hurried away before he'd appeared. Alan had laughed it off when he returned to the workshop, but Freda could see the trip to West Street had unnerved him. Only Lemuel seemed unconcerned.

Alan really should speak to Sarah about all of this, Freda thought. Only last week she'd overheard her friend talking about planning to take the children to Whitstable, to show them the seaside and where Mummy and Daddy had visited when they were first married. Buster might be too young to understand, but he would love to splash in the sea; and Georgina, it seemed, had asked about their wedding and been enthralled by the story. However much it would delight the children, though, a trip like that would cost money – money that would be better spent getting Alan away from the clutches of Frank Unthank and his mob. But then Sarah deserved a treat. She'd been acting rather down lately, and it was hard to get her alone for one of their friendly chats.

Freda was still deep in her thoughts when a black car momentarily blocked out the sunlight coming through the lace curtains of the bay window, making her jump. Thankfully it was Douglas, and in the passenger seat of the vehicle was Anthony Forsythe.

Freda rushed out to help, and had to laugh as she saw that Douglas had again used a hearse from his business. Anthony seemed unimpressed by his new landlady's joviality.

'You must have had heads turning, arriving at the hospital in this,' she said as Douglas greeted her.

'It brightens what can sometimes be a gloomy day,' Douglas replied as he opened the passenger door and helped Anthony onto the pavement. 'Can you get the crutches, please, Freda? They're in the back. I'll come back for the bags once we've got this young man settled.'

Freda hurriedly did as he asked, trying not to think about what was usually loaded and unloaded out of this particular door. 'Here you are,' she said, doing her best to help Anthony prop a crutch under each arm. 'Can you manage?'

'Do you think they'd have let me out if I couldn't?' he growled as he gingerly moved up the short pathway to the front door. The step over the threshold was a little trickier, but he made it. He paused in the hallway and then looked towards Freda, waiting to be told where to go next.

'Just in here,' she said, pointing towards the open door. 'We thought you'd be more comfortable in the front room. Douglas and his wife Betty lent us a bed and we brought down a chest of drawers from the spare room upstairs. If you need anything else, please just say so.'

Anthony turned to Douglas, who had just walked through the door carrying a canvas holdall. 'It's very good of you to go to all this trouble for me. I'm grateful,' he said gruffly.

'Don't mention it,' Douglas said, giving him a slap on the back, which momentarily had Anthony hanging tightly onto the crutches as they started to slip on the linoleum. 'We all help each other out around here. I'll be getting back, if you don't need any more help. We are a little short staffed, what with David having the day off for the wedding. Give the bride and groom my best wishes, and we will see you this evening at the reception,' he said to Freda, closing the front door as he left.

'I've put the armchair here next to the wireless, so you don't have to move much. Shall I unpack your bag for you?' Freda asked as she reached for the holdall.

'No!' Anthony said, reaching to stop her and letting a crutch crash to the floor. 'I can manage. You get off to your wedding.'

Freda rubbed her arm where he'd grabbed her. It wasn't so much the harshness of his touch . . . no. It was something else . . . something intimate and warm, and somehow familiar. Feeling rather puzzled, she started to leave the room. 'I have some sandwiches for you. They're only potted paste, but it's filling. I'll make a cup of tea and then I'll have to scoot, or I'll miss the service. I can come back to help you later on if you like?'

Anthony hesitated a moment, and then managed a smile. 'No, you've done more than enough for me, and I can make my own tea. You hurry along,' he said, putting his weight on his good leg to reach down for the fallen crutch. 'Oh, and Freda . . .'

Freda stopped in her tracks. 'Yes?'

'You look very beautiful in your finery. It makes a nice change from your Woolworths uniform.'

She put her hand to her face as she felt her cheeks start to burn. 'Thank you.' He'd noticed her at work was all she could think as she picked up her handbag. She hurried from the house, trying to make sense of her feelings.

Sarah had lost count of the number of compliments she'd received from family and friends as she stood in the grounds of St Paulinus after the wedding service. She had to admit she felt like a queen in the smart red suit with its matching accessories. She couldn't wait to find out what Alan thought of her new outfit. No one would know it was second-hand, she'd thought earlier when she'd given a quick twirl in her Nan's bedroom while getting herself ready.

There'd not been a dry eye in the place as George and Maureen spoke their vows to each other; Sarah couldn't help but think her mum would be proud of her family, and was hopefully looking down on them with a smile. She knew Irene would have approved of her outfit, and the smart hairstyle. Maisie had laboured over it for more than an hour before stepping back and announcing that Alan would be a fool if he didn't fall in love with his wife all over again. Sarah just hoped he'd notice her, as he'd not been near nor by her since walking his mum down the aisle, then joining his relatives after the service.

'Don't forget you're supposed to be taking the photographs, love,' Ruby said as she joined her granddaughter. 'I'd hate not to have something to remember the day by. Georgina looked as pretty as a picture walking down the aisle behind her nanny Maureen. As for young Buster . . .' She roared with laughter.

Sarah smiled indulgently. 'Perhaps he was a little young to be a pageboy and stand still that long. His impersonation of an aeroplane roaring up and down the aisle was quite impressive, though.'

She looked at Ruby's outfit admiringly. 'I must say, your coat looks splendid.'

'It looks as good as new – and look at this,' she said, pointing to her head. 'Maisie added a band of the velvet trimming to my hat, so it looks as though the whole outfit was made at the same time.'

'She's a clever lass and no mistake.'

Sarah agreed as she took her dad's Box Brownie camera from its battered case. 'This old thing has recorded so many family occasions,' she smiled, feeling nostalgic. 'If only it could talk, it could tell some stories.'

'It does talk in a way, as it gives us memories to hold onto when our loved ones are no longer with us,' Ruby said, glancing over to the corner of the graveyard where her first husband had been laid to rest. She also thought of Sarah's mother, Irene, who was buried very nearby. Thumping her chest hard and trying not to cry, she put an arm around her eldest granddaughter to give her a squeeze. Tapping her head gently, she added, 'We may keep our memories up here, but this little box gives us something to smile over. Don't ever feel sad about anything, my love.'

Sarah kissed Ruby's cheek, wondering as she did if her nan knew anything of what was going on between her and Alan. No doubt she'd picked up on the tension between them and would be asking questions before too long. 'Weddings are emotional occasions, I think. It's all that looking back and remembering other times. Well, I'd best go record some more memories, or I'll have the happy couple after me,' Sarah said, heading off round the side of the church to where the wedding party had gathered. It was a relatively small group, with more friends and associates of her Dad's being invited to the evening reception at the Prince of Wales pub.

Freda had been kept busy once she'd arrived at the church. Maisie had informed her she had a headache coming on and would appreciate some help with her brood, and she knew Freda was the ideal person to keep them under control. Although proud that her child-herding skills were being called upon, Freda was a little resentful that she wasn't able to chat with people she hadn't seen in a while. She'd also wanted to have a quiet word with Alan, as Lemuel, when she'd seen him as she hurried past the workshop on her way to the church, had told her there'd been another demand from Frank Unthank in the morning post. He'd assured her the workshop was in good hands while the family were at the wedding, and had even turned down George's invitation to attend the reception later. Deep in thought, Freda found herself almost tripping over a small headstone. Someone grabbed her elbow before she fell.

'Watch it, kid, or you'll lose your hat,' a familiar voice exclaimed.

'Alan! The very person I wanted to see.'

'Where else would I be but at my mother's wedding?' he smiled.

'It's been a lovely day, and your mum looks smashing. So does George, come to that. You don't look as good, though,' she added, knowing that she could get away with such a comment, having known Alan for many a year.

'I managed to get a haircut after you pestered me to do so,' he grinned, running his hand over the short back and sides he'd managed to have only minutes before the barber shop closed.

'You look as though you've not slept in an age,' Freda pointed out. She didn't like to see Alan, who was like a brother to her, looking like this. 'You need to take better care of yourself, or you'll be looking older than your new stepfather.'

'I could say the same of you. You've been perkier. I

hope it has nothing to do with all this business with Unthank?'

She decided not to tell Alan what Lemuel had told her. It could wait until tomorrow. There was no point in worrying him more. 'A bit, but I've got me mates to look out for me,' she smiled back, straightening his tie a little. 'I'll have you know someone told me I was beautiful,' she joked with just a little embarrassment showing, as her cheeks turned pink.

'You are beautiful,' Alan said, giving his favourite friend a gentle kiss on the cheek before whispering in her ear, 'Just tell him, whoever he is, that if he messes with you, kid, he'll have me to answer to.'

Freda looked up into his eyes, knowing she loved him as much as she loved her own brother. 'Don't you worry about me. Why not go and find that glamorous wife of yours and tell her how beautiful she looks? Look, here she comes now.'

Alan's eyes clouded for a moment as he moved away from Freda, the guilt of his money problems weighing heavy on his mind. He could hardly look his wife in the eye, let alone speak to her. In turn Sarah seemed to have turned cold towards him, as if she sensed he had let the family down in some way. 'I have to go and speak to my mother. She's worried about getting to the reception on time,' he said, walking away from Freda and his wife.

'Hello, Sarah – I was just saying to Alan how lovely you look. Have you taken many photographs yet? It does seem funny, your dad not being the one with the camera today.'

Sarah simply nodded and did her best not to speak in

anger, or to let Freda see how her hands were shaking as she held the camera – the camera that had just recorded Freda and Alan standing close together. They'd looked so intimate. She'd wanted to run away when she'd rounded the corner of the building and overheard her husband tell Freda she was beautiful. When was the last time he'd spoken to her like that? No wonder he'd hurried away after seeing her approach. And he hadn't even looked at her, let alone noticed her new outfit. 'I must press on,' she said, doing her utmost to smile at the person who was ruining her life, the person who she'd thought was one of her best friends and who was now standing there like butter wouldn't melt in her mouth. If she was braver she would say something, but then it could spoil the happy occasion.

How Sarah managed to cope as she took photograph after photograph of her dad's happy day, she never knew. Even when slipping into the dark vestry to place a new film in the camera, she didn't take the opportunity to cry. She was determined that whatever her husband did with . . . with someone she'd once loved like a sister, she would not act like a victim. She would need to make plans, and show the world she could cope and do what was best for her and the children.

Sarah's resolve did not weaken as the day progressed, and by the time Betty arrived with Douglas and their two eldest daughters she was feeling determined to make the day a success for her father and stepmother. Several glasses of sherry during the afternoon had helped considerably. The camera had been passed back to her dad, who was planning to take it with him on his honeymoon. Sarah was chatting to him and Maureen about their plans when Betty joined them.

'I hear the wedding went very well,' Betty said, giving Maureen a hug and grinning at George, who was loosening his tie and opening the button of his starched collar.

'It was lovely,' Sarah said. 'The children managed not to misbehave too much, and the best man didn't lose the ring.'

'The men didn't even overdo the boozing at the stag night. I had full expectations of them having been in a fight and turning up at the altar with black eyes,' Maureen said as she linked her arm through her new husband's. 'All in all, it's been a wonderful day, and come ten o'clock we are heading off on our honeymoon. I can't wait . . . I mean, I can't wait to get to Ramsgate and the guesthouse,' she said, looking slightly flustered.

Betty chose to ignore Maureen's embarrassment. 'I've never been to Ramsgate. I hear it is very nice. Are you driving there tonight? It's rather a long way.'

'We are staying at the Wheatley Hotel tonight, and then setting off in the morning. My boss at Vickers has supplied the petrol, so we are able to use the car,' George explained. 'Nothing but the best for my wife.'

Betty looked at Sarah and sighed with delight. It was wonderful to see these two finding love in the autumn of their lives. 'We will miss you at Woolworths while you're away, Maureen.'

'Oh, that reminds me. If you look in the cupboard under the sink, you'll find a tin of biscuits. I knocked up a batch and put them away so you could have one with your tea each day,' Maureen said to her boss. 'Make sure you get to them before my stand-in finds them, or you'll not see a crumb,' she added sternly.

'I was hoping to cut back, but as you've made them specially for me, I'll do my best to enjoy them,' Betty laughed before patting her stomach. 'I had a problem doing up this skirt. I blame your good cooking, Maureen.'

Sarah glanced at Betty's pretty skirt. Its fine dusky blue pleats fell to her calves and rustled around her legs as she moved. Betty was wearing a short-sleeved white fitted blouse and a blue brooch, looking casual yet quite chic. She had filled out a little, Sarah thought, and wondered about the reason. Perhaps it was more than Maureen's baking that was to blame? She'd have to have a chat when they were alone.

'You must show me the wedding photographs when they've been developed,' Betty said to George, who promised that Maureen would drop them into the office at Woolworths to show Betty after the honeymoon. He then led his new bride away to chat with the band, who were just setting up on a small stage at one end of the hall behind the public house.

'Now we are alone, I can ask you about Alan. Have there been any developments?' Betty asked. 'Did you speak to him about your fears?'

Sarah looked around before answering. The last thing she wanted was for someone to overhear, especially as Vera Munro was one of the guests and the biggest gossip in Erith. Vera would love nothing more than to spread the news that there was trouble afoot in the Gilbert family. 'Alan came home late last night after Dad's stag do. I pretended to be asleep,' she said, looking ashamed.

'I'd been round Nan's until Bob came back, and then I decided to go home for the night. For one foolish moment I decided to have it all out with him – I even left the kiddies at Nan's, so they'd not hear. Then I chickened out. Was that bad of me?'

'No doubt I'd have done the same under the circumstances,' Betty said. 'It's best to leave things well alone until after the wedding. You don't need the attention.' She nodded politely to Vera as the woman passed by.

'But then something happened at the church,' Sarah whispered, and quickly explained how she'd seen Freda and Alan's intimate moment. 'I took a photograph of them together.'

'Oh my,' Betty said, putting her hand to her mouth. 'That could be embarrassing if the wrong person saw the photograph. Would your dad not show them to Maureen when he's had them developed? He might even show them to others without realizing the implications of Freda and Alan being together.'

'Gosh, I'd not given that a thought,' Sarah said, looking worried. 'What should I do?'

Betty thought for a few seconds. 'You must offer to take the film to be developed so that they are ready when the happy couple return home. Perhaps you could put them in an album. We have some for sale in the store.'

Sarah frowned. 'Surely that photograph would still be seen.'

Betty couldn't believe her ears. 'For goodness' sake, Sarah. You have to remove the incriminating photograph. In fact, you can give it to me, and I'll keep it safe.'

'That sounds like a plan. If I take the film to the chemist,

I can collect it during my break and it need never go home with me.'

They both sighed with relief as a deep voice said from behind them. 'The way you two have your heads together, anyone would think you were plotting something.'

Both women jumped and turned to face Mike Jackson, who had been George's best man.

'You must excuse me – I need to powder my nose,' Sarah said, hurrying away so he didn't spot her guilty expression.

The band had started to tune up as Sarah crossed the busy hall, stopping to say hello to guests on the way. She had just put her hand on the door to the ladies' when the announcement was made for the bride and groom to take to the floor for the first dance of the evening. Looking back, she saw her dad take Maureen into his arms as the bandleader sang the first words of 'I'll See You in My Dreams'. Sarah fled into the ladies' room, blinded by tears as the emotion of the day overcame her, and memories flooded back of her own wedding and others. Dreams might start in the hall of this pub, but they could also be dashed to the ground and lost forever, she thought as she reached for her handkerchief.

'Sarah! Are you all right?' a familiar voice asked, making her freeze on the spot. It was Freda.

Feeling as though Freda were her enemy, the woman who could ruin her marriage and deny her children the chance to live with both parents under one roof, she did her utmost to pull herself together. She'd made a promise not to cause a scene during the wedding, and she'd not go back on her word. 'I'm fine. It's just the occasion getting to me a little. I'll be as right as rain in a minute.'

Freda leant into the mirror a little to check her make-up, and reached into her handbag for a comb. 'I can understand that. When you think of what happened to Maisie's brother out there during Ruby's wedding, it reminds us that horrid things can happen at weddings as well as good things. I must say your outfit looked smashing. I hardly recognized you in the church,' she said, determined not to let Sarah's earlier coldness affect their friendship.

'Thank you,' was all Sarah could think to say before going to the sink and running cold water over her wrists to cool herself down. She was hoping that if she stood here long enough, Freda would leave, and then she could take a few minutes to pull herself together.

'Oh, by the way,' Freda smiled, unaware of Sarah's inner thoughts, 'Betty wants to enter me for the *New Bond* cover girl competition. She said to ask you if you would take my photograph while you have George's camera. I told her I'm not pretty enough to be on the cover of the Woolworths magazine, but she insisted it had to be someone from the branch and I was the one. What do you think?'

Sarah was only half listening as Freda spoke. Instead she was trying to work out why it was that Alan had decided to choose Freda over his own wife and to put his marriage in jeopardy.

'Sarah . . . ?'

'Oh yes, I agree,' Sarah muttered distractedly.

Freda looked puzzled. 'You agree I'm not pretty enough for the cover of *The New Bond*?'

'No . . . I mean yes . . . I mean, of course I'll take your photograph. I'll fetch the camera and we can go outside and take it now, if you wish?' Sarah said, knowing she couldn't refuse.

Freda flung her arms around her friend and gave her a hug. 'Thank you so much. I don't know what I'd have done if you'd said no. I'd die of embarrassment going to the photographer up the road from Woolies for a formal sitting.'

Sarah flinched, thinking that Freda had most likely been this close to Alan.

'I'll go find my cardigan and see you outside in ten minutes, if that gives you enough time. We'd best do it now before we start dancing, or my hair will be back to my usual mess.'

'Freda . . .' Sarah called as Freda reached the door. 'Freda . . . what do you think of my Alan?' she asked, not knowing if Freda would lie or tell the truth.

Freda cocked her head to one side and grinned. 'I love him to bits. In fact, if you weren't around, I'd marry him in a flash,' she laughed before hurrying out.

Sarah stood still, looking into the mirror on the wall. She could hear a tap dripping and outside a round of applause, no doubt for her dad and Maureen as they finished the first dance. The woman who looked back at her through the cracked glass was a stranger to her. A white-faced ghost who could see into the future; a future without a husband she loved very much. There was sure to be a fight – but would she win, or would she walk away alone?

Maureen had been coaxed by friends to sing the final song of the evening. Amongst cheers and shouts of good wishes, she had a quick word with the leader of the small band then grabbed hold of her new husband, pulling him onto the stage to stand beside her. Fuelled by a few pints of best bitter, he beamed at the guests and slipped his arm around his new bride as she broke into the popular song, 'Goodnight Sweetheart'. As Sarah watched, thinking back to when the same song had been sung by Alan, it was as if the clock had stopped before going back in time. Alan appeared beside his mum and took over the song as the happy couple stepped down to the dance floor and joined the crowd.

'You should be up there as well,' Freda said as she appeared at Sarah's elbow, followed by Betty and Maisie.

Sarah shook her head and did her utmost to ignore Freda by linking her arms through those of her two other friends. She swayed to the song, trying hard not to show her feelings.

'Would one of you charming ladies like to dance?' said Mike Jackson as he held out his arms. 'My wife has abandoned me to dance with Myfi, and I'm all alone,' he grinned.

'Mike Jackson, you old smoothie. What would you do if we all said yes?' Maisie guffawed.

'I'd deem it an honour,' he laughed as David Carlisle arrived at his side along with Douglas Billington. Both men pulled him to one side to whisper in his ear as best they could with so much noise around them.

Sarah could see Mike frown before looking towards Alan, who was still on the stage.

'Has something happened?' she asked, raising her voice so she could be heard.

'There's been some kind of altercation up at Alan's workshop. Whoever it was burst in and tried to set fire to the building. Someone's been injured.'

Freda, who had been listening, cried out in horror and leapt towards the stage, pulling Alan down towards her. Hand in hand, they hurried from the hall, followed by the other men.

Maisie grabbed Sarah's arm. 'I think we should go too,' she said. 'Come on, Betty – Sarah needs our support right now. Whatever happened up the road, it seems our Freda and Alan are in the thick of it.'

'What's going on, love?' Ruby asked, coming over to her granddaughter's side. Sarah dragged her attention away from her departing husband and Freda and turned to her grandmother.

'I don't know, Nan, but I'm going to find out. Can you keep an eye on the kids for us? I don't think they should be up at the workshop to see whatever has happened, as we don't know what's going on yet.'

'You hurry along,' Maureen said, joining the women. 'Your dad's going up the road as well to see what can be done. The children – all of them – will be as right as ninepence with us,' she added, looking to Sarah's friends, who were urging her to hurry. 'You get along there – and make sure that my son doesn't put himself in danger.'

8

The women rushed from the Prince of Wales pub and hurried the short distance up Crayford Road to where Alan's workshop stood. Mike Jackson, although off duty, was already questioning two of his colleagues, who were keeping a small crowd of inquisitive neighbours back while firemen unrolled a hosepipe. He was shouting instructions as he pulled off his jacket and tie.

'Where's Lemuel?' Alan cried above the noise.

'He went back in,' a woman screamed, pointing to the open doors.

'Sadie?' Freda said in surprise, as she saw the distressed woman being comforted by a neighbour.

Sarah pushed past Freda and faced Sadie. 'What the hell is going on? And why are you here in my husband's workshop?' she demanded as they heard a loud crash from inside the building.

'Stay back, Alan,' Mike called out as he grabbed Alan by the arm to stop him going into the building.

'I can't let Lemuel die in there,' Alan cried in anguish. 'Let go of me!' He pulled free and headed for the doorway, from where smoke was billowing.

Sadie screamed for Lemuel as Sarah did the same for her husband. Freda echoed her cries.

'This is madness,' Mike said as he was stopped from going after his friend.The small crowd watched as flames could be seen coming from the roof at the back of the building, lighting up the night sky.

Sarah turned back to Sadie, who by now was sobbing uncontrollably. 'What were you doing in my husband's workshop?' she demanded again, almost at her wits' end, wondering if Alan was all right. 'Has this got something to do with you?'

'Yes . . . I mean, no . . .' Sadie stuttered before starting to sob once more.

Sarah was so angry that she took Sadie by the shoulders and gave her a good shake. 'Tell me – you've got to tell me what happened!'

Sadie gave her a fearful look as if she'd done something wrong. 'I came up to bring a bite to eat for Lemuel. He sleeps here, you know. We was just chatting, like, and then we heard someone break open the door and start to come in. Lem turned off the light and we sat and waited . . .'

'A likely story,' Maisie sneered.

Sadie ignored her words and continued, all the time looking towards the open door of the workshop and the black choking smoke pouring out, hoping that at any minute Lemuel would appear. 'The next thing we heard was a bang, and then we saw flames. Whoever it was who'd broken in had started a fire. Lem grabbed me and pushed me towards the door, telling me to get to safety and call for help before he went for whoever it was who'd started the fire. I just ran and shouted for help as loud as I could. I've not seen him since,' she finished before dissolving into sobs again.

Who would set fire to the workshop? Sarah thought to herself as she left Sadie to be cared for by a neighbour and joined Mike Jackson, who was describing the layout of the building to a fireman who was preparing to go inside.

'There are two people in the building – Alan and Lemuel. Lemuel's been in there the longest. Unless he's managed to escape there might also be a third person in there who broke in and started the fire.'

'What's going on?' a familiar voice demanded. 'Sadie! What are you doing here, my girl?'

Freda groaned inwardly. It was Vera Munro, and she was bound to have something to say about all this. 'The workshop's on fire,' she explained, stating the obvious. 'Your Sadie's all right, so there's no need to worry.'

'But why on earth would she be here?'

'I was visiting Lemuel,' Sadie told her defiantly. Of course it would enrage Vera, but at this point Sadie no longer cared.

'Is that right?' Vera hissed at her granddaughter.

Sadie raised her chin and looked Vera in the face, her hands twisting the handkerchief Betty had passed to her. 'Yes. Lemuel is a friend – a very good friend – and neither you nor anyone else is going to stop me being his friend,' she said, her voice raw with emotion.

Vera sneered and then, to the horror of everyone watching, she spat at Sadie, making them all step back in shock. 'You're no better than you ought to be, Sadie Munro.

Already an unmarried mother, and now carrying on with a darkie. You're scum, just like your mother was.'

'Well, the apples didn't fall far from the tree, did they?' Sadie flung back at the bitter old woman. 'It all had to start somewhere.'

'Now, now, ladies,' Douglas said, attempted to calm them. 'There are men inside that burning building who we should be thinking about right now. Let's leave family discussions to another time, shall we?'

'As for you, Douglas Billington, you're only here to fill a few coffins for your business. There's always a profit to be made for Billington and Carlisle when people die,' Vera shot back at him.

There was an audible gasp from the crowd, and Maisie, unable to hold back, stepped forward and slapped Vera across the face. 'Someone should 'ave done that to you years ago, you interfering old bag,' she said furiously.

'Look what she did to me,' Vera screeched, looking in turn at each of the faces surrounding her. No one made a comment until Betty stepped forward. 'I'm afraid you asked for that, Vera. Emotions are high here just now as we wait to hear what's happened to our friends. Why not take yourself back home, out of the way? You can apologize to Maisie later.'

Vera's mouth opened and closed without a sound coming out. 'Me, apologize to that trollop? Why Betty Billington, you've gone down in my estimations. Next one of you will be giving house room to the darkie – if he survives,' she sneered, giving a nod of her head that showed she hoped Lemuel had died in the fire.

'What a good idea. Thank you for suggesting it Vera.

When Lemuel comes out of there, he's welcome to use one of my spare rooms if someone else doesn't beat me to it. Lemuel is well liked in Erith.'

Vera looked disgusted. 'I've heard enough. Come along, Sadie; we are going home. I'll be locking my door tonight in case we are murdered in our beds. There are some unsavoury people in the area and I want none of it.' She grabbed the sleeve of Sadie's cardigan, but her granddaughter pulled away.

'I'm staying here, Nan. I want to know how Lemuel is. I'll come home later.'

'Then you'll find the door locked and your bags on the doorstep,' Vera snapped back, before flouncing off.

'Blimey. I've never seen Vera walk away from something without seeing it through ter the end,' Maisie remarked.

'Can we please stop all this bickering? My husband is in there somewhere!' Sarah shouted, causing the women to fall silent.

Freda hurried over to the firemen to see if she could help. Mike Jackson was nearby, and she could see his frustration as the minutes ticked by. The roar as part of the roof caved in near the front of the workshop made them all jump. There was now no chance the men could get out of the front door. 'Mike, there's a small back entrance to the building. Alan usually keeps it locked, but from what I can see, that part of the building isn't alight. We can go down between the houses and along the back alley. It's a small chance, but worth trying.'

Mike spoke to a fireman, who pulled out a hand-sized axe. 'Will you show us the way, Freda? I have an idea of where to go, but it would save time if you were with us.'

Freda looked down at her smart outfit. What the heck, lives mattered here, and the wedding was all but over. 'Follow me,' she called over her shoulder as she started to run down Crayford Road to a narrow alleyway between the terraced houses. She could hear Mike and one of the firemen following behind her, and ran as fast as she could.

'It's a bit overgrown,' Mike said as they stopped at the rear of the workshop, where Freda pointed to a narrow door covered by a bramble bush and long grass.

'That won't take long to clear,' the fireman said as he set to with the axe and forced the weeds aside with his gloved hands. 'Now stand back,' he advised before hacking at the wooden structure. 'Keep clear there inside!' he bellowed, in case Alan or Lemuel were nearby.

It didn't take long to break in through the wooden door, and with Mike stepping in to help pull piece of wood away with his bare hands they soon made a large enough hole to climb through. Even then, smoke had found the gap and was filtering out into the alleyway, causing the three of them to cough and their eyes to stream.

'I'll go,' Freda said as she shoved in front of the two men. 'I'm smaller than both of you, and I can start to look for Alan and Lemuel while you break more of the door away.'

Mike's years of experience screamed at him not to let a young slip of a girl do what was, after all, a man's job. But before he had time to argue, Freda had disappeared through the gap in the door.

Freda took a deep breath as she squirmed and wriggled her way through the gap and into the workshop. She'd expected to be able to find her friends with ease, but instead found herself stepping into a strange and almost silent world where all she could hear was the crackle of burning wood. Thick, black, acrid smoke stung her eyes and filled her very being, to the point that she wondered if she would ever get out alive.

'Alan,' she shouted, before pulling her jacket up over her mouth and nose. A faint groan from nearby had her feeling her way a little to the right until she all but stumbled over a large pair of feet. 'Alan? Lemuel?' She reached down, feeling her way towards the head of the person lying on the concrete floor. Up close, she could tell it was neither of her two friends, and she pulled back as the stranger groaned again and tried to grab her hand.

'Kid . . . is that you . . . ?' Alan called faintly from nearby.

'Oh, thank God,' Freda said aloud as she counted her steps over to where she'd heard Alan's voice. 'Oh Alan,' she sobbed as she found him, and they clung together for a few seconds. 'Mike and a fireman are breaking down the back door. You can't get out the front way as the roof has caved in and blocked . . .' She started to cough and covered her mouth for a little while. 'Did you know there's someone else over there on the floor?'

'Yes, we've been trying to move an oil drum away . . . away from the worst of the fire . . . before it blew,' he gasped. 'Lemuel's here moving Bessie . . .'

Even with her throat aching and her eyes streaming, she managed to laugh. Alan's old bike, Bessie, meant the world to him. 'We need to go *now* . . . before the fire spreads more. Keep to the wall and feel your way along as far as you can . . .' she coughed. 'What about that bloke on the floor . . . ?

Alan cleared his throat before telling her to get out and they'd follow.

Almost tripping over the man for a second time, Freda felt her way back towards the door just as Mike and the fireman appeared through the smoke. Leaning in close to Mike, she told him what she knew and then made her way back outside where she fell onto the dirt path, gasping for air. Someone forced water through her lips before splashing her face. She rubbed her eyes to clear the stinging.

'Don't do that, love, you could make things worse,' a kindly person said as they passed her a wet towel so she could wipe her face.

'Where are they? They should be coming out by now,' she said, looking back over her shoulder. 'Please can someone go and look?' she pleaded a second before there was an almighty roar, followed by screams that carried over from those standing at the front of the workshop.

Freda felt her heart skip a beat. 'Please God, let them be safe,' she said aloud before getting to her feet, heading towards the door, ignoring the calls to keep back. Then she froze on the spot as Mike staggered out, holding the legs of the stranger she'd almost tripped over. Alan followed behind holding the other end of the man, who had come to and was starting to protest.

'Thank God,' Freda said. The man seemed to be becoming more agitated by the second. Alan gave him a hard punch to the jaw, and his body went limp.

'Don't look at me like that,' he said in a rasping voice,

seeing Freda's shocked expression. 'This is the bastard who started the fire.'

Freda hurried to help drag the man out of the way as Lemuel's head appeared in the doorway. 'Can you give me a hand, man?' he called to Mike, who was wiping his smoke-stained brow with a white handkerchief. Between them they dragged the bicycles belonging to Anthony to safety, and Lemuel went back into the burning building.

'Lem, no – it's not worth it,' Alan called out before trying to follow him. Mike and Freda held him back. 'Don't be foolish! Think of your wife and children,' Mike shouted above the roar of the fire.

Lemuel was soon back, pulling Alan's motorbike through the small door aided by the fireman.

'Oh, you've saved Bessie,' Freda exclaimed, feeling tears start to prick her eyes. This time they weren't caused by the smoke.

'That was a damn fool thing to do,' Alan snapped, but they all knew he was grateful.

As they stood in the alleyway, more police and firemen joined them, taking over and making sure everyone was safe.

Alan slung his arm around Freda's shoulders as they returned to family and friends and gave her a big hug in front of them all. 'You're a hero, kid,' he said, planting a large kiss on her cheek. 'What would I have done without you?'

Freda shrugged, aware of the hurt look Sarah gave her before taking her husband in her arms and hugging him. 'Alan Gilbert, you could have died,' Sarah scolded him.

'I had to do something. Lemuel was still in there. I couldn't leave him to die,' he exclaimed, pulling away from her.

'At least everyone is safe,' she said.

Alan gave her a tired look. Could she not show a little compassion? 'My livelihood has gone. Please try to look just a little upset.'

Sarah was taken aback by his harsh words. 'At least Bessie survived,' she beamed, trying to show how much she really cared. 'I can ask Betty again if she'd take you on,' she added, dismissing what Betty had said to her before. Alan needed to be working back at Woolworths, needing a job more than ever.

Alan frowned before rubbing his grimy face and with both hands and giving a big sigh. 'You've been discussing my business with Betty? What have you told her?'

'Only that your dream had not really come to fruition,' she said, looking around for her friend.

'Just leave it alone, Sarah. You know nothing about my business. The workshop is man's work, not some little job you go to when it pleases you to earn pin money,' he told her, feeling angry that his wife had been discussing their private business with someone – even if that someone was a good friend of the family. She also had no idea of what was going on with the workshop. 'Thank goodness Freda seems to understand how important the workshop is to me.'

Sarah looked at the man in front of her, not recognizing him as the man she loved and had married. 'I'm sorry if you feel I've done wrong. I was only trying to help,' she replied, doing her utmost not to cry. She was sad that the workshop had all but burnt to the ground, but she was just trying to help and was already looking to the future. A future that mattered because they had children and she had her own dreams of the four of them together. If she could get their marriage back on an even keel then her worries about Freda would be in the past.

'Just leave it, Sarah,' he said as he turned to where Mike stood with a fellow police officer.

'I know you are exhausted from what you've been through, but it's important that you tell us anything you know about the fire. We can speak to Lemuel and the other man after we have your information,' Mike said as he nodded to his colleague to take notes.

'There's not much to say, really,' Alan told him. 'I came here from the reception, so I arrived around the same time you did. Lem will be able to tell you what led up to the fire starting. It looks as though Sadie Munro was with him at the time, so she may be of help.'

Mike raised his eyebrows but didn't comment on why the girl had been in the workshop. He knew from past experience that Vera Munro would have plenty to say on the subject. 'What about the other chap we found in the building?' He leant over to where his colleague pointed to his notes. 'A Mr Freddie Unthank . . . was he a customer?'

Alan froze. 'Unthank? I thought I recognized the chap, but with all that was going on I didn't give it much thought. I was more concerned with everyone's safety,' he said, waving over to where Lemuel was sitting on the pavement resting alongside Freda and beckoning for them to join him. 'Lem – did you know that chap was one of the Unthanks?'

Lemuel nodded, a grim look on his face. 'I thought as much.'

'I'd seen him when I went to Frank Unthank's office in West Street,' Freda chipped in. 'Was he there looking for Alan?' she asked Lemuel.

'No – he was surprised to find me there alone with Sadie. We caught him inside with a can of petrol. He'd already struck a match when I spotted him,' he said, looking embarrassed to be mentioning Sadie. 'We did our best to put it out, but it was futile.'

Mike gave Freda a sideways look. So he'd been right. Something was going on when he found Freda at Unthank's. 'How come he was still in the building, if he was up to no good?'

Lemuel rubbed the knuckles of his left hand and grinned. 'He tripped over and knocked himself out.'

Sarah looked from Freda to Lemuel and Alan. How was it that they all knew what was going on while she, the wife of the owner, was completely in the dark?

Freda opened her front door and crept slowly inside. She didn't wish to wake Anthony. The last thing she wanted was a grumpy man making comments about her staying out late.

She took off her shoes, and had all but passed the closed door to the front room when it opened, making her jump. 'I'm sorry – did I wake you? I tried to be as quiet as I could.'

'I was waiting up for you,' he said, sounding concerned. 'There seems to have been something going on a few streets away, and I was worried you'd not be able to get home.' Then, looking closely at the bedraggled figure standing in front of him, he burst out laughing. 'It must have been a merry affair.'

Freda froze. This was one of the times when she wished her road didn't have electric lighting and she could have skulked away to her bedroom without anyone seeing the frightful state she was now in. Despite her best efforts, there was a wobble in her voice as she answered Anthony. 'There was a fire at my friend's motorbike workshop. The person who did it must have known he'd not be there, as his father was getting married – it was written about in our local newspaper. He has lost his business and his livelihood. Now, if you will excuse me, I'd like to have a wash and go to my bed. It has been a long and tiring day,' she said, her voice all but a whisper. The Unthanks had done this to show Alan they meant business when he hadn't paid his debt in full. What would they do next?

'Come and sit down,' Anthony urged her. Leaning heavily on his crutch, he took her hand and led her to the armchair she'd placed by the bay window. 'I'm going to make you a hot drink. You look as though you need it. No, I can manage,' he said as she started to object. 'I have one leg that works, and with my sturdy wooden support I will find my way to the kitchen and make your drink. You are not to move. Not even to wash your face,' he threatened as she started to object. He leant against the door and waved the crutch in her direction. 'Rest for a few minutes. I'll want to know all about your day when I return – and I don't mean how pretty the bridesmaids looked.'

Freda leant back in the armchair and closed her eyes, her thoughts drifting back over the final stages of this exhausting evening.

Rather than watch the fire burn out in what remained of the workshop, most of those at the scene had returned to the Prince of Wales, where the wedding reception was coming to an end. Sitting in the public bar, they had been fortified with drinks by the landlady, who had made hot tea for those who were past drinking alcohol.

Freda had joined Sadie, who was sitting looking glum. 'I don't think Nan will want me back home. She made that clear when I ran after her. She told me I can come to collect Arthur in the morning and muttered about letting her down once and for all. She wouldn't talk to me any more, as she'd left Arthur with her neighbour,' She gave a deep sigh. 'He's just a friend,' she added, looking across the bar to where Lemuel was deep in conversation with Mike Jackson. They'd walked into the pub together after seeing Freddie Unthank carted off to Erith police station. As if he could feel Sadie's eyes on him, Lemuel looked up and gave her a smile. Freda thought that his expression, and Sadie's pleased response, spoke volumes.

'Look, Sadie,' Freda offered, 'I do have the small back bedroom going begging. It would suit you and Arthur at a squeeze. I can't offer you the larger bedroom as I'm advertising it for a new lodger and, to be fair, I don't think you could afford it what with only having your part-time job. I'd like to let you stay for free, but . . .'

Sadie looked shocked. 'You'd do that for me and my Arthur? It's not as if we are good friends or anything. It's right decent of you,' she said, leaping up to give Freda a hug.

'You can kip down on my settee tonight until you get yourself sorted out,' Maisie added. 'It'll give Freda a chance to get the room aired and ready fer you and the kiddy. I feel a bit responsible as it was me who goaded yer nan. Blame one too many sherries.'

Sadie looked between the two friends. 'I'm lost for words,' she said, looking grateful.

'Well, it ain't your fault yer nan's an old battleaxe,' Maisie said, not mincing her words.

'Mind you,' Freda put in, 'I don't want no funny business under my roof. As much as I like Lemuel and consider him a good friend, he's not to come around to my house unless I'm there. Do you understand?'

Sadie nodded vigorously, her blonde curls shaking. 'I'll not do anything to upset you. I'll never forget what you've done for me,' she added with gratitude shining from her eyes.

'I wonder where Lemuel will be laying his head tonight? I hear he was kipping down in Alan's workshop,' Maisie said thoughtfully.

'I'll put the lad up,' Ruby called from where she'd been sitting at the next table, sipping a port and lemon. 'My Bob'll agree with me. He's chatted with him a few times when he's popped into the workshop to see Alan. Do you know if his property was saved from the fire?'

'He's got his rucksack with him now, and he didn't have much else, from what I recall. You could say he was travelling light,' Freda said. 'The only problem is, I'm not sure he can pay his board and keep.' She leant a little closer to Ruby so that those around them couldn't hear. 'He was doing bits and pieces for Alan and kipping down in the workshop, as money was short.'

'I'll not be asking him for money. He was there to help Alan, and Alan being family means we owe Lemuel our thanks. If he wants, I can find him a few jobs around the place that I've nagged Bob to get on with for an age – and he can help out up the allotments. With two of them, we won't have to get rid of one of the plots. It was getting a bit much for Bob on his own,' she explained as she saw Freda's quizzical expression. 'We're both getting on a bit, you know. Look, here come the bride and groom. They must be ready to leave for their honeymoon,' she added as she got up to go to her son and daughter-in-law.

Freda saw Ruby wince as she got to her feet. It saddened her to think that Ruby and Bob were getting older. Ruby was an institution in Alexandra Road. She'd make sure to ask Lemuel to keep an eye out for her while he was staying at number thirteen.

'Hot tea; and I made you a sandwich,' a voice said from far off.

Freda came to from her thoughts and sat up, taking the cup and saucer. 'Thanks. This is just what the doctor ordered,' she said, giving Anthony a smile. 'It's me that should be looking after you, not the other way around,' she added as he sat down on the edge of his bed and placed the crutch down beside him.

'You look all in. I'm not that incapacitated I can't make a cuppa and a sarnie,' he said, taking one of the Spam sandwiches from the tray he'd carried in with his spare hand.

'Oh my goodness,' Freda spluttered, almost dropping her cup. 'Your bikes. I forgot to tell you about your bikes. You must have been wondering what happened to them?'

'You mean my bikes were at the workshop that burnt down?' he said, turning pale and placing his half-eaten sandwich back on the plate.

'Yes. Alan and Lemuel had fixed the one I damaged when I ran into you,' she said, feeling her cheeks burn at the thought of their accident. 'The others had been put there for safekeeping after your landlady told us to take them.'

Anthony was silent as he thought of his bikes. Then he shrugged. 'They don't matter. They are only things, and it's not as if I'll be able to ride for a long time. At least no one was injured, and that's what counts.'

Freda could see that he was disappointed, but any thoughts she'd had of him being unfriendly and miserable in the past were washed away as she witnessed his compassion for those who could have been injured. He's not as bad as I imagined him to be, she thought. She smiled at him. 'Don't worry – I saved your bikes. We got them out, along with Bessie,' she grinned.

Anthony perked up. 'Really? That's a huge relief. I hope Bessie wasn't injured?'

'A couple of dents, but the old girl will live.'

'I take it Bessie isn't a woman?' he asked.

Freda giggled. 'She's Alan's pride and joy, and he treats her like his best girl,' she said, and went on to explain how the motorbike had once belonged to Alan's late father.

Anthony listened quietly. 'It must be good to have something belonging to your father. Mine died when I was a toddler, and my mother not long after. I've got nothing to remember them by,' he said, without seeking sympathy.

'I'm the same,' Freda said. 'Me mum only died a few years back, but we weren't close. Dad died when I was younger. He was a smashing bloke,' she said, just a little misty-eyed.

'You are lucky to have memories,' he said, smiling.

'You didn't have any other family?' Freda asked, not wanting him to know that Betty had told her he'd been in a children's home.

'No,' he said without explaining more. 'Drink your tea before it gets cold, and eat your sandwich.'

'I'm not really very hungry. Here – you have it,' she said, holding out her plate and watching him tuck in. 'Can I ask you something?'

Anthony gave her a wary look.

'It's not personal – well, not really. I just wondered why you had so many bicycles. Are you thinking of setting up in business, or something?'

He laughed, looking relieved. 'It's my hobby. I like to cycle.'

'But so many bikes . . .' she said with a grin. 'Do you wear them out?'

'No; but I like to ride in races, and it's best to have a spare or two.'

'I suppose it hasn't helped, having your leg injured. Do you belong to a riding club? I've seen groups of people out on their bikes of a weekend. There must be a club of sorts round here somewhere. You could join when you're up to it. That's if head office doesn't move you on to another store. You trainees get around,' she grinned before finishing her tea. 'Another?'

'Not for me, thanks,' he said, waving away the plate. 'Mrs Billington informed me that my time at the Erith store will be extended because of being off work due to the accident.'

'That's good,' Freda said, without thinking it might make her look a little forward.

Anthony was thoughtful. 'I've been told there's a cycling section of Erith Sports Club. I made a few tentative enquiries before my . . . our . . . the accident. I thought it would be a way to find a training partner. I had one while working at the Liverpool branch, and it helped me stay focused.'

Freda was confused. 'A training partner, just to go cycling . . . why would you need that? I know I'm tired, so forgive me if I appear a little confused.'

Anthony laughed. 'I didn't explain myself very well. I participate competitively in races and cycling events. It is something that gives me an interest; otherwise I'd go home from work to another dingy room, and sit and think about where my life is going. Not that this is a dingy room,' he added quickly.

'Oh! I had no idea about your hobby. I had you down

as just another of the annoying trainees who come and go through our doors. We've had quite a few in the past couple of years. Are you any good – at this racing, I mean?'

Anthony laughed, and agreed that some of the younger trainees were annoying. 'Yes – without blowing my own trumpet, I've done quite well. In fact . . .'

'Go on, please tell me,' Freda said as he fell silent and looked more than a little embarrassed. 'I am interested – honest I am.'

'There's a chance I could be competing in the next Olympic Games. Well, I should say there was, before I had the accident. I may have missed the boat now.'

Freda felt a pang of guilt. 'Isn't it next year? Surely there's time for you to get well and participate? I've never known someone who took part in the Olympics. Is it right that they are holding them in London?' she asked, excited at the prospect of such an important event taking place almost on their doorstep. 'You've got to get well for this – you really have to,' she added earnestly. 'I'd come along and cheer you on.'

He laughed at her enthusiasm. 'It's not just a case of turning up. I would have to compete in other trials and reach a certain level of competence before the selection committee invited me to participate. But now it's not going to happen, and none of this is your fault,' he added sternly as the smile on Freda's face disappeared.

'But your bikes are safe and look as good as new. I checked them over to make sure. The landlord of the Prince of Wales has put them all in his shed for safe-keeping. We can collect them tomorrow and put them in my back garden, and you will soon be back on your feet,' she added earnestly. 'I didn't want to see them damaged, as they mean so much to you.'

The look of happiness on Anthony's face had her heart pumping nineteen to the dozen. 'I'm so relieved, I could kiss you,' he said, giving her a big grin.

Freda's first thought was that she wished he would, and she was surprised by the feelings coursing through her body. Instead, she said, 'Shall we have another cup of tea to celebrate?'

'I'll make it. It's the least I can do,' he said as he pulled himself to his feet. Grabbing the crutch, he left the room to put the kettle on once more, but on returning a few minutes later, he found Freda sleeping soundly. Reaching for the eiderdown on his bed, he tucked it round her and went out to turn off the kettle.

He had never imagined, when Freda sent him flying from his bicycle outside the Woolworths store, that she would change his life so much. With luck, perhaps he could stay around to change hers – if she'd let him.

9

~

Freda stepped into Betty Billington's office with some trepidation. Although they were good friends, she knew that during working hours at Woolworths, Betty could be a formidable boss. It was Monday morning and she'd only been in the building for half an hour. 'You wanted to see me?' she asked, trying to assess whether Betty's expression suggested there was something wrong.

'Come in and sit down,' Betty said as she closed a file on the desk and removed her spectacles. 'I hope you've recovered from that terrible fire. It was such a shame George and Maureen's wedding reception was spoilt, but at least no one was hurt.'

Freda breathed a sigh of relief. Why was it she always felt worried when being summoned to the manageress's office? It must be because it brought back memories of schooldays, she thought to herself.

'I went to the workshop to help out on Sunday, but there wasn't much I could do. Your Douglas was there, and David Carlisle too, helping Alan clear up the mess. And Mike Jackson popped in to check up on a few things.'

'I take it he was on duty?' Betty asked, looking

thoughtful. 'Was there any news about the man who set fire to the building?'

Freda shrugged her shoulders. Mike had already mentioned the coincidence of her having been at Frank Unthank's office, and then his son turning up the worse for wear at the workshop on Saturday night; he had actually asked her if there was a connection. She'd laughed it off as pure coincidence, but Mike was no fool, and she knew he'd want to know more very soon. 'I didn't ask, but I would think he's still locked up. Lemuel caught him in the act, after all,' she said, feeling uncomfortable and hoping Betty didn't ask any more questions. She didn't like having to keep things quiet, but until Alan solved his money problems and spoke to his family, she'd have to go along with things – and that meant keeping his secret, as it wasn't hers to share. 'Is Sarah not in work today?' she asked, hoping to change the subject.

Betty frowned. 'Under the circumstances, she's helping her husband.'

'Oh, of course she would be,' Freda stuttered, wondering why Betty had such a serious expression on her face.

'You're very close to Alan, aren't you?'

'He's like a big brother to me,' Freda smiled. 'I'd do anything for him.'

'It was very brave of you to go into the burning workshop to look for him. I must say, I was as surprised as Sarah was when you disappeared round the back of the building like that rather than simply advising Mike or one of the firemen.'

'I didn't think about it,' Freda answered. 'I've had some experience of the Fire Service during the war, and besides,

Alan was in there somewhere and I was worried about him.'

Betty nodded thoughtfully. 'Just be careful, Freda,' she said as she reached for a card on her desk and picked it up.

Freda frowned. 'That's my card from the staff noticeboard in the canteen. Is there something wrong with it?'

'On the contrary,' Betty smiled. 'I took it down because I have a new staff member who I feel would be suitable as your new lodger.'

'I take it you know Sadie Munro and young Arthur have moved into my small back bedroom?' Freda said.

'It was good of you to take her in. Goodness knows Vera Munro can be an obstinate woman. I really felt for Sadie when I witnessed her grandmother telling her off like that. I do wonder, though, if you'll be able to cope with a full-time job and a house full of guests? I'd hate for you to overdo things and make yourself ill.'

Freda relaxed. Betty always looked out for her staff and friends. 'Thank you. I had been wondering about asking Sadie to take on some of the day-to-day housework and cooking for my lodgers, in exchange for a lower rent. I know she finds it hard to make ends meet, and it would give me time to help Alan out once he finds a new workshop.' Betty's smile froze, and at once Freda sensed that she'd said the wrong thing. 'Is there something wrong?'

'Well . . . I do feel you should give Alan and Sarah some time to themselves, Freda. It has been a difficult time, and now they have to plan for their future. It's no secret that Sarah is keen for Alan to return to Woolworths, and he did enjoy working here before the outbreak of war,' she said, although privately she still thought it wouldn't work out.

Freda couldn't believe what she was hearing. The Alan she knew and loved relished working for himself, even if recently he'd become down in the dumps over the mess with the Unthanks. It wouldn't be right for her to argue with her boss, so she simply nodded her head and kept her thoughts to herself. 'You said you knew someone who would be interested in my spare room?' she asked, indicating the card Betty still held in her hand.

'Oh, yes,' Betty said as if her thoughts too had been elsewhere. 'Effie Dyer, who you and I discussed the other day, is looking for somewhere to live. She comes from the Kent coast and it seems she expected to live with a relative in Erith, but it all fell through. She is working on the vegetable counter at the moment. Would you take it from here?' She handed the postcard to Freda as her telephone started to ring.

Freda mumbled her agreement, not sure what to say to Betty as this was the young woman she'd seen coming out of the house of ill repute when they'd gone to collect Anthony's belongings. She left the office to head back downstairs to the shop floor, where she was supervising the counter staff. She'd pop over to the counter where fresh vegetables were being sold and see if she could catch Effie and have a few words. Deep in thought, she didn't at first hear her name being called until someone poked her in the back and wheezed, 'Didn't you hear me call you?'

'Oh, Ruby, I'm sorry. I was miles away. Are you all right? You look a little flushed.'

Ruby leant against a nearby counter and dabbed at her

hot face with her handkerchief. 'It's a bit on the warm side out there, and I hurried to catch you up as I wanted a word.'

Freda reached for a chair that was kept for customers and made the older woman sit down, although she protested. 'Couldn't it wait until later, when I was home? You'd have only needed to cross the road to have a word,' she scolded.

'No, not really. It's a bit on the embarrassing side,' Ruby all but whispered, looking from left to right. 'You've got a man living with you, and he might have overheard.'

Freda felt her face twitch as she tried not to smile. 'Anthony doesn't live with me,' she explained. 'He's a lodger, and rents my front room. It's all above board. Why do you mention it– has Vera been saying things? I fully expect her to start stirring things up, now her Sadie's moved in with me.'

'I know what you mean about Vera, but so far she's kept her distance. No doubt she will turn up on my doorstep to moan before long, when she hears that I've given Lemuel a room. No – it's just that what I've got to ask you, I can't really say in front of a man.'

Freda was intrigued, and leant closer so that no one could overhear them. 'What's the problem?'

'It's that Lemuel. I don't know how to say this, but I've got a problem with him . . .' Ruby looked a little ashamed.

Freda was surprised; she hadn't imagined Ruby as someone who would have a problem with black men. There'd been a few men coming off the ships over the years, and to Freda's knowledge Ruby had always treated everyone fairly – not like some she could think of who would call out names, or even cross the street rather than interact with a person from foreign shores. She also remembered the card she'd seen in the boarding house the other day. The words 'no darkies' still made her feel ashamed that someone in her adopted town could be so uncaring. Perhaps it was Ruby's age that was the problem? 'Ruby, Lemuel is no different to us, you know,' she explained, carefully picking her words.

'I know that, you daft 'apporth. It's just that I was doing some washing and though I'd run his few bits through while I had some hot water, and what I see made my heart ache for him.'

If Freda hadn't been intrigued before, she was now. 'Come on, Ruby – spit it out,' she hissed, as she spotted an assistant waving to her for help. 'I'm going to have to go in a minute.'

'It was his unmentionables. They're so threadbare, I thought I'd treat him to some new ones, but I have no idea what size he wears. I have his ration book so I can use his coupons, but it's to be my treat for all he's done. I thought you'd know about sizes seeing as you've served on all the counters here in Woolies.'

Freda couldn't help but burst out laughing. 'Oh Ruby, you had me thinking all sorts,' she giggled. 'Look, I've got to get cracking or Betty will give me the sack for chatting. Leave it with me, and I'll sort out what's needed. I'll pop over later,' she said, giving the older woman a kiss on the cheek. 'I want to ask Bob's advice about something, so there's no time like the present – or after I finish work, at any rate.'

Ruby got to her feet, giving a wince as she did so. 'Don't

look at me like that. I'm all right,' she said as she saw Freda about to say something. 'It's just me old bones. I'll expect you about half past six.'

Freda watched as she walked away. There was most definitely something wrong with Ruby, she thought with concern. Sarah didn't seem very talkative these days, so perhaps she'd pop over to see Maisie in her tea break and kill two birds with one stone. After watching Ruby leave the store, she headed over to where a young assistant had been trying to get her attention.

'Please, Miss, we haven't got any paper bags,' the girl said with her hand still in the air.

Freda thought how strange it was that the younger shop assistants treated her like a grown-up when she still felt as though she was that shy sixteen-year-old who had walked through the staff entrance not so many years ago. A lot of water had gone under the bridge since those days. 'You can put your hand down, Jeannie. You aren't at school now.' She smiled gently, not wishing to intimidate the young girl, who hadn't long started her full-time job at Woolworths. 'When you had your tour of the store on your first day, do you remember being shown the stock room?'

'Yes, miss, it's upstairs,' Jeannie said, lowering her arm.

'Then take yourself up there and ask someone to give you a box of bags. Bring them down and place them under the counter on the shelf. Do you think you can do that?' she asked as the girl started to look flustered. 'There's no need to rush,' she added, as the girl looked ready to run off. 'Do you know where Effie is? I believe she started here about the same time as you.'

'Yes, Miss. That's her over there. She's a bit on the stuck-up side. She don't talk to anyone when we go for our breaks,' Jeannie said, before hurrying off to collect her paper bags.

Freda looked over to where the girl was pointing and took a deep breath. She felt uncomfortable about giving a room to Effie if she was up to no good.

''Ello, love. We don't usually see you at this time of the afternoon. Is something up?' Maisie said, looking up from her sewing machine as Freda entered her shop. 'Why aren't you in work?'

Freda threw herself into the chair that was used by customers while Maisie waited on them. 'It's my tea break. I wanted to ask you something – a few things really.'

'Fire away, but if you don't mind I'll carry on sewing while you talk. I've got a pile of orders to work through, and with the shop being quiet this afternoon I thought I'd get cracking.'

Freda nodded and leant back in the chair, looking around at the shop. It might be small, but Maisie had worked wonders, filling it from floor to ceiling with second-hand clothing as well as items she'd made either from scratch, or by remodelling clothes she picked up from jumble sales, or took from customers in part exchange. 'It always smells so nice in here. Almost as good as Alan's workshop – or what it did smell like,' she added sadly.

'I'm not sure 'ow clean clothes can sniff like oily engines,' Maisie said good-naturedly. 'Mind you, it smells more like burnt wood now. I do feel sorry for 'im. That workshop was his dream, and now it's gone. At least he's got another job ter go to.'

'Has he? I didn't know,' Freda said, looking more alert than when she'd arrived. 'Has he got another workshop? I hope it's nearby, so I can go and help him.'

'I meant, surely Betty will 'ave 'im back at Woolworths.'

Freda scowled. 'He'll never go back there. It would nigh on kill him being trapped inside a shop, now he's been his own boss.'

'You seem certain. Sarah seems to think he'll go back,' Maisie snipped the frayed cuff off a child's coat, watching Freda to see if there was a reaction.

'Then Sarah doesn't know her own husband very well,' Freda threw back at her, not realizing she'd given the wrong signal to her friend. 'Anyway, that's not what I came over here to talk about. I saw Ruby earlier and she's after buying some underwear for Lemuel, but she doesn't know his size. I thought you'd be able to guess, what with having a husband and working with clothes.'

Maisie roared with laughter. 'I'm not one for sizing up men's underpants, but I'd say he was a bit bigger in the waist department than my David, if that's any 'elp?'

'Not really, as I have no idea what size your David is,' Freda snorted, joining in with Maisie's infectious laugh.

'Hang on a mo.' Maisie got up from her seat and started rummaging in a large wicker hamper in the corner of the room. 'I picked up a lot of men's stuff a while ago. I was after the suit and overcoat to cut down, but there was some shirts and men's vests and stuff as well. The suit was a bit on the large size, so chances are so are the shirts and stuff.

Bingo!' she shouted, pulling out a large pair of men's underpants. 'I reckon these'll suit him down ter the ground. They look bigger than what my David would wear.'

Freda didn't know where to look. She had never been this close to men's undergarments before. 'Are they clean?' she asked, wrinkling her nose.

'Everything in here was washed and ironed before being delivered. The man's wife was quite respectable.'

'Is the owner of the clothes . . . ?'

'Dead as a door nail, but it wasn't anything catching,' Maisie grinned.

Freda shuddered. 'Goodness, Maisie, I don't know how you can touch things like that. It makes my skin crawl,' she said, rubbing her arms and pulling a face.

Maisie hooted with laughter. 'Blimey, Freda, anyone would think I'd popped next door ter the undertaker's shop and pinched the pants off a still-warm corpse. The lady who brought in the clothes was very presentable, and it's no different to you selling clothes you no longer need.'

Freda looked unconvinced. 'I'm not sure I'd want to sell on my unwanted knickers, though,' she said, looking a little closer at the garment Maisie was waving in the air. 'But they do look decent quality, and if Ruby was to give them a good boil . . .'

'No one would be any the wiser – not that anyone will be looking at Lemuel's undergarments,' Maisie grinned. 'Speaking of which, how is Sadie getting on now she'd moved into your gaff?'

Her friend's inclusion of the two names in one breath was not lost on Freda. 'Nothing's going to go on under my roof,' she sniffed primly. 'I've no doubt Vera will be spreading rumours, but if Lemuel wishes to come courting Sadie, then he doesn't put one foot on the staircase that leads to her bedroom.'

Maisie hooted with laughter. 'Gawd, Freda, you sound like you was born back when Queen Victoria was on her throne. And there's you wiv a man sleeping in yer front room.'

Freda blushed. In the few days that Anthony had been staying at the house, she'd seen him in a better light. Certainly not like the usual annoying trainee managers who came and went at the Erith branch of Woolworths. 'He's a nice man. We've had a few chats about his bicycles. Did you know, he could be competing in next year's Olympic Games – that's if his leg heals in time and he does well in a few races. He called them bike trials,' she said, nodding her head as she remembered his words. 'It does sound exciting,' she added, her eyes shining.

Maisie was interested – all the more so if this meant Freda wasn't chasing after Alan Gilbert. Perhaps Sarah had got it wrong about Alan and Freda? She'd have to give this some serious thought. The last thing she wanted was to see Sarah and Alan's marriage fail for something that hadn't happened. It would make them as bad as Vera Munro – God forbid. 'I can't say it's my cup of tea, but good luck to the chap. If me and David can 'elp in any way, you've only got ter shout. It's not often someone living in Erith, and a Woolworths worker at that, gets ter go ter the Olympics. D'yer think we can go and watch?'

Freda was thrilled that her friend was so interested. 'I hadn't given it a thought, but we can find out if Anthony gets chosen to compete. He's got to get back on his feet first, though. But if he does, perhaps the children would like to watch? From the little I know, the Olympics are held in different places all around the world. Who knows when they will be back in London after next year?'

Maisie smiled at Freda's enthusiasm. 'P'raps you should ask Anthony,' she said.

Freda, not realizing that Maisie was humouring her, nodded enthusiastically. 'I must get back to the store. Can I collect the men's things when I leave work?'

'I'll 'ave them all parcelled up for you. You can tell Ruby she can 'ave them for what they cost me. It's not the usual stuff I'd sell, and they'd no doubt be used fer dusters otherwise.'

Freda giggled. 'Fancy using those for dusters. I'll stick to the ones from Woolworths, ta very much.'

'Me too, but beggars can't be choosers. Why, that new lodger of yours might have some he could donate for you ter polish your furniture,' Maisie smiled, knowing her teasing would embarrass Freda no end.

Freda turned bright red and hurried away to get back to work before she was missed, although her mind was on Anthony. She hadn't given a thought to how he would cope with his washing while he was incapacitated. Perhaps she should offer to do it for him. After all, it would be the neighbourly thing to do, wouldn't it?

Sarah took the large envelope of photographs, and thanked the woman behind the chemist's counter.

Her dad had been insistent that he would settle the bill for developing the wedding photos, so she hadn't needed to pay anything on collection for the prints. Tucking the invoice into her handbag, she decided to treat herself to fifteen minutes alone to look through the photographs – and where better than the Oak Tea Room in Hedley Mitchell's, the only store in Erith that was larger than Woolworths.

Crossing busy Pier Road, she was deep in thought until she spotted a familiar figure coming out of Maisie's Modes. It was Freda. Sarah had no wish to speak with her at that particular moment. In the days since the fire at Alan's workshop she'd done nothing but think about that evening, and how Freda had been lauded by everyone for leading the rescuers to the back entrance of the workshop and then going inside to help. Why on earth hadn't she thought of that entrance herself? Hadn't she been there only days before, and opened that door to let in some air? Sarah could have kicked herself for not thinking of it. Instead she'd been worried sick and was being taken care of by her friends. Why, oh why, wasn't she brave and fearless like Freda? At least then Alan would be full of praise for her – and perhaps he would forget about Freda. No wonder the pair of them are so close, thought Sarah with a sigh.

Keeping her head down, she hurried across the road and into the safety of the tea room before Freda called out. The girl seemed to have no shame about her dalliance with Alan, and brazenly acted as if nothing had changed in their close circle of family and friends.

'I can fit you in at the small table near the window, Miss, but you won't hear the orchestra so well,' a young waitress told her.

'That will suit me fine,' Sarah said, and then added, 'I

have a bit of a headache,' as she saw the woman's reproachful look. It wasn't as if the orchestra was very good, consisting as it did of three elderly ladies beating a Brahms lullaby to death.

Thankfully there was a heavy lace curtain at the window, so she wouldn't be spotted by anyone coming and going from the Woolworths store across the road. She glanced briefly at the menu. 'Just a pot of tea, please, and a jug of hot water,' she smiled at the waitress. At the prices Mitchell's charged these days, squeezing a second cup out of the pot would justify her spending the money.

Taking the envelope of photographs from her bag, she opened it and set the photos in front of her. She had mixed feelings about her dad and Maureen's special day. First, she was overjoyed that her dad had found love again since her mum's tragic death during the last year of the war. However, the fact that he was marrying her husband's own mother had been a cause for concern. She loved Maureen dearly, but how would it be if she and Alan ended their marriage and he chose to continue his life with Freda? With the family links being so close, they would always be in each other's pockets.

Putting her thoughts to one side, she picked up the black-and-white pictures that recorded the day. She hoped she'd not made a mess of using the camera. Her dad had shown her numerous times how to hold it, and she had encouraged people to move into the best positions to compose a good photograph. She prayed she'd not chopped everyone's heads off, or left someone out. It was quite a responsibility being in charge of recording the happy event.

Not realizing she'd been holding her breath, she let out a big sigh as she saw Maureen beaming from the first picture. The bride stepped from the car that had taken her and Alan to the church. Helping Maureen out was Alan, looking nervous as he held the car door open while offering his mother his hand. His tie was a little askew, but he still looked very smart. Her heart ached as she ran her finger over the outline of his face. 'I'll fight for you, my love, but only if I know you still want me. I'll not hang around to see you with another,' she whispered. Quickly she put the photograph to one side and smiled at the next picture, which showed her dad holding hands with his grandchildren, Georgina and Buster. That was certainly one for framing and giving to Nan, she thought, before moving on to the first photograph of her dad and Maureen together as they signed the register in the vestry. The vicar had been quite firm that she was only to take the one photograph, and she'd hoped it wasn't blurred. Along with Mike Jackson as best man, she had signed the document as an official witness. The vicar had cheekily suggested he take a photograph of the four of them, being quite taken with the idea of a woman being the official photographer for the occasion. There she was, beaming back from beside Mike, who'd had permission to wear his dress uniform as he was attending the wedding of a town councillor. There was talk of George Caselton being the mayor of Erith before too long. Wouldn't her mum have loved that, Sarah thought with a smile.

'Ah, I do love a good wedding,' the waitress said as she placed a silver tray on the table, removing the teapots and milk jug along with a delicate cup and saucer. 'Was it your wedding?' she asked, picking up the empty tray.

'No, it was my dad's wedding,' Sarah replied, turning the photo of the happy couple so the girl could see. 'My mum, his first wife, died a few years ago.'

'Why, that's Councillor Caselton,' the girl said, looking closer. 'You say he's your dad?'

Sarah was puzzled. 'Yes – do you know him?'

'I'd say I do. He managed to help me and my two kids move into one of those new prefabs up on Watts Bridge, near the Cinder Path. We'd been turned down before as we had a room with my cousin, Gert, but it was short-term and the council people didn't want to help us.'

Sarah felt her chest swell with pride. 'He's only been a councillor for a couple of years. He's very dedicated. I'm glad he was able to help you.'

'I'll never forget him for how he helped us. People can be kind, you know,' the waitress said, tucking the tray under her arm. 'See that branch of Woolworths over the road? There were some people in there who came to my rescue in the early days of the war. I was at my wits' end, having escaped from a nasty situation, like, and they not only fed me but found me somewhere to live. Bloody good people. Anyway, you give my best to your dad and his new wife. He probably won't remember me, but my name is Jessie – Jessie Arnold I'm known as these days, since getting hitched. Give me ten minutes and I'll bring you a fresh pot of tea. No charge, as this hoity-toity lot won't notice. Sod the hot water,' she giggled as she turned to leave the table.

'Hang on a minute,' Sarah said, as a memory bubbled to the surface of her mind. 'Were you the young kid we found hiding in the storeroom when we were trapped by the unexploded bomb that came down on the tobacconist over the road? It must have been six or seven years ago, if I remember correctly.'

'Blow me down with a feather – fancy you remembering all of that. I take it you was stuck there as well?'

'I worked at Woolworths. I still do, but I'm part-time now I have two children, and I help out in the office.'

'Why, you girls were lovely to me. What you thought of why I was hiding there I'll never know, but it didn't matter, as it was Woolies that turned the corner for me. I've had a good life since then. Please give my regards to your mates, won't you? There was a young girl not much older than me who worked there. I've thought of her often, as someone said she'd run away from home and come to Erith.'

Sarah frowned. 'That will be Freda. She still works over the road. You should come in and see her. I'm sure she'd like to say hello.'

'No, I'd feel daft if she didn't know who I was. You are lucky, working in such a nice place and having such friends.'

'I'll tell them about you. But can you answer a question for me?'

'Fire away – but if it's about the rock-hard scones, you'll need to see the manageress,' Jessie grinned.

'I just wondered why you didn't apply for a job in Woolworths? I'd think it was more up your street than here. It's a bit on the posh side, if you don't take offence at me saying so,' Sarah grinned. 'I always feel I should be on my best behaviour when I come in.'

Jessie grinned back. 'I was too frightened, to be honest, what with the way I was found hiding there. But meeting you and remembering how nice everyone was . . . well,

I may just pop over and ask about a job. Thank you for suggesting it. I'm grateful,' she smiled. 'You're a decent lot over there.'

Sarah smiled to herself as she poured her tea. She'd be sure to remind Betty of the frightened young girl they had discovered way back in . . . why, it must have been the Christmas of 1941, if she wasn't mistaken. She returned to the pile of photographs, feeling a warm glow as she looked at all the people who had turned up to wish her dad and Maureen well on their happy day. It was only when she reached the one she'd taken of Alan and Freda together that her face fell.

There was no denying they had been deep in conversation when she'd lifted her camera. The photo in front of her had caught them just as they started to hug each other. She placed it into her pocket, not sure what to do. The last photograph on the pile was face up on the table, and Sarah froze. It was Freda beaming into the camera. The photograph she'd taken of her, for the *New Bond* staff competition.

Freda looked fresh-faced and happy as she smiled into the camera lens, but all Sarah could see was the woman who was carrying on with her husband. Checking no one was watching, she picked up the photo and tore it into small pieces – and then took the negative from the packet and slipped it into her pocket to cut up and throw away once she was home. 'I'll play no part in helping you become a *New Bond* cover girl,' she muttered to herself as she stirred her tea.

*

Freda headed back into Woolworths and ran upstairs to the staffroom, where she pulled on her overall. She was a few minutes late. Betty ran a tight ship, and would not be amused if she knew her supervisors were slacking. With six new staff members, including Effie, working behind the counters, Freda had been tasked with checking on four of the younger women to see if they understood what was expected of them. She also had to move them between the various counters, so that they gained experience and Freda could see where they were best suited. She decided to start on the counter that she disliked most – vegetables. Not only was it hefty work, as the women had to tip sacks of potatoes and other seasonal veg onto the counter, but it was also messy. In the colder months the women complained of having to handle the wet muddy spuds. Even though gloves were provided, the women still complained and everyone preferred to work on the other counters. Freda's one fear was sticking her finger into a slug. She'd done it once and screamed aloud, frightening customers who were queueing to be served. These days, if she ventured anywhere near the long counter that ran across the width of the store, she stayed alert to the horrible slimy things, which seemed to be attracted to her.

Keeping one eye on the vegetables, she called out to Effie for her to join her once she'd finished serving her customer. Freda carried a clipboard so she could follow the checklist for each of the young girls. Betty had already made several comments relating to Effie's good timekeeping and clean appearance. Freda frowned, thinking back to when she had spotted the young girl leaving the house in Wheatley Terrace. Why had she even been inside that property? And she'd looked none too happy as she left.

'You wanted to speak to me, Miss Smith?' Effie Dyer said as she approached the side of the counter where Freda stood.

'There's no need to look so worried,' Freda said kindly as she looked at the young girl, who reminded her so much of herself when she'd first joined F. W. Woolworths. A little too thin, with high cheekbones and blonde hair scraped back in a thin ribbon, Effie looked at her with large, rather scared blue eyes. 'I only wanted to check how you were getting on, and if you had any concerns?'

The tension in the girl's face disappeared and was replaced with a smile of relief. 'I thought I'd done something wrong,' she said. 'I like my job and want to do the best I can.'

Freda nodded encouragingly. 'That's what I like to hear. I've been assigned the task of looking after you and the three other new members of staff, so if you have a problem, or just want to ask a question, then come and find me.'

Effie nodded her head by way of thanks. 'I just want to find somewhere decent to live; but that's not Woolworths' problem. There was a card on the staffroom noticeboard and I mentioned it to Mrs Billington, but now it's been taken down . . . It mentioned being local to the store, which would have been handy. I do oversleep sometimes,' she added, immediately looking ashamed for saying so.

Freda laughed. She'd had the same problem, so could sympathize. On cold mornings, when there was ice inside the window frame and she knew she'd need to boil a kettle in order to wash before dressing, she too would linger under the blankets. Being rescued by Sarah and her family and then living with Ruby had made all the difference. Perhaps it was now her turn to help out another young woman? Despite her reservations, and before she could change her mind, Freda said, 'I was the one who placed the card on the noticeboard, and the room is still available. If you'd like to wait back after work we can have a chat, if you like?' She could see the girl was interested, but then a shadow fell over her face.

'But you're a boss here. Would it be all right for me to rent a room from you?'

For the first time, Freda felt grown up. Amongst her friends she was the youngest, and they'd always watched out for her. Now she could do the same for a younger person. 'Don't worry about it,' she smiled. 'I do have a couple of other lodgers, including one of our trainee managers.'

Effie visibly shrank, and the light left her eyes. 'A man lives in your house?'

Freda could see the girl found that a problem. 'Everyone has their own room with a key, and my other lodger is a young woman with her little son. I'm very choosy about who I allow to live in my home,' she said reassuringly. 'Why don't we have that chat after work, and if all goes well you can come and see the room?'

The girl thought for a moment, and gradually the smile came back to her face. 'Yes, I'd like that. Thank you.'

Freda watched her go back to serving the customers, and made a note on her clipboard. She'd pop upstairs to the office and have a word with Betty if she was free. She liked Effie, but she still couldn't shake the image of her scuttling away from that dodgy-looking house in Wheatley Terrace. It would be good to discuss her fears with someone else now that the girl might be living under her roof. She'd not like to be known for taking in someone with loose morals.

10

~

Sarah, with much on her mind, decided not to head home straight away after her cup of tea in Hedley Mitchell's. The atmosphere at home was tense, with Alan sitting deep in thought most of the time, apart from when he walked to the pub for a pint. Sarah felt as though she was walking on eggshells and had taken to sending the children to a neighbour who usually looked after them when she worked, rather than them having to play quietly so as not to upset their brooding father.

With help from friends and neighbours, it had taken only a few hours to clear the workshop space of debris. All that remained was a burnt-out shell, although they'd managed to salvage some of the tools and equipment, now being stored in their shed. Sarah had tentatively suggested she bring Alan's accounts up to date and help with any other paperwork that had survived the fire, but he'd dismissed her offers of help with a wave of the hand. Her suggestion of making an appointment to see Betty about returning to work at Woolworths had been met with barely hidden contempt. Sarah could appreciate that since Alan had left his trainee manager's job at the start of the war

– and had gone on to join the RAF and seen so much action – he didn't feel as though he could return to a mundane job. He'd told her enough times that he wanted to be his own boss. That was all well and good, but he now had responsibilities and needed to consider his family. She was at her wits' end trying to find a way to turn her husband back to the young man she'd fallen in love with. Whatever she tried or said was dismissed or ignored. She was beginning to feel as though their marriage was over and not worth rescuing. However, something deep inside was telling her to fight for her man. But how?

Sarah walked into Woolworths, stopping to chat with a few customers and staff who enquired about the fire. People meant well, but she just wanted her life to get back to normal. Would it ever, with Alan now out of work and barely willing to talk to her? Excusing herself, she hurried upstairs to Betty's office and entered after tapping on the door.

'Sarah, my love, I was just thinking about you,' Betty exclaimed, hurrying around the desk to hug her friend closely. 'Now sit yourself down and tell me – what has happened since I last saw you? I was expecting Alan to come in to see me. You know the door will always be open at Woolworths for him to return.'

Sarah sat in the chair opposite Betty and gave a big sigh. 'I've tried, Betty – oh, how I've tried – but he just doesn't seem interested in returning to a steady job with prospects. The problem is I have no idea what he wants to do next. He just won't talk to me,' she said, shrugging her shoulders. 'Honestly, I could wring his neck!'

Betty burst out laughing. 'I'm sorry; but I was thinking

back to all the times you've been in here crying over Alan. Why, I do believe you've grown up – not that I think tears are a bad thing sometimes.'

Sarah was startled by Betty's words, then joined in with her friend's laughter. 'I do think you're right. There's a time for tears, and there's a time for rolling up one's sleeves and getting stuck in.'

'You could be right,' Betty said, thinking of her step-daughters and how she'd had to learn quickly about bringing up two girls and then having a child herself. 'There are days when I thank God I have a job to go to and can leave my family in the care of our housekeeper. Do you know, I seriously considered boarding school for a while? Then I realized I'd be distraught at not having them to come home to every evening.'

'We are a pair,' Sarah declared, knowing just how Betty was feeling. The Woolworths manageress had tackled a growing family and a new husband in the same way: she'd rolled up her sleeves and taken up the reins, running a busy store when the male staff went off to war. 'We deserve medals,' she chuckled.

'I have something better,' Betty said, giving her a wink before pulling open a drawer of the desk and taking out a cake tin adorned with pictures of the King's coronation. 'Maureen gave me a gift before she went on her honey-moon. She told me not to eat it all at once – she knows how I love a fruit cake, but she told me they were biscuits, so it was such a surprise when I opened the tin. She is a dear,' Betty said, patting her stomach. 'I have to be so careful at my age, so I've been savouring one slice each day.'

Sarah peered into the tin, looking puzzled. 'Wherever did she get all that dried fruit from to make a cake? Come to think of it, how did she manage to find the fruit for that beautiful wedding cake she made?'

Betty tapped the side of her nose. 'I believe our Maisie had a hand in this. It seems she knows someone working on the docks . . .'

'Thank goodness for Maisie. Who'd have thought that this long after the end of the war we would still have shortages? There was a time I'd not have looked at anything remotely dodgy,' Sarah said as she took the proffered slice.

'I won't tell if you don't,' Betty grinned. 'I do think we deserve a cup of tea to wash this down,' she said, placing her slice of cake on top of the tin and hurrying to the office door, where she called out to a passing assistant to kindly fetch two cups of tea. She left the door ajar and went back to her seat.

'Oh, I have the wedding photographs in my bag,' Sarah said, reaching for the envelope and passing them to Betty, who wiped her hands on her handkerchief before looking at the pictures.

'You've taken some very good photographs, Sarah,' Betty said as she turned each one over after looking carefully at the wedding guests. 'I would love to have attended the service, but with Douglas working and it being a busy day here, it wasn't to be. However, you've done such a good job I almost feel as though I was there.'

Sarah beamed with pride. 'I can tell you, it was a relief to see they looked all right. I was sure I'd chop off people's heads or miss something important . . . I haven't missed someone out, have I?' she asked as Betty checked back through the pile, apparently looking for something.

'It doesn't matter. You probably didn't have time to take a photograph of Freda for the cover girl competition for the staff magazine. Or perhaps it didn't come out,' she asked as she saw Sarah squirm in her seat before looking down into her lap in embarrassment. 'Is there something you've not told me?' Betty asked.

'I tore it up,' Sarah muttered.

'Well, there's bound to be a couple of spoilt photographs,' Betty consoled her.

Sarah knew she couldn't lie to Betty. 'It was a nice photograph, but . . . but . . .' She couldn't finish her words as large tears dropped onto her lap.

'Now, come along, Sarah, what did we say about tears not ten minutes ago? You can confide in me if there is a problem.'

Sarah shook her head and gulped, trying hard to stop the tears. 'This is different. Betty, I don't think Alan loves me any more. I'm sure now that Alan and Freda are in love . . . She wants to steal my husband,' she said, reaching into her pocket and pulling out the photograph of Freda in Alan's arms outside the church.

Outside the door, Freda froze in shock. Wanting to speak to Betty about Effie, she'd relieved her colleague of the tea tray, saying that she'd take it up to the office. She'd been about to bump open the door with her elbow when she'd heard Sarah start to cry. She heard everything that was said inside the room as clearly as if she'd been standing next to her friends. How could Sarah believe she wanted to steal her husband? Why would she even think such a thing? Feeling indignant, Freda barged into the room and put the tea down, slopping much of it into the saucers. 'I heard everything you said, and it's not true. I'm not stealing your husband away from you! Why would you say such a thing?'

Betty leapt to her feet and hurriedly closed the office door before steering Freda to her seat and encouraging the girl to sit down. 'Please keep your voices down,' she said sternly. 'I don't wish your private problems to be overheard and shared by the staff. Now, I shall leave you alone while you sort this out,' she added, picking up her handbag.

'No! Please stay. I have nothing to say that can't be heard by you or any other member of staff,' Freda said firmly. 'Alan is like a brother to me, and has been ever since I came to Erith. Just as you've been like the sister I never had. Please believe me. I'm not telling lies,' she said turning to face Sarah, who was staring coldly at her.

'Then what about this? What about the times when you and Alan are whispering together? What about all the times you are at the workshop alone? Why was it you who had to go and rescue Alan from the fire? Why . . . ?' Sarah stopped asking questions and threw the photograph across the desk as Betty placed a hand on her shoulder.

Freda felt helpless. She knew she couldn't tell Sarah about Alan's money problems with the workshop and Frank Unthank. It wasn't her place to do so; but she didn't want Sarah to think that anything was going on between her and Alan. She picked up the photograph and smiled for a moment, recalling the conversation she'd had with Alan at the wedding. Slowly a thought crossed her mind.

'It's not what it seems . . .' She looked at Sarah beseechingly, but knew she couldn't break a confidence. 'You need to speak to Alan. Ask him to explain what's been going on . . .'

'Don't you think I've tried to speak to my husband?' Sarah fired back. 'He never wants to speak to me. He clams up as soon as I walk into the room, he turns his back on me in bed and then he doesn't seem to sleep. He's the ghost of the man I married, and you seem to be at the bottom of everything that's gone wrong.'

Freda wanted to blurt out that, along with Lemuel, she'd been trying to help Alan – and that meant she was helping Sarah, Georgina and Buster as well. Instead she stood up and faced Betty and Sarah. 'I'm sorry. I need to get back downstairs, but please believe me: I've never stolen another woman's husband. I'm sad you'd think I was capable of such a thing,' she said before leaving the room.

Outside in the passage, she leant against the wall and took a deep gulp of air. It would be oh, so easy to walk out of the building and never return, but she was made of sterner stuff. She would see this through to the bitter end, even if it meant losing her friends along the way. If only Alan would explain everything to his wife, but his stupid pride and stubbornness meant he ignored both her pleas and Lemuel's words of advice. Alan's answer was always that once he'd settled his debts and he was back running his business, then life would be as it was before.

*

'Blimey, what have you got there, girl?' Bob said as he let Freda in the door and took the heavy parcel from her so she could take off her cardigan and hang it up.

'It's something for Ruby. Can you give it to her?' Freda asked as she followed him up the hall and into the living room, where Ruby was listening to the radio. 'I'm not interrupting you, am I?' she asked as Ruby leant over to turn down the volume.

'It's only the news. They're saying Princess Elizabeth's wedding will be in November. I reckon that'll be a sight for sore eyes, don't you? All those toffs wearing their diamond tiaras and ballgowns,' Ruby sighed.

'I'd love to watch it, but I doubt they'll be sending me an invitation,' Freda said as she felt the teapot. 'I think I can squeeze one out of there.'

'I'll make a fresh pot,' Bob said as he placed Freda's parcel on the table. 'This is for you, love,' he added.

'What are you doing buying me presents and wasting your money?' Ruby asked as she stared at the parcel wrapped in brown paper and tied neatly with a new piece of white string. 'This looks like Maisie's handiwork.'

'It's the unmentionables for Lemuel,' Freda explained. 'I went to see Maisie to ask her advice about men's sizes, and she had these items. She reckons they will fit him. They're second-hand, but all very clean.'

Ruby picked at the knot until the string fell away and the brown paper unfolded. 'These look as good as new,' she exclaimed as she held up a pair of men's long johns. 'They may be a bit much for this weather, but come the winter he'll be glad of a bit of protection under his trousers.'

Freda nodded, but didn't say anything.

'And what's the matter with you? You would normally be falling about at something like this.' Ruby waved the underwear in front of her.

'I'm fine. Just a bit tired,' Freda answered, knowing she would never tell Ruby what had happened in Betty's office that afternoon. If her old friend sided with her granddaughter, which was likely to happen as blood was thicker than water, then Freda would be in danger of losing all her friends in one afternoon. Granted, Maisie was yet to hear, but Freda felt sure she'd side with Sarah too.

What had happened for her life to unravel like this? She had been loyal to Alan, thinking she would be helping his family, and now she was being cast as a scarlet woman. 'I wanted to pick your brain about something,' she said, thinking it best to change the subject before Ruby wheedled her secret from her like someone working a winkle out of its shell with a pin.

Ruby frowned. There was something upsetting the girl, but she'd not push for an explanation yet. Best to keep an eye on her, and have a shoulder ready for her to cry on if necessary. She just hoped it had nothing to do with what Maureen had mentioned a while back in Maisie's shop. Thank goodness Freda lived just across the road and could be watched. 'Fire away – my brain's not up to much these days but I'll help if I can.' She winced as she moved to make herself more comfortable in the wooden upright chair by the table.

'Are you in pain? Perhaps you should see the doctor.' Freda knew Ruby wasn't one for doctors.

Ruby shrugged off the advice. 'I'll be fine. It's only my back, and it is much better when I get into bed. It's just my old bones protesting. Nothing for you to worry your young head about.'

'If you're sure,' Freda said, but sounded unconvinced. She must find a moment to have a word with Bob and George about Ruby's aches and pains. That's if they hadn't turned their backs on her once Sarah told them she was an adulteress, she thought glumly. Shaking the uncomfortable thought from her head, she said, 'It's about a house in Wheatley Terrace – the one at the end of the row with dirty windows and no garden. I was told it's a . . .' She couldn't bring herself to say the words in front of Ruby.

'A knocking shop?' Bob said, bringing in the tea tray.

'Bob Jackson, mind your mouth in front of a young lady,' Ruby admonished him.

'It's what I meant, though. I'd seen people come and go from the house and had my suspicions,' she said, trying not to notice Bob's grin in case she encouraged him to laugh and joined in. Despite her worries about Alan and Sarah, she usually couldn't ignore Bob when he joked about and made them laugh.

'I know the house you mean,' Ruby said as she gave Bob a glare. 'I'd call it a house of ill repute. The old girl who owns the place also offers another service for young women. I'd have it shut down if I could. In fact, I'm going to have a word with my George when he's home from his honeymoon to see if he can influence the council to do something.' Ruby paused, deep in thought. 'Perhaps she sees what she does as a service to those women, but it isn't right, killing those poor little babies.'

'Now, now, Ruby, you know that what goes on there is all hearsay. I hope you're not getting all this from Vera.'

Freda watched as Bob and Ruby discussed the goings-on in the house which she'd seen Effie leave only a few weeks before. 'You mean it's not just a knock . . . a house of ill-repute?' she asked.

'If it was just that I'd turn a blind eye, but word is she offers a service to women who want to get rid of their unborn babies.'

Freda felt sick and her head started to spin just enough for her to grab the edge of the table. After the day she'd had, to hear that abortions were being carried out only a couple of streets away made her feel ill.

'Why did you ask, Freda?' Ruby said. 'You look worried. You're not asking about that house for a reason, are you?'

Freda laughed shakily, and took a drink of hot tea. 'No; it's just that I saw a new staff member come out of there a few weeks back, and I wondered what was going on.'

Ruby shook her head in disgust. 'You'd best steer well clear of that one. Either way it doesn't bode well.'

Bob agreed. 'Ruby's right, love. Keep away from her. Best to stick with your own kind who won't drag you into anything nasty.'

Freda sighed. Now wasn't the time to say that Effie was visiting later for a chat about her vacant room. After her run-in with Sarah, she'd decided to tell Effie to come to her house rather than have their chat at work. All she'd wanted to do was escape once the closing bell rang in the store. As for 'her own kind' . . . well, not many of her friends seemed very supportive at the moment. However she felt about Effie she would have to offer her the room or Betty would be upset. She'd taken the girl on at Woolworths, and was a good judge of character. The way things were going, Betty might be the only friend she would have left in the weeks to come.

'This is it,' Freda said as she steered Effie into the bedroom at the top of the stairs. 'It's not much of a view from the window out over the back gardens, but you do get the sun in the morning, which is nice. As I said before, you can use the kitchen whenever you want, and the living room. The front room's out of use for now while Anthony is here. He injured his leg, so he has to have a room downstairs. I'll introduce you to him later, along with Sadie and Arthur, my other lodgers.'

'You seem to have a full house,' Effie said as she peered out of the tall window. 'Are you sure you have room for me as well? Won't Anthony want his room back when he's better?'

Freda laughed. She liked the young girl more by the minute – that's if she ignored seeing her in Wheatley Terrace. Effie was polite and seemed interested in the house and the way Freda organized her lodgers. 'He's only here until he's back on his feet. I felt a little responsible, because in a way I was the one to blame for his injury.'

'Blimey – how did you do that?' the girl said, before putting a hand over her mouth. 'Sorry. So much for me being on my best behaviour. I don't swear that often, honest I don't.'

'It doesn't bother me, but don't go doing it at work, or you could be in trouble with Betty.'

'Mrs Billington, do you mean? Do you know her that well, to call her Betty? Does she come here?' Effie said in awe.

'I've known Mrs Billington since she was Miss Billington. I know it does sound strange – but it's a lovely story, and she's a lovely lady when you get to know her,' Freda smiled. 'I'll tell you all about it one day. And yes, I caused Anthony's injury when I knocked him off his bike while I was riding my friend's motorbike. There's no need to look at me like that. I rode a bike during the war for the Fire Service. I'll tell you all about that as well.'

Effie's eye shone. 'Does that mean you'll let me rent the room?'

'Well, we have a few things to sort out. Let's go downstairs and have a cup of cocoa while we chat. Sadie's making a bite to eat for us all for our dinner. If you want to stay for a while, I'm sure we can stretch it a bit further.'

'I'd love to, if it's not putting anyone out? I was going to pick up a bag of chips on the way back to my digs. Some proper food would be nice for once.'

'Doesn't your current landlady feed you?'

Effie looked embarrassed. 'I only pay for my room, as she charges a lot and I'd had a debt to pay off – but I make sure I eat at work in the lunch break. Well, I did until the cook went off on her holidays. The new cook can't even boil a spud.'

Freda roared with laughter. 'Maureen will be back in

a few days. She's on her honeymoon. I've missed her cooking as well.'

'What? The old girl's only just got herself married? There's hope for me then,' Effie said, without any spite in her voice.

'It's her second marriage. She lost her husband a long time ago. She is now married to Councillor George Caselton. He's Sarah Gilbert's father. You've probably seen Sarah, she works in the office at Woolworths. Her nan lives over the road at number thirteen. I used to lodge there when I first came to live in Erith.'

'Blimey, everyone seems to know each other at Woolworths,' Effie said, forgetting to apologize for her language. 'You're like one big happy family.'

Not so happy at the moment, Freda thought to herself as she followed the girl downstairs.

'Hello – who are you?' Effie said as she bent down to chat with Sadie's son Arthur, who was sitting on the floor lining up a row of wooden motor cars.

Arthur looked up and gave her a toothy grin before returning to his toys.

'He's not one for talking much,' Sadie called from the kitchen. 'I put it down to living with my nan for far too long. He could never get a word in edgeways.'

'Sadie, this is Effie. She may be taking the room next to yours.'

Sadie wiped her hand on the cotton pinafore she was wearing, and came into the room to shake hands. 'Pleased to meet you. It'll be nice to have another waif and stray living here.'

'Waif and stray?' Effie asked, after saying hello.

'Our Freda is one of those kindly souls who lets people come into her house to live when they've nowhere else to go. If it wasn't for her, me and the nipper would be sleeping in one of those dosshouses down West Street way. She's a good one, is Freda.'

Freda dismissed Sadie's words with a flap of her hand. 'Now you're being silly. My friend Molly was very good to me; she gave me this house after she married. I'm just passing my good luck on to others. Besides, I couldn't run this house on my wages, so it makes sense to have a few lodgers.'

'Someone gave you this house?' Effie asked in wonderment.

'Yes, as I say, my friend Molly got married and moved away. She was also left her late parents' house, so, being a generous soul, she gave this house to me.'

'Molly also got married to the film star Johnny Johnson,' Sadie said, making Effie's jaws almost hit the ground.

'Blimey, I've seen him at the pictures,' Effie said in amazement. 'Whatever are you going to tell me next? I can't keep up with all this excitement,' she grinned.

'Blimey,' echoed a young voice from the floor.

Effie covered her mouth again in horror, but Sadie burst into laughter.

'What's all the laughter about?' Anthony asked as he limped gingerly into the room, leaning heavily on one crutch.

'Young Arthur's learnt a new word,' Freda said, thinking that if the little boy were hers, she wouldn't be amused by such language. 'Perhaps we should all be a little more circumspect with what we say around the child?' she suggested, knowing this sounded like something Betty would say.

'I'm sorry, it's my fault. I'll be more careful next time. That's if there is a next time,' Effie said, looking to where Freda had started to take cups and saucers from a cupboard for their cocoa.

'We will have to have a little chat after our dinner,' Freda said, giving her a warm smile. She knew that Effie would fit in very well with the other residents, but she was still worried about the young girl's connection with the house on Wheatley Terrace.

'So we might have a newcomer,' Anthony said as he sat in the chair that Effie had quickly pulled out for him. 'Haven't I seen you somewhere before?'

Effie shrugged her shoulders and went over to help Freda. 'Probably around the town,' she said, dismissing his question.

Anthony frowned. 'No, it's more specific than that. It'll come to me, given time,' he said as he leant over to take a motor car that Arthur was holding out to him. 'You didn't happen to live round Wheatley Terrace, did you?' he asked.

Freda saw Effie freeze for a moment before she laughed off the comment by saying, 'Never heard of it. Shall I hand the drinks out, Freda?'

'Yes, please. We may as well sit down at the table. Dinner will be ready soon. I've asked Effie to stay for a bite to eat, Sadie. I take it you've cooked enough for an army again?' Freda said, wondering why Effie had lied to Anthony. Was she right to give the girl a room in her house, however pleasant she was? She decided to give her the benefit of the doubt for now . . .

'There's plenty here. I cooked up some extra potato and cabbage so we can have bubble and squeak tomorrow.'

'I don't want to put you out,' Effie said, looking worried.

'It's fine,' Sadie said, reaching behind her to where a trug had been left on a side table. 'Lemuel was round earlier. He's left us a couple of cabbages and some carrots. He's been paying his way by digging over Bob's allotments. Ruby told him to give us a share of the latest crop. He didn't stop,' she added, quickly knowing that Freda would not approve.

'Lemuel? That's a funny name,' Effie said as she sipped her cocoa. 'Is it foreign?'

'It's from the Bible,' Sadie explained softly. 'Lemuel is my friend. We are walking out together,' she added, raising her chin a little in case anyone was going to question why she would do such a thing.

'That's nice, but it's still a very unusual name for a mother to give her son. I've never heard it before,' Effie said as she cocked her head to one side to think about it.

'Lemuel comes from the West Indies,' Sadie explained.

'What, you mean he's a black man?' Effie asked in amazement. 'You're walking out with a black man . . . ?'

'We love each other,' Sadie said. 'Do you find something wrong in that?'

'No, not me. The few I've met have been lovely blokes.'

Freda watched the exchange between the two young women and started to wonder where young Effie had met these foreign men. Lemuel was unusual in having lived in England since the war. Most others were working on the ships that came up the Thames to the docks. Some lodged in the roads around Wheatley Terrace, renting a bed by the night until joining another ship setting out to foreign lands. Again, Wheatley Terrace had cropped up. What did it mean?

'Hello, Mike – are you here on official business, or to take my husband for a pint?' Sarah asked, as Mike Jackson removed his helmet and stepped over the threshold of the little house in Crayford Road.

Mike looked serious as he followed her into the living room that led straight from the front door. 'I'm afraid it's official business this time, Sarah, but I do have time for a cuppa if you're asking.'

'Consider the kettle already on.' She smiled at the family friend. 'How's Gwyneth? I've not seen her since the wedding. Even then we didn't have time to swap more than a few words. I thought she wasn't looking her usual glowing self.'

Mike sat down in one of the two armchairs set each side of the unlit fireplace. It was another warm day, and he pulled out a handkerchief to mop his brow. 'We've both been waiting patiently for Gwyneth to fall for our first child. Each month she seems to get more upset when it doesn't happen. As much as we both love Myfi, and as you know we have formally adopted her, it's not quite the same as having a child of our own. Gwyneth blames herself, but I do wonder if it has something to do with my age. I did mention it to our doctor when I was there seeing him about my bad chest, but he dismissed me as if I was an idiot. I just know I would give my right arm to make Gwyneth happy,' he said sadly.

Sarah thought a lot of Mike. Being the son of Bob Jackson, who was now married to her nan, Mike was like an uncle to her, although having a younger wife he didn't act his age. 'I'm sure it will happen,' she said, not knowing what else to say. 'It's early days. Let me put the water in the teapot and then I'll give Alan a shout. He's out the back tinkering with Bessie. The wedding photographs are on the sideboard, if you'd like to look at them?'

'I would,' he said getting up. 'George and Maureen must be due back soon,' he called back as Sarah returned to the kitchen.

'This evening. We had a postcard from them yesterday. They've had a lovely time, even if they did set off a little late because of the fire. They say that Sea View Guest House is comfortable and the landlady very welcoming. I wonder . . .'

'What do you wonder?' Mike said as he saw Sarah turn and give him a thoughtful smile.

'Why don't you take Gwyneth away for a few days? We can have Myfi here. She can top and tail with Georgina. I know Georgie would love it as she idolizes your girl.'

Mike thought for a moment. 'You may have something there. A few days in the sun may make Gwyneth forget all this baby stuff for a while. I'll have a word with your dad about the details. Thanks for that.'

Sarah smiled to herself as she headed out the back of the house to call her husband in. Perhaps a short time to themselves, enjoying each other's company, would solve their problem. If only it was that simple for her own marriage.

Alan held out his hand as he entered the room. 'Mike,

it's good to see you. I've not had a chance to thank you for all you did on the night of the fire.'

Mike returned the handshake. 'It's all part of the service, old chap. I'm thankful everyone got out alive, even though your business suffered; have you found somewhere else to work yet?'

Sarah watched the jovial chatter between the two men. In the case of her husband, it was all false. She'd seen him put on this happy façade on several occasions, switching it off again when the visitor had left the house. In some ways she wished Maureen still lived with them, as she would soon see through it and demand an explanation for his moodiness.

'I've not as yet, but there's a few irons in the fire. Early days and all that,' Alan said, sitting down opposite the policeman.

'At least you're keeping your hand in, working on Bessie.'

Sarah sighed to herself. The only reason Alan went into their small back garden and tinkered with the motorbike was to avoid speaking to her. If she went out with a cup of tea, he would turn his back. If she tried to start a conversation, he became morose, and only when pushed would he answer in words of one syllable. It was a relief to go to work for a few hours to escape the tension in the house. There was also the nagging problem of money. Alan hadn't offered her any housekeeping since a few weeks before the fire, and she'd all but used up the money she'd put aside for treats for the children and a possible holiday at the seaside.

She pulled herself back to the present, where Mike

had started to talk about the intruder who had started the fire. She could see Alan was squirming in his seat and taking sideways glances in her direction. 'I'm not sure what you're getting at, Mike,' he said, looking like a rabbit trying to dodge the headlights of one of his beloved motorbikes.

'It's the connection between Freda being rescued from Frank Unthank's office the other week, and then his son turning up and setting fire to your workshop on the night of the wedding. The wedding and the family connections were well documented in the *Erith Observer*, so I could imagine a burglar taking his chances.'

'I'd thought the same. It was a lovely article about the forthcoming wedding, and your dad being a councillor, as well as mentioning the workshop, but this could have been an open invitation for any of our homes to be visited by a thief.' Sarah tried to convey sympathy with her expression as she spoke to Alan. All she received was a glare for her troubles.

'No doubt he thought the building would be empty until being caught by Lemuel Powell, but for the life of me I can't see how it all fits together . . .' Mike added thoughtfully. 'That's why I decided to come and have a chat in case I'm missing something.' He looked expectantly at Alan.

Seeing Alan was not about to say anything, Sarah spoke. 'But why do you mention Freda? She doesn't work for the garage or own a share. She's just a friend,' Sarah added, watching to see if even a flicker of shame crossed her husband's face. Instead he leant forward, elbows on knees, and placed his face in his hands.

'You say Freda was rescued. Did something happen?' Sarah asked, ignoring Alan and his reluctance to speak.

'I don't think she will mind me telling you that I spotted Alan's motorbike outside Unthank's office in West Street. There was a crowd of kids hanging about, so I went to check all was well. That's when I spotted Freda through the window being given a hard time, and from what I could see it could have turned nasty. It was none of my business why she was there, as she appeared to be unharmed, and I didn't want to press charges; so I left it there.'

'What is Frank Unthank's business?' Sarah asked. 'I know the name but I'm not sure what he does.'

'He has his finger in a lot of pies, but seems to avoid getting on the wrong side of the law most of the time. He's known mainly as a moneylender and businessman,' Mike explained.

'A moneylender, you say? I wonder if Freda has been borrowing money?' she said thoughtfully. 'If she hadn't paid the man back on time, he may have threatened her . . . but then why would he go to the workshop and not her house to collect his debt? Freda hasn't invested in the workshop, has she, Alan?'

'Don't be daft,' Alan all but snapped back, before remembering that Mike was watching him. 'The kid's got enough on her plate renting out rooms in that house of hers.'

'Then perhaps she is in debt because of the house. It was foolhardy of Molly Missons to pass the house to a young woman like Freda and expect her to be able to maintain the upkeep. It must be almost twice the size of this place, and more suited to a family.' She almost added 'like ours', but that would have sounded like sour grapes. Although she had to admit to herself, she'd been more than a little envious when Freda was given the house, especially when their family of four, plus living as they were with Maureen at the time, were squeezed here in a two-up, two-down terraced property.

'They are larger houses, I'll give you that, but Freda should be doing all right, as she's always had a couple of lodgers. She's not said anything to you about money problems?' Mike asked, looking at Sarah. 'I know you girls have all been close since moving to Erith.'

Sarah felt uncomfortable. She was not about to tell Mike that she believed Freda was carrying on with Alan. 'We've not socialized as much lately as we used to, what with me being busy with the children and Freda having her lodgers to care for. Even at work we seem to have been on different shifts and breaks.' She wasn't about to add that she'd made sure of late to avoid Freda in the staff canteen, being sick of all the false pretence between them. God forbid she should snap and confront Freda in front of her colleagues. Sarah wasn't one to wash her dirty linen in public. 'Alan's seen more of her than I have,' she smiled politely, hoping Alan would take over the conversation. He stayed quiet.

Mike looked at his notebook. 'I don't feel as though I'm much further forward,' he said. 'I thought perhaps you could come up with something more.'

Sarah frowned. 'Do you think the Unthanks believed the motorbike Freda was driving belonged to her?'

'Why would that make any difference?' Alan sighed.

'If they did and Freda was in debt, then they would go looking for it, to perhaps take away in lieu of payment or to damage and teach her a lesson.'

'You could have something there,' Mike said, adding to his notes.

'This is preposterous. You can't put the blame for something like this on Freda,' Alan blurted out.

'It all makes sense, and with Unthank junior not telling us why he was in your workshop that night, it's all we have to go on. That's if you can't remember anything else?' Mike said, giving Alan a look that said, 'prove me wrong'. 'Perhaps if you do think of anything more, you'll come down the station and let me know? We've enough to go on to charge Unthank. Although it would be good to know what's all behind it all, if only to put a stop to Frank Unthank running around Erith and having his heavies set fire to innocent people's property.'

Sarah looked between her husband and the police sergeant. It was as if Mike was waiting for Alan to tell him something they didn't already know, whereas Alan was trying to hide something he did know . . . All she could think was that her husband was having an affair, and the pair were not only keeping their sordid secret from all and sundry, but Freda was in some way behind the family business going up in flames.

Freda Smith had a lot to answer for, Sarah thought to herself as she pinned a smile to her face and saw Mike to the door.

11

Freda looked at the clock over the mantelpiece. It was almost ten o'clock, but it felt later. It had been a long day; so much had happened, and not all of it good. At least she had a new lodger, which would help her build up her lost savings. Best of all was that Effie seemed to get on well with Sadie and Anthony, and wanted to muck in with the meals and other chores.

She reached for the envelope Effie had left behind. Inside were the names of two people Freda could write to for references and below that her next of kin, who seemed to be a sister living in nearby Belvedere. Freda had asked why Effie wasn't able to live with her family, and had been told the sister had a young family and was in rented accommodation – consequently there wasn't room for Effie. That all seemed reasonable enough, and so Freda had offered the girl the room in her house on a three-month trial. There was the issue of Freda having seen Effie coming from that house in Wheatley Terrace, but on reflection she had decided to let it alone for now.

Checking the front and back doors were locked, she called out to Anthony, who was in his room. 'I'm making a drink – would you like one?' They'd taken to having a hot drink together last thing at night; Freda looked forward to this companionable time. Usually she asked more about his bike riding and told him about her life in Erith, not just her day at Woolworths but also how she helped out with the Brownies and Girl Guides.

'I'll be out in a minute,' he called back as Freda went through to the living room. Of late Anthony had been taking short walks up and down the bottom end of Alexandra Road, trusting his injured leg, although he was using a walking stick and relying on a crutch at times when the injured limb was paining him.

Freda thought of the couple of weeks Anthony had spent in her home. At the time of the accident she'd not been keen on him at all as he came across as brusque and unfriendly to her when they worked under the same roof – although he might have been tagging along to be like the other trainees. However, he'd fitted in so comfortably, not just with her but with Sadie and young Arthur too, and she had the feeling that with Effie joining them they'd rub along almost like a family. But at some point he was bound to say he was fit enough be to on his way and, when his training was completed at the Erith branch of Woolworths, he could easily be moved to a store the other side of the country. The thought made her sad; she felt as though he had become, if not a firm friend, then someone who fitted into her life and didn't cause any waves, which she was grateful for at that moment. But it would be ages yet, surely?

Freda now looked forward to coming home in the evening and closing her front door on the outside world, knowing that she could enjoy a pleasant evening with friendly people. Occasionally Lemuel joined them, or Freda would care for Arthur, allowing Sadie and Lemuel to go out on their own. The thought made her smile. It was nice to witness a burgeoning romance, even though she felt there could be rocky times ahead for them both, even if only caused by people who didn't understand that the colour of a person's skin meant nothing at all, especially when a couple were in love. One of these people was Sadie's own grandmother, Vera.

'You look as though you're miles away,' Anthony said as he joined her. 'Is there something on your mind? There have been moments lately when I thought you had the troubles of the world on your shoulders. Is there anything I can help you with?'

Freda wasn't about to tell him how she'd become involved in Alan's problems or that Sarah thought she was having an affair with her husband, so she shrugged her shoulders. 'Nothing for you to worry about,' she smiled.

'I'm here if you want to chat,' he said. 'I'm like a gypsy in your life, wandering in before I hit the highway waving goodbye, so you can tell me anything and I'll take it with me when I go.' He grinned. 'Speaking of which, I have some news to give you.'

Freda felt as though she'd been punched in the stomach. 'You're leaving so soon?' she asked, surprised by how unhappy that made her feel. 'I thought you'd be staying with me – I mean, staying here in my house – much longer. What's happened? Aren't you happy with your room?'

The smile on Anthony's face disappeared as he saw

how unhappy Freda had become. 'Here, here,' he said as one large tear dropped onto her cheek. Reaching into his pocket, he pulled out a clean handkerchief and wiped away the tear while looking closely to see if any more threatened to fall. 'I didn't realize I'd had such a profound effect on you,' he laughed, trying to lighten her mood.

'I'm sorry. I've had a bit of a rotten day, and your news was the final straw,' she said, taking a step away, as being so close to him was doing something strange to her heart beat.

'Sit down,' he commanded, pulling a chair out from the table with one hand while leaning on his walking stick.

'I've got the cocoa to make . . .'

'Sit down and do as I say,' he commanded with a smile before sitting down across the table from her. 'Now, what made you think I was leaving?'

Freda felt fragile. It was hard to stop her bottom lip from wobbling. She was always the first to laugh when Sarah started to cry. The friends often said Sarah could cry at the drop of a hat and be smiling the next minute, whereas Freda was far more level-headed. 'I thought you were going to say you were leaving because you were talking about waving goodbye and . . .'

'Do you want me to leave?' he asked gently.

His question opened the floodgates and Freda found herself sobbing her heart out into the edge of the embroidered linen tablecloth that had been a gift from Maisie. As she calmed down and straightened the damp tablecloth, she gave him a watery smile. 'Gosh, you must think me an utter idiot. It's just that I've had a horrid day and I think I've lost all my friends and I can't say why and the only thing that is keeping me happy at the moment is knowing I can come home to a happy house and . . . and . . . when you said you had news about leaving . . .'

Anthony left his seat and hurried as best he could to her side to pull her to him, which caused her to start crying once more. 'I've never known anyone cry so much,' he grinned as he tried to lift her mood. 'Even that angry young woman who ran me down never shed a tear, and there I was lying in the road groaning and bleeding. And, if I recall, I swore rather a lot as well.'

Freda pulled back and rubbed her eyes with her hands. 'I didn't hear you swear once,' she said indignantly.

He laughed and brushed a few strands of hair from her face with one finger. 'I thought that would stop the tears. Now sit yourself down and I'll make the cocoa – no, I'll do it,' he said as she went to protest. 'Then we are going to have a serious talk with you telling me everything that has happened to you, and I'll tell you why I'm not leaving here any day soon.'

Anthony sat quietly as Freda explained what had happened with Alan, and how Sarah assumed she was carrying on with Alan, and how it had all got out of hand. She told him about what she'd overheard that day outside Betty's office. 'She even threw away the photograph of me that was meant to be for the staff magazine cover girl competition,' Freda said, taking a deep breath as she finished speaking.

'There must have been something to make Sarah believe you were up to no good with her husband. These accusations aren't usually plucked out of thin air,' he said, looking puzzled.

'I can only think it's my fondness for motorbikes. It was Alan's bike I was riding when we had our accident. Alan treats me like his kid sister; his nickname for me is "kid",' she added. 'And when he was demobbed and started his motorbike repair business rather than return to Woolworths – he was a trainee manager like you – I started going there to help out. We always joked that when he made it big I could go and work for him. I think I told you that I was a part-time despatch rider for the Fire Service during the war, so I've always had a love for motorbikes and getting my hands mucky. Sarah isn't like that, and although she supports him wanting to have a business, she's not a bit interested in motorbikes and repairing things. She even accused me of being the one who led the rescuers in to save Alan, as if I'd done something wrong. I was only trying to help as I knew the layout of the building. Perhaps that has made her question us being close. Although nothing has ever happened,' she added firmly. 'You do believe me, don't you?'

'I do believe you. I've not known you long, but I can tell you are an honest person.'

Freda felt awful and looked down into her lap. She'd not said anything about Alan's problems with Frank Unthank, or the part she'd played in them. So far she'd not told a soul about it, and the guilt lay heavy on her mind. 'Look, there is something else. I promised Alan I'd never tell a soul, but if I don't say something I'm going to burst. I know Alan is so down with the guilt that I fear for his health.'

'If you feel you can trust me, I'll keep your secret. If you don't want to tell me, I'll still support you and be a friend.'

'But you're bound to go away at some point . . .' she said with a shake in her voice.

Anthony gazed at Freda for a few seconds before shaking his head solemnly. 'I have a feeling I'm going to accept the job I've been offered and hang around for a while. I like Erith, and I like the people who live here.'

'A job? You're going to leave Woolworths? How can you waste all that training? Why, you could have your own store one day and be like Betty Billington.'

'I don't think the tweed suits would be my style,' he said seriously, making her laugh.

'What kind of work would you do?' she asked, looking to where he'd propped his walking stick against the table.

'It was Mrs Billington's idea. She wrote me a letter. I'll show you later. She suggested that I stay with the Erith store and take an office-based job which would give me time to regain my strength and then, if I wished, I could resume my general training at a later date. She seems to think I'd not need any more store training and once I'd mastered the office side of store work, I could be offered an assistant manager's position.'

Freda felt her chest swell with pride. Well done Betty for thinking of her staff. Then a thought came to her. 'Isn't Sarah classed as a store manager?' That would put the cat amongst the pigeons, if Anthony took her job away, and no doubt with Anthony being her lodger she'd end up being blamed. The mood Sarah was in lately, she would still find fault with Freda even if she were a saint.

'I believe she is more assistant to the manageress, but I intend to ask, as I'd not wish to tread on anyone's toes.'

Freda flashed him a look of thanks. 'I'm pleased your

news means you are staying in Erith. Will you be looking for new accommodation? I only ask as I was thinking of turning this room into a bedroom and hiring it out on a permanent basis, if you'd be interested.'

'I'm not so sure. I've heard the landlady is prone to tears, and I'd run out of handkerchiefs very quickly. But if I could help her smile again, I'd most certainly think seriously about staying here.'

Freda held out her hand to shake his. 'Then it's a deal,' she said.

'Only if you tell me what the problem is with Alan's workshop. I don't mean that it burnt to the ground in the fire, but why you are so protective of him and the business. My gut tells me there is more.'

Freda lowered her hand and did her best not to meet his gaze as she thought of what he wanted to know.

'I'm not asking because I'm nosy, but because I want to help you. It looks as though I'll be staying in Erith, and I'll need somewhere to store my bikes and have them kept in tip-top condition. Alan could be the man to do that. That's if he intends to start up again?'

Freda's eyes glowed with excitement. 'We'd be so grateful if you really mean it?' she said, before continuing with suggestions for his bikes.

Anthony held his hand up to stop her excited chatter. 'First I want to know everything. I can't afford to have something happen to my bikes, or my friends. If there's anything illegal going on, or if you are in danger, I want – no, I *need* to know right now.'

'I'll make some fresh cocoa,' Freda said. 'It's going to be a while before you see your bed.'

'Before you disappear into the kitchen, I have this for you – that's if you're interested?'

Freda took a pale blue deckle-edged card from him and read the words carefully. 'It's an invitation to join the Thames Road Cycle Club for a dinner dance, to be held at the Electricity Showroom in Pier Road,' she said, her eyes shining with excitement. 'Are you inviting me to go as your partner?'

'If you'd like to?'

'I'd like that very much,' she replied. Perhaps at last something good was happening in her life. She hurried to make their cocoa, wondering what she could wear to this very special dance – special because Anthony had invited her as his partner.

'You're back! It's wonderful to see you. How is married life?' Betty asked Maureen before clapping a hand across her mouth as her cheeks turned pink.

The new Mrs Caselton roared with laughter. 'You're not the first to ask, and it is blooming marvellous, thank you very much. I must also thank you for allowing me to extend my time off. We couldn't go away with everything that happened the night of the wedding reception; it wouldn't have been fair to leave Alan and Sarah to all that mess. Besides, the pair of us wouldn't have slept much wondering what was going on.' She snorted as she realized what she had said. 'Thank goodness I wasn't some young bride on her first honeymoon, or what you've just asked me and what I've just said could have had other meanings. Dear me, it is good to be back,' she said, wiping her eyes as she continued to laugh.

Betty joined in with her laughter. 'But you're early. Are you that keen to leave your husband at home and come to work?'

'He left an hour before me, as there will be a lot to catch up on. He's off to a council meeting this evening. The honeymoon is well and truly over,' she grinned.

'Even so, you didn't have to come in early,' Betty said as Maureen slid a cup of coffee to her over the serving counter.

'To be honest, I wanted a word with you before our Sarah comes in. Can you spare me five minutes, please?'

Betty gave a quick look at the clock on the canteen wall. She'd arrived early herself to have a word with the supervisor of the cleaning staff, but it could wait. She had a good idea what Maureen wanted to discuss, and it was nothing to do with catering supplies or how many staff lunches were required. 'By all means. Shall we sit down?' she said, picking up her drink and walking to a nearby table.

Maureen eased herself into the wooden seat. The old injury she'd sustained in the same attack that killed George's first wife during enemy action on the New Cross Woolworths store still gave her trouble in cold and also warm weather. She could tell today would be a warm one. 'It's about Sarah and Alan. Something's not right between them. What with you knowing her so well, I wondered if she'd said anything to you. When I popped round there last night with gifts for the children you could have cut the air between them with a knife, it was so tense. Oh, they pretended there was nothing wrong, but I wasn't born yesterday.'

'It must be the strain of the workshop fire,' Betty said, not wishing to say anything that would have Maureen marching off to confront her family. 'With so much uncertainty about the business's future, Alan is bound not to be his usual happy self. Give them time; it will all blow over, and things will go back to normal.'

'So you don't think there is a problem in their marriage?' Maureen said, picking up on Betty's words.

'I would be betraying a confidence if I were to say anything. I find myself in a difficult situation at the moment. I so want to help, but my hands are tied. I'm having problems understanding what is going on with my friends . . .'

'I appreciate your loyalty, Betty, but if you can't speak, can you at least nod your head if I ask you whether you believe what's being said – about my son carrying on with Freda Smith?'

Betty hated what she was about to do, but Maureen was as good a friend and loyal staff member as every one of the women involved. She couldn't let any one of them down, or she'd be failing as a friend and their manager. She looked Maureen straight in the eye and nodded to confirm her suspicions. She'd thought long and hard since the day Freda had burst in on her conversation with Sarah. Something had to be going on for the girl to deny it so strongly. It wasn't in Freda's nature to act in such a fashion. There's no smoke without fire, she thought to herself, using one of Ruby's favourite sayings, but she hated herself for becoming involved.

'Thank you. I know it took a lot for you to do that, but I'll never tell Sarah and Alan I've spoken to you. I overheard something being said at the workshop not long before the fire, and I should have tackled the pair of them at the time. My God, I could knock their blooming heads together. I was going to have a word with Ruby about it all, but it's not fair to burden an old lady with such news. I did wonder if she was suspicious, but nothing's ever been said. It's not a good thing to start married life by upsetting my mother-in-law,' she smiled.

'Ruby would no doubt dish out good advice, but I agree she should not be bothered at the moment. If, and I hope it never happens, the marriage fails, then it will be up to Alan and Sarah to inform their family and close friends. Until then, we can only be supportive and kind – and try not to take sides.' However, she felt as though she had by confirming her thoughts with that nod of her head.

Maureen digested Betty's words. 'I knew you'd understand. Thank you for sparing me some time. I just keep thinking about those poor little kiddies, if Alan and Sarah go their separate ways. It would break my heart, but Georgie and Buster . . . well . . .' She sighed. 'I'd best keep myself busy, it doesn't do to brood too much.'

'That's the ticket,' Betty said as she finished her coffee. 'I can only imagine what you and George must be going through, as it affects both your children, but you must try and not let it affect your own marriage. Talk to George, don't bottle it up, and promise me you will speak to me again if you need a shoulder to cry on. I know you have a telephone at your house, so if it is easier for you, please do telephone me at home and we can have a chat.'

'Thank you; it has helped to unburden myself. I'd best get my skates on and start cooking before the hordes arrive,' Maureen said, although Betty could see she was still pondering the problem.

Back in her office, Betty opened her diary and made a few notes, crossing out two appointments. Picking up the telephone, she dialled the number of her husband's business. 'Douglas? Can you spare me an hour around midday? No, my dear, it can't wait until this evening. I need you to reserve a table at the Oaks and arrange for David and Maisie to join us. Tell them it is important.'

Freda and Effie entered the staff canteen together, having met on the staircase leading from the shop floor. Although she'd trusted her gut feeling and offered Effie the room, Freda still wanted to question the girl about her connection to Wheatley Terrace. If she didn't, soon it would be too late and the whole thing could become the elephant in the room. The fact that Anthony also seemed to have recognized Effie made it seem all the more important to get to the bottom of things. Where better than over a cup of tea and a slice of something nice prepared by Maureen now she was back at work?

'Hello, Maureen, how was Ramsgate?' Freda asked as the older woman slid two cups across the counter.

'Very nice, thank you,' Maureen said without a smile. 'Did you want something to eat with that?'

'Yes please, I'll have a cheese sandwich. What would you like, Effie? Oh, Maureen, I don't think you've met

Effie. She's going to be renting a room from me. I'll have a full house then,' she grinned, as Effie nodded hello and asked for the same.

Maureen turned to Effie and gave her a welcoming nod along with a smile.

'I don't think that one likes you much,' Effie said as they sat down. 'The way you spoke I thought you knew her.'

'I do,' Freda said glumly. Clearly Maureen must have spoken to Sarah and believed what had been said. 'Perhaps she's having an off day. I'd be the same if I was back to work after a lovely holiday. Now, tell me more about where you lived before you came to Erith,' she said, trying hard not to feel hurt about the way Maureen had snubbed her. She prayed Alan would explain everything to his family soon.

'There's nothing much to tell you. I've been sleeping at my sister's place in Belvedere, but it's not been easy, as she doesn't have the room and her husband and landlord have grumbled about an extra person staying. I rented at another place, but it didn't work out.'

'Oh, was that in Wheatley Terrace? I thought I saw you coming out of a house when I was walking down that street,' Freda said casually.

Effie gave her a puzzled stare. 'You must have been mistaken. I've never been near that house,' she said before tucking into her sandwich and lifting up a discarded newspaper. 'Look, they've named the date for the Princess's wedding. Isn't it exciting?'

Hmm, so that's how it's going to be, Freda thought to herself. It's funny how I never mentioned which house, but she knew what I meant. 'Yes, I'd love to go along and watch, wouldn't you?'

The girls chatted on until the bell rang to signal the end of the tea break. As they hurried along the long passageway to go back downstairs, Betty called out to Freda from the open door of her office. 'Can you spare me a minute, Freda?'

Freda straightened her overall and stepped into the room, closing the door behind her.

'Take a seat, Freda,' Betty said as she closed a ledger that lay in front of her. 'I wanted to ask if you'd come to a decision about letting your spare room to our new staff member, Effie?'

Freda felt herself relax. She'd expected Betty to ask about her relationship with Alan. Everyone seemed fixated on their friendship of late. 'I've had a chat, and she came to see the room yesterday evening. She will be moving in on Sunday,' she explained, deciding not to mention seeing Effie at Wheatley Terrace. Betty was at last being friendly, and she didn't wish to antagonize her by saying the wrong thing.

Betty made a note on a pad and put a large tick next to it. 'There was something else . . .'

Here it comes, Freda thought, feeling her stomach lurch.

'I'm sending off a few words about Maureen and George's wedding along with one of the splendid photographs taken by Sarah to the editor of *The New Bond* magazine. You'll remember I did wish to enter you for the cover girl competition. Do you have a photograph at home we could use?' she asked, making no mention of the fact that Sarah had destroyed the photograph she'd taken at the wedding.

'I have a nice one taken with the Brownies, but it's not really glamorous like the ones we see on the cover of the magazine. Does it matter that I'm in my Brown Owl uniform?'

'No, that wouldn't be right at all. I know they will arrange a professional photograph of the chosen staff member, but it would be a help if the one submitted was as, er . . . as nice as possible. Do you think you can arrange this?'

'I could ask Sarah to take the photograph, if she still has George's camera,' Freda suggested, and was surprised by Betty's startled expression.

'No, that wouldn't do at all.'

Freda knew then that Betty had taken Sarah's side over the misunderstanding. 'Betty, as I've already told you, I have not had any romantic involvement with Alan. He is a friend, a very good friend – and that's all. Sarah is putting one and one together and making ten.'

Betty looked sad. 'Look at this from where I'm sitting, and also from Sarah's point of view. There is more wrong with their marriage than the workshop fire. If you know something, please tell me now, so we can inform Sarah and put an end to this sorry mess. You owe it to your friends not to keep things from them.'

Freda felt as though she'd been pushed into a corner with no way of escaping without hurting someone. 'I can't, Betty. Believe me when I say I am not involved with Alan. But I promised I'd keep his secret, and as much as I admire and respect you, I will not break my word and tell any of our friends. I'll do my best to have a photograph taken that is suitable for you to send to the staff magazine,' she added as she stood up to leave the office. 'Please don't tell Sarah what I've just told you. As you say, it is their problem and I feel it is down to Alan to talk to his wife.'

How Freda got through the morning, she never knew. Fortunately, the store was busy, and she stepped onto the crockery counter to help out as they had a staff member off sick. She pinned a smile to her face and chatted to the customers as if she didn't have a care in the world, while inside she was weeping for the loss of the friends who no longer seemed to believe her – and for the secret she could not share with them. Skipping her lunch break in case she bumped into Sarah or Betty, and not wanting to go into the staff canteen because of Maureen being there, she worked on, looking forward to the bell that would announce end of trading for the day. She would be able to head to her own little house and close her front door on the world. At least there Anthony would believe her. Roll on five thirty, she thought to herself.

Betty hurried out of the store at dead on midday. She didn't want to be late for her luncheon appointment. She appreciated that her husband, as well as Maisie and David Carlisle, were busy people. Asking them to leave their businesses halfway through the day was highly unusual.

'There she is,' Maisie said as she lit a cigarette. 'We was about ter give up and go back ter work.'

'We couldn't do that, as I've already ordered lunch. Douglas ordered for you, Betty. Now, perhaps you would tell us what this is all about?' David said as he kissed Betty on the cheek and pulled her chair out for her.

'I've got a good idea,' Maisie winked. 'Would it have anything ter do with the mystery of the fire in the workshop – and with Alan and Freda?'

Betty was shocked, even though she knew Maisie was joking. 'A tad too close for comfort, my dear,' she said as she refused a cigarette from her husband. 'We seem to be the only ones in our little group of friends who are not involved in this horrid business.'

Douglas looked confused. 'Is this the business of the workshop or the friendship of Freda and Alan? Surely Mike and Gwyneth Jackson aren't involved, and they are as much friends as we are?'

'Darling, Mike is our local police sergeant. I'm afraid he is involved in an official capacity,' Betty sighed. 'I just wondered what you all thought of this business. Let's put our heads together about the fire. I for one think it strange that it happened on the night many of the townsfolk knew the family would be together at the wedding reception.'

'Surely Mike is already investigating this? I saw Alan in the pub the other night, and a sorry state he looked as well. He told me they will charge the chap who was caught starting the fire, but then he shrugged off my questions,' David said. 'He still seemed to be in shock about the whole episode.'

'Well, wouldn't you be?' Maisie asked. 'What would you two be doing, if your undertaker's business went up in flames?'

'I'd be devastated – but I'd also be looking for temporary

premises to carry on trading, so as not to disappoint my customers.'

'But what if you didn't have any customers? Sarah as good as told me the workshop was empty only weeks before the fire,' Betty said thoughtfully.

'You're saying he could have set the fire himself ter get the insurance money?' Maisie pondered. 'He picked the right time – but why do it and endanger Lemuel's life, when he's known the chap fer years? You'd 'av ter be pretty desperate ter do such a thing.'

'No, no. I'm not saying Alan arranged for the building to be burnt to the ground. God forbid!' Betty said, looking horrified. 'No, I'm saying that perhaps there's a reason Alan's business has not been doing well; and perhaps whoever caused it decided to destroy the evidence.'

'Have you been reading those crime novels you sell in Woolworths that young Freda is so passionate about?' Douglas asked, giving his wife a gentle smile. 'You've got to admit your idea is pretty far-fetched, my love.'

Maisie stubbed out her cigarette as a waitress arrived with their food, and grimaced at the pilchard salads placed in from of them. Stabbing the unappetizing meal with a fork, she stopped and thought for a moment. 'You know how Freda has always hung around Alan . . .'

'They've been great mates for years,' David said. 'She's always at the workshop and she's very loyal to him.'

'So, what if Freda knows something about Alan's business . . .' Betty added.

'And he's sworn her to secrecy?' Douglas suggested.

'Bingo!' Maisie declared, stabbing the pilchard on her plate. 'That's why the pair of 'em always have their 'eads together whispering, and why Sarah thinks they are carrying on . . .'

'It all makes sense,' Betty said. 'But what can we do without accosting Alan and forcing him to inform us what happened to cause this sorry state of affairs? And furthermore, how can we convince Sarah to trust Alan again?'

The four friends were thoughtful as they ate their food. Waving away the dessert menu and requesting coffee, they made small talk until Douglas thumped the table. 'Why the hell didn't I think of it earlier? David, we have the empty shop premises where we store the . . .'

'The brass handles and coffins?' Maisie said, grinning as she saw Douglas's attempt not to mention his business in case the other diners overheard.

'Well, yes. We have plans to set up a florist's shop, as it would fit hand in glove with our other work, but we've been that busy there's not been time.'

'In essence it is a generous idea. However, I'm not sure a motorbike repair workshop would fit into a retail premises,' Betty said, patting his hand.

David Carlisle grinned at the two women. 'There's a small yard at the back he could make use of, and then he could use the shop front as an office. I'm assuming George Caselton sorted out insurance and suchlike, and now he is home from his honeymoon he will chase everything up. It was George who did all the paperwork when his son-in-law started the business. Alan may be good with his hands, but he has no head for business matters. In Alan's frame of mind, he wouldn't have thought of such things.'

'And wiv Sarah's only thoughts being about her husband

having an affair wiv Freda, she's as much use as a chocolate teapot right now,' Maisie declared.

Betty laughed. 'I couldn't have put it any better myself. How do we approach this? I doubt Alan will accept charity?'

'Leave it with me,' David said. 'I'll nab George and have a word. I'll not mention our theory of what's behind all this. I'll simply say they can have use of the premises for as long as they want, and at a nominal rent once they are up and running again. As for the rest of the business with Sarah and Freda – let's just be friends to all concerned, and not take sides.'

'An excellent suggestion, David, well done. If you could inform George, and I'll have a word with Maureen about the shop and suggest she is kinder to Freda until we know the whole story. I'd hate there to be a fight in the staff canteen. Now, if you don't mind I have a store to run; and don't you both have a funeral to attend to?'

'Good grief,' Douglas exclaimed. 'We are supposed to be burying old Mrs Green in half an hour. If we don't put our skates on we will be in trouble with the vicar.'

Freda all but slammed the door behind her as she arrived home. The day was hot and sultry, and she felt tired and limp. She was glad to be home, but recent events lay heavily on her mind.

'Welcome home,' Anthony said, as he stuck his head around the door of the kitchen. 'Dinner is ready, so go wash your hands or whatever it is you women do and I'll put it on the table.'

Freda perked up at once. 'Where is Sadie this evening?'

'She's looking after Maisie's children and has Arthur with her.'

'Oh, that's good. As much as I enjoy their company, it will be good to have a quiet evening. I'm exhausted.' She went to the kitchen tap and washed her hands under the cold running water before splashing her face and neck. 'That feels better,' she said, taking the towel from him and going into the living room to sit down. 'What are we eating?'

'Sadie made Scotch eggs, and there are tomatoes and cucumber from the box Lemuel brought in from Bob's allotment. Sadie sliced the cucumber and mixed it with an onion, then soaked them in vinegar. I've had mine and enjoyed it all. It's a rare treat to be fed such good food. I've always had to fend for myself before now. I take it your day hasn't been good?'

Freda explained about Maureen's attitude, and how cold Betty had been towards her.

'You can't blame them when they don't know the truth,' Anthony said as he watched her tuck into her meal. 'Am I really the only person who knows the truth?'

'Apart from Alan, although Lemuel knows about the business with Frank Unthank, yes. Please don't get any silly ideas in your head about telling Betty. Alan would be so disappointed, and he doesn't need this right now.'

'I won't,' he assured her. 'You really are a good friend to put up with so much when you could so easily tell your friends the truth. I'd kill for a friend like that.'

Freda put her fork down and gave him a smile. 'You do have a friend right here.'

There was a sudden stillness in the air as they gazed at each other. It ceased only when Freda said, 'My biggest problem at this moment is to find a nice photograph to give to Betty for that wretched cover girl competition. I don't think I have one that will suit the occasion.'

Anthony grinned. 'Finish your meal. I'll not be more than a few minutes.'

Freda was thoughtful as she finished her meal. It would be delightful to have a romance with Anthony, but at the moment she felt as though every friendship she'd ever touched turned to dust, and previous romances had hurt her deeply.

True to his word, he appeared just as Freda was taking her empty plate to the kitchen. 'This should solve your problem,' he said, showing her a camera. 'You go put on your prettiest frock and powder your nose, and then I'll take your photograph.'

'But where can we take it?' she asked, looking around.

'Why don't we take a stroll down to the river front and find a nice spot there?'

'But your leg . . . ?'

'The doctor has told me I can extend the distance I walk each day. If I tire, then we can stop for a drink along the way. In a few weeks I'm going to be able to take short bike rides. Would you care to come with me and make sure I don't get hit by mad women on motorbikes?'

'I'd like that,' she grinned before dashing upstairs to change. As she peered into the mirror of her dressing table, she had a sudden thought. Perhaps Anthony being around would be a blessing in disguise? With Anthony taking her to the bike club dance, and them being seen out together cycling, her friends would think she had a beau. It would stop all the unpleasantness, and give Alan time to sort out this business with Frank Unthank. As she headed back downstairs, she thanked her lucky stars that Anthony had moved into her house.

12

November 1947

'No! It will be too dangerous to sleep out on the pavements of London overnight. Anything could happen to you girls. It's not safe to be in London,' Bob said as Sarah, Maisie and Freda sat looking downcast, while Ruby tutted in disapproval.

'Young women should not be alone in London in amongst the crowds. I remember what it was like when the old King died, and we went up to pay our respects. I was pushed and shoved all over the place, and that was by people who were grieving. God only knows what it would be like with them celebrating a royal wedding.'

'But all the people I know who went ter London on VE Day said it was fun and there wasn't any problems,' Maisie said. 'We stayed here for your wedding and someone was killed,' she added, knowing she was pushing her point a little too hard.

'That's a different thing completely, and well you know it,' Ruby said, putting her hands on her hips and then wincing.

'Are you all right, Nan?' Sarah said as she noticed a flash of pain cross Ruby's face.

'I'm an old woman. That's what's wrong with me,' she said, dismissing the girl's concerns. 'And don't try to get round me by being nice,' she added. 'I know what you're up to.' The three girls had the good grace to look ashamed.

'What can we do to have your blessing for us to go to London to watch the wedding?' Freda asked Bob, who seemed not to have noticed Ruby's pain. Even though she no longer lived under Ruby and Bob's roof, she knew better than to incur their disapproval.

It had been touch and go for a while after Sarah's outburst in Betty's office, but in the months that had followed Freda had found that Betty and even Maureen had mellowed towards her. Maisie had seemed her old self, and it had been she who proposed their trip to London to wave and cheer with the rest of the country as the young Princess was married. Freda had wondered why, but thought it prudent to keep her head down. She was just pleased not to be the cause of so much unhappiness. As much as she still longed to reassure Sarah that her relationship with Alan was purely platonic, she had to keep being careful, as the problem of Frank Unthank hung heavy over their heads. But time had crept by, and she'd spent much of her leisure time helping Anthony regain the strength in his damaged leg. She'd even taken short bicycle rides with him and accompanied him to a few dances. They remained strictly friends, although it suited her to have Maisie and Sarah think she was romantically attached to the young man. Perhaps that was why their attitude towards her had mellowed. Besides, she rather enjoyed Anthony's company.

Bob sat and thought carefully about Freda's question. He loved these girls like they were all his granddaughters, and he never wanted any harm to befall them. When he thought back to Freda going into that fire, it still put the fear of God in him. He'd been one of the first to scold her, even though he was proud of her for showing such courage. 'If I had a choice, I'd want you to stay here where I can see you. We could go to the pub to celebrate and if we wanted to watch the wedding, I've heard it will be shown at the Odeon before too long. However –' he said quickly, looking at the disappointment in her eyes – 'however, I'm not an unreasonable man, so instead I'd say that as there are a group of you going together, I'll give you my blessing as long as there are two men in your party. What do Alan and your dad say about this?' he asked, turning to Sarah.

Sarah felt herself blush under Bob's scrutiny. 'Alan's not really bothered, as long as I find someone to look after Georgina and Buster. He's going to be busy working at the shop and getting it decorated,' she added quickly, in case her friends questioned Alan's attitude. None of them dared. 'I've not mentioned it to Dad.'

'So, you'd like me to have the kiddies for the day?' Ruby asked, trying not to smile, although she felt she'd been stitched up like a kipper.

'But where are we going to find two men?' Maisie wailed. 'My David has the kiddies, and he could also be called in to work if too many people pop their clogs that day.'

Sarah laughed. 'Maisie, your David works in the office, so no need for the dramatics.'

Maisie shrugged her shoulders. 'Yer never know,' she grinned.

'We could invite Sadie to join us, as long as someone can care for young Arthur,' Freda suggested, looking at Ruby.

Ruby bristled. 'Not that I mind having Arthur, but the poor little lad has his own grandmother,' she said, thinking of Vera. 'It's about time she stopped moaning about her daughter's romance with Lemuel.'

'But you know she's not going to accept him. And if we could get Sadie to join us then Lemuel would come along, and we'd have one of the men Bob insists we ought to bring with us,' Sarah said, in the wheedling voice she'd used since childhood to twist her nan around her little finger. 'Please, Nan,' she grinned, trying not to laugh.

Ruby sighed dramatically, and Sarah rushed to give her a hug. 'I'm happier knowing Lemuel will be with you. And speaking of the devil,' she said, turning to greet him as he entered through the back door.

Lemuel looked at the expectant faces smiling in his direction. 'I feel you are wanting me to do something?' he grinned. 'Your washing isn't dry yet, Mrs C. I checked on my way in from the shed. I have cleaned your gardening tools and hung them up,' he said, nodding in Bob's direction.

Bob and Ruby both protested. 'Lad, you don't have to do all these odd jobs for us,' Bob scolded.

Lemuel shook his head. 'My mother would not be happy

if she knew her son was not helping out. As a lad she would chase me around the house with her broom if I was cheeky, and if I hadn't completed my allotted chores. I live by what my mother taught me, and now I have another mother,' he grinned, putting his large arm round Ruby's shoulders. 'What a funny family we look, with me being twice the size of you and you having the wrong colour of skin,' he teased.

Ruby compared her pale white arm to that of Lemuel's deep brown one. 'I can't see what you're going on about, lad. We are both the same inside and out.'

Lemuel roared with laughter and hugged his landlady. 'My mother is so like you, Mrs C. Perhaps one day you will meet each other.'

'I'm not one for travelling. A trip to the coast is enough for me. You invite your family to visit us. They are more than welcome to stay here. In fact, next time you write I will give you a letter to put into the envelope, so your mother knows she is welcome.'

Lemuel reached into his pocket for a handkerchief and blew loudly into it. 'Everyone has been so kind to me. It has been a long time since I saw my family. My brother James and my sister Esther and her family are saving hard to come to England, but my mother . . . I too will save hard and send her the money. They will have a good life in this blessed country,' he said emotionally.

'And they will be welcome. Now, I do believe these girls have something to ask you.' Ruby nodded towards Sarah to speak.

Lemuel listened with interest as the three girls explained their trip to see the royal procession, and how they wanted

Sadie and Lemuel to join them. 'We will see the Royal Family?' he asked in wonderment.

'There's going to be many royal families from around the world,' Sarah said. 'This country may be hard up since the war, but we know how to celebrate a wedding.'

'Then I thank you – and I'll make sure all the ladies are looked after while I'm with them,' he assured Ruby and Bob. 'I will go and tell Sadie right now.'

'Tell her I'll have Arthur while she's in London,' Ruby called after him.

'Lemuel's a nice lad,' Bob smiled. 'We are all the better for knowing him. The things he's told me about his childhood in Trinidad – I've written some of it down to tell the kiddies when they are older.'

'Why, you talk as if Lemuel won't be here for long,' Ruby scolded him.

Sarah shivered and rubbed her arms. It felt as though someone, or something, had walked over her grave.

'It's good of you to come with us,' Freda said as she sat next to Anthony on a wooden bench at Erith train station.

'Did I have much choice?' He grinned. 'With Lemuel informing me none of you could go to London if you didn't have adequate protection, I couldn't really refuse.'

'Budge up, you two. A mother of five needs to sit down, as her varicose veins are playing up,' Maisie said as she squeezed in between them.

'Don't listen to her,' Freda scoffed. 'If she's got varicose veins in those legs I'm Charlie's aunt. She'd not be able to totter about in those shoes, either. How the heck do you intend to be on your feet all tonight and most of tomorrow in those?' she demanded.

Maisie reached for her cigarettes. 'I was born wearing high heels,' she grinned. 'So, what's the plan for tonight?'

'I'm not sure. Sarah's got the details. I'm just going to follow you all. You know what I'm like when we've been to London,' Freda said. 'Once I forgot to get off the underground train and had no idea where I was going. I had to get off at the next stop and wait for them to find me. I've never been so frightened in my life,' she said to Anthony, who roared with laughter.

'Perhaps we should tie a piece of string to your belt, and one of us always hang on to the other end,' he suggested.

'Nah, she needs a label tied to the lapel of her coat,' Maisie hooted with laughter. 'Mind you, we won't lose you with that hat stuck on your head, will we?'

Freda was indignant. 'I knitted this specially for the wedding,' she said, patting the top of the bright red beret. 'I have a white scarf and blue mittens. I thought it would be patriotic.'

'You look very smart,' Anthony said, giving her hand a squeeze. 'But if you do get lost, can you wave your beret up high?'

'Oh, you!' Freda gave his arm a playful punch. 'You're as bad as Maisie.'

'The train's coming,' Sarah called out, starting to herd the friends together. 'Don't forget your bags,' she added as she grabbed one of Maisie's. 'Whatever have you got in here? It weighs a ton.'

'Two bottles of gin, a fruit cake and a clean pair of

knickers,' she responded. 'We can't celebrate a wedding without all the essentials.'

'She is joking . . . isn't she?' Anthony asked, as he helped Freda into the carriage and put their bags on the overhead luggage rack.

'You never know with Maisie,' she replied.

As the train moved out of the station, Freda wiped the grimy window. The journey in the packed carriage reminded her of when she had first come to Erith, wondering what lay ahead. So much had happened to her in the nine years since she'd left Birmingham.

'A penny for them?'

'I beg your pardon?' Freda said, startled by Anthony speaking close to her ear.

'A penny for your thoughts. You were miles away.'

'Oh – I was just thinking how I travelled on this same train line nine years ago when I came to Erith. I had no idea what lay ahead, or even if I'd stay long.'

'And now you have a whole new life,' he said, watching her animated face as she spoke of the past.

'I do. I've been very lucky. Oh, look. Do you see that poster over there?' she asked as the train pulled into Belvedere, the first stop on the Charing Cross line. 'I saw a similar one on my journey in 1938, advertising the Kent coast. I'd never been to the seaside and I decided there and then that once I'd settled and found my brother – that was the reason I came to Erith – I would go to the seaside.'

Anthony watched as she explained about her brother, then excitedly told him of her first trip to the coast and how she'd travelled down the Thames on a paddle steamer called the *Kentish Queen*.

'What's up?' she asked as she stopped to draw breath and saw him smiling at her.

'Nothing,' he said. 'Nothing at all. I'd like to go on one of those trips.'

'Perhaps next year in the summer? It's lovely when you can stand on the deck and feel the breeze in your hair. It's so exciting!'

'I may be rather busy next summer.'

'Why? They're not sending you to another store, are they? It's only been a few months since you've started back to work,' she said, looking disappointed.

Anthony was touched by her alarm. 'I'll still be working at the Erith store and I'll still be lodging with you. That's if you don't mind a chap sleeping in your front room for so long.'

Freda chuckled. 'I've told you, the room is yours now and I'm calling it the downstairs bedroom. You pay rent, so none of your cheek or you'll get your marching orders.'

Anthony joined in with the laughter. 'The thing is, I'm going to be really busy. I had a chat with the selection committee, and they are still prepared to consider me as part of the team for the Olympics. It means doing well in a few of the trials and a hell of a lot of training, but I'd like to give it a shot. It's not every day the Olympics come to London. It's a chance in a lifetime for someone like me to do something worthwhile.'

Freda gave a whoop of delight. 'Did you hear that, you lot? Anthony's going to compete in the Olympics!'

'Man, that's good news,' Lemuel said as he leant over from his seat beside Sadie, pumped Anthony's hand up and down and slapped him on the back. 'To think we will know someone who might be in the Olympics.'

'What can we do ter help you?' Maisie asked. 'It must be expensive having ter have all the clobber to wear, as well as the right bikes and suchlike?'

'He has four bikes already,' Freda explained. 'They're in my back garden under a tarpaulin.'

Sarah looked thoughtful. 'I don't know much about this kind of thing, although my Alan used to follow the motorbike racing. The riders seemed to have a team of mechanics to support them. Is it the same for cyclists?'

Anthony looked at their faces, all eager and interested in his news. 'It helps to have supporters, and yes, my bikes will have to be fine-tuned to get the best out of them – but as for a team, I don't think so. I'm answerable to the officials, though.'

'We should do some fundraising to get you what you need ter win a gold medal,' Maisie said. 'I reckon the staff at Woolworths would be up to chipping in. That would be a good start.'

'I'll come out riding with you,' Freda offered. 'But I'm not sure I ride fast enough to race you.'

'The company would be good. I'll be out early in the morning before work and then again in the evening, come rain or sun.'

'Blimey, that'll ruin your love life,' Maisie chuckled.

Freda could have curled up and died. 'We're only friends, Maisie,' she sighed.

Maisie simply nodded and grinned. 'What else can we do ter help, Anthony?'

'You could stop calling me Anthony for a start. I much prefer Tony.'

'But you never said . . .' Freda faltered.

'We didn't exactly start off the best of friends, and by the time we were on speaking terms it seemed too trivial to mention.'

'You idiot,' Freda laughed.

Sarah was still looking serious. 'It's good to have fund-raising, but you need at least one mechanic who can keep the bikes in tip-top condition. I'll have a word with my husband, Alan, to see if he would help out.'

Freda froze at the mention of Alan's name. Although Sarah was now civil towards her and they'd shared a couple of outings to the cinema with friends, the two of them were still not as close as they had been. Alan's name was avoided at all costs. When Freda had visited Alan to find out if Frank Unthank had pestered him again for the money he still owed, she had made sure Sarah was not around. Alan still refused to tell his wife about his problems, and as far as Freda could tell the couple were still distant. Alan had mentioned that the insurance company was slowly investigating the incident before considering a payout, and George had told him it could still be a few months. However, he would be honour-bound to pay off Unthank who, once he knew of the new premises, was bound to come knocking. They'd both agreed it was only a matter of time, as Alan had received three letters from the man's office reminding him of his debt and telling him to expect a visit. Alan had burnt the letters before Sarah found them. Perhaps being interested in Anthony . . . Tony's . . . Olympic dream would be enough to bring them together? 'You know, it was Lemuel who worked on the bike I damaged when I ran into Tony. It was when he was helping Alan just before the fire,' she added, feeling as though she'd overstepped the mark by bringing back the memories of that awful night.

'I could help again, if Alan had space in his new yard?'

'We'd have to speak to him, but I do believe he'd be interested,' Sarah said with a gleam in her eye.

'We wouldn't expect him to pay for anything,' Freda added, hoping it would help.

'I wish I could help in some way,' Sadie said wistfully.

'But you can. You are such a wonderful cook, and Tony will need feeding up – and all the work around the house you do will help no end.'

Sadie brightened up. 'We are going to be a proper team, aren't we?' she grinned.

'Team Tony,' Maisie exclaimed.

'Team Tony!' they echoed in unison as the train came to a halt at Woolwich Dockyard. They all budged up close together as the workers piled onto the train.

'When do we get off?' Tony asked.

'The end of the line – Charing Cross. Then we head ter Lyons Corner House for some nosh, after which we find our way over ter Westminster Abbey ter stake our claim on the pavement, where we can watch all the nobs arriving for the wedding,' Maisie explained.

'That sounds fine with me, but what if we get split up? There will be so many people wanting to see the wedding,' Tony said.

Sadie giggled and pointed towards Lemuel. 'Just follow the tall man with the blue-and-white striped bobble hat.'

Lemuel grinned and pulled the hat down over his ears. 'I wondered why you knitted this for me.'

'Are you pleased to have everyone helping with your plans for the Olympics?' Freda asked Tony quietly as the excited chatter intensified around them. 'I don't want you to feel we are interfering.'

Tony draped his arm round her shoulders in a friendly manner, making more room for the woman on the other side, who was more than filling the seat. 'I can't believe so many people want to support me. I've never known this before. Usually it's been just me and my bike. Granted, I have friends who also cycle; but they have their own families to go home to.'

Freda gave him a friendly kiss on the cheek. 'Well. You have all of us now, so like it or lump it, you're stuck with us for the duration.'

'You make it sound like a war.'

'Think of it more as a battle. A battle to win a gold medal,' she smiled, before becoming aware of eyes on them; Sarah had stopped speaking, and was watching what would appear to be two lovers' having an intimate conversation, to anyone not listening to the couple. Freda could almost see her thinking that perhaps she'd been wrong in accusing Freda of carrying on with Alan. Time would tell, but Freda knew there and then that she would let Sarah believe she was in love with her lodger, even though, for now, they were just good friends.

'Blimey, it's bloody freezing,' Maisie said as she tightened her scarf around her head and pulled up the collar of her coat. 'Whose idea was it ter come and wave at the 'appy couple?'

'Yours,' Freda and Sarah answered in unison.

'Is she still moaning about the cold?' Sadie asked from just behind them, where she had snuggled up against Lemuel, who was now snoring gently. 'Did you know that more people die at this time of night than any other time?'

'You're a bundle of fun. Where'd you get that happy snippet from? Don't tell me. I suppose it was your nan?'

'I think it was,' Sadie giggled. 'God, I'm going to turn out just like her one day, if I keep saying things like that. It's been rather peaceful not having to put up with Nan's opinions.'

'Don't worry; we'll drown you in a bucket of water if that 'appens,' Maisie said. 'Does anyone 'ave any food left? It may just warm me up a bit,' she added as she tugged at the blanket the girls were sharing. 'Has this thing shrunk or are you hogging it all, Sarah? Me feet are bloody freezing.'

'Serves you right. You should have worn something more suitable,' Sarah huffed. She wasn't going to admit that even with a pair of Alan's woollen socks on underneath her boots, her toes had gone numb. She'd even worn a vest under her jumper and put on the spare cardigan from her shopping bag. 'Perhaps we should get up and move about a little?' she suggested.

'Or we could open the gin . . . ?' Maisie replied.

'Oh, Maisie,' Sarah gasped. 'Surely even you can't drink gin at four o'clock in the morning?'

'I'd vote for the gin,' Sadie piped up. 'I can't move to get up, as Lemuel is sleeping.'

'Trust a man ter be able to sleep on a pavement,' Maisie sniffed. 'By the way, where has Tony gone?'

'He went off to stretch his legs, and I wish I'd have gone with him. It's impossible to sleep with you lot moaning all the time. Why don't you try to get your head down for a couple more hours?'

'Nah, I'm wide awake now,' Maisie said, struggling to her feet and causing her friends to collapse around her like a row of dominoes.

'Watch it,' Freda grumbled. She too stood up, and brushed away a few dried leaves that had caught in her coat. 'I was comfortable until you started pushing and shoving.'

Sarah closed the umbrella she'd been using to shelter her head from the shuffling people behind them. 'I'm going for a walk to stretch my legs. Will you save my place, please?'

Maisie moved the blanket and her bag – and just in time, as a man made to take the place. 'Oi! I 'ope you'd jump in me grave just as quick,' she snarled, causing him to hop hastily out of the way. 'Stay 'ere fer a while, Sarah, until Tony gets back? And then I'll come with you. I could do wiv a wee.'

Freda was shocked by the way Maisie had spoken to the man. 'I don't think that was called for, do you?'

Maisie shrugged her shoulders and didn't seem bothered. 'We got here early and found a decent place to park ourselves. I'm not 'aving anyone pinch our spot just cos Sarah's moved. We will have ter fight tooth and nail to 'ang onto this place once the crowds get thicker. We've bagged one of the best views and will see all the toffs as they arrive at Westminster Abbey, and 'opefully the Royal Family as well as the bride and groom.'

'Surely there isn't room for any more people?' said Sarah, gazing along the length of the queue.

'You wait and see. Wiv us being so close to the Abbey, people will be fighting to get a good view. P'raps it's time we all stood up, or we're likely ter get trampled on. Give those two a shout,' she said, nodding to where Sadie was still cuddled up close to Lemuel.

Freda tapped Sadie's leg and called to them to get up. 'Tony will need to be able to see Lemuel in order to get back to us. I must say, it was a good idea to knit such a colourful hat. Perhaps we should all have had one,' she grinned, and was rewarded by Maisie giving her a glare.

'I'll stick to red lipstick if yer don't mind,' she said, reaching into her handbag for her powder compact. 'You could do with running a comb through yer hair. Now you've got a fella in tow, you need ter think of such things.'

It was Freda's turn to glare. 'He's not my fella, as you put it. Tony is my lodger and, I like to think, a friend as well.' All the same, she dug in her bag for a brush and then copied Maisie's lead by touching up her lips, although she turned her back so Maisie couldn't rib her any more than she had already. Thankfully Sarah hadn't heard the exchange, as she was watching a family squeeze through the crowd. Freda still wanted her friend to carry on thinking she was in love with Tony.

'Now that is a good idea,' Maisie laughed as a middle-aged woman planted a wooden stool close by and helped an older woman to sit down. 'I'll most likely kill someone for a seat by the end of the day,' she said to the older woman. 'P'raps I should trade a drop of gin fer a sit down,' she guffawed.

'She can't hear a word you're saying,' the younger woman replied. 'Deaf as a post, and her eyesight's none too good. I don't know why she wanted to come with me.'

'Oh, bless her, she didn't want to miss the wedding,' Sarah said. 'I wish my mum was here to see all the pageantry.'

'Me too; mine would have loved it,' Maisie said, the smile leaving her face at the memory of her mum.

'I'd like to have been here with my mum too,' Freda joined in, feeling suddenly tearful. 'We never did much together, but she'd have liked all this.'

'What – all three of you have lost your mums?' the woman said, looking aghast. 'Bloody Hitler. I still curse him every day, even though the war has been over and done with for a while. Was it enemy action?' she asked looking at the three girls.

Maisie and Sarah nodded, looking sad. Freda shook her head and said, 'No, mine was very ill. You should cherish your mum. You'll miss her when she's gone.'

'Can we open the gin now?' Maisie asked.

'Mind your backs, excuse me!' Tony called as he edged through the thickening crowd to where the friends stood. In each hand he held three mugs of steaming tea.

'How the heck did you manage that?' Freda asked as she helped distribute the drinks amongst the group of friends.

'I found a stand with a chap selling tea. I've paid a ten bob deposit on the mugs, so hang onto them.'

Freda looked to where the elderly woman was watching them.

'She may have bad eyesight, but she can smell tea a mile off,' the daughter laughed.

Freda didn't think twice as she passed her mug to the woman. 'Here – you two share this. I'll have a sip from his,' she said, smiling at Tony, aware that again Sarah was watching.

Tony slung his free arm round her shoulders and handed over the tea. 'You go first,' he said.

'They seem to be getting rather cosy,' Maisie whispered to Sarah. 'I like him, so let's 'ope things work out for her. Then you can stop your worrying.'

'I may have jumped the gun with my worries,' Sarah confessed. 'But even if Alan isn't carrying on with Freda, why is he acting the way he is? It's like being married to a stranger . . .'

'I didn't expect to 'ave ter do all this walking,' Maisie moaned as she stopped to kick off her shoes and pick them up.

'Stop your moaning. You want to see the bride and groom come out on the balcony and wave to the crowds, don't you?' Freda snapped. She too was so tired her bones ached, but she'd not miss a single part of this magical day. 'Here, give me your arm and let's join in with the singing,' she added as the girls linked arms and they joined in with 'Maybe It's Because I'm a Londoner'.

'Where are we going?' Lemuel asked as he walked behind the girls, still holding onto Sadie's hand. 'I thought the wedding was over?'

'We walk to Buckingham Palace and wait for the Royal

Family to come out onto the balcony,' Sadie explained. She'd noticed the way he'd watched royalty alight from limousines and carriages to go into Westminster Abbey, and listened intently as those around tried to identify the people.

'I never expected to see our King and Queen even once – and now we will see them a second time? My mother and sister will want to know all about this. I shall have to write a very long letter.'

'Why don't we cut out the pages from the newspapers and put them in the envelope? There will be loads of them on sale by tomorrow. I'll help you,' she said, and was rewarded with a squeeze from his large hand.

'You are a good woman, Sadie Munro. I hope you too will have a wonderful wedding one day.'

'Is that a proposal?' she said, smiling up at him.

A cloud passed over his face. 'Hurry, or we will lose the others,' he said.

Sadie started to hasten her pace in order to keep up with his longer strides. 'Please, I can't keep up with you,' she said, trying to catch his hand to slow him down. 'What have I done to upset you? Please, Lemuel – I'll get lost in the crowd . . .'

Lemuel slowed his pace, then stopped and turned to face Sadie as the crowd of well-wishers continued to hurry. 'You haven't upset me, Sadie. You could never do that.'

'Then what has happened for you to try and get away from me?' she gasped, still trying to catch her breath. 'I thought we were joking, and then . . .'

'Then I realized that we could never marry.'

'But why not? I thought you had feelings for me?'

'I do. But it wouldn't be fair to you to be married to someone like me,' he said, standing so close that she could feel his heart beating as she laid a hand on his chest.

'You mean someone who treats me like a lady, is kind and considerate and who makes me feel like the most cherished person in the whole wide world? Oh, Lem. I know you are thinking that we were born so many miles apart, and that people will look down on us for coming from different races; but I don't care about any of that. Our friends accept us as a couple, and Arthur adores you. I've made some bad choices in the past, but I know that being with you is the best thing that has ever happened to me. And I don't care about my Nan's attitude. She can go to hell for all I care. You and Arthur are my family, and I don't give a damn about anyone else.'

Lemuel shook his head. 'If that was the only problem, I'd say blow everyone else and be on my knee proposing to you in the proper manner.'

'Then what is it, Lem?' she asked. He put his hands on her shoulders to protect her as the jubilant crowds continued to jostle them. 'I'd rather know. I hate secrets. Even if what you have to say to me forces a wedge between us, I'd rather know. A relationship based on secrets is not a healthy one.'

'Go on, give her a kiss or I'll do it for you,' an elderly man said, slapping Lemuel on the back as he passed by.

Lemuel gave him a polite smile before leaning towards Sadie so she could hear him above the sound of a group of people singing 'The Lambeth Walk' as they danced around the couple. 'I have a wife and daughter back home.'

'What?' Sadie asked, not believing her ears. 'Did you say . . .'

'I said, I have a wife and daughter back home in Trinidad.'

Sadie couldn't believe her ears. This man who worked hard and strove for perfection in all he did. This man, who encouraged her to attend church on a Sunday. This man had a wife and child . . . ? Sadie pulled away from Lemuel and hurried into the crowd. She knew her friends were now far up ahead of her, and she had to find them. She didn't look back to see Lemuel, who was standing with stooped shoulders, watching her go.

'There you are,' Freda said as Sadie fell into step next to her. 'Where's Lemuel?'

'He's back there a way. I hurried to be with you all.'

Freda gave her a sideways look as they approached Buckingham Palace and pushed and shoved until they could see the front of the building. 'Are you all right? I know it's been a long day, but you look as white as a sheet. Are you feeling sick or dizzy?'

Sadie shook her head, 'No, I'll be fine. I probably need something to eat,' she said as she put her trembling hands to her face, thinking of what Lemuel had just told her. 'I'll be fine in a minute. I just . . .' Sadie slumped against Freda and slowly slid to the ground as darkness engulfed her.

'Get back, get back,' Maisie commanded as she took control of the situation. 'Get back and give her some air.'

Freda loosened the top button of Sadie's coat and fanned her face with a *My Weekly* magazine she had folded in her pocket. Sarah folded the blanket she'd slung over her shoulder into a pillow to tuck under the girl's head.

'Here, let me shove some of this under her nose,' Maisie instructed Freda as she pulled the top off a small bottle of smelling salts and waved it back and forth under the stricken girl's nose.

Sadie came round quickly, fighting hard to get away from the smell. 'Let me go, let me go,' she mumbled, waving her arms about.

'Sadie, Sadie – calm down. We are here with you,' Freda soothed her as she took the girl in her arms and rocked her slowly back and forth until she calmed down. 'That's better. Now, lie there for a little while until you are back with us properly.'

Maisie and Sarah bent down next to Sadie as she took deep gulps of air. The crowds parted around them, still streaming towards Buckingham Palace.

'I didn't know you carried a first aid kit,' Sarah said approvingly.

'I don't. I put the smelling salts in me bag in case you had a fit of crying. I know what you're like at weddings, and the way you've been recently, it made sense to be prepared.'

'Has it shown that much?' Sarah asked.

'It has,' Maisie replied. 'Now, how about you pass me my bag and we crack open a bottle of that gin? I reckon Sadie could do with a swig.'

'No!' Sadie said. 'I can't have any of that.'

'It's all right, yer nan's not here to judge you,' Maisie grinned, knowing how Vera Munro frowned on people who drank spirits, even if she was partial to a sherry or three herself. 'Come on, a drop of mother's ruin won't hurt you.'

'I think it will,' Sarah said, as she watched Sadie shy away from the bottle as if it would poison her. 'I have a feeling our Sadie is expecting . . .'

Sadie looked at the three faces staring down at her in shock, and began to cry. 'Please, you can't say anything to . . .' She looked to where Lemuel was bearing down on them, his face full of concern. 'Don't say anything . . . please. Not yet.'

'Someone had best say something soon, or everyone will guess what's going on,' Maisie said, shaking her head.

13

'I hope those girls are having a good time up in London,' Ruby said as she switched off the wireless. 'The news report was very interesting, but it's not the same as being there.'

'You should have gone up with the girls. They'd have looked after you.'

'What, and sleep on the pavement in November? No, the days of me travelling to London are well and truly over. I should coco! We had a good trip up there back when the old King died. Now, that was a solemn occasion. It took hours just to reach the building where he was resting. It was a beautiful coffin, and the candles at each corner were enormous. There'll not be another state funeral in our lifetime,' she said to herself as she reached for her knitting.

'You never know, there could be another one. If there is, I'll take you to London to pay your respects,' Bob said generously.

'It's very good of you, Bob, but the King's still young so it won't be in our lifetime, more's the pity. I do like a good funeral.'

'What time are we expecting them all back?' Bob asked, looking at the mahogany clock that ticked loudly on the mantelpiece.

'Our Sarah said they'll get back as soon as they've seen the bride and groom waving from the balcony of Buckingham Palace; but I would think all and sundry will be after catching a train home, so they may have to wait a while. And if they are late, it doesn't matter. The nippers are all right sleeping here like they did last night. I'll put them to bed at their usual time. Speaking of which, they are a bit too quiet in the front room.'

'I'll go and check up on them, love,' Bob said easing himself out of his armchair. 'Then I'm going to water the vegetables. I've been spoilt having Lemuel here doing it for me.'

'He's a nice lad,' Ruby said with a smile on her face. 'I'll miss him when he goes.'

Bob turned back at the door. 'He hasn't said he's moving away, has he? I've got used to having him around. I've learnt things about his home country that I never learnt when I was at school.'

'No, he's got no plans, but I get the impression he's soft on young Sadie and you never know, there might be wedding bells on the horizon.'

'Blimey – that'll upset Vera,' Bob grinned, before going off to see to the great-grandchildren.

'It certainly will,' Ruby said to herself as she counted the stitches on the needle before starting to knit another row. The silver lining to Vera's prejudice against Lemuel was that she never visited number thirteen these days; however, it meant she was liable to swoop at any time if she spotted Ruby going about her shopping in the town. 'The silly woman should come to her senses and accept the lad,' Ruby muttered angrily as she dropped a stitch.

'Ruby, I think you ought to come and have a look at Georgina. The poor cock's burning up.'

Ruby threw down her knitting and hurried into the front room, where Sarah and Alan's eldest child lay on the sofa. 'Nanna,' she said. 'I want my mummy.'

Ruby winced as she bent over the child and felt her forehead with the back of her hand. 'There, there, lovey. Grumps is going to get a drink of water for you while I find a blanket to tuck you up. Mummy won't be much longer. She went to London to see the Queen. Do you remember how we spoke about it earlier, and you drew a lovely picture?'

The child screwed up her eyes as she tried to think but then gave up. 'I want my mummy,' she said as she started to grizzle.

Ruby gave her a quick cuddle and hurried from the room to find Bob. 'I don't like the look of her at all. I think we should get the doctor. Can you use the telephone to speak to him while I sit with her?'

'But the telephone's in the same room – she may get upset if she hears me.'

'Then speak quietly,' Ruby hissed.

Ruby propped her great-granddaughter on her lap and rocked her gently while talking to Arthur and Buster, who had been playing on Ruby's best rag rug with a set of wooden building bricks Bob had made for when they came visiting. She could hear Bob repeating their address and then placing the black Bakelite receiver back down.

'He will be along shortly. I'll shut the dog out in the kitchen and put the front door on the latch in case we don't hear him,' he said, patting Ruby gently on the shoulder before leaving the room with a backward glance that showed how worried he was.

'A nice man is going to come and take a look at you,' Ruby explained as Georgina started to cry. 'He will make you feel better very soon. Do you remember Doctor Gregson, when he made Buster better after he fell over and hurt his arm? Well, he's going to make you better too,' she said as she watched her great-granddaughter's eyelids start to droop. 'That's it, love, you have a little snooze.' She pulled the blanket up around Georgina's shoulders and continued to rock her gently.

'Coo-ee, it's only me,' a familiar voice called out as the front door rattled and then closed. 'I thought I'd pop by, knowing your lodger's not at home,' Vera said as she poked her head round the door to the front room. 'Whatever's happening here?' she asked, seeing Ruby's expression. 'Is the girl ill?'

'Bob's just called the doctor,' Ruby said as Vera hurried over and felt Georgina's face.

'She's burning up. I'll get a damp flannel. We need to cool her down while we wait for the doctor. Did Bob tell him it's urgent? The poor little cock doesn't look too good at all. I'll get that flannel and have Bob ring the doctor back . . .'

'It came on so quickly . . .' was all Ruby could say as Vera flew into action. Whatever she'd said about Vera Munro in the past, she took it all back. Ruby had never been so pleased as she was right now to see her cantankerous neighbour.

She continued to soothe the child until Vera returned carrying an enamel pudding bowl and a clean flannel, followed by Bob, who went straight to the telephone and picked up the handpiece.

Wringing out the cloth, Vera bathed Georgina's face. 'Can you slip her out of her blouse and flannel petticoat? She will feel so much better if we cool her down.'

'You're a natural, Vera,' Ruby said as she unbuttoned the child's clothing.

'I did it for our Sadie when she was around this age,' her friend replied. 'I had no choice.'

'I don't remember much about Sadie when she was a kiddie. Was she still with her mum back then?'

Vera nodded as she held the wrung-out cloth against the back of the child's neck. 'There, there, you'll soon feel much better,' she said gently. 'It was before Sadie came to live with me and her mother sodded off for good. If I hadn't gone to see the child that day, chances are we'd have lost her. Her mother was drunk out of her mind and carrying on with some sailor.'

'I've never known you call her your daughter, Vera.'

'I stopped calling her that many years ago, and even though she met her maker years since on, I'll not mourn her. Sadie's my family, and young Arthur here,' she said, smiling at the young lad, who was still contentedly playing with his building bricks alongside Buster.

Ruby knew it wasn't the time or place to say anything, but she couldn't resist asking. 'Then why turn your back on your Sadie and Arthur just because of her friendship with Lemuel? I've got to know the man, and he's a true gentleman. I'd have him join my family at the drop of a hat,' she said, seeing a flash of anger cross Vera's face.

'After what Sadie's mother put us through, with her running after anything in trousers, I had to make a decision to bring my granddaughter up in a respectable household. She did well at school and had a good office job in London until her little problem with her boss, but we managed to remain respectable to the outside world. But her walking out with a darkie is too much even for me. No one would call me a fussy woman, but even I couldn't see a marriage with the likes of a man like that working out. People would point their fingers and talk about us behind our backs.'

'So instead you have turned your back on your granddaughter and her son? You'll miss out on seeing this charming little lad grow up, and you won't be there to be a great-grandmother to any other children that may come along.'

Vera shook her head until her hat almost fell off. 'No, it's not like that at all, Ruby. You shouldn't twist my words.'

'Well, think on, Vera, before it's too late and you end up a lonely old woman, rather than a proud grandmother of a woman with a loving and hard-working husband who would do anything for his wife . . .'

Vera sat fiddling with the flannel before dropping it into the bowl and getting to her feet. 'I'll just go and refresh this water,' she said, hurrying out of the room.

Bob turned from the telephone where he'd been speaking to the doctor's wife. 'He's on his way. He'd been having his tea, but his wife explained it was important so he's coming straight away.'

'Well, he'd best get his skates on as this poor kiddie needs to be in hospital,' Vera said as she returned, pushing past Bob. 'If I'm not mistaken, this is scarlet fever. I suggest you let the child's parents know as soon as possible. You never know how it might turn out.'

For once, Bob didn't pull a face at Ruby as he usually did when Vera started on with her scaremongering. This time, he looked at his wife with fear in his eyes.

'Gosh, what a wonderful day. I'm so glad we decided to make the journey. You don't see a Princess get married every day of the week,' Sarah said as the four girls walked with arms linked towards Charing Cross station. 'I'll remember today for the rest of my life,' she added with a yawn. 'Thank goodness my Georgina is staying with Nan – otherwise she'd have me up all night with her questions. She really wanted to come with us, but sleeping on the pavements isn't right for a seven-year-old.'

'She'd not have seen much standing in amongst the crowds. That's why I told Claudette and Bessie they should stay 'ome. My younger ones didn't really understand, which was handy,' Maisie said as she stopped to take her cigarettes from her bag. 'Oh, bugger. I 'aven't got any matches left, and I left me lighter at 'ome in case I lost it.'

'Hang on, I have some,' Freda said as she stopped to take her handbag from her shoulder. She opened it to delve inside. 'A Brown Owl is always prepared . . . Oh no!'

'Hey, you bugger, come back with that right now,' Maisie bellowed as a thin, weedy-looking man spotted an opportunity to grab Freda's handbag and took off, dodging in between the weary walkers. Maisie and Freda set off in hot pursuit, with Maisie yelling at the top of her voice for people to stop the chap while Sarah stayed with Sadie, who was still feeling weak.

'What's going on? Where are the others?' Tony asked as he caught up with Sarah.

She quickly explained and, without a second thought, he ran after them as fast as his bad leg allowed, pushing and shoving past protesting walkers. Her caught up with Maisie first, who was sitting on the kerb rubbing her ankle.

'I broke the heel on my shoe and twisted my ankle,' she said angrily. 'I 'ad the bloke by his collar when it 'appened. Don't worry about me. You go and help Freda in case he hurts her. He's a wily bugger. I did manage to get a punch in before I fell,' she grinned.

Tony only stopped for a moment. Lemuel, who had lingered earlier to take a look inside a bicycle shop, hadn't been far behind him – by now he would have caught up with Sarah and Sadie. In a matter of minutes they'd find Maisie and be able to help her.

Tony scanned the crowd ahead for Freda as he pushed and shoved his way through, shouting 'excuse me' and 'sorry' as he went. After no more than a hundred feet he pulled up suddenly as a crowd stood around what looked like a fight. Hearing Freda screaming like a banshee, he leant in to grab her arm. Just at that moment, a policeman did the same.

'Don't let him go,' she gasped out loud. 'That's the man who pinched my handbag.'

Tony let go of Freda and managed to grab hold of the man, who saw his chance to escape, still holding onto Freda's bag. 'Oh, no, you don't, mate,' he said, as the thief continued to wriggle until a bystander stepped in to help Tony. By now his leg ached like hell and he hoped it hadn't impeded his recovery too much, but then he immediately felt bad as Freda could have been hurt. Lemuel appeared by his side and quickly saw what was going on. He took hold of the thief so that Tony could concentrate on Freda.

'You look a right mess,' he said as he helped straighten her coat before handing her bag back to her. 'Why the hell did you chase after this fellow? He could have hurt you.'

Freda was still breathing heavily and trying to catch her breath. 'We caught him,' she grinned. 'Is Maisie all right?'

'Maisie will be fine once she stops mourning the damage to her shoes. You did tell her she should have worn something more sensible to go walking all over London. She learnt the hard way.'

Freda frowned. 'You seem angry with me. There's no need.'

'There's every need. That chap could have hurt you, and all because of a handbag. I didn't think you were one for possessions. I'll never forgive myself for not staying with you.'

Freda felt wounded that he thought her so superficial that she'd put her life in danger for chasing after someone who'd pinched her old bag. Taking her bag from his hand, she opened it and pulled out a tarnished powder compact. 'It doesn't look much, does it? But I'd go after anyone who tried to pinch it. This is all I have to remember my mum by, and it was all I could think about when that piece of scum took my bag. He was stealing a memory, and it made me angry. That's why I laid into him when I caught him up.'

Tony reached out and touched the side of her face. 'You're going to have a right old shiner there by tomorrow. It might be an idea to tell people you're taking up boxing . . . I can understand why you chased after him. The pull from lost loved ones must be strong. I can only imagine how that must feel. It's just that . . . It's just that the thought of something happening to you almost ripped my insides out. I thought I might lose you.'

Freda wasn't sure she had heard correctly. Was Tony saying he loved her? Granted they were friends, and she thought a lot of him, but they'd never even exchanged one kiss or spoken of their feelings. 'But, Tony . . .'

He pulled her into his arms and held her close while Freda stood still, looking over his shoulder to where she could see Sadie and Sarah hurrying towards them. The look on Sarah's face spoke volumes. Freda kissed Tony's cheek. 'Oh Tony,' she sighed, knowing that she wanted all the mess with Alan to be done and dusted before she started a romance. She knew she had strong feelings for him, but didn't want her growing love to be tainted with everything else that was happening. Going by the look on Sarah's face, it was clear that she thought there was more between Freda and Tony than there really was. At least Sarah's obsession about Freda being overly fond of Alan would stop, if Sarah thought there was something going on between her and Tony. Feeling like a fraud, she linked her arm through his. 'Let's see if the policeman needs my details, and then we can head for home.'

Maisie arrived, limping, but refusing to remove her one remaining shoe. 'Does anyone fancy hailing a taxi cab ter the station? I'm going ter find a telephone box and place a call through ter David to collect me at Erith. Anyone fancy joining me?'

The two men declined, leaving the four women to jump into the vehicle that pulled over once Maisie had placed two fingers between her lips and given a shrill whistle. 'See you both on the platform,' she called from the open window as they sped away, with the cab driver tooting his horn as he weaved between the happy crowds.

Maisie hurried frantically towards the platform, where her friends were meeting up for the homeward-bound train.

'Slow down, we've got ten minutes before the train's due out,' Sarah grinned. 'I dread to think what colour your feet are,' she added as she spotted that Maisie was running barefoot. The smile faded as she saw the look of panic on her friend's face. 'Whatever's wrong?'

Maisie stopped in front of her concerned friends and leant against Lemuel, gasping for air. 'Something's 'appened back 'ome. David told me as much as he could before my money ran out. Your dad will be at the station to pick you up, Sarah.'

'My dad? Why not Alan?' Sarah asked, trying to make sense of the little Maisie had said.

'He can't, as he's up the 'ospital.'

Sarah's face turned pale. 'What has happened? Has Alan hurt himself? My God. Please tell me what's happened,' she all but screamed as her voice was almost drowned out by the incoming steam train.

'Alan's fine. He's up there with Maureen and Ruby. It seems your Georgie took poorly.'

'Poorly? She was fine yesterday when we left,' Sarah said as Lemuel opened the train door, and Tony helped her up the steps and into a window seat. 'I have to be with her,' she continued frantically. 'She'll be scared on her own . . .'

Freda took her hand and patted it gently. 'Her daddy, her nanny, and her great-nanny are with her, and she will be in good hands,' she said, trying to calm Sarah. 'We will be pulling into Erith station in an hour.'

'An hour?' Sarah said, pulling away and burying her face in both hands.

'Fer heaven's sake, Sarah, don't you go getting all hysterical on us. All's being done what can be done, and if there are any developments, yer dad and David will be able ter tell us when we reach Erith. Bob and yer dad are at number thirteen in case there is a telephone call, and they will let David know. Bob and Vera are looking after the little ones so the men can run people about.'

'But petrol?' Sarah asked.

'My nan?' Sadie asked at the same time.

Maisie gave a snort of laughter as she delved into her bag, then thought better of it under the circumstances.

'Sorry . . . here, you finish off the gin. It'll make you feel better,' she said, passing over the bottle, which still held two inches of alcohol in the bottom.

'No thank you. I can't really go into the cottage hospital with the smell of gin on my breath, can I? But I appreciate the offer,' she said, seeing the glance Maisie gave Freda.

'The thing is, Sarah . . . she's not in the cottage hospital.'

'What do you mean, she's not in the cottage hospital? Where is she?' Sarah demanded.

'They've taken her to West Hill in Dartford.'

Sarah frowned. 'West Hill? Nan still calls that the workhouse, just like her mum used to. But why would our Georgina be there? How much will it cost? If we are unable to pay then Dad will sort it out,' she said before bursting into tears.

Maisie found herself trying not to laugh, but Sarah thinking the hospital was still a workhouse really did take the biscuit. She should try to remain serious, she thought as she took a deep breath, knowing that it was her nerves making her laugh. 'It's an isolation hospital. The doctor took one look at her and called the ambulance.'

'Isolation . . . ? I don't understand.'

'They think she may have scarlet fever.'

'That's contagious, and Arthur has spent the last two days at Ruby's house,' Sadie said, looking as distressed as Sarah.

'I think we should all calm down and wait until your dad tells us more,' Freda said, although she too felt panic rising in her stomach. She'd heard a fair amount about scarlet fever from customers at Woolworths, and she knew that not only could it spread like wildfire, but it could be a killer too. With the families being so close, Maisie's kiddies, as well as Mike and Gwyneth's daughter, Myfi, would often meet at number thirteen and play with Georgina and Buster. Whatever would they hear when they reached home? How were the other children?

'God, why won't this train go any faster?' Sarah asked as she checked her watch. 'I wish I'd had time to speak to my dad. Perhaps I should have done, and then we could have caught the next train.'

'Then you'd have been home even later – we all would,' Sadie said, thinking that she wanted nothing more than to be holding her son in her arms and thanking her nan for helping Ruby. It was time to start to build bridges, even if Vera would be shocked by what she told her. Sadie would be needing her family even more pretty soon.

'I'll never leave the children on their own again,' Sarah said as she fell into Alan's arms after running from her dad's car and into the hospital, demanding a nurse tell her where to find her daughter. She'd found Ruby, Maureen and Alan sitting quietly on a long, hard wooden bench. Empty teacups lay on a small table in front of them.

'Don't say that,' Maureen said. 'None of us know these things are going to happen.'

'Mum's right,' Alan said as he held her close. 'Why, I fell out of a tree right in front of Mum and Dad when I was a nipper. I'd have still fallen out of it if I'd been on my own.'

'Although you'd have probably climbed higher if you'd been alone,' Maureen said, trying to lighten the tense atmosphere.

Sarah nodded, and wiped her eyes with the handkerchief Ruby had passed to her. 'Tell me what happened – right from the beginning, and please don't leave anything out.'

They filled her in. 'So if it hadn't been for Vera hurrying up the doctor and nagging us all, we could have still been at home worrying over the poor child. I should have noticed something earlier – then she might not be so poorly now,' Ruby said, starting to look upset.

'Mum, it wasn't your fault. These things happen,' George said. 'Look, it could be a really long wait. Why don't I take you home to Bob? I can use the telephone in reception to ring you if there's any news. You look all in,' he said to Ruby. 'Me and Maureen will stay here as long as we are allowed.'

'You're right, and no doubt Bob will be fretting.' Ruby stood up, wincing as she always did these days. 'There's no need to look at me like that. I'm just a bit stiff,' she scolded George. 'Now, you two,' she added, giving Sarah and Alan both a kiss on the cheek. 'Be brave, and give my great-grandchild a big kiss from me when they let you go in to see her.'

'Thank you for all you've done, Nan. I wouldn't have known what to do if Georgie had been home with me. You and Vera and Bob, well, you've been marvellous,' Sarah said, putting on a brave smile. 'I'll see you later.'

'I'll walk out to the car to see them off,' Maureen said, knowing that Sarah and Alan would want to be alone to talk. She knew the pair were still under a lot of strain, and she feared the worst for their marriage. Perhaps if little Georgie pulled through, this would bring them together again – but more than anything else just now, Maureen feared for her granddaughter. She would walk to the chapel after she'd waved goodbye to George and Ruby, and say a little prayer.

'I'm pleased you're here,' Alan said as he reached for Sarah's hand and squeezed it tight. 'The family mean well, but I prefer it when it's just the two of us against the world.'

Sarah really wanted to ask him why, if that was case, he had shut her out all these months – and why he was so close to Freda. Instead she squeezed his hand back and replied, 'I prefer it when it's the two of us as well.'

She shivered as she sat waiting for what he would say next. The room was a pale green with dark, almost black painted woodwork. The worn, rubber floor covering was practical if dull. The only sound came from a tall, thin sash window, which rattled slightly in the wind that had not long started to blow.

'Cold?'

'A little.'

'Come closer and share my coat,' he said, holding open the front of his overcoat as she snuggled in.

'I can't recall the last time I did this,' she murmured as she breathed in his masculine odour along with a faint smell of the washing soap she used for their laundry.

'We should do it more often,' he murmured into her hair.

'I'd be fighting Buster off. You know how much he loves

his daddy,' she smiled up to him. 'Just like I do.' She waited for him to reply and declare his love, but he stayed silent. 'Alan, you are supposed to say you love me too,' she said as her throat tightened with emotion. She sat up, and pulled away.

Alan groaned and ran a hand through his hair. 'Everything is such a mess, Sarah. I don't feel worthy of your love right now.'

'But why? What has changed to make you feel like this? You need to talk to me, Alan, so that I can share your problems and we can work through them together. Does this have something to do with the workshop? You know that the insurance Dad took out will cover what the owner of the building needs for recompense – and with Douglas Billington offering you that shop and yard, it won't be long before you are up and running again.' She wanted to remind him again that there was always a job for him at Woolworths, but she didn't wish to enrage him.

'Let's not talk about it now, eh?' he sighed.

'But when can we talk about it? And exactly what is this "it" we aren't supposed to talk about? Freda seems to know, going by how close and secretive you two seem to have been. At least I know now that you aren't having an affair with her . . .'

'What are you talking about?' he sighed.

'Freda and Tony – Anthony – have become very close. I've noticed it during the time we've been in London.'

Alan simply shook his head and got up to leave, just as a doctor entered the waiting room followed by a worried-looking Maureen. 'Mr and Mrs Gilbert? I have news about Georgina.'

Sarah reached for Alan's hand, all thoughts of their earlier harsh words forgotten. 'Please – tell us how she is?'

'Our initial suspicions are unfounded, but she is still a very sick little girl.'

'What suspicions?' Maureen asked as she followed the doctor into the waiting room.

'The symptoms Georgina showed could be a number of things, but we have ruled out scarlet fever, which I believe was your worry,' he said, turning to Maureen.

'That was her great grandmother's thought, too,' Maureen explained, 'but does it matter what it is named? We just want her well again.'

Sarah could have kissed Maureen for getting straight to the point. 'Can I see her, please?' Sarah asked urgently.

'First a few questions, if you don't mind,' he said, sitting down opposite her and holding a pen to a clipboard. 'Can you tell me what she ate, and anything unusual she did, during the last twenty-four hours?'

'I was in London watching the royal wedding,' Sarah said, feeling as though she'd let her daughter down by being away. 'She slept at her great-grandmother's house last night. That was Mrs Jackson, who was with us until just now,' she added. If only her nan hadn't left – she could have answered some of the questions.

'I had the children this morning,' Maureen said, 'and I took them to work. I'm the cook at Erith Woolworths.'

'Then I collected them,' Alan said, 'and we went to my new business premises in Erith. They played while I took a few measurements. After that we went up to the allotment to help Sarah's, Mrs Gilbert's, grandfather dig over the ground and prepare it for the next season of vegetables.' He looked at Sarah, who smiled at him, glad that he had involved the children with his work. 'After that we went back to Mrs Jackson's house, where they had their tea and I went home as I had paperwork to finish.' He didn't add that he'd popped in to the Prince of Wales for a swift half, as it didn't sound like the actions of a responsible parent. 'It couldn't have been long after that when she was taken ill.'

'That's all very helpful. My immediate thoughts are that she came into contact with a substance that has caused a problem. However, there's also a chance she ate something that has disagreed with her, although her younger brother is perfectly fine. Now, if you'd like to follow me, you can have a quick visit. We have her in a separate building where we keep patients in isolation, as they may be contagious. I'm of the impression this isn't the case with Georgina but, as she is sleeping, perhaps you should just look into her room and then leave. She was given an emetic to clear her system, which has helped immeasurably. If you'll follow me . . .'

Alan took Sarah's hand, and they followed the doctor from the room. Maureen looked on, hoping against hope that the little girl they all loved so much would be all right – and that this scare would be a turning point for the couple. Only an idiot couldn't have noticed the cracks in their marriage, and she'd not stand by and see two of the people she loved most in the world suffer so much. She'd been silent so far. However, if this continued, she'd not keep quiet for much longer.

*

'Come in for some tea,' Freda said, as Lemuel turned to go across the road to number thirteen. 'It's a bit on the late side for a meal, but I think we could all do with something to eat. I did ask Effie if she could have something ready for us that could be kept warm in the oven.'

'If it's not too much trouble, I'd like that, thank you. I don't feel I should be under Ruby and Bob's feet while they are worried about the child,' Lemuel said. Freda, Tony and Sadie went into the house and he followed, avoiding eye contact with Sadie.

'Hello, you lot, did you have a good time? Let me pour you a cuppa, and then I want to hear all about the wedding,' Effie said excitedly. 'Mrs Billington had her husband put a wireless in the staff canteen, and some of us got to listen to the service. Oh, Princess Elizabeth sounded so nervous – and Prince Philip – did you know he's been made a prince? Well, he sounded so handsome . . .' She chattered on from the kitchen as the four friends took off their coats and made themselves comfortable around the table.

'How can someone sound handsome?' Tony chuckled.

'Don't be horrid,' Freda said as she threw her knitted mittens at him. 'I know exactly what Effie meant. He has a strong voice.'

'And he speaks so nicely . . .' Sadie chipped in, albeit rather sadly. 'I hope they have a long and happy life together.'

'We can all toast the happy couple,' Effie said as she passed round the tea. 'It's not champagne, but it's just as nice,' she added.

Tony got to his feet and in a very posh voice said, 'To the happy couple. May they live long and prosper.'

'The happy couple,' they all chanted.

'I didn't know you could speak as posh as that,' Freda said to Tony. 'Perhaps you should use that voice when you accept your gold medal at the Olympics.'

'The Olympics? Isn't that next year?' Effie asked as she carried a meat pie into the room and placed it in the middle of the table. 'It's more kidney and carrot that steak and kidney, but for all that it's tasty. I've got some mash to go with it,' she added, hurrying to the kitchen and coming back with a dish of potatoes. 'Now, what's all this about the Olympics? And did you know an ambulance went to your friend's house across the road this afternoon?'

Freda smiled to herself. Effie was such a joy to have in the house, and never stopped chatting. The one subject she never mentioned was her link to that house in Wheatley Terrace, which had weighed heavily on Freda's mind but now didn't seem so important . . . While the girl dished up the food, Freda told her about Georgina's illness; then Tony explained why they had mentioned the Olympics.

'So you've got a year to get fit and learn how to ride a bike faster than anyone else,' Effie said, making the task sound easy.

Tony laughed. 'Nine months, and before then I have to prove to the selectors that I'm worthy of a place in the team by doing well in a few cycling trials. So, once I've eaten this, I shall help with the washing up and then be off to my bed. I take it you still want to join me when I go out for my training rides?' he asked Freda.

'Certainly,' she said, forking potato into her mouth.

'Then be ready at half past five tomorrow morning, as that's when we start,' he replied before thumping Freda on the back as she started to choke after his words sunk home.

'At least you'll be fit, Freda,' Effie chuckled.

With their meal finished, Freda insisted that Lemuel and Sadie needn't help with the washing up, and left them alone in the dining room. As the others headed to the kitchen with the dirty plates, there was silence for a while as the couple struggled to think of where to begin.

It was Sadie who took the bull by the horns. 'It will be wonderful to see Tony compete in the Olympics. I recall Nan telling me about the earlier one when she was a small child.'

'I didn't know that there had been another in this country. Then it is surely a fine honour to be invited a second time,' Lemuel said politely.

'I suppose you'll miss the Olympics if Tony competes, as you will have gone home by then to be with your wife and child?' Sadie said, knowing that she had to ask the question. His answer was bound to break her heart, but she couldn't leave something like this left unsaid.

'Sadie, I . . .' Lemuel began, but seemed unable to continue.

'We need to talk about this, Lemuel. You see, I have a vested interest in your future – as does Arthur, who has come to love you. And also . . .'

Lemuel frowned. 'Also?'

'Also . . . our unborn child. It's early days, but I know the signs. My body is telling me that I'm to expect a happy event.'

Lemuel beamed and reached across the table to take her hand, but she quickly pulled it away.

'You have to be honest with me, Lemuel. I've never loved anyone the way I love you, and we both know that a future for us and any children we bring into the world will be hard. Many people will be harsher with their words than my nan.'

'I know. I have seen how people react to the colour of my skin without looking below the surface to know the man.'

Sadie looked serious as she listened to his reply. 'I would be prepared to live with that. However, what I can't do is live with you without a wedding ring on my finger, and knowing there is another woman and child back in your home country. You have to be honest with me right now. If you aren't, then I'll have no choice but to move back in with Nan and beg her forgiveness. I'll also have to stop this pregnancy, and that means making a visit to a woman round in Wheatley Terrace. It's an open secret she helps women out of sticky situations. It goes against everything I've ever believed in, but you'd leave me with no choice . . .'

So intent was she in making Lemuel understanding her feelings that Sadie didn't notice Effie and Freda coming into the room. She was startled by the younger woman's outburst.

'No! Give your baby away . . . leave it on the doorstep of the church . . . but please, don't go to that house.' Her voice broke and she slumped into one of the vacated seats at the table, with a concerned Freda fussing around her. Tony fetched a cup of water from the kitchen as Effie's sobs overwhelmed her.

'I'm sorry. I never meant to upset you – or anyone else, come to that,' Sadie said, glancing at Lemuel.

'You're not to blame for me getting so upset. Would you mind if I explained?' Effie said as she accepted a handkerchief from Freda and wiped her eyes.

'You don't have to if you don't want to,' Freda said, although she very much wanted to hear what Effie had to say.

'I'd like to tell you all, as it's played so heavily on my mind. Truly, I feel something should be done – but I have no idea where to turn.'

'I'll put the kettle on,' Tony said.

'Take your time,' Freda said gently to Effie as she sat beside her, ready to give her a hug if she broke down again.

'You did ask me why I couldn't live at my sister's place in Belvedere. It's because she has taken on our other sister's children. The landlord is none too happy with so many in the few rooms as it is, but with the four extra little ones . . .'

'What happened to your other sister?' Sadie asked, although she'd part guessed what would be said.

'Dora found herself in the family way again, and her husband told her to be rid of it. He didn't want a fifth child – even said it wasn't his. He told her where to go and gave her the money.'

Freda shuddered. It was a common problem. Even though there were places a woman could go for help, some women still used the back-street abortionists through ignorance and not wishing to ask for help from charities. 'I take it the . . . the procedure didn't go well?'

'The first I knew was when I visited and found her in pain. There was blood everywhere. I called for an ambulance, but she died the next day. Her husband scarpered after telling me to hand the four boys over to Barnardo's – I refused. A week later, we heard he'd died in a fight down by the docks. Good riddance to him,' she spat out.

'So why were you in Wheatley Terrace? I spotted you leaving the house,' Freda explained.

'I saw you there too, but it must have been another day – I was in hospital when Freda was there,' Tony said from the kitchen.

Effie nodded. 'I was so angry, I went to the house a few times, trying to speak to the woman who'd butchered my sister. The last time I was there I managed to get in when someone left the building. I gave her what for – and she laughed at me. She told me she was offering a service, and my sister had been unlucky. I'm afraid I acted in quite an unladylike way; I clobbered her one, right on the nose. Then I legged it in case someone came to her defence. I was petrified after that, in case she sent someone after me. Fortunately, she hasn't, but I'd still like to see her serve time for what she did to our Dora.'

Freda was thoughtful as Tony carried in the tea tray, and they helped themselves to a cuppa. 'How would you feel about speaking to a policeman?'

'I'm not so sure about that. My family aren't ones for talking to coppers. Do you think it would help?'

'It could help others not make the same mistake,' Freda said, looking towards Sadie, who kept her head down as she stirred her tea. 'If it helps, you could talk to our friend Mike Jackson – he's Bob's son, from over the road. Mike could advise you. I suggest you don't mention you thumped her one, though,' she added with a small smile.

'All right, I'll speak to him. But I'm not going down the cop shop.'

'I'll have Mike pop in here for an informal chat. Has your other sister looked into finding somewhere else to live so she has room for all the kiddies?'

'I don't think so . . .' Effie said.

'You know Sarah's dad is a local councillor? Belvedere may be a bit out of his area, but he'll know how things work. Let me have a word with him.'

'Blimey, I did all right moving in here,' Effie joked before looking serious. 'Thank you; I'm really grateful,' she said, and looked at Sadie. 'Perhaps you ought to ask Freda for some advice?'

'I'm going to give it to the pair of them once we have some time to ourselves. Perhaps you two would like to take your tea to your bedrooms?' Freda said, looking at Effie and Tony.

'I'm ready for bed, so that's a good idea,' Tony said, wishing them all goodnight and heading to the front room. Effie did likewise, and went upstairs.

Freda topped up Sadie and Lemuel's cups, and gave them both a smile. 'You can tell me to mind my own business, but I'll not stand by and see the pair of you mess up your lives. It's patently obvious you were made for each other – and yet there are barriers forming between you.'

Lemuel took Sadie's hand. 'I don't want to lose you, Sadie.'

'But you said you have a wife and child back in Trinidad . . .'

Freda was horrified. 'This is news! You've not mentioned that before, Lem. Why not tell us about your wife?'

'My wife left me some years ago, and took our child with her to live with another man. It was before I came to England. I am ashamed that she would do such a thing, so I do not talk of it. My sister, Esther, has seen my daughter, and she passes my letters to her.' He reached into his jacket for his wallet and pulled out a small photograph. 'This is my girl. Her name is Elizabeth, after the royal Princess. She is fourteen and a young woman now.'

'She is beautiful,' Sadie said softly, gazing at the image. 'But . . . your wife?'

'My sister says she has married again.'

'Well, then you must be divorced, and are free to marry,' Freda said with a big sigh of relief. 'Haven't you ever checked with anyone?'

Lemuel gave them both a blank look. 'I've never had a reason to check before.'

The two women burst out laughing.

Freda picked up her cup of tea. 'Now we've got that out of the way, I'm going to leave you to sort out the rest for yourself.'

Lemuel again looked confused. 'The rest?'

'Do you not wish to make an honest woman of Sadie?'

'I thought she knew that I want that very much.' Lemuel smiled.

'Oh, for heaven's sake, Lemuel! You have to show her, and make some plans. Just remember, I'd like an invitation to the wedding,' Freda said, as she left the happy couple to themselves. She'd not climbed more than a few steps upstairs when there was a knock at the door. In all that had happened at home, she'd forgotten about young Georgina. She just hoped whoever was knocking wasn't bring bad news.

'Thank goodness you're still up,' Bob said, slightly out of breath.

'Come in, Bob. Do you have news?'

'I won't, if you don't mind. Ruby's got a brew on the go and I want to get back. She's still a bit weepy after what happened. I just wanted to let you know. I'll pop up to Maisie's and let her know as well.'

'Let us know what?' Freda said, more than a little impatiently.

'She's going to be all right,' he said, reaching into his pocket for his handkerchief and blowing his nose loudly.

'Thank goodness,' Freda said, grinning from ear to ear. 'That's the best news ever.'

14

December 24th, 1947

'What a miserable day for a wedding,' Betty said as she gazed from the window of her first-floor office over Pier Road to the bustling crowds below. 'At least it's not as bad as last winter's snow.'

Sarah shivered. 'I'd not want that weather back in a million years. I suppose it is romantic to have a Christmas Eve wedding, but I'd not say it's my favourite time of the year to get married.'

Betty coughed politely and tried not to laugh as she held out her left hand to show Sarah a glittering eternity ring that sat neatly above her wedding band and engagement ring.

'Oh, my goodness – what a beauty,' Sarah said, before colouring up as she realized what she had just said. 'What I mean is, you chose your wedding day, whereas Sadie and Lemuel had no choice what with her . . .'

'Expecting a happy event?' Betty suggested as she watched Sarah gaze with longing at the ring. 'Douglas surprised me with this last night. He had seen me admiring it when we went to Gamage's to buy presents for the children for Christmas. The dear man must have gone back and purchased it while I was choosing new underwear for the girls.'

'You're a lucky woman,' Sarah sighed wistfully.

'I am,' Betty said, aware that the Gilberts were still struggling, even though Alan was now working from the shop close to Billington and Carlisle's. 'Now, let me get my handbag and we can slip off and have a quick glass of sherry to celebrate Alan's new business finally opening.'

'And I feel Christmas Eve is a strange day to celebrate opening a business as well, especially with Lemuel working for him. The poor man had to go in and help this morning even though he's getting married this afternoon,' Sarah said, shrugging her shoulders. 'But I dare not question Alan's judgement, as he can still be a little snappy with me.'

'Best not to. This shop could be the making of him, and if it gives work to Lemuel, then all the better. I do like the man, and he will make Sadie very happy.'

Sarah followed Betty as they left her office and headed to the entrance of the Woolworths store. 'How do you feel about him being a coloured man, and Sadie being white?'

'Lemuel is a good man, and people will see that. I don't expect there to be a problem. Why, look how he has been accepted into our circle of friends, and we are no different to others in this town.'

Sarah shook her head at Betty's innocence on this topic. Sadie had told her of the taunts thrown at her when walking out on Lemuel's arm, and Sarah had seen for herself the signs in the windows of lodging houses declaring 'no blacks'. Fortunately, Sadie's love for this kind, gentle man outweighed any negativity.

Betty waved to one of the supervisors to indicate she was leaving the store before catching Sarah at the front door. The two women stopped to look at the Christmas display in the main window. Betty sighed. 'I thought by now we'd be in a position to have vibrant displays that enticed shoppers to come in and buy our products. This damnable austerity wasn't expected, and is becoming a bind. It makes one wonder who should be running our country.'

Sarah raised her eyebrows before chuckling. 'Crikey, Betty, the way you speak you'll be humming "The Red Flag" next. I do agree we should think more about brightening our window display. For some reason, I imagined having a window dresser would mean more attractive displays. Shall we have a word with her, do you think?'

'Yes, we should. I've been a little remiss in leaving the woman to get on with things. Life seems so busy right now, and I never seem to be able to shake off this tiredness. I'm fine – it's nothing to worry about,' she said quickly, noticing Sarah's concerned look. 'We should think about an Easter display and discuss it with the window dresser. I do know we did better when left to our own devices. Why, Freda and her Brownies did a really impressive display during the war, coming up with their knitted chickens and papier-mâché eggs for Easter,' she said as they crossed Pier Road and headed towards the High Street. This was where Alan Gilbert's new shop premises were to be found, alongside Billington and Carlisle and Maisie's Modes.

'If you're sure you're all right?' Sarah said, ignoring Betty's bright reply about the Easter window display.

Betty quickly changed the subject. 'It is satisfying to know our husbands will be working side by side in the High Street.' She smiled. She didn't add that her husband and David had begged Alan to take on the empty shop and yard for a peppercorn rent, in order for it not to run into disrepair. Alan had fallen hook, line and sinker for his friends' words and had set to with a vigour that they'd not seen in him for many months, painting the shop and clearing weeds from the yard behind the property.

Sarah nodded her head in agreement. Deep down, she felt there was still something keeping Alan from her. They had little to say to one another at home. It felt as though he was in another world, far away from her, when he sat staring into space. He ignored the children too, and refused to join in with family pursuits. Perhaps the resurrection of his workshop would be the new start they needed, both in business and their life together.

'This is very jolly,' Ruby said, as she accepted another glass of sherry from George. 'I must make this my last or I'll be falling flat on my face in church, and that wouldn't do.'

George tried not to smile, knowing his mother was on her third sweet sherry and, already slightly unsteady on her feet, she had taken the only seat available in Alan's shop front. 'Well, if you can't enjoy yourself celebrating a wedding as well as a new family business, when can you? Bob can hold you upright if you feel out of sorts in the church. Here comes Sarah, so I'll leave you in her capable hands. I need to see Alan about something out in the yard,' he said, kissing Betty's cheek before crushing his daughter in a bear hug.

'Dad,' she squealed. 'I'm not a child any more.'

'You'll always be my little girl,' he told her, giving Betty a wink, which embarrassed Sarah even more.

'I'm sorry that Maureen had to work,' Betty said to George. 'If you like, I will slip back and relieve her in the staff kitchen for a little while so she can come and look around.'

'I'll go,' Sarah said, knowing that it wouldn't be seemly for the store manager to be seen in the canteen serving her staff.

'No,' Freda exclaimed as she walked into the shop from the workshop area behind the counter and overheard Betty's words. 'I feel bad enough having the day off on one of our busiest times of the year. I don't have to leave for the church with Sadie for another couple for hours.'

'You can all stay where you are,' Gwyneth Jackson announced loudly from where she stood by her husband's side. 'I've wished everyone good luck with the business move and, not being one for drinking sherry, I could kill a cup of tea.'

'Do you think you ought to?' Sergeant Mike fussed.

'I'll be fine, dear,' she said, giving him a smile that spoke volumes.

Ruby, who had been watching the conversation with

interest, slapped her leg with glee. 'So, the holiday to Ramsgate worked?' she asked with a broad smile. 'A bit of sea air and not having to think about work must have hit the spot. I knew it would.'

'Nan!' Sarah exclaimed, feeling her face turn red. 'I think we should be a little more circumspect, don't you?' she hissed, seeing a few strangers turn to stare as they looked around the shop. 'Now's not the time or the place for such things.'

'It's always the time and the place for news of new life,' Ruby answered back. 'I'm right pleased for the pair of you,' she added, leaving her seat to hug Gwyneth first and then her stepson, Mike.

'We were going to announce it to you all on Christmas Day,' Mike explained. 'Myfi is so excited – it's been hard to keep the secret.'

'You look very happy as well,' Betty said as she shook his hand. 'Oh dear, I'll be losing one of my valued staff members; but on this occasion, I can forgive you,' she said as she kissed Gwyneth's cheek. 'Now, are you sure you don't mind relieving Maureen for a short while? I do have something to show her, and it would be nice to do it in front of her family and friends. Although that will mean you'll miss my news . . .' she said, putting a hand to her mouth in consternation.

'Let me go. I know where everything is, as I helped out when Maureen's leg was bad,' Sadie said, reaching for her coat. 'You've all been so good to me, it's the least I can do.'

'But your wedding dress,' Sarah faltered. She knew the girl's frock had seen better days, but it wasn't right that she should be serving tea in her wedding attire.

Sadie burst out laughing. 'This isn't my wedding dress. I wasn't going to come here and risk getting grease on it. Freda and I have our dresses ready to get into when we leave here. Besides, I didn't want Lemuel to see me in my finery until I walked down the aisle.'

'He shouldn't even see you before the wedding,' a voice said from the doorway. 'But then, with the stable door being locked after the horse has bolted, it doesn't really matter, does it?'

'I thought you'd appear before too long, Vera Munro,' Ruby said. 'Let's face it, you'd turn up at the opening of a jar of jam.'

'I am the girl's grandmother,' Vera sniffed. 'I'd decided to go to her wedding and went looking for her. It's a fine thing when I'm not invited to my own flesh and blood's nuptials.'

'Oh, Nan, you were invited! I saw you open the envelope and put it on the mantelpiece,' Sadie said, glancing to Ruby for support as Lemuel reached out and took her hand.

'You are very welcome to be a special guest at our wedding, Mrs Munro,' he said politely, giving her one of his sincere smiles.

'Vera Munro, I saw that invitation on your mantelpiece too,' Ruby huffed. She had no patience when the woman started to play her silly games.

'Oh, I thought it was a Christmas card,' Vera replied, noticing a spark of anger in Ruby's eyes. 'What do you mean by special guest?' she asked, looking up at Lemuel, who stood a good foot taller than she did.

Sadie answered for him. 'As Arthur is too young to give

me away, I wanted you to walk me down the aisle. I know you don't approve of my circumstances, but I love Lemuel, and he loves me and little Arthur. I just want to be part of a happy family – and that includes you, Nan,' she added, looking beseechingly at the old woman. 'I want my happy ever after, just like the fairy stories you read to me when I was a little one.'

Sarah held her breath, along with others in the room. Was Sadie's wish about to come true? She too had hoped for a happy ever after, but with Alan blowing hot and cold, she had no idea how her future would pan out. Looking at the young woman holding hands with her intended, she felt quite tearful. She wished Alan was by her side, lovingly holding her hand. She jumped as a hand was placed on her shoulder. Thinking it was her dad, she turned and smiled. It was Alan. Perhaps the moment had melted the ice around his heart, and he was showing some affection towards her.

'Can I squeeze by?' he asked. 'I need to open another bottle of sherry. You'd like a tipple, wouldn't you?' he asked Vera, who was still summoning up a response to her granddaughter's request.

'Too true,' Vera said, her usually stern face breaking into a grin. 'It's not every day I get to walk my granddaughter down the aisle.'

An audible sigh rippled through the room as the guests started to chat amongst themselves, once more confident that Vera Munro would not be causing a problem.

'Mind you . . .'

Heads turned, and waited.

Vera smiled, knowing she had an audience. 'Mind you,

it is not right that my granddaughter starts her married life in one room, however nice it is,' she added, seeing Freda frown in her direction. 'You can have the top floor in my house. It will need a lick of paint, so you may as well do the whole house,' she added, as Lemuel shook her hand and gave her a kiss on the cheek. 'Let no one say that Vera Munro is afraid to have a darkie living under her roof.'

Sadie glanced at Lemuel, who simply grinned. In his book it was a step in the right direction. He secretly liked his grandmother-in-law's forthright nature.

'She's a rum one and no mistake,' George said, tapping his pipe out on a wall in the yard behind Alan's shop.

Douglas Billington nodded. 'One never knows what will come out of that woman's mouth.'

'Let me guess . . . you must be talking about our Vera,' Alan laughed as he joined them, carrying a tray full of pints of best bitter. 'I thought these would go down better than sherry.'

'You can say that again,' George said as he sat down on a bench that had been set up against the back wall of the shop. 'At least we can enjoy this away from the womenfolk without the snow we had this time last year. Why, every time I cleared our path the damn stuff came down again.'

'Is that brother of mine still moaning about last year's snow?' Mike Jackson grinned as he joined them, already holding a glass of beer.

'I'd not thought of you and George being related now that Ruby and Bob are married,' Douglas said as he thought of the family connections. 'I suppose that makes

Mike your uncle,' he said to Alan, who was looking confused.

'Don't muddle me any more than I am already.' Alan ran a hand through his hair. 'What with George here marrying my mother, it means he is my stepfather as well as my father-in-law. I'm fast losing track of this family. Whatever you do, Douglas, don't have any of your daughters marrying into our family when they are old enough, or confusion will reign forever.'

George joined in with the laughter, all the time watching Alan closely. He knew his wife, Maureen, was worried about the lad, and he in turn was worried about the state his daughter, Sarah, was getting herself into over any small thing. The pair had never said anything, but he'd gathered their marriage was having problems. In turn young Freda seemed to be on edge around Sarah, and that just didn't seem right. No, it wasn't right at all. He'd promised Maureen he'd have a word with Alan before Christmas, and with it now being Christmas Eve, his wife was nagging him every chance she had. She wanted the air cleared before they all sat down at Ruby and Bob's dinner table come Christmas Day.

'What relation will Mike and Gwyneth's baby be to us all when it comes along?' George said, faking a worried look.

Mike roared with laughter. 'Let's not think about it. However, I'd like to say thank you for recommending we take a trip to the Sea View guesthouse in Ramsgate. That weekend and the sea air worked wonders, if you know what I mean,' he said, giving them all a wink.

'I thought I'd find you all out here.' Freda grinned as

she poked her head out of the back door. 'Maureen's arrived, and Betty wants to say something to you all.'

'Alan was showing us where the workshop shed will be situated,' George said by way of an excuse, as the men started to follow Freda back inside. 'Alan, would you give me a minute?' he asked, putting a hand on his son-in-law's shoulder.

Alan looked back to where everyone else had disappeared. 'We'd better not be long . . .'

'We won't,' George assured him as he put his glass of beer down and reached for his pipe. He fiddled with it as he considered what to say first. 'Your mum and I have been discussing your situation,' he started, noticing the flash of concern cross Alan's face. 'We know things haven't been going well. Is there anything we can do to help?'

Alan wasn't sure what George was getting at. Had George heard about the run-in with Frank Unthank? Perhaps Freda had let something slip. It had been a while since the fire, and so far the Unthank gang had left them alone. There again, perhaps it was his mum who'd seen that there was a frosty air between him and Sarah these days. Women noticed these things, and he'd found it hard to act the good husband, knowing he'd kept his money problems to himself. He was beginning to regret doing that. But then again, Sarah had not made things easy, always going on about plans for the future and suggesting he return to working at Woolworths. Then of course there was their darling daughter, who was fighting fit after scaring them all half to death. Who'd have thought eating those berries up the allotment could cause her to be so ill?

'Alan?'

'Sorry, George, I was miles away. I've a million and one things on my mind right now. As for whether you and Mum can help out, why, you've been more than generous with this business already. I'm that relieved the insurance company paid out, even if it did all go on paying off the landlord of the workshop. I'd have hated for you to be out of pocket. And as for this place, if you'd not turned up with Mike and Lemuel to help paint the shop and build the counter, we'd not have opened on time. Then to stand guarantor so we could have an account at the warehouse – well, you went above and beyond. I'll never be able to stop saying thank you.'

George felt a lump form in his throat. This wasn't what he'd expected to hear. Alan was, he felt, still hiding something, but if he didn't want to say anything, he couldn't help the lad. 'You're family. We both want to see you and Sarah and the kiddies happy. It goes without saying we'll do all we can. The fire wasn't your fault and the burglar will hopefully serve time for what he did when it goes to court. Now is the time to look to the future.'

The mention of the fire made Alan shudder. 'We'll do our best to make you proud,' was all he could add. Word on the street was that Unthank had bigger fish to fry these days, but Alan knew that he'd soon be around to collect his dues. At least George hadn't asked anything that would mean he knew about his money problems.

'There's something else,' George said, as Alan turned to go inside. 'Maureen wanted me to mention about Freda.'

'What about Freda?' Alan asked sharply.

'Your mum says it's unfair to have her turning up to

help you out all the time, now she's helping Tony with his training. She's out morning and night either timing his rides or joining him on your old bike. It's important he does well in the time trials and hopefully the Olympics. Well, we just thought with her not being able to be in two places at once as well as hold her job down in Woolworths, you should think about not accepting her help so much. We thought . . . well, we thought perhaps you could take on Lemuel full time, and we'd contribute towards his wages until such time that the business could swim on its own.'

Alan was lost for words. He still owed Freda money, and she loved her time helping out. How could he tell her she was no longer needed? That said, he would love Lemuel to be full time, as he was a boon to the business. The idea they would repair bicycles and sell accessories, as well as continuing with the motorbike repairs, was all down to him. 'I know you are right, George, and Lemuel could well do with a proper job now he's to be a family man, but it doesn't seem fair what with Mum still working at Woolworths. If you can afford to be generous, why not have Mum give up her job instead?'

George roared with laughter and relief. He'd done his wife's bidding and made the offer. 'You mum will never stop working for Woolworths. She likes that job far too much. Why, she is the queen of that staff canteen,' he chuckled. 'I will tell her, though. Now, let's get inside and see what all the fuss is about. I know it's a mild day, but I'm feeling a bit on the chilly side.'

'I'll pay you back as soon as I can, sir,' Alan said, following him inside. Knowing George had again put his hand in his pocket to help get the shop ready for opening, he felt as though his debts were rising rather than disappearing.

'Ladies and gentlemen,' Betty said, using her authoritative voice to make herself heard. 'I know we have already toasted Alan on his new business venture but there is other family news, and may I add there are more congratulations in order. Some of you are aware of the Woolworths monthly staff magazine. A favourite feature in the magazine is the wedding announcements, and this month we have two friends in the *New Bond*: first, Maureen and George Caselton . . .' She held up the open magazine for all to see. As the applause and cheers died down, Betty again opened her mouth to speak as she laughed at the happy comments coming from her friends. 'There is one more surprise, and this time it is for Freda.'

'Me?' Freda said, looking puzzled.

'You've not sneaked off and married Tony, have you?' Maureen joked.

Freda felt herself start to blush. Tony, standing by her side, looked just as embarrassed. 'I'm sorry. My friends do like to joke,' she said quietly, so only he could hear. Tony's response was to give her a quick hug followed by a wink, which caused more merriment amongst those present.

'Please, a little hush,' Betty called out. 'I'd like to introduce the cover girl for this issue, Miss Freda Smith,' she said, waving the magazine in the air and showing the photo of Freda that Tony had taken some time before.

'I knew you'd never hand it in to Mrs Billington, so I did it for you,' he whispered as she put her hand to her mouth in shock before grinning.

'Well, well, well,' Maureen said as she took a copy of the magazine from Betty to look more closely at the weddings page. 'Who'd have thought two Erith Woolies women would get into the same issue, when we hardly ever have one staff member get a mention?'

'But, like buses, they come along in threes,' Sarah called out, before whipping the magazine from her mother-in-law's hand. 'Usually Woolworths award staff members who have served the company for twenty-one years. But with the war, and her being such a shy, unassuming person, our Betty here slipped the net,' she smiled as she flicked through the pages. Eventually she came to a full-page photograph of Betty Billington. 'Betty started working for F. W. Woolworths when she was a mere slip of a girl, only a few years after the first war. Twenty-five years later, she is still with us, and very pleased we are too. I know that head office is planning something special for our Betty, but for now, here she is – in the same magazine as Maureen and Freda.'

'Oh my,' Betty said, as she reached for her husband's hand. 'We were going to make our own special announcement tomorrow evening at Maureen and George's Christmas tea party, but it seems as though we should be saying something now.' She looked up at Douglas, who stood proudly by her side. 'There will be another little Billington joining our family next year.'

'What – not another late baby! Who'd have thought it?' Vera said out loud, causing more mirth while she looked on disapprovingly.

'Just like buses coming along in threes, it seems we three friends also produce babies in threes,' Gwyneth said as she kissed Betty and Sadie. 'What a wonderful day, and we still have a wedding to celebrate. Life is certainly good.'

Sarah found herself alongside her husband and Maisie as she gave her best wishes to Betty and Douglas. 'So, your expanding waistline was not down to Maureen's baking?' she grinned.

'To begin with, it was – but then Douglas and I decided that if another little one was to join us it wouldn't be a bad thing after all, and we let Nature take its course. This time, however, I'm prepared to take time away from Woolworths and see if I'm ready to return after the baby has been born. Head office have been marvellous, and assured me they can't do without me,' she chuckled.

'I'd best start making maternity wear,' Maisie joked. 'There's a limit ter how much we can make do and mend with our old clothes. Yer never know, our Sarah here could be next – what do you think, Alan?'

'About what?' Alan asked, as he'd been congratulating Douglas. 'If you mean another baby for us, I don't think now is the time,' he said, doing his utmost not to meet Sarah's gaze.

'Nah, I meant going back to Woolworths and taking over from Betty,' Maisie grinned, completely forgetting the friction between husband and wife in the excitement of the moment.

Betty, knowing of Sarah's despair, tried to make light of the conversation. 'I have a very short shortlist of likely candidates to cover for me while I'm off. Tony will be one, but let us keep it between ourselves for the moment. The lad has enough on his plate working towards the

Olympics. There's time enough to decide. However, it would be nice to keep it in the family, so to speak.' She sighed, looking to where Freda and Tony had their heads together looking at the *New Bond*. 'I have high hopes there . . .'

Sarah couldn't believe her ears. Yet again, Freda seemed to be the one getting what should have been her, Sarah Gilbert's, dream – a loving relationship. If only Alan had taken the manager's job at Woolworths, and then there might have been a chance of more children. Instead her husband acted like a stranger to her, closer to Freda than to his own wife, and three of her friends were expecting babies instead of her. Life just wasn't fair, she thought to herself as unshed tears began to gather. It was time to leave.

'Excuse me, I need some air,' she said, pushing through the many people she knew so well as she headed towards the front door of the shop. Behind her she could hear Alan call after her as he followed. Exiting the building in a hurry, she became aware of a short, stocky man with dark hair, wearing a long black coat. He was followed by two men she could only describe as looking like thugs. What were they doing here?

'I'm sorry, the business is closed today. This is a private celebration,' she tried to explain as the man with the long coat shoved past her, ignoring her words. The tension and disappointment that had been burning inside her burst in a torrent of anger. 'Excuse me, I am speaking to you,' she said, poking him in the back before grabbing the collar of his coat. 'I told you. This is a private event. Please leave right now.'

The man spun on his heels and hissed into her face as the two thugs closed in. 'Let go of me, woman, or you'll end up regretting the day you laid a finger on Frank Unthank.'

Sarah was aware of a sudden silence. This time it wasn't because of one of Vera's silly comments, but something more palpable. She shivered as the air around her filled with menace tinged with fear. However, she stood her ground. Despite her personal problems with her husband, this business was his and it was built with the love and support of his family and friends. No one was going to barge in like this man was trying to do. Sarah wrinkled her nose as the odour of stale onions and cologne filled her nostrils. 'I have no idea who you are, but I do know every person on our guest list, and it does not include anyone called Frank Unthank. Nor does it include these gentlemen,' she hissed back, placing her hands on her hips. 'Now, I suggest you all clear off out of here before I call the police.'

Bob, who up to now had been sitting quietly beside Ruby, was on his feet and standing alongside Mike, who had joined Sarah on the pavement outside the shop. 'Now, Mr Unthank, we don't want no bother. This is a family celebration. If you have business with Alan Gilbert, or anyone else on the premises, I suggest you come back another day, if you don't mind.'

Sarah frowned as she spotted Freda reaching for Alan's arm to hold him back. Something was going on here that she didn't know about . . . something more than her concerns about Alan and Freda being close. A thought came to her. 'The man who caused the fire in my husband's workshop – he was an Unthank. Any relation to you?' she asked, giving the short, bulky man a steely stare.

Frank Unthank shrugged his shoulders. 'My youngest son. He was a fool to get caught. He will pay his dues, serve his time and be back working with me before too long – mark my words.' He glared, looking over Sarah's shoulder to where Alan stood. 'That's another score that needs settling. I'll bide my time. However, I'm here to deliver this,' he said, taking a white envelope from his pocket and holding it out to Alan. Sarah watched as Alan stepped forward and took it without saying one word.

'Follow that to the letter – or else your little girl friend could have an accident. She made me promises she hasn't kept,' Unthank said, pointing to an ashen-faced Freda before returning his gaze to Sarah. 'Nice to meet you, Mrs Gilbert. Perhaps we will meet again.' He nodded towards the premises behind her. 'And it's a nice place you have here. You'd best take better care of it than you did of your workshop.' With an unpleasant smile, he turned away.

Sarah threw herself at her husband, beating his chest with her fists. 'What's this all about? I demand you tell me right now. Why is he after you? And you . . .' she said, looking to where Freda stood frozen to the spot. 'Are you carrying on with my husband?'

By now, nearly everyone in the workshop was gazing out at the scene through the open doors. Betty hurriedly whispered in Douglas's ear, then he banged his hand on the counter for attention. 'Ladies and gentlemen – may I have your attention, please? The time is fast approaching for Lemuel and Sadie's wedding. I suggest that the bride and her family go back to Freda's to prepare. Perhaps Alan and those who are in the know about what has just happened here can stay and have a discussion.'

'That's a good idea,' Mike Jackson said. 'Gwyneth – would you walk Vera and Sadie back to the house? I think you should stay, Freda,' he added as she went to follow the women. 'Let's clear the air, shall we?'

Freda nodded, and did her best not to look to where Sarah was being comforted by her father.

'I have to get back to the staff canteen,' Maureen said, giving Betty a beseeching look.

'Stay here,' Betty advised her as she reached for her handbag. 'I'll have the canteen covered even if I have to roll my sleeves up and do it myself.' She patted Maureen's arm. 'Your family is more important than work right now.'

Maureen gave Betty a kiss on her powdered cheek before the Woolworths manageress ushered Vera and the wedding party from the shop.

'I'll go and 'elp Sadie in case she needs stitching into her frock. As much as I'd like to stay and find out what the hell is going on, I think someone should keep an eye on Vera and her tongue, or the whole town will know something's afoot. Stay here,' Maisie instructed her husband. 'You may be needed, but please don't get into any fights.' She turned to Ruby. 'Do you want to come with me?'

'I'd best do that, as it'll take more than one person to keep Vera quiet,' Ruby said as Bob helped her into her coat. She straightened up with a visible effort after being seated for so long. 'I take it you know some of what's been going on here?' she asked her husband, giving him a disapproving look.

'I have a feeling I know part, but not all the picture,' he said, looking at Freda, who nodded her head.

'You'd better not have been up to no good, Bob Jackson,' Ruby scolded. 'I know the Unthank family from old, and there's many a person come to no good after upsetting them. I couldn't bear it if anything happened to one of my loved ones.'

Bob gave Ruby a quick hug. 'Now you're talking daft. We just need to clear up a few things, and then I'll be at the church.'

'Well, don't forget you need to come home for a shave and to put your best suit on. You are not going to church looking like that,' she said, poking him in the chest.

Bob looked down at what he was wearing. It was his second-best suit, and a new pullover Ruby had knitted only weeks ago. He knew better than to argue.

'Anyone else coming with us?' Maisie asked.

'I'm staying here – I want to know everything,' Sarah said as she pulled away from her dad and poured herself a glass of sherry from the bottle on the shop counter. 'I'm not leaving until it all comes out.' She glared at Alan and Freda.

'I'd best get going; I'm not really part of this,' Tony said, picking up his jacket.

'No, I want you to stay. You're my friend and I want you here beside me. I don't like keeping secrets,' Freda said.

Sarah gave a harsh laugh, poured herself another sherry and raised the glass. 'Here's to secrets,' she declared with a catch in her voice.

Maureen took the glass from her and led her to a chair.

'Come on, love – I have a feeling you'll need a clear head if you want to get to the bottom of whatever's been going on. You don't want to have a headache when those kiddies of yours wake you up at the crack of dawn tomorrow to tell you Father Christmas has arrived.'

Sarah gave her mother-in-law a weak smile. Saying nothing, she sat down to see what would unfold. Never in her life had she felt so tired or miserable, and it wasn't the sherry causing it.

Freda perched herself on the edge of the long wooden counter. She would back Alan up if the going got tough. She could see Sarah deep in thought, and was glad Maureen was there to calm her down. She didn't blame her friend – and yes, she still thought of Sarah as her friend, although this business had come between them even if Sarah didn't know what was behind the fire in the workshop or the reason Alan had changed in so many ways. Only the new shop and the thought of a light at the end of the tunnel had cheered him in past weeks.

'Alan, am I right in thinking I'm the only one besides Sarah who hasn't a clue what's been going on here?' Maureen asked. 'I overheard something between you and Freda and should have tackled the pair of you at the time. I wish I had.'

Sarah looked to Tony and raised a questioning eyebrow.

'I only know what Freda has told me,' he apologized.

David Carlisle and Douglas Billington looked at each other before David spoke. 'Along with our wives, we felt something wasn't right. We had a chat and wanted to help. Hence offering you the premises for your business,' he said. 'We will stand by you, even if it means breaking the law. Friends come first.'

'Now come on, lads. No one is talking about breaking the law. I'm thinking Alan and Freda are just in a bit of a fix. Isn't that what Mike and I came across down in West Street a while back?' Bob gave Freda an encouraging smile. 'Why don't you start by telling us what happened to you?'

Before Freda could respond, Alan walked into the middle of the room. He'd been leaning against the wall, watching his friends and family discuss his life. 'I should speak, as I'm the one who caused all this mess. No,' he said as Freda tried to interrupt, 'I'll tell everything.'

Sarah watched her husband as he explained how his workshop had started to go downhill after the GPO took away the contract for the maintenance and repair of their fleet of motorbikes. He had tried his utmost to find more work, and a glimmer of hope had come with the offer to bid for a smaller company's fleet maintenance. But it had meant stocking up on parts, and he had needed money.

'You should have come to me, Alan,' George said, as he shook his head in sadness. 'That's what family are for.'

'I wanted to sink or swim on my own,' Alan replied.

'You could have told me . . .' Sarah said in disbelief. 'You could have told me the business was in trouble. We could have thought this through together . . . That's what married couples are meant to do – not keep secrets from one another.'

Alan ran his hand through his hair as he shook his head. 'I thought I had the answer. I was told about someone who would give me a loan. It seemed the perfect answer. I'd borrow the money. Stock up on spares and win the new contract. No one need know, and the business would soon be thriving again,' he said with a pleading look to Sarah.

'But why tell Freda when you couldn't tell me?' she wailed.

'Alan didn't tell me. I found out, and I tackled him face to face,' Freda said. 'Then I made things worse. I tried to pay off some of the loan using my savings, but I angered Frank Unthank even more.'

'You paid off some of my debt? Why didn't you tell me?' Alan said with a look of horror on his face.

'Because it was the afternoon I knocked Tony off his bicycle, and with Lemuel arriving and promising to help, I thought it was best kept quiet. The money doesn't matter.'

'And I begged her not to say anything,' Alan said, looking embarrassed.

'I told Tony. The secret was chewing me up inside and I didn't know who to turn to,' Freda added, as Tony reached out and squeezed her hand to reassure her.

'I was happy to be your confidant,' he said.

'Surely you knew how much money was owed?' Maureen asked with a shocked look on her face. 'Didn't the man send you letters and statements? That would be the businesslike thing to do.'

'Frank Unthank doesn't do things by the book,' Mike Jackson said. 'He works outside the law, but no one has so far stepped forward with enough information for us to nab him. He deals in threats and violence. That's the language he knows best.'

It was Lemuel's turn to step forward. 'I have seen the paperwork,' he said to Maureen. 'Unthank does not send statements – he sends threats, and with hundreds of pounds added for interest, the sum more than trebled. Not long after that the workshop caught fire. His son, who broke in, didn't know I'd be there. The workshop should have been empty with you all at the wedding reception.'

'I assume Unthank is even more angry, now that his son's had his collar felt and will go to prison,' Bob said thoughtfully. 'How long do you think he'll get, son?' he asked Mike.

'Six months at the most. He has a good solicitor, and from what I've been told their angle is that he went in through an open door and was helping himself to a few things when the fire started.'

Alan groaned. 'Six months or six years, Unthank will be just as angry. I need him off my back or he'll go for my family next. He said as much today.'

'Then we pay him what he wants regardless of the interest, and that way he has no argument with any of us,' George said. 'I've got the money and it's yours. It will come to you both when I'm gone, so you may as well have it now. I don't want to be attending your funerals any time soon. That's not the natural progression of life. Now, what's the tally?'

Alan went to a small safe under the counter and pulled out a folder. Without saying a word, he passed it to George Caselton. He couldn't have looked any more ashamed if he'd tried.

Sarah looked over her dad's shoulder as he slid out a

bundle of papers and looked at the latest. 'How much?' she all but screamed. 'Five thousand pounds? That's twice as much as a nice little house would cost. Whatever have you done to us, Alan?'

Alan gave her a look that begged her for forgiveness. 'I only borrowed four hundred pounds. I'd paid some back, but he kept piling on the interest.'

'I knocked fifty pounds off that sum,' Freda said, horrified at how much the money Alan owed Unthank had grown. 'That was on the day you rescued me at Unthank's office,' she said to Mike and Bob.

George raised his hand to silence them. 'Mike, David, Douglas – will you accompany me to visit Mr Unthank. I'll give him a personal cheque, and we can put this sorry business to bed before we celebrate Christmas.'

'I'll pay you back . . .' Alan started to apologize.

'There's no need. I'd rather have a son in-law who's alive than a grave to visit. As I said before, the money would go to you both eventually, so I'd rather it be made use of now than sit in the bank. Don't you agree, my love?' he said, looking to where Maureen was wiping her eyes.

'I dare not think what could have happened,' she sniffed. 'Thank you, George. At least this sorry business is done and dusted.'

'But it's not,' Sarah said, rising from her chair and facing Alan. 'You may not have been carrying on with Freda, as I feared, but what you've done is just as bad. If you don't mind,' she said, turning to George and Maureen, 'I'd like to come and stay with you for a while, and bring the children. I don't want to sleep under the same roof as a man who doesn't love me enough to confide in me. I'll go home now and pack.'

'I'll help you, love,' Maureen said as she followed Sarah to the door. 'No, Alan,' she said as her son made to go after them. 'Let it be for now, eh? Given time, Sarah may just forgive you. I'll make sure you get to see the children on Christmas morning,' she added, looking close to tears again.

'Sarah . . . ?' Freda said. 'I'm sorry I couldn't tell you anything. I promised Alan I wouldn't . . .'

Sarah gave Freda a hard look. 'You may not have been carrying on with my husband as I thought, but you did enough to ruin my marriage. Please . . . please just keep away from me,' she said before hurrying from the shop.

Alan slumped onto Sarah's vacated seat, a picture of abject misery. 'What the hell do I do now?' he groaned.

'What you do, son, is you get yourself cleaned up and you make sure this fine man here gets to church on time. Nothing is going to spoil his wedding day, and as best man it's your duty to see it doesn't. Give our Sarah time, and she'll come around.'

'I don't feel like going to a wedding, not after all this,' Freda said, looking sad.

George wagged his finger at the young woman. 'You are going, and you will enjoy yourself. Aren't you a bridesmaid? It would be a fine thing if the bride walked down the aisle with her bridesmaid missing. That would give Vera Munro something to gossip about, and no one needs that happening.'

Freda gulped back the lump that had formed in her throat and agreed.

'I'll make sure she does a good job, sir,' Tony said as he took Freda's hand and gave it a squeeze.

'Take care of her. She's a good kid,' Alan said.

'I'll do that,' Tony said with a gentle smile. 'I'll do that for as long as it takes.'

15

July 1948

'Oh Betty, he's adorable, and so like his handsome daddy,' Freda cooed as she held young master Billington in her arms. A fluff of blond hair peeped out from a soft lemon bonnet, which Freda was pleased to see was one she'd knitted herself. 'I can't believe he's already a month old; look how he's grown. You are so lucky, Betty,' she added as she kissed the baby's little button nose and handed him back to his smiling mother.

'I hope you don't mind me taking over the office like this, Tony?' Betty said as she handed the baby to Maureen, who was holding out her arms for a cuddle. 'As it was, I fought my way through the store as customers and staff recognized me. Why, I've only been gone four months, for heaven's sake.'

'You have no idea how much you are loved,' Maureen said as she sighed over the baby. 'May I take him to the staff canteen to show the girls? I'll send back a bun and a cup of tea,' she added, knowing that would tempt Betty.

'Is it bad of me to say yes so quickly? I feel as though

I'm trading my son in for a sticky bun!' Betty grinned.

'You've always been partial to a bun,' Maureen said as she left the room with the baby, who had started to wail. 'I'll have none of that, young man. You might have your mum wrapped round your tiny finger, but it won't wash with me. Now, let's introduce you to everyone,' she could be heard saying as she disappeared down the corridor.

Freda and Betty chuckled as Tony looked horrified. 'I think I'd rather have a sticky bun, if you don't mind. I'd not know what to do with a crying baby.'

'You'll be fine when it's your own,' Betty smiled. 'Douglas even changed a nappy the other day.' She was about to describe how their son had been sick on Douglas's best suit when she saw the embarrassed look Freda gave Tony. Hmm, so something was going on between Freda and Tony. She was pleased, as it was about time Freda met a decent lad – and from all she knew about Tony, he was very decent indeed. She shrugged her shoulders. 'Oh well – you'll find out one day, I'm sure. Now, how are you coping as our temporary manager?'

'I'll leave you to it,' Freda said, giving Betty a kiss on the cheek. 'I should be down on the shop floor. I'll see you at the christening on Sunday.'

Tony grinned as Freda closed the door behind the pair. 'I've not burnt the store down yet, and the takings haven't gone missing,' he laughed.

Betty tapped the wooden desk with her fingers. 'Touch wood,' she laughed.

'Even though you trained me so well, I feel as though there aren't enough hours in the day. How did you cope?'

'Before I married – I take it Freda told you I married

late in life? Well, before I married, I would still be here working late into the night. I was of the opinion that everything had to be done, and done properly. Gradually, I mellowed. Running this store through the war and making good friends, as well as meeting Douglas, had me re-evaluate my life. Make good use of your staff. We have good supervisors, and the trainee managers that come and go have to learn to pull their weight. It's all down to delegation. Don't forget that you also have some experienced staff in the office. Sarah must be a godsend to you.'

Tony, who had been jotting down Betty's suggestions, didn't answer.

'Sarah is helping you, isn't she?'

'I don't wish to cause problems, as I know she is a good friend of yours . . .'

'We are speaking as managers of F. W. Woolworths, Tony, so please don't hold back. I assume you have a staffing problem?'

Tony nodded. 'I feel as though I've failed, and in my early days as a temporary manager if Sarah had done something wrong, I could probably handle it. It's more that she turns up and goes through the motions of working, without doing much at all. What she does is good, and she scrapes by. The wages go out on time and paperwork gets sent to head office . . . It's as if the light has gone out inside her. Yes, that's it. Her light has gone out. Does that sound dramatic?'

Betty thought for a moment. 'No, I really don't think you're being dramatic. Since Christmas Eve, Sarah's life has changed beyond comprehension. She was born to be a wife and mother and does that job admirably, far better than I could ever do. No, I'm right,' she added as Tony started to protest. 'No, I get by. I have staff at home to help me. Whereas Sarah is now without her husband. I know she has moved in with her dad and Maureen, but that is not where she should be. I thought it would all have blown over by now, what with George having paid off Alan's debt and Frank Unthank's son being sentenced and locked up for setting fire to the workshop . . .' She stopped speaking as she thought of what the future would be like if Alan and Sarah were to divorce. She'd never known anyone have a divorce before, and in their close circle the ripples of the young couple's separation could be catastrophic. She jumped as Freda tapped on the door and entered with a tray of tea.

'I'm only bringing this because Betty is visiting. Don't think I'm going to make a habit of serving you tea,' she said with a cheeky grin to Tony.

'Be off with you, woman, before I give you your cards,' he replied with a laugh.

Betty felt warmth spread through her as she hoped Freda had at long last found her soul mate. 'Now, I have a little news for you,' she said after thanking Freda and watching her leave the room. 'I've spoken with head office, and in light of you representing our country in the Olympic Games I have gained permission for you to take next week off for more training before you head off to Windsor.'

Tony looked at Betty in amazement. 'But how . . . ? I mean, I don't know how to thank you. I've been training all the hours God gives, but the gift of an extra week off work would be . . . I really don't deserve this after being off sick with my bad leg for so long. The last thing I want to do is jeopardize my job.'

Betty smiled. It warmed her heart to see that Tony was so hard-working and conscientious. The country's future was sound with young men like this. 'Considering it was a Woolworths employee who was partially to blame for your accident, I don't feel the company should in any way comment on your time off sick. Besides, it all worked out well in the end. I have to confess to having a hand in asking for you to have more time off. I quite liked seeing Freda and Maureen featured in *The New Bond* and thought it would look rather good to have another staff member mentioned in the staff magazine when they win a gold medal for Great Britain.'

Tony chuckled. 'You are a ruthless woman, Mrs Billington. I just hope I can bring honours back to Erith.'

'Just do your best, Tony. We are all proud of you here in Erith, in our little family.'

A cloud passed over the young man's face as he digested Betty's words.

Betty noticed, and passed a plate of biscuits across the table. 'You know, I was completely alone, with no family to speak of, until I was welcomed into Sarah's family. Along with Freda and Maisie, we became part of something very special. I can see the same is happening to you, so please, forget the past and enjoy the present.'

'I will; thank you. Speaking of the present, if I'm not here, who will steer this ship?'

'I'm coming back to cover for you,' Betty declared.

'But you've only just . . .' Tony looked sheepish, not knowing which words to used.

'Safely delivered a baby boy?' Betty suggested. 'I'm fit and I'm healthy and as it will be for just the few weeks, I can go back to caring for my child afterwards. I intend to have our Sarah step into the breach as well. It may help her . . .'

They looked at each other, wondering if Betty's plan would work.

'Yer know you've got to snap out of this, Sarah,' Maisie muttered between pursed lips that held half a dozen dress-making pins. 'Yer not the only woman whose husband's let her down. Why, it's not as if he's robbed a bank or carried on wiv some floozie. Yer would have something to complain about if that 'appened.'

Sarah ran her hands across the paper pattern her friend was pinning to a heavy white satin fabric. Satisfied there wasn't a kink in the delicate tissue paper, she nodded to Maisie, who pinned the pattern to the satin. 'Alan had secrets he decided not to share with me, and instead took Freda into his confidence. Why, even Lemuel knew, and he'd not been in town more than a few days.'

'Oh, come off it, Sarah. Alan and Lem knew each other during the war, and that would be a special friendship, with what those men had to put up with in the RAF during the Battle of Britain.'

Sarah shrugged her shoulders. 'I suppose so. But I was still the last to know he had problems, when I should have been the first.'

'P'raps he knew how you'd react . . .' Maisie said, holding her breath in case she'd gone too far.

Sarah bristled. 'I don't know what you're going on about. I've always been a fair-minded and reasonable person,' she sniffed.

'Then stop going around like a wet weekend and concentrate on yer job and family. Yer can't expect everyone to carry you through life. Wiv Tony off to compete in the Olympics, you need to be pulling your weight more at Woolies.'

'I don't wish to continue this conversation,' Sarah sniffed. 'Let's talk about something else. Why don't you tell me who this wedding dress is for?'

Maisie grinned to herself, knowing her words had hit home. With luck, Sarah would take note. Underneath it all she was a decent sort and would snap out of her melancholy. 'It's not fer anyone in particular. Since Princess Elizabeth's wedding last year people keep asking if I sell wedding gowns, so as I'd got this piece of satin on the cheap, I decided to run up a dress and see how it goes. I've a few second-hand bridesmaid frocks on the hangers, and a good few outfits for the mother of the bride. Who knows, it might just take off, and it could be a nice little money-spinner. I've 'ad a few wedding dresses given ter me, but I'd not sell them second-hand. They can be unpicked and turned into christening gowns. I might donate one ter Sadie and Lem. What do yer think?'

Sarah shuddered. 'Second-hand wedding dress, second-hand marriage woes. No thanks. You're doing the right thing unpicking them, although I'm not so sure giving one to Sadie is a good idea. There may not be a christening.'

'Why not? Lem's the most religious man I know, and

these days Sadie attends the Northend Baptist mission with him. Who'd have thought that?'

'It's to do with her being born out of wedlock, and of course young Jacob was well on the way before their wedding. The church won't christen the new baby. Nan told me that Vera's going to have a word with the elders to see what can be done about it.'

'Then I'll make up a christening gown and keep it ter one side. No God-fearing man in his right mind is going to go against Vera Munro's request,' Maisie said with a grin.

Sarah chuckled. 'Nan said as much to me. Talking of Nan, I don't think she's very well. I tackled her about it last week when she had the children. She told me to mind my own business and said she was as fit as the day she first moved to number thirteen, Alexandra Road as a young bride.'

'Blimey, no one's that fit,' Maisie guffawed, then cursed as she pricked her finger. 'Sod it, there's blood on the fabric. I'll 'ave ter cut round that bit.'

Sarah froze as a shocked look crossed her face. 'Blood and tears,' she whispered.

'You don't believe all that rubbish, do yer?' Maisie said, although she shuddered as she quickly chopped away the offending piece of fabric and then reached for her first-aid tin to get a plaster.

'That's why no one carries red and white flowers, and blood on the wedding dress is just as bad. Perhaps we should sew a little horseshoe into the hem of the gown to give some extra luck. I have a couple that were on my wedding cake. You can have one of those.'

Maisie nodded in agreement, although she wasn't so sure Sarah and Alan's marriage had been that lucky of late.

Freda looked round her at the small room in the guest-house. 'I have to share?' she asked, seeing the room furnished with bunk beds.

'You're lucky to have a room at all with so many visitors in the town for the racing. Do you want it or not?'

'I'll take it,' Freda said quickly. There'd be no chance of her finding other accommodation, as the cycling events were due to start within a couple of days. 'Am I able to do some washing and ironing?' she asked hopefully. She planned to launder Tony's cycling clothes, to give him one less thing to think about while he prepared to compete.

'You'll have to take your turn, as some of the other wives are wanting to wash their husbands' clothes as well. You can use the kitchen to make your man's food as well.'

Freda frowned. 'I'm not married.'

The woman folded her arms across her chest, and a stern look appeared on her face.

'Oh, it's nothing like that,' Freda said as her face flushed with colour. 'Tony is a good friend and work colleague. He's here to compete for Great Britain and doesn't have family to help him.'

The woman's face softened. 'I didn't think you looked the sort to live in sin,' she nodded approvingly.

'I'd not like it under my roof either,' Freda said as she

went on to explain how she too took in paying guests. 'My friend, Tony, and I work at Woolworths and usually my guests are employees of the company.'

'Then it's all above board and respectable. I've always found people who work in Woolies to be very nice. Very nice indeed. Now, if you want to get settled in, I'll put the kettle on and we can have a cup of tea while we get acquainted. I'll tell you which buses you can catch to where the cycling events are being held.'

Freda nodded. She didn't like to say she had a detailed map that Tony had drawn for her. 'That would be nice, although I won't need to take the bus as I have my bicycle with me. I brought it with me on the train.'

'A competitor yourself, are you?'

Freda chuckled. 'No, I prefer a motorbike; I rode one during the war. But I've been keeping Tony company while he trains, and now I cycle a lot. I can also put my hand to a few repairs to Tony's bikes.' She didn't add that she missed helping Alan out, and being able to assist Tony was a small way to ease the pain of what happened at Christmas.

'You are an interesting young woman. We are going to get on fine.'

Freda was as good as her word and spent an hour with the landlady, coming away with the best places to shop for fresh produce and being shown where to store her food in the kitchen. She'd packed a couple of plates along with knives and forks, and planned to take food for Tony's lunch each day. She knew from past experience that he would forget all about eating, instead preferring to put as much training in as possible.

Not having visited this part of England before, Freda was keen to see something of Windsor town before heading to the Great Park, where the cycling events would be held. Her dream was to see the Royal Family and to be able to tell Ruby all about it. However, to be on the safe side she would purchase a few picture postcards with views of the castle. Such a shame she'd forgotten to ask Betty if there was a Woolworths branch in the town. She could have used the camera George had lent her to take a photograph. That would amuse her friends.

Thanking her lucky stars she'd packed a rain mac, she swung her leg over the bicycle and headed off in the summer drizzle, keeping the meandering Thames in sight and looking up at the castle that dominated the little town. She couldn't help noticing how different the river was here to the wide expanse of water in her home town. There wasn't one overhead crane, or any docks, let alone a ship. Instead she could see a few small landing stages and pleasure boats already plying their trade for the busy tourists. It would be fun to take a trip on this part of the Thames and compare it to when she'd been on the *Kentish Queen* on trips down to the seaside towns of Margate and Ramsgate. If there was time, she could treat Tony to a few hours on the river. She hoped her friend would like the trips as much as she did.

Spotting a small grocer's shop, she stopped to pick up provisions for their lunch and was soon on her way again as the rain stopped and the sun started to shine.

'That hit the spot,' Tony said as he lay back on a grassy bank after demolishing a plate of fresh ham slices and salad. 'I don't know what I'd have done without you here to help me. I must be the cleanest and most well-fed competitor in the camp.'

'I'm doing my bit for King and country,' Freda grinned. 'And if it means you win a medal, then all the better.'

'Don't hold your breath,' Tony muttered. 'The best cyclists in the world are here. I'm just one of the lads making up the numbers.'

Freda was shocked by the way he thought. She knew that to compete and win one had to focus on being number one and aim for the top spot. She was thoughtful as they cleared away the remains of the picnic lunch and prepared to mount their bicycles so Tony could show her the best place to view tomorrow's race. The rain had eased off for their picnic meal, but the overcast sky threatened another downpour. She was keen to see the start of the race tomorrow, but then how would she know if he had won a medal? It would have been wonderful to see the whole race, and to wave and cheer him on and keep him focused on winning. After the months of accompanying him on long training sessions, she had faith in his ability. She needed to give him a personal prize to keep him focused. Looking across the field, she could just see the river, and an idea came to her. Tapping Tony on the arm to get his attention away from strapping the picnic blanket to the back of her saddle, she gave a big smile as he turned around. 'I want to give you a special treat, so you try your hardest tomorrow. It will keep you focused,' she added as Tony stood looking into her eyes with a slightly puzzled expression. 'I want to . . . that is, I thought . . .'

Tony brushed a stray hair from her face with one finger before placing it under her chin and bringing her lips closer to his for a gentle kiss. Then he pulled her close. Taken by surprise, Freda sighed and enjoyed the moment, surprised by her sudden strong feelings for Tony. 'Oh my,' she murmured as their lips parted.

'I've wanted to do that for so long,' he said, still holding her close. 'Now I'm completely focused.'

'To think I was going to promise you a trip on the Thames as an incentive to try harder,' she whispered.

'I have my prize,' he said as he kissed her again.

Freda spent the rest of the day in a dream. Whatever she was doing, she couldn't forget Tony's kiss. Handwashing his cycling kit later that evening, she was miles away and didn't hear her landlady ask a question.

'The girl looks to be in love,' a fellow guest laughed as she waited in line to use the kitchen sink. 'She 'az a certain bloom to her cheeks, do you think?' The Frenchwoman smiled. 'I remember this so well. These days I remember more the washing of his underclothes.'

The women laughed, and Freda did her best to concentrate on what was happening around her. Today had changed everything as far as she was concerned. Perhaps for him it had only been a spur-of-the-moment kiss, but how would it be when they returned home to Erith? Living in the same house could be uncomfortable if it weren't for her two other lodgers, Effie and Dulcie, who worked at Woolworths too and had taken Sadie's room when she married Lemuel and moved back to her nan's house. She wasn't sure she could trust herself. 'Goodness, what would Ruby and Vera make of that?' she thought to herself as she put Tony's clothing through the mangle. She draped the wet clothes over a hanging rack before using the pulley to raise it to the ceiling of the kitchen to dry. The rain had started to fall again, but if tomorrow was dry she could hang the washing outside on the line before she left to watch the race.

Bidding the other women goodnight, she went upstairs for an early night, intent on being ready for what lay ahead on race day. Try as she might, she tossed and turned before falling asleep as the dawn chorus started and then dreaming of Tony's kiss.

Waking late, she decided to forgo breakfast and hurry to where Tony had told her would be a good place to view the race. She climbed up a grassy bank that bordered a turn in the road and settled down on a blanket to wait, tucking into a sandwich the landlady had thrust into her hand, wrapped in greaseproof paper, as she dashed from the house. There were many people milling around and nearby was a large van manned by people from the BBC, who seemed to be covering the race. Out of interest, and knowing Bob and Ruby Jackson would be intrigued to know she'd seen what happened when news was sent to their wireless set, she wandered over to take a closer look.

A man holding a microphone with a long lead trailing from inside the vehicle spotted her and stepped forward. 'Good morning, madam. Would you care to tell our listeners which country you are supporting in this race?'

Freda took a step back in fear as the microphone was held close to her face. The man nodded, encouraging her to speak.

'Er, I'm here to cheer on the Great Britain team. I have a friend in the race, Tony Forsythe. And my name is Freda

Smith, from Erith in Kent,' she added proudly, wondering if Ruby and Bob were listening. Wouldn't they be surprised!

'Kent? That's a long way to cycle,' the chap laughed as he noticed her bicycle lying on the grass nearby.

'Oh no, we are staying here in Windsor until tomorrow,' she said with a smile.

'Well, good luck to Tony Forsythe and his young lady who are staying here in Windsor. If you'd been at the start, you'd have seen Prince Philip start the race with a pistol,' he laughed as he took the microphone away.

Freda was mortified. Why, anyone who was listening to this BBC programme would think she was . . . she was sharing a bed with Tony. She had to correct the man before her friends thought the worse of her. She hurried forward, trying to catch his attention as he interviewed a man wearing an official's badge. In the distance she heard the roar of a crowd, and with others on the grass bank she turned to watch as the first in the race appeared at the corner. Where was Tony?

'Here comes the Italian in the lead by twenty yards, followed by the French . . . and is that a British shirt I see . . . ?'

Freda pushed forward as she heard the announcer's excited words. Surely that wasn't Tony? He'd told her it was best not to be too far forward in the early part of the race. But perhaps he was doing better than he thought he would at this stage. Oh, how she wished she'd listened properly when he spoke about the race with her friends' husbands.

As she watched, squinting to see if Tony was there, she noticed two cyclists crash into each other and quickly scramble to their feet before squaring up to each other. Other cyclists steered round them, and a race official's car pulled up to see to the problem. Trying to calm the situation, one official guided the men towards the side of the road while another tried to clear the debris, causing approaching racers to swerve. Freda gasped as cyclist after cyclist crashed into each other – amongst them she spotted Tony as he flew over the handlebars of his best bike. He landed on top of one of the Swiss cyclists. With thoughts only of his safety, Freda fled down the grassy bank and through the crowd that now lined the route.

'Tony,' she shrieked as she got within shouting distance and could see someone helping him to his feet.

'Freda?' Tony looked around until he saw her pushing through the melee of officials and injured cyclists.

'Oh Tony, I thought you'd been hurt,' she sobbed as she threw herself into his arms.

He held her tight, kissing away her tears, oblivious to the interested glances thrown in their direction.

'Is that it? After all your hard work and preparation,' she sobbed. 'Can't you get back on your bike and finish the race?' She looked at the mangled heap of frames, spokes and wheels and tried to work out which part of it was Tony's beloved bicycle.

'It doesn't matter, there's always next time,' Tony smiled as he slung his arm around her shoulders and slowly hobbled back to the grassy verge, where they were met by the gentleman from the BBC.

'Sir, how do you feel knowing you're out of the race and there isn't another Olympic Games for four more years?'

Tony roared with laughter, causing Freda to cuff away her tears and give him a questioning look. 'I feel better than I have in years.'

'But, sir, you were down to finish in the last ten. You could have been a contender for a medal . . .' the man said, not understanding the grin on Tony's face.

'Did you bump your head?' Freda asked, trying to check him over.

'No, just this damned leg's giving me trouble again,' he said, kissing the tip of her nose.

'But Tony . . .'

Tony hushed her with a kiss, ignoring the questions from the commentator and the microphone so close to their faces. 'Freda Smith, I'd get down on one knee if I thought I could get up again. You will have to accept my proposal standing up.'

'Tony . . . ?'

'Ladies and gentlemen, things are hotting up here at the Olympic Games in Windsor Home Park. Forget the racing – we have a proposal of marriage in the offing . . .' the excited presenter shouted down the microphone before poking it back in Tony's face.

Tony never noticed as he stood facing Freda. 'I thank the day you ran me down in Pier Road. You are obstinate, bossy and downright irritating at times, but I love you, Freda Smith, and I want you to be my wife as soon as possible. Will you marry me?'

This time the tears in Freda's eyes were tears of happiness. 'Oh yes, please, Tony. Can we marry today?' she laughed.

'I think all your friends would have something to say

about that,' he grinned back, holding out his hand. 'Come on – let's get back home and tell everyone, shall we?'

Freda took his hand and they walked away as the BBC presenter stood watching them, lost for words.

16

'Where is everyone?' Freda asked as she banged hard on the front door of number thirteen. 'It's only eight o'clock, so Ruby can't be in bed yet. I do hope there's nothing wrong.'

'Perhaps they've gone out somewhere,' Tony said as he peered through the bay window. 'I can't see anything.'

'You wouldn't. The curtains are drawn, which in itself is strange on a summer evening . . . Oh, Tony. Perhaps someone has died?' She gasped, thinking of times when neighbours had passed away and everyone in the street had closed their curtains as a mark of respect on the day of the funeral. Had Ruby's aches and pains been something serious?

'Someone would have got word to us, or Vera would have been down here by now,' Tony said, putting his arm round her shoulder.

Freda liked the feeling, and leant into him a little more. 'We may as well go home, then. I so wanted them to hear our news! It will just have to wait.'

The couple crossed the road to Freda's house and let themselves in, heading straight to the kitchen.

'Oh hello, you two. How did the race go?' Effie asked as she reached for two cups and saucers from the cupboard and placed them on a tray next to her own. 'I've not heard anything about the Olympics. I've been at my sister's, as there is news about that woman from Wheatley Terrace. Sergeant Jackson let me know that she's been arrested for performing illegal abortions.'

'Oh, that's good news. At least no other woman will suffer at her hands; although for some it is too late,' Freda added, thinking of Effie's sister.

'Yes, but someone will pay for it,' Effie said, trying valiantly to keep a smile on her face. 'I was just making my tea. We have fresh eggs and vegetables courtesy of Ruby and Bob.'

Tony agreed with what Effie had said. 'And it sounds as though Ruby is fine, if she delivered these,' he said, looking at the bowl of eggs on the table.

'Why wouldn't she be?'

'We stopped off to see her and Bob and there was no one home,' Freda explained, not wanting to say that Tony had asked her to marry him until she had told her closer friends.

'That's because they are all up at Vera Munro's house. There's some kind of party going on.'

Freda and Tony looked at each other in surprise. 'Vera's having a party?' Freda asked incredulously.

'I think it's Sadie and Lemuel's party. I don't know any more than that. They did invite me, but I said I was going to my sister's after work. Why don't you walk up there? I'll not go now, as I was planning on having an early night after my bath,' she said, glancing to where she'd draped her towel and washbag over the back of a chair.

'Then we will leave you to it,' Freda said, thinking it was time she did something about having a proper bathroom in the house, just as Ruby and Bob had done, by bricking up the doors of the coal house and outside toilet to create a small bathroom off the kitchen. The building work would be messy, but she might just be able to arrange it if the price wasn't too much. It was then she realized the decision would no longer be hers alone. When she married Tony, he might well take on such tasks. She liked that thought. 'Come on, Tony, we can eat later,' she said, taking his hand and pulling him from the room. If Effie noticed how close the pair now were, she didn't say anything.

'Crikey, whatever is all that noise?' Freda asked as they reached the gate to Vera's house, which was further up Alexandra Road halfway between Maisie's double-fronted home and Ruby's house at number thirteen. 'I know Vera has had a piano in her front room all the years I've known her, but I've never known it be played. It's usually shrouded in its green chenille cover with photographs on top.'

'That song doesn't seem to be the kind Vera would join in with, either,' Tony said as he opened the gate and ushered Freda towards the front door. It swung open as she reached for the door knocker.

'Hello, Lemuel, what's all this about?' she asked as she looked up to the tall, handsome, dark-skinned man who was beaming down at her.

He roared with laughter, and held out his hand in greeting. 'Ma'am, you pay me the greatest compliment a man can have. I'm not Lemuel, I am his younger brother, James.'

Freda froze; the likeness was amazing. As she stood dumbfounded, with one foot on the doorstep, she could see that James was slightly fuller in the face and, if it was possible, a good couple of inches taller. Giving herself a shake, she held out her hand and introduced herself and Tony, adding, 'I've never seen such a close likeness between siblings.'

'Wait until you see my sister,' he guffawed.

Freda liked this man immediately. But how had it been kept a secret that Lemuel's brother was to visit? Vera's inability to keep secrets was well known.

The couple were ushered through to the living room, where Sadie and Lemuel greeted them with surprise. 'I thought you weren't due back for another couple of days?' Sadie said, looking a picture with her freshly styled hair and wearing a bright yellow cotton summer frock. 'I'm so pleased you are able to join us. Let me introduce you to my mother-in-law, Cynthia, and my sister-in-law, Esther,' she said, leading Freda to a row of chairs where a rotund lady was chatting to Ruby and Vera. 'This is Freda, who we've been telling you about. She lives down the road opposite Ruby's house. It's her lodger who took part in the Olympic Games,' she said as Freda made her hellos, shook the hands of the two women and squeezed onto a chair next to Ruby.

'This is a big surprise,' Freda said. 'We've heard so much from Lemuel about his family, and to see you all sitting here is just wonderful.' One of Esther's children toddled up to her and climbed onto her lap.

'It was a big surprise for Lemuel,' Cynthia said. 'We have been corresponding with our new daughter-in-law, and her grandmother graciously invited us to visit. Esther's husband had to stay to look after their business, but as soon as James knew how much I wanted to come to England, he sold his car and his own business and paid for our trip. It is a dream come true,' she smiled benignly. 'I now have just one wish left, then I can die a happy woman.'

'My goodness, that sounds a bit drastic,' Ruby said. 'I hope it is something worth popping your clogs for?'

Sadie explained what 'popping your clogs' meant, and Cynthia burst into laughter. 'Oh my, I am going to like living here in England,' she said, much to Vera's consternation.

'I'm not sure we can put you up,' she said, looking horrified. 'We've only got the one spare room, and that's for young Arthur and Jacob Donald.'

'Donald? Do you meant Sadie and Lemuel have named their kiddie after your Don? That's a nice thing to do,' Ruby nodded approvingly.

'Jacob Donald, after both the grandparents,' Cynthia added, mopping her eyes with a handkerchief. 'My Jacob would have been so proud to think how well our children have done. His dream has been fulfilled, even though he is no longer here to see it. That just leaves my dream.'

Sadie knelt down in front of Cynthia and took her hand. 'Why don't you tell everyone your dream? Then perhaps we can help.'

Cynthia blew her nose and smiled. 'I'd like to meet one of the Royal Family. It doesn't have to be our King. I just need to know that they are real.'

'Of course they are real,' Vera scoffed. 'What makes you think they aren't?'

'When I was very young, I was told the royals were make-believe people. Just like the stories in my books were made up. There is part of me that still wants proof. Perhaps now I'm here in England, I should visit London and knock on their door?'

'I doubt they'd let you in, so you may as well save your train fare,' Vera sniffed.

Lemuel, who had been close by listening to his mother, clapped his hands together. 'I can show you they are real,' he said, going to the sideboard and pulling out a large envelope. 'I had meant to send these to you.' he explained, pulling out pages of newspaper reports of the wedding of Princess Elizabeth. 'Look, we were there watching the wedding.' He spread out one of the larger pages of a newspaper. 'See that corner . . . we all stood there as the King and Queen went past in a carriage after the wedding.'

Sarah appeared from the kitchen and peered over his shoulder as he knelt down, holding out the pages. 'That's right, and we slept on that pavement overnight so that we didn't miss seeing Princess Elizabeth travel to the church with her father. It was magical,' she said to Cynthia. 'I'll remember that day all my life.'

'Mother, we should have visited last year – then we could have gone to London to watch,' Esther scolded.

'But the time was not right,' Cynthia nodded wisely. 'The time was not right for us. But to think I now have a grandson whose parents have seen the King and Queen! If only they had spoken to you.'

Freda couldn't contain herself any longer. 'That was

the day that Lemuel and Sadie truly fell in love. I saw it happen,' she explained. 'But if you want to meet someone who has touched a royal hand, he is here in this room. Tony,' she called, and Tony looked up from where he'd been chatting with David Carlisle. 'This is my intended. He met Prince Philip only yesterday, and shook him by the hand.'

Tony shook hands with Cynthia, who then wouldn't let go of his hand and stroked it gently. He explained about Prince Philip meeting the cyclists in the Olympic event before using a pistol to start the race. He finished by explaining that he had fallen off his bike in the crash.

Maisie, who was more interested in what she'd heard Freda say, stopped laying out food and came to her side. 'What did you just say about Tony, Freda?'

Freda grinned. 'I said Tony met Prince Philip . . .'

'Not that bit, you idiot – the part where you said, "this is my intended". I did hear that right, didn't I?' she shrieked.

Freda suddenly felt shy as all eyes turned towards her, and she looked to Tony for support.

'Yes, I asked Freda to marry me just after I fell off my bike. The fact she said yes more than made up for crashing out of the Olympics,' Tony said, slipping an arm round Freda's shoulders. 'Hopefully the wedding will be soon, as there's nothing to wait for.'

Amongst the cheers and hugs, Ruby pulled Freda to one side to give her a cuddle. 'I'm as pleased as if you were my own granddaughter,' she said. 'I hope your brother Lenny will be here to give you away?'

Freda slapped a hand to her mouth. 'I hadn't given that

a thought. I'll have to write to Sally and find out when he is home. With him being my only living blood relative – apart from his and Sally's two kiddies, that is – I must have him by my side. What a fool I am for not thinking things out properly,' she said. 'I hope Tony will understand.'

'If he doesn't, then he's not the man for you. Not that I think that for one moment,' Ruby said. 'Why don't you come over for your dinner tomorrow, and you can use my telephone to speak to Sally? That would be so much better than writing a letter. Then you can visit so they can meet Tony. Even if Lenny is away at sea, Tony can still get to know Sally and the children.'

Freda thought for a moment before bursting into tears. 'I've just realized that at long last, Tony is going to have a family,' she sobbed.

'It's so good of you to come with me, Ruby,' Freda said as they walked up the high street to Maisie's Modes. 'With you and Maisie advising me on what to wear for my wedding, I shouldn't go far wrong.'

'I deem it an honour, my love. You're like family, so it's only right I give you all the help I can. Besides, you know I like a wedding and a party afterwards. Even at my age I can manage a knees-up,' she grinned, before thanking a woman who held the door to the shop for them as she walked out. 'Put the kettle on, the bride is here,' she called to where Maisie was handing a parcel to her last customer of the day.

'Blimey, you're in good spirits,' Maisie grinned. 'I take it someone has booked the date?'

Freda removed her coat and hat and hung them on a hook on the wall. 'Things have moved on a bit since we last saw you,' she said, rolling her eyes skywards.

'Don't tell me – you've changed your plans and want a gold coach to take you ter the registry office?' Maisie said, roaring with laughter at her own joke.

'It's almost as bad as that,' Ruby said as she went to where Maisie kept her kettle and shook it to check it contained enough water for their drink. 'I've brought some biscuits, as no doubt you're out of them.'

'I didn't stop for anything to eat midday, if that's what yer mean,' Maisie grinned. 'Now stop fiddling with that kettle and sit down, so you can both bring me up to date wiv what's been 'appening.'

'There's not to be a registry office wedding,' Freda said, waiting to see her friend's expression.

'Oh, bloody 'ell, has he changed his mind? I 'ope it wasn't my fault as I told Tony when he marries you, he takes on all of us as well as the local Brownie and Girl Guide groups.'

'Oh, Maisie, he'd love all of that. He's already talking about helping out with the local youth club to teach the kids how to maintain their bikes as well as take them for rides at the weekend. No, it's something bigger than that . . .'

'Come one, Freda. Don't keep me in suspense,' Maisie all but screamed. 'Are you up the duff and putting it all off until after the birth?' She knew just how to embarrass her young friend, and succeeded as she saw Freda blush a deep red.

'No, be serious,' she scolded. 'As my brother Lenny is

away until September, we plan to have the wedding then. And . . .' she stopped and smiled. 'And it's going to be a church wedding at St Paulinus, just like many of you have had,' she grinned.

Maisie clapped her hands together in delight. 'Now, that's more like it. I never saw you as someone who would dash off to do it on the quick dressed in a suit.'

Ruby smiled. Maisie had some blunt ways of speaking, but she'd hit the nail on the head with that comment. 'I'm here in my official capacity as honorary grandmother, and after having a word with Bob we both decided we wanted to pay for the wedding gown and all the bridesmaids' dresses,' she said, looking at Freda's shocked face. 'And I don't want any arguments. This'll be the last big wedding for a while until all the grandkids grow up, so I want to spoil you.'

Freda burst into tears and threw herself into Ruby's arms. 'I don't know how to thank you,' she sobbed. 'I came here thinking Maisie may have something second-hand that could be altered, and to ask her to be my chief bridesmaid, what with you being the eldest,' she added with a cheeky grin. 'I never expected to be told you'd be treating me like a granddaughter.'

'Blimey, you can stop these tears fer a start. It's like 'aving Sarah here. She's usually the first to start blubbing. Crikey, talk of the devil and she will appear. Here she comes,' Maisie laughed as Sarah let herself into the shop.

'Hello everyone,' Sarah said as she went to kiss her nan's cheek.

'I'm glad you could get here, love,' Ruby said. 'I thought

it was time you and Freda made things up, considering she's going to be getting married soon and needs all the help we can give her.'

Freda gave Sarah a shy look, not sure how she would take Ruby's advice. 'I'd like us to be friends,' she said quietly. 'At no time did I want to hurt you.'

'Yer could say she was stuck between a rock and a hard place. In a way, Alan shouldn't have made her promise not ter say anything. Like a bloody fool, she did his bidding. He's got a lot ter answer for,' Maisie said pointedly.

Sarah and Freda looked at each other, both observing how the other was reacting to Maisie's words.

'Well, someone speak, we can't stand here all day,' Ruby said, looking at the three women who meant so much to her. The kettle started to whistle. 'I'll get that, shall I?'

'I want you to be one of my bridesmaids, along with Georgina,' Freda said, trying the break the ice. 'Tony and I are going to get married in a church now we have time to plan. Lenny's ship's not back until the end of August so we've booked St Paulinus for the third Saturday in September. Please say we can be friends again,' she begged, holding out her hand to Sarah.

'Yer supposed ter say something now,' Maisie said as she nudged Sarah. 'Oh, bloody 'ell, I just knew she was going ter cry – and now you've got me starting,' she sniffed, before holding her arms wide. The three of them hugged tightly before breaking apart and laughing.

'I just want to say one thing,' Sarah said.

'Please do. Get it out in the open,' Freda urged.

'First, I feel as though we should be making a toast in champagne,' Sarah said, giving a small smile.

'We'll have to make do with tea,' Ruby said, appearing with a tray and handing out the mugs.

'What are we toasting, apart from friendship?' Maisie asked.

Sarah raised her mug into the air. 'Bloody men!' she declared. 'And in particular, bloody Alan.'

'Sarah Gilbert, I've never heard you swear before. Whatever would your mother have said?' Ruby gasped.

The four women fell about laughing, as they knew only too well what the late Irene Caselton would have said to women swearing.

'Bloody Alan,' Freda said, clinking her mug against Sarah's. 'Here's to friendship.'

Once Ruby's stash of biscuits had been consumed, Maisie pulled out a notebook and licked the end of her pencil. 'Right, let's get this show on the road. Shall we make a list of bridesmaids?'

'I want you two. Oh, and Sadie and our Sally. Then there's Georgina, your four girls, Myfi, and I suppose I should ask Gwyneth and Betty's older two girls . . .'

'Blimey. You're going to have more people walking down the aisle than in the congregation at this rate. I make that unlucky for some, thirteen,' Maisie said. This wedding will look more like a circus act than a serious occasion.'

'But I want all of you to be with me when I marry my Tony. I want it to be a perfect day that we will remember forever.'

'And I agree, it would be a marvellous idea. Do you have any suggestions, Nan?'

Ruby had wandered away from where the girls were

standing and was rooting though a pile of fabric. 'You've been busy, Maisie. Is this earmarked for anything?' she asked, holding up a bolt of cream-coloured cotton.

'I bought it wiv a job lot of furnishing fabric from a company that went out of business. That's curtain lining. Why, d'yer want some curtains made up?'

'No, but the little girls would look very pretty in matching cotton frocks. You could have some pretty sashes made from whatever fabric you chose for the adult attendants.'

Freda was thrilled. 'It's a marvellous idea, and the children can wear the frocks afterwards. What do you think?' she asked her two friends as her eyes shone with excitement.

'That's a blinder of an idea, Ruby,' Maisie said. 'Hang on a minute, I've had a thought,' she said, pulling open a cardboard box. 'These old frocks came in – don't ask from where,' she grinned. 'I spotted a monstrosity that must have come from the last war but, picked apart, it might just do to trim the little ones' frocks.' She pulled out dress after dress until she gave a yell of success. 'Here it is. Look, a hideous thing, but the embroidered overskirt would make very pretty sashes.'

'Oh my, I see what you mean,' Sarah said as she shook out the old dress and held it up for them all to approve. 'I'll come over in the evenings and help you with the dresses, Maisie. How about you, Freda? Perhaps we could take a trip up to Woolwich market together to look for some fabric for the adult bridesmaids.'

'I'd like that,' Freda said. 'And perhaps we could just have the grown-ups escort me, and the little ones can sit in the congregation, so it doesn't look too much like a circus,' she grinned.

'Better still – why not just have the little ones? There's nothing nicer than to see a young bride surrounded by small children on her wedding day.'

'Ruby's right, you know,' Maisie said as she picked at the biscuit crumbs left on the plate. We can be there to 'elp you but it would be wonderful ter see you with our kiddies as you get married.'

'Then I agree,' Freda said. 'Although I want you both close by my side in case I get cold feet or something,' she added nervously.

'The three musketeers,' Ruby smiled. 'It's good to see you all friends again.'

'I want to apologize for being so horrid to you, Freda,' Sarah said. 'I should have known that you'd be loyal to Alan as a friend and would never have an affair with him. I don't know what possessed me to think that.'

'I'd have been the same in your position,' Freda answered. 'I lost count of the number of times I wanted to tell you what was going on, but he made me promise. If I'd said anything, I would have been the one to break bad news and see you split up.'

'That's all down to Alan, and look where it's got him. He lives alone in his mother's house while his wife and children are streets away.'

'Will you take him back?' Maisie asked.

'Oh, yes, I'd have him back like a shot, but first Alan has got to realize he misses me and loves me. And I've got to know we can trust each other. I've seen a few glimmers of the old Alan when he's come to collect the children, and I know that if I bide my time, he will come back to me.'

'Blimey, Sarah, it sounds as though you've got it all planned,' Maisie grinned. 'You're a tough cookie, as the Yanks say in those crime movies. If you didn't cry at the drop of a hat you could be scary.'

'That's my girl,' Ruby said as she reached for her coat. 'I'm going to love you and leave you, or my old man will have bought up a whole litter of puppies if left to his own devices.'

'Don't tell me you've caved in over the greyhound puppy?' Sarah laughed.

'I have, but I've given Mike and George strict instructions that if anything should happen to Bob then it's theirs, as I want nothing to do with it.'

'Oh, Nan, don't talk like that,' Sarah exclaimed.

'It'll happen to us all sooner or later, my love, so don't you go fretting. I just don't see myself as a greyhound trainer, that's all,' Ruby laughed as she swung her coat over her shoulders before doubling up in pain.

'Nan,' Sarah shouted. Maisie reached the older woman first.

'Now, it's about time yer told us all what's the matter wiv yer. I've seen yer in pain a few times now, and it's about time yer confessed so that we can 'elp.'

'I don't know. I get these jabbing pains sometimes. They come and go, but I'm all right at night when I'm lying down – and I'm all right now, so you've no need to worry about me,' Ruby said, brushing Maisie aside.

'Oh, no, you don't, Mrs Jackson,' Maisie said, taking Ruby's coat from her and laying it down. 'Now, you tell me where it hurts,' she said as she ran her hands carefully up Ruby's back before frowning and feeling her waist. 'What the bloody 'ell 'ave you got on under yer frock?'

'Just my undergarments,' Ruby said, struggling away from her. 'There's no need to fuss.'

'I am fussing, whether you like it or not. Now tell me again what you have on under that frock.'

Ruby looked embarrassed. 'It don't seem right me telling you what's under my clothes.'

'If you don't tell me I'll take a look,' Maisie threatened, much to the horror of Freda and Sarah.

'It's just my corset,' Ruby said, looking embarrassed.

'And you wear it every day until you go ter bed?'

'What if I do? A woman wants to look good for her husband.'

'Not by wearing a heavy-duty corset every bloody day. Wiv all those whale bones in it, you must be in agony,' Maisie scolded her.

'Have you been doing this for Bob?' Sarah asked, trying not to smile.

'Yes,' Ruby said, looking miserable. 'He never saw me as a young girl, and I thought if I could get my figure back, he'd be proud of me.'

'God, Ruby, there's not a prouder man than your Bob,' Maisie scolded her. Now, do me a favour, will you?'

Ruby nodded her head, looking ashamed.

'Get yourself into that back room and take off your corset, and promise me you'll never wear it again.'

Ruby hurried off as Maisie pulled out her wedding dress patterns. 'Tell me what takes yer fancy, and we can start to get cracking on the most important dress of yer life,' she said, spreading them over her worktable.

Freda scanned the envelopes, with their line drawings of elegant models wearing full-length bridal gowns. It took only seconds for her to point to one design. 'That's the one I like. It's the dress I've dreamt of wearing.'

Ruby appeared, holding out a salmon-pink bundle with lacy edges. 'Here, you take it, then I'll not be trying to truss myself up in it ever again. I must say it's nice to feel loose and free again.'

Maisie took the corset and guffawed. 'Bloody heck, Ruby, you've got half a whale in this corset. Look at the number of bones sticking out of it. No wonder you've been in pain. I promise I'll find it a good 'ome,' she said, throwing it into a nearby box. 'Now, come here and see the dress design that Freda's chosen.'

'Oh my, that will look lovely on you. Do you think you can run this up for her in time, Maisie? We've only got a few weeks to go,' Ruby said as she lifted the pattern closer to her face to look at the detail on the flowing skirt and bodice. 'You'll look a treat, and your Tony will have eyes only for you.'

Maisie gave Sarah a wink and went to where her tailor's dummy was covered in a sheet. 'Ta-da!' she exclaimed, pulling the sheet away to show the very same gown. 'It was one I was making as a sample. What do you think?'

As Freda and Ruby exclaimed at the design, Sarah felt a shiver run through her body as she recalled the splash of blood on the fabric. The hairs stood up on her neck as she whispered to herself, 'Blood and tears.'

17

~

September 18th, 1948

'It is traditional to have a couple of pints before the wedding ceremony,' Alan said as he slid a glass of best bitter across the table to Tony, who was looking particularly nervous as he loosened his tie. 'We wait here for the others, then head off to the church in plenty of time to see your blushing bride arrive on the arm of her brother.'

Tony nodded, too nervous to speak, and took a gulp of his beer. 'I'm not a drinker as a rule, but I'd not want to spoil a tradition,' he said.

Alan raised his hand as he spotted Douglas Billington walk into the Prince of Wales alongside Bob Jackson and David Carlisle. 'Over here, lads. Where's Mike?'

'He'll be along shortly after he's dropped Gwyneth at St Paulinus,' David said, as he checked who wanted drinks.

Tony jumped to his feet. 'I'm supposed to be there first. The vicar told me not to be late,' he said as David grabbed his arm.

'Hold your horses,' David laughed. 'They are going early to check the flowers and take the buttonholes. The women spent last night preparing them, freshly delivered from Bob's allotment. They roped me in as well. If I ever see another chrysanthemum it will be too soon,' he grinned. 'Here are yours,' he said, holding out a small cardboard box to the groom, and to Alan, who was the best man.

'And you an undertaker,' Alan laughed. 'I'd have thought you were used to flowers.'

The men settled down to give Tony advice about married life, which was all taken in good sport. Mike added his views on babies now that he was a proud father to their six-month-old baby son, Robert.

'I wished I'd been told this,' Alan said ruefully, as he accepted a second pint. 'At least then my wife wouldn't be living under a different roof to me.'

Bob shook his head. 'Son, we've all been over this a hundred times. You did what you thought was right at the time. However, you should have confided in your wife before it all got out of hand.'

'Is there a chance you'll get back together again?' Douglas Billington asked. 'I know my Betty's been most supportive of Sarah, to the point I was threatened never to keep a secret. I almost caved in and told her what gift I'd bought her for our wedding anniversary, when she sensed I was up to something. I'm not a fan of secrets. Wasn't it your wedding anniversary recently, Alan? How did you handle that, what with living in different houses?'

Alan gave them all a blank look before slapping his hand against his forehead. 'Bugger me, I've messed up again. Here's me thinking that if I play my cards right today, she might start to look at me favourably – and I forgot not only our anniversary, but also her birthday. We married on Sarah's twenty-first birthday, the day war broke out,' he explained to Tony.

Bob started to grin. 'You can thank your step-grandfather-in-law for saving your bacon. Ruby reminded me of the day. We picked some flowers, and I forged your signature on a couple of cards. Ruby had the two kiddies make their own cards, so all's right with the world there.'

'Jesus,' Alan swore. 'You may just have saved my marriage. Cheers, Bob,' he said, raising his glass.

'I never took you for someone who could forge a signature, although I'm not sure, being an ex-copper, you should be talking about it,' David joked. 'Talking of coppers, here's our Mike,' he added, as Mike appeared from the public bar with a grim look on his face. 'Cheer up, mate, it might never happen.'

'It has,' Mike said. 'Freddie Unthank is out of prison. I've just bumped into him and his brother at the bar. To be honest, he should have been locked up for at least two years for arson. However, his father has some powerful friends, and with Freddie's dodgy ticker he was let out on compassionate grounds.'

'Dodgy ticker, my backside,' Bob huffed. 'He's fitter than our Tony here, and that's saying something. No one with a bad heart would be in here knocking back whisky before lunch. No, they are up to something.'

'I suggest we head for the church now, in case those thugs intend to cause trouble at the wedding,' Douglas said looking over his shoulder to where the two brothers could be heard talking loudly above the other drinkers.

Alan shrugged his shoulders. 'They wouldn't know we

were going to a wedding, and Freddie was locked up fair and square.'

Mike shook his head. 'The Unthanks will want to get back at you, Lemuel and Freda for giving evidence against them. They are sore losers. Mark my words, this is not over yet.'

'Freda and Tony's wedding announcement was listed in *The Erith Observer*, so all and sundry will know her friends will be with her today,' Bob said, looking worried. 'Mike, can you ring the station and tell them there could be trouble? Meanwhile, we need to get to the church and warn our male friends about impending problems. However, let's not tell the womenfolk just yet. It could all blow over, and there's no need to spoil the day. Come on, drink up, we need to be on our way.'

Leaving the pub, Mike Jackson looked back and saw the Unthank brothers were watching them closely. This was not going to blow over any day soon, he thought grimly.

'Keep still, I'm trying to make sure your veil is pinned securely. It will only take one of the little ones stepping on the edge, and the whole lot will be off your head and on the floor. My goodness, I've never known such a wriggly bride,' Maisie scolded.

'I'm only trying to see if Tony's inside?' Freda said, trying to peer through the church door. 'I had a dream that he wouldn't turn up. Wouldn't that be embarrassing?' she asked with a nervous giggle.

'Oh, he'll be there all right. I gave my David strict

instructions ter get him here, in one piece – and sober. I know what those blokes are like when they get together,' she tutted, sticking another hair grip into the smart French pleat underneath the voluminous veil.

Ruby popped her head into the church, and came back with a smile on her face. 'All is as it should be, thank goodness.'

'Oh good, Tony's in there,' Freda said, giving a huge sigh of relief.

Ruby gave her a frown. 'I meant my Bob and that blooming greyhound. Do you know he wanted to bring it with him? Seems the puppy would have missed a meal if it had been left behind, and going by my daft husband, that could have lost him the Greyhound Derby in a year or two's time due to being undernourished. Honestly, the man has gone barmy over this dog. If only he knew that I'd been slipping it a few biscuits, and it helped Nellie finish off our scraps from the table most days. At the rate it eats it won't be able to walk, let alone race around the course chasing a rabbit.'

'Ruby, you are a one,' Betty said as she pulled out the full skirts of Freda's gown and stepped back to view her handiwork. 'Now don't you look a picture,' she said, pulling out a clean handkerchief and dabbing at her eyes.

Freda looked to Maisie and then Sarah, who was trying to make the youngest bridesmaids behave themselves. The three girls all burst out laughing.

'Whatever is wrong?' Betty asked. 'Do I have a mark on my nose or something?'

Freda leant forward and kissed Betty's cheek. 'Dearest Betty. Think of all the years you've kept a supply of clean handkerchiefs in your desk drawer for when one of us needs to wipe away our tears. This is the first time we've ever seen you need to use one for that reason.'

Betty joined in with their laughter. 'I can assure you that there have been times when I've reached for a handkerchief. You've never been around to see. I tend to cry in private. Now, I'm going into the church, as I'm not needed here. Will you join me, Ruby?'

'Just a minute, love, I want to give this to our Freda,' she said, giving Freda a hug and a kiss on the cheek. 'Who'd have thought the day you came into my house for a steak and kidney pudding dinner, you'd become a part of my life? I'm that pleased you hung around and didn't leave Erith. Here, tuck this up your sleeve. It's for good luck,' she said, handing over a small silver horseshoe tied to a thin piece of blue ribbon. 'This can be your something blue. Do you have the rest?'

'The something new is my dress, and the something old is my veil, as it's second-hand,' Freda explained, touched by Ruby's words.

'The something borrowed is my sixpenny necklace,' Sarah said as Freda touched the chain at her throat. 'It means a lot to me, and as it is part of Woolworths and Freda is part of our lives, it's only right she wear it today.'

'I remember when Alan gave that to you after he nicknamed you Sixpenny Sarah as everything used to cost sixpence at Woolworths, and that's where you both met,' Freda said as her eyes shone with happiness.

'Oh, you've set me off again,' Betty sniffed as she took Ruby's arm to help her into church.

'I'm on the verge myself,' Ruby said before wagging

her finger at the girls. 'Now, if you fall out again, I'm going to bang your heads together. Hear me? As for you, you little ragamuffin,' she said, turning to where Freda's brother Lenny was waiting patiently to walk his sister down the aisle, 'I will never forget the trouble you put us through all those years ago. But you've not turned out so bad for all that,' she added, patting his arm. 'Come on, Betty, let's get ourselves settled before the organist starts playing.'

'Oh, Ruby,' Maisie called out to the old woman. 'I 'ope yer not wearing that old corset, are you? I swear yer left 'alf the whale bones on my sewing-room floor when yer went.'

Ruby roared with laughter and wagged her finger at Maisie. 'Don't you ever change, Maisie Carlisle . . .'

Maisie snorted with laughter. 'As if I would, Ruby. Come on, Sarah, let's take the kiddies inside ready to wait fer their aunty Freda. I won't rest until I see them all walking in line behind her.'

Freda smiled as her two best friends disappeared in a flurry of small, identically dressed children.

Lenny took his sister's arm as they stepped towards the church door. 'If I've not told you already today, I just want to say you're as pretty as a picture, and I know our mum and dad would be as proud as punch of you. Thank you for waiting for me to be on leave so I could give you away.'

Freda wasn't so sure about her mum being interested in anything she did, but her dad was a different kettle of fish. 'We've been lucky in so many ways,' she said. 'Come on, let's get down that aisle so I can become Mrs Anthony Forsythe and start my married life.'

Lenny looked behind him as they stepped through the church door. 'Oh, we seem to have a couple of latecomers,' he said as he spotted two men standing by the lychgate.

Freda looked over her shoulder through the layers of veil that now obscured her vision. She froze in horror for a moment as she recognized Freddie Unthank and his brother. What were they doing here? She'd given a statement on the night of the fire, and it was her evidence that had helped put Freddie behind bars. They could only be here to spoil her wedding day, and she'd not stand for it. She had to tell Alan and Mike what she'd seen. But first she had to get married. Composing herself, she turned away from the two men, determined they wouldn't ruin her special day. 'Come on, let's get inside right now and, Lenny, close the door behind us please.'

'This is your secret surprise,' Tony said as the car pulled up alongside the jetty at the Erith river front. 'I remembered what you told me, and decided that I'd do my utmost to bring you your dream on the day of our wedding.'

The couple had left the church in a shower of confetti and rice, and much to Freda's relief there'd been no sign of Freddie or his brother. It had been a beautiful service and the little bridesmaids had all behaved perfectly. Freda had spotted Betty and Sarah dabbing their eyes throughout the ceremony, and she had to admit that she'd cried with happiness too when the vicar had announced that she and Tony were now man and wife. After Sarah had taken some photographs outside the church, she and Tony had climbed into the car lent to them by George, and Tony had driven them to their wedding reception.

Freda peered from the car window. 'But it's the Running Horse pub.' Her stomach churned as she thought back to how Maisie and David had almost been killed the day a landmine went off close to the pub, and she shuddered to think of the lost lives. A shiver ran down her spine, almost as if someone had walked over her grave. She tried to give herself a talking to. If Tony had been thoughtful enough to plan their reception in this pub, she would have to grin and bear it. She'd not wish to disappoint him by showing she was unhappy with his choice. Hadn't she just vowed to love, honour and obey her husband?

'You're looking the wrong way,' Tony said, giving her a nudge as she turned to looked towards the river.

'Oh, my goodness,' she shrieked. 'Is that the *Kentish Queen*?'

'No, this is the *Medway Maid*. We did our best to book the *Queen*, but the owner's been ill, so I failed on that count,' he said as he helped her from the car.

'Don't ever say that,' she gasped. 'You could never fail me, Tony. So, does this mean we are going on the river? How long we will be gone, what about our guests? I thought my surprise would be a reception at the Prince of Wales – gosh, I'm so sorry for asking so many questions, I can't believe we are going on the river!' She shrieked with delight before throwing her arms round her husband's neck. 'I don't deserve such a wonderful husband.'

'And I don't deserve such an adorable wife,' he replied, nuzzling her neck. 'Come on, let's go on board and I'll show you the rest of the surprise.'

'There's more?' she asked as she lifted her voluminous skirts and headed down the short jetty, the breeze catching her veil so it flowed out behind her. 'I'm not sure I'm wearing the best outfit for this kind of outing, but I'll manage,' she added as a deckhand took her arm and helped her aboard.

Grasping her hand, Tony led her down a short flight of steps. Below deck there was a room complete with bar, and a table laden with food. 'This is for your friends and family,' he said, watching her face as the penny dropped.

'We are having our wedding reception on board? Oh my, I can't believe this is actually happening.'

'Come and see this,' Tony said, getting caught up in her excitement. He led her back up the steps to the deck at the stern of the paddle steamer, where a piano had been set up. An open area bordered by bench seats formed a makeshift dance floor.

'It's perfect,' Freda sighed as she grabbed his hands and spun him around the deck until, feeling dizzy, they stopped, laughing fit to burst.

Cheers from the jetty made them to look to where their guests were arriving in a charabanc. The newlyweds went down the gangplank to greet their guests and were soon caught up in the good wishes from their friends and family.

'All right, kid?' Alan said as he kissed her cheek and shook Tony's hand.

'I'm more than all right,' she grinned back. 'I take it you had a hand in helping Tony arrange this?'

'I only did what you deserved. Tony knew what he wanted, and I helped him achieve it. I'm sorry for putting you through so much, kid. I've been a bloody idiot, but hopefully now we can all move on with our lives,' he said, glancing over to where Sarah had arrived with their children. 'Will you excuse me? There's someone I need to speak to,' he said, giving them both a grin. 'Wish me luck.'

As Alan started to move through the crowd of guests, Freda hurried after him. 'Hang on a minute, Alan, I want to tell you something. You're going to think I'm daft, but I swear I saw the Unthank brothers outside the church . . .'

Alan didn't want to worry Freda, as it would only spoil her big day. 'You must have imagined it,' he grinned. 'Freddie Unthank is still locked up in jail. Just enjoy your wedding day, and don't give it another thought.' He gave her a playful punch on the arm.

Freda shrugged her shoulders. 'With all this floating around my face, I probably imagined it,' she said, tugging at the veil that seemed to have a life of its own in the river breeze. 'Forget I said anything,' she smiled back.

Tony claimed his bride as the pianist started to play, and they took to the dance floor just as the pleasure boat set sail down the Thames. 'By the way, the answer is Margate,' he whispered in her ear.

'Oh Tony, you old romantic, what a thing to say to a woman,' she giggled.

'I thought you'd want to know where we are heading.'

'I never gave it a thought. Will we have time to go to Dreamland?'

'No, the steamer only has time to turn and come back, but after the weekend I'm taking you to Ramsgate to stay at Sea View guesthouse, where George and Maureen stayed on their honeymoon. It's their gift to us.'

Freda was lost for words. As the day progressed she mingled with her guests and danced until her feet ached. She moved around the boat, spending time with Lemuel and his family, chatting about their homeland, and then sat catching up with her sister-in-law, Sally. Everyone was having a wonderful time, and all too soon the boat was turning at the seaside town of Margate and heading back up river to Erith, where it would put down anchor mid-river for the party to continue.

Alan swept his wife around the dance floor. The conversation was pleasant, but he was no further forward than when he had boarded the boat. Over Sarah's shoulder he could see Lemuel dancing with Sadie. It did his heart good to know his old mate from his RAF days was in love and settled. As the music stopped there was a call for Maureen to give them a few songs. It was then he had an idea. Making his excuses, he joined his mum and whispered in her ear. Maureen nodded, knowing the song meant a lot to Alan, and bent to speak to the pianist. Soon, people were humming to the strands of a song known well to friends who worked in the Erith store.

'What is this song?' Cynthia asked Sadie, who had just joined her mother-in-law and her nan.

'Oh, it's so romantic,' Sadie smiled. 'The song is an American one and is about a man who met his sweetheart in a five and ten cent store. That's what they called Woolworths in America. I'm told that when Alan proposed to Sarah in the middle of Erith Woolworths, someone started to sing the song, just like a musical.'

'Now that is romantic,' Cynthia said as she leant over to explain the song to her daughter. 'Lemuel and James, now this is how a man romances a woman. Take note, both of you.'

The two brothers ribbed their mother good-naturedly about their singing prowess, but did attempt to catch a line or two of the song as the guests all joined in with Maureen.

Alan looked to where his wife was sitting, and she smiled back and nodded. Was it the sign he'd been waiting for? Taking over from his mum, he sat down next to the pianist and soon the haunting introduction to 'I'll See You in My Dreams' flowed across the boat and his rich, musical voice sang the plaintive words. For friends in the know, it was obvious Alan was singing to Sarah.

He'd just stood to go to her side when something caught his eye. He looked towards the wheelhouse on the upper deck and saw Freddie Unthank standing alongside his brother – but what really caused him to freeze with fear was that the fact that Freddie was holding a gun. He stood up and forced himself to walk calmly towards his wife. It looked to everyone present as though he was going to join her and continue the song. Along the way he passed Mike and David, and encouraging the guests to join in with the song he was able to whisper to the two men, alerting them to what he'd seen.

As the song came to an end, he started to sing 'The Lambeth Walk', encouraging guests to get to their feet for the jolly dance. With luck this would stop the Unthanks being able to take aim at Freda. Even the younger children lined up and copied the steps from their parents. Alan reached Sarah and pulled her close, whispering to her to take their children and do their best to hide away before he hurried to the steps to the wheelhouse, close to where he'd just seen the Unthank brothers. On the opposite side of the boat, Mike and David were doing the same. Mike stepped forward and challenged the Unthanks, and Alan took his chance to start his approach from the opposite side. With luck, and having the element of surprise, the three of them would be able to overcome the two men. In between them was the captain of the boat, unaware of what was going on. Suddenly Freddie raised his gun, and shouted at Mike to stand still. Alan dived in from Freddie's blind side, and the gun went off as the men piled into each other.

As the guests heard the gunshot they rushed to take shelter, screaming to children and loved ones to hurry. Lemuel and James, seeing the struggle taking place in the wheelhouse, leapt up the steps, followed by David and Douglas. The men quickly overpowered the Unthank brothers, pinning them to the deck. It was then that Alan realized the boat was not steering a steady course and instead was veering to one side, heading for a tugboat moored in the river. Looking towards the wheelhouse, he saw that the captain was slumped over the wheel, causing the boat to change direction at an alarming speed. He shouted out a warning, but it was too late. In only seconds, the pleasure boat hit the tug and rocked violently from side to side. Guests who were still on the outer deck were thrown over the edge of the railings and hurled into the dirty, grey river.

Alan looked around him in horror. The Unthanks, dragging David and Mike with them, had disappeared into the water. Loud screams from the deck below told him that women and children had also gone overboard. How had such a happy event turned into complete horror? Reaching the captain, Alan pulled him away from the wheel and laid him on the deck. He could see the man was breathing and, thank goodness, not badly injured. He heard a shout from one of the crew who, realizing what had happened, rushed over and seized the wheel, tugging it hard to correct the boat's direction. The boat shuddered as it changed course and Alan heard further cries from the decks outside, but the boat was soon back under control. Leaving the deckhand to see to the captain, Alan hurried back to the dance floor, where just moments before he and the other guests had been enjoying Freda and Tony's special day.

Alan scanned the dance area looking for his wife and children but couldn't see them. Panicking now, he leant over the side rail and spotted David Carlisle holding up two small children. Relief rushed through him as he realized that Buster and Georgina were safe. He spotted Douglas, who was labouring with the lifeless shape of a man. 'Sarah,' he called out, continuing to search the dark waters for his wife. Then he saw her, struggling to stay above water. Without thinking, he dived in to save her.

Looking back, Freda couldn't remember exactly how those in the water were pulled to safety. Her abiding memory was of trying to rip off her veil and wedding gown as they dragged her under the water, pulling her down and down. Telling herself not to panic and to hold her breath, she wriggled out of her dress and immediately felt herself come up to the surface, where hands grabbed her and pulled her back onto the boat. It was still listing dangerously to one side. Maisie rushed over to her and wrapped her in a coat, then helped her walk as best she could on the uneven deck. 'Who is in the water?' she asked with chattering teeth.

Maisie wanted to answer, 'Too many to count,' but she could see Freda was in shock. With relief Maisie could see her own family was safe and, as she watched, David was pulled aboard with Georgina and Myfi, who were sobbing hysterically.

'Arthur, Arthur,' Sadie started to scream, as hands held her back from throwing herself into the water. 'My Arthur fell in,' she cried.

Maisie, who was still comforting Freda and had been given the two children by David, had her hands full. Unable to help, she watched in despair as both Lemuel and James jumped into the water, followed by Tony, swimming to where there were still youngsters in the river. Beside her, Freda started to scream and then to sob uncontrollably.

18

~

October 11th, 1948

Mike Jackson sat in silence as the police vehicle sped away from the graveyard and headed towards the cottage hospital. He was afraid that, having just said goodbye to one friend, there could be more bad news waiting for the three women when they arrived. Nobody spoke as the car moved through the streets of Erith and drew up at the entrance to the hospital, where Mike helped them out of the car.

'They want to speak to you both in the sister's office before you go onto the ward,' Mike said, looking at Sarah and Freda.

'Can I stay wiv them?' Maisie asked. 'They might need me . . .'

Mike nodded, although Sarah and Freda didn't speak. Their pale faces and vacant eyes spoke volumes.

'We had to go to the funeral to say our goodbyes and pay our respects to a man who saved our kiddies,' Maisie said anxiously to Mike. 'I pray we did the right thing, and nothing has changed for the worse while we were away. Perhaps we should 'ave stayed here?'

Sarah looked up. 'We had to say thank you. It was the least we could do. He saved a life, and paid with his own.'

Freda's body shook as the tears came. 'I can't believe my actions have caused the deaths of three people. I must be such a bad person . . .'

Maisie led her to a wooden seat and pushed her into it. 'Now, Freda Forsythe, you listen ter me. You are not a bad person. If anything, you are the good one in all of this. You 'elped Alan. You 'elped Tony find friends and a wife. You've 'elped a lot of people, and should never blame yerself, or you'll 'ave me ter answer to. Do you 'ear me? It's the Unthanks who are ter blame in all of this.'

Freda nodded slowly. 'Yes, I hear you,' she said, choking back more tears. 'Where's Betty with her clean handkerchiefs when we need them?' she sniffed.

'I just want to see Alan,' Sarah fretted. 'Where's the doctor? If the doctor doesn't get here soon, I'm going to go to the ward, and not wait for what he has to say. I hate to think he's alone.'

'He's not alone. Maureen's in there with him as well, so you've no need to worry,' Mike said gently.

'But I do worry,' Sarah said. 'I want to be with him. Please – let's go into the ward now, shall we?' she said as Freda stood up and joined her. 'There's time for talking later.'

Sarah took Freda's arm and they went into the small ward, where there was only one bed occupied of the four. Even with the curtains drawn, they could see three people by Alan's bed, talking quietly to a doctor in a white coat.

'Ah, Mrs Gilbert,' the doctor said, pulling a seat forward for her. We have some news for you.'

Sarah sat down next to Maureen, who squeezed her

hand as she leant over to kiss her husband's cheek. 'I'm here, my love.'

'Sarah?' Alan called as he turned his heavily bandaged head toward her voice.

'You're awake. Oh, Alan, you're back with us,' she cried out. 'When did this happen?'

'Just after the three of you left for the . . . for the funeral,' Maureen said, aware that Alan didn't know what had happened in the aftermath of the pleasure boat colliding with the tug.

Maureen budged over so that Sarah was as close to her husband as possible.

'Alan, darling, do you remember much about the boat trip . . . ?'

'Not much,' he murmured. One of his blue eyes was hidden by bandages, but he was looking at her with the other. 'There was a lot of water and I could feel myself going under . . . Strong hands grabbed at me. I thought it was one of the fellas helping me but then he started to punch at me, and I went under again. When the hands found me a second time, I started . . . I started to fight back – and then it went dark . . . I think it may have been someone else trying to save me. Was it Lemuel?'

Tony sat at the other side of the bed in his dressing gown, and one arm in plaster. 'We think it was, Alan. We saw him in the river, before . . .' He looked to the doctor, who nodded for him to go on. 'We think Lemuel helped you before he was lost in the river. He rescued young Arthur for Sadie, and then went on to bring other children to safe hands. There were only you and James left in the water by then.'

Alan groaned. 'No, please don't tell me Lem has died. He had so much to look forward to. It should have been me. I'm the one who messed up and lost my family.'

Maureen patted her son's arm and got to her feet. 'It's time we all left you so you can be alone with Sarah. It's early days, but you have much to talk about, son,' she said as she kissed him and left the room followed by Freda and Tony.

'Mr Gilbert, we have more tests to run, but it is my opinion that you will in time recover from your injuries. There will be a few scars, but we all carry them in life, and you should be proud to carry yours. I'll leave you with your wife,' the doctor said, patting Alan's shoulder before closing the door to the outside world so the couple could be alone.

Alan reached out and Sarah leant close, taking him into her arms. 'Please forgive me, Sarah. I couldn't bear a life without you.'

Sarah kissed him gently. She could feel the Alan she loved and knew so well was back with her. 'There's nothing to forgive. You just need to concentrate on getting well and strong again. We have the Woolworths Christmas party in ten weeks' time. I want you there entertaining the old soldiers and singing my favourite songs, just like you used to,' she said, speaking gently as his grip on her tightened.

'Tell Betty I'm ready to return to the store. I'm giving up on running a workshop. It's just not worth the hassle, with people like the Unthanks ruling Erith.'

'You'll do no such thing.' Sarah scolded. 'The Unthank brothers perished in the accident, and Frank Unthank is under arrest for many other crimes. He's a shattered man, having lost his sons. In a way I have some sympathy, as it must be so awful to lose a son. Cynthia hasn't taken Lemuel's death well, and neither has Sadie. Both women are beside themselves with grief. We will all miss him,' she said, as Alan gripped her even tighter. 'James has stepped in to take care of the business as his brother loved it so much. When you are ready, he will hand it back. It's kept him going since the accident.'

Alan was quiet for a while, and when he spoke again it was hesitant. 'What about us . . . ?'

She kissed him gently. 'As for us, we will look to the future, and you will build your empire. Why, it could be as large as Woolworths one day. Gilbert and Son has a nice ring to it.'

'Gilbert and Wife sounds even better,' he said, returning her kiss. 'And I promise you there will be roses round the door of our own home one day, just like you've dreamt of for so long.'

'I don't need roses, Alan. I have you.'

Acknowledgements

First, I really must thank my husband Michael for his unstinting support – his nagging to get my words written, his wanting to chat about World War Two events while I'm watching *Coronation Street*, and for driving me to author events and book signings. I don't know how he does it, as I know that if the tables were turned, I'd be a hopeless partner of an author.

I've recently returned from a rather lovely Romantic Novelists' Association event where the 2019 Joan Hessayon Award was announced. This is an annual event where the previous year's New Writers' Scheme graduates receive their certificates and the winning book and author is announced. For me this brings back many happy memories of my graduation year, as it was in the same year that I met my agent, Caroline Sheldon. This led, after all Caroline's hard work, to Pan Macmillan offering that first contract – and *The Woolworths Girls* was born. I've had the support and help of many wonderful editors along the way, as well as the team at ED Public Relations. Thank you all from the bottom of my heart.

The Woolworths series would be hard to write if it

were not for the Woolworths Museum curated by Mr Paul Seaton. Paul patiently answers my questions, ensuring I can tell my stories knowing (hopefully) that the smallest detail is correct. Thank you, Paul.

I thank my readers, along with the people of Erith, where my books are set. Without you all sharing your memories of Woolies, the town, and what life was like 'way back when' I wouldn't have half the content of each book. Thank you for the many emails, tweets, Facebook messages and chats, as well as such lovely letters. Your support means the world to me and makes me the luckiest author in the world to have such fabulous readers.

Thank you,

Elaine xx

Dear Reader

Dear Reader,

It doesn't seem five minutes since I was writing about 'the girls' as the war came to an end. So many of you asked for another book so we could see what happened next in the lives of the people of Erith. I was thrilled to be able to revisit the town of my birth, this time in 1947–8. To be able to research how our country had moved on from the war was a new step for me, and in some ways it was a sad trip. Would my characters all succeed in life or would their dreams come to nothing? The girls' lives were in my hands and I hope I didn't fail them.

There were so many weddings in this book, as well as one funeral, that I could easily have changed the title to that of a certain well-known film – perhaps the working-class version?

Writing about weddings reminds me of those I've attended over the years, as well as my own. It seems only yesterday that I was busy making bridesmaids dresses and planning that special day. My mum had passed away only months before, and my fondest memory is of my dad's family stepping in to make sure my husband and I had a lovely day. Dad decided he didn't need to attend the rehearsal and then asked me at the door of the church what he had to do, and Uncle Nobby appeared at the hairdresser's to escort me home – I was going to catch the bus! Auntie Joan and Auntie Maureen arrived at the house to help me dress, while Auntie May hurried down the aisle to the vestry to be with Dad while we signed the register, so he didn't feel alone. Auntie Doll was there at the reception and I remember her talking to me about mum and keeping her very much part of that day in 1972.

My sister Pamela, my cousin Jill and my husband's little sister Karen looked pretty in their dresses of lavender and lilac satin – fortunately my stitching held up on the day. My eleven-year-old brother was one of the ushers and was caught on cine film throwing the empty confetti box rather than the confetti!

It was a lovely September day. The sun shone and yes there were tears, but there was hope and joy as we all thought of Mum looking down on us and smiling. Now, with the passing of time and so many of my family no longer here, I can look back and smile fondly at the memories and know that I was lucky to have such a wonderful family. Cousins keep in touch from around the world, and although we don't meet up often, we all share happy memories.

How was your wedding? Please do visit my Facebook

author page and let me know. I love to chat with readers and share stories.

Until next time,

Elaine
xx